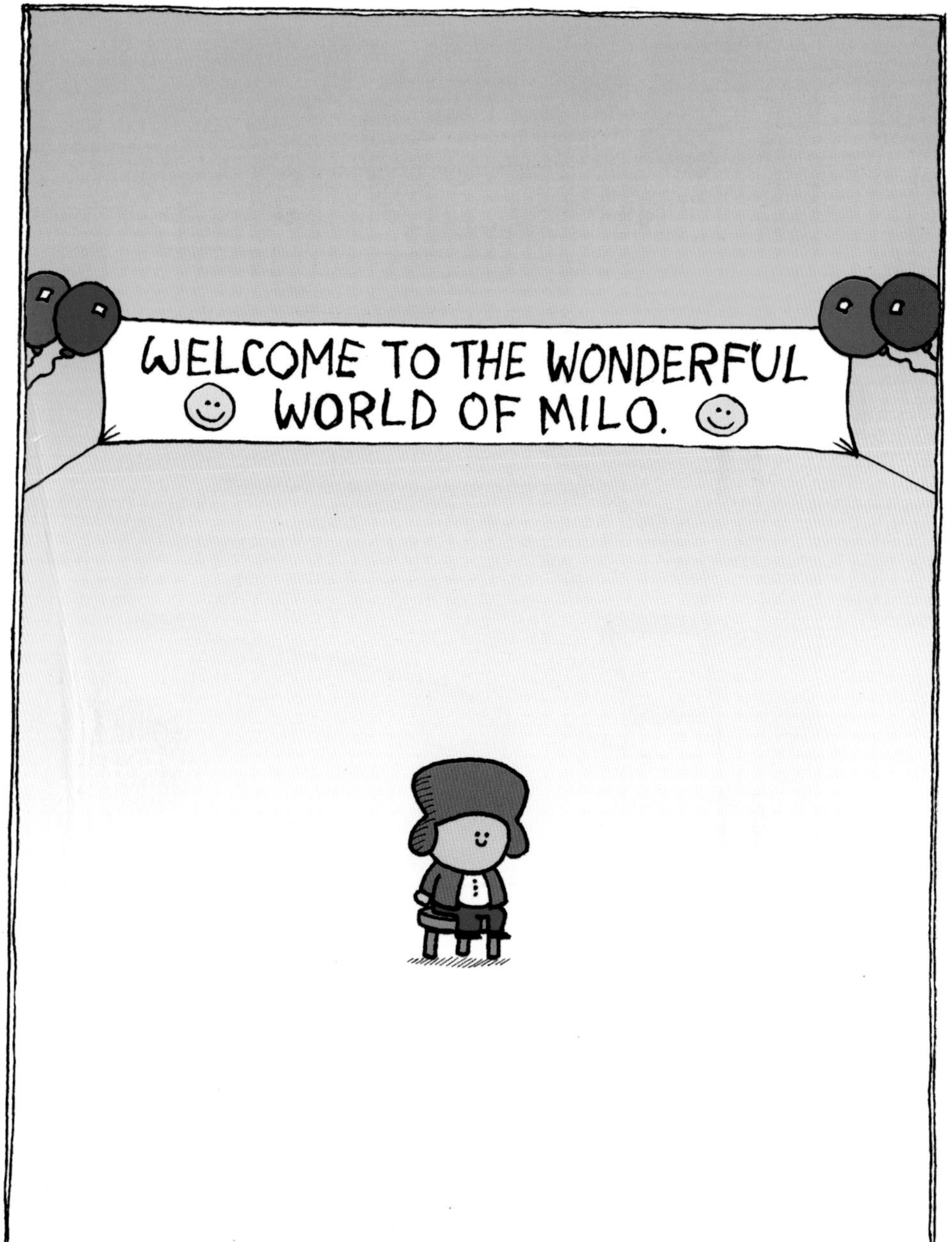
WELCOME TO THE WONDERFUL WORLD OF MILO.

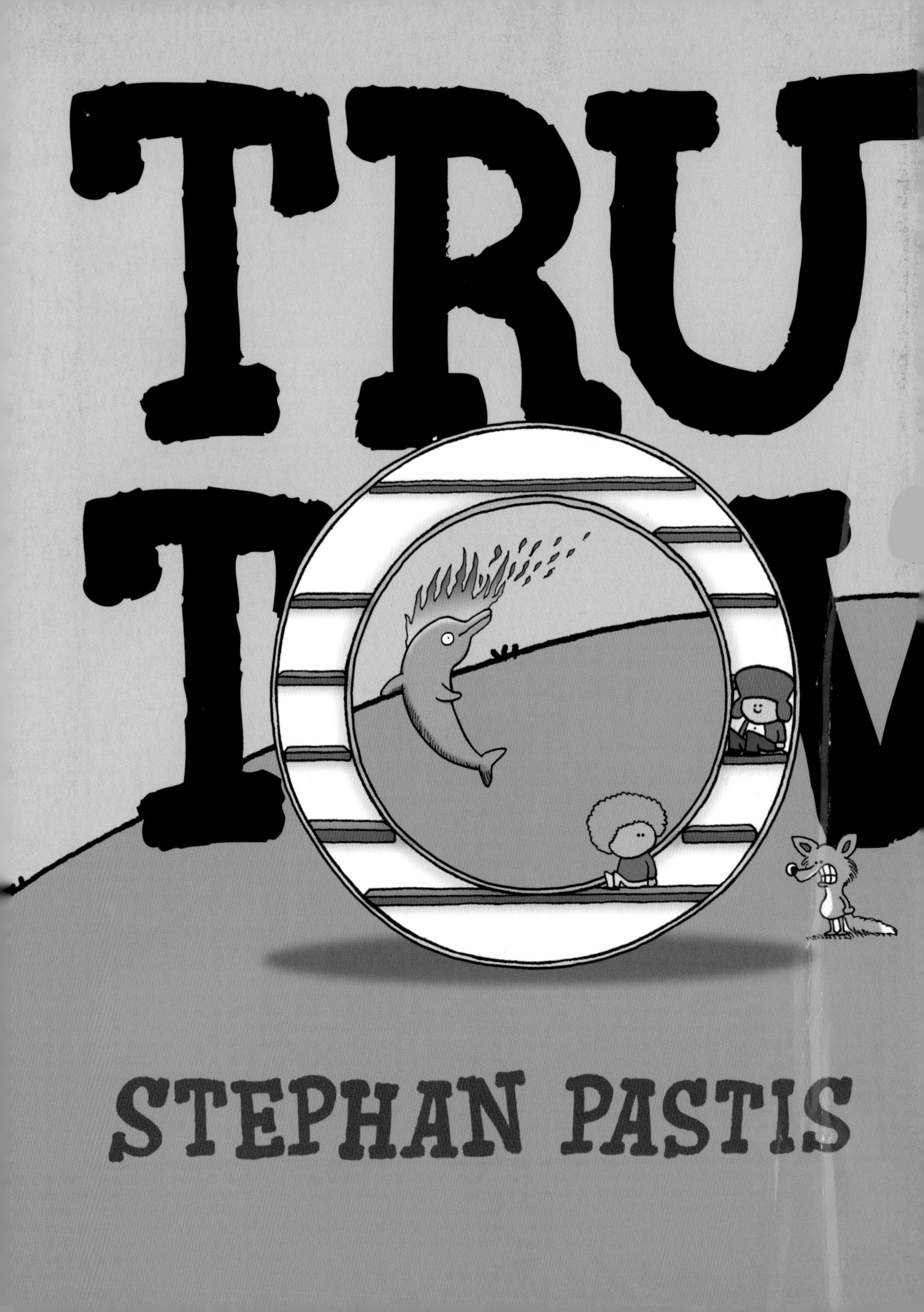
TRU
STEPHAN PASTIS

THE WHY-WHY'S GONE BYE-BYE

ALADDIN | New York | London | Toronto | Sydney | New Delhi

ALADDIN / An imprint of Simon & Schuster Children's Publishing Division / 1230 Avenue of the Americas, New York, New York 10020 / First Aladdin edition August 2022 / Copyright © 2022 by Stephan Pastis / All rights reserved, including the right of reproduction in whole or in part in any form. / ALADDIN and related logo are registered trademarks of Simon & Schuster, Inc. / For information about special discounts for bulk purchases, please contact Simon & Schuster Special Sales at 1-866-506-1949 or business@simonandschuster.com. / The Simon & Schuster Speakers Bureau can bring authors to your live event. For more information or to book an event contact the Simon & Schuster Speakers Bureau at 1-866-248-3049 or visit our website at www.simonspeakers.com. / Designed by Karin Paprocki and Stephan Pastis / The illustrations for this book were rendered digitally. / The text of this book was hand-lettered and set in Bodoni. / Manufactured in China 0522 SCP / 2 4 6 8 10 9 7 5 3 1 / Library of Congress Control Number 2021944661 / ISBN 9781534496149 (hardcover) / ISBN 9781534496132 (paperback) / ISBN 9781534496156 (ebook)

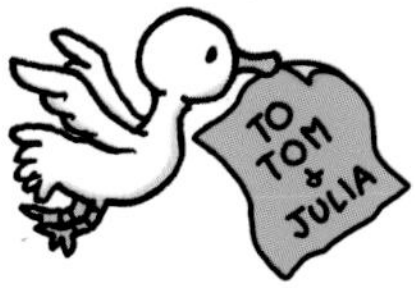
TO
TOM
&
JULIA

PROLOGUE

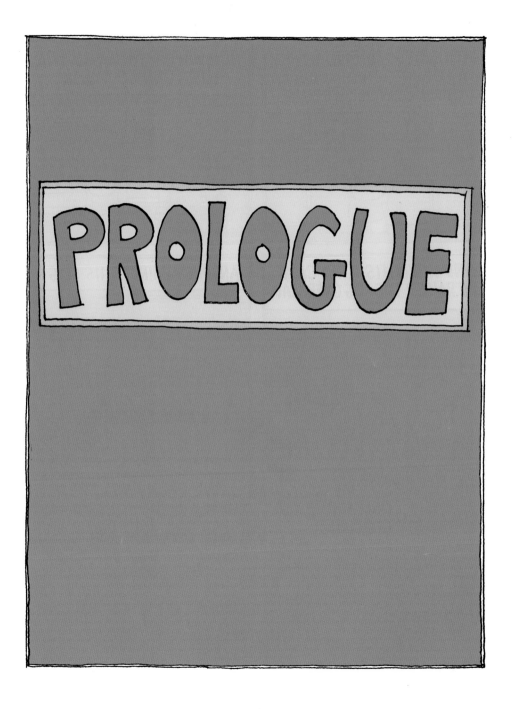

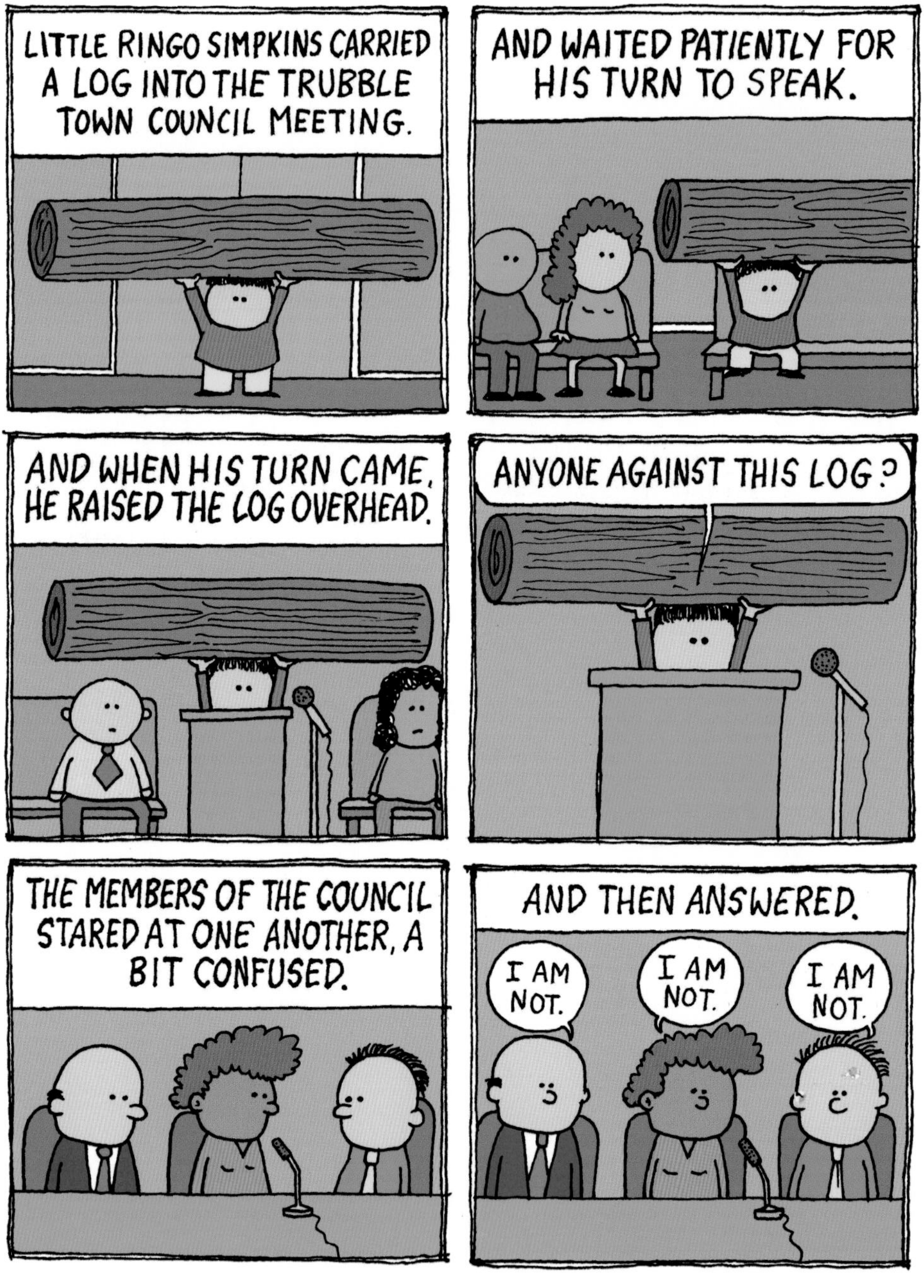
LITTLE RINGO SIMPKINS CARRIED A LOG INTO THE TRUBBLE TOWN COUNCIL MEETING.
AND WAITED PATIENTLY FOR HIS TURN TO SPEAK.
AND WHEN HIS TURN CAME, HE RAISED THE LOG OVERHEAD.
ANYONE AGAINST THIS LOG?
THE MEMBERS OF THE COUNCIL STARED AT ONE ANOTHER, A BIT CONFUSED.
AND THEN ANSWERED.
I AM NOT.
I AM NOT.
I AM NOT.

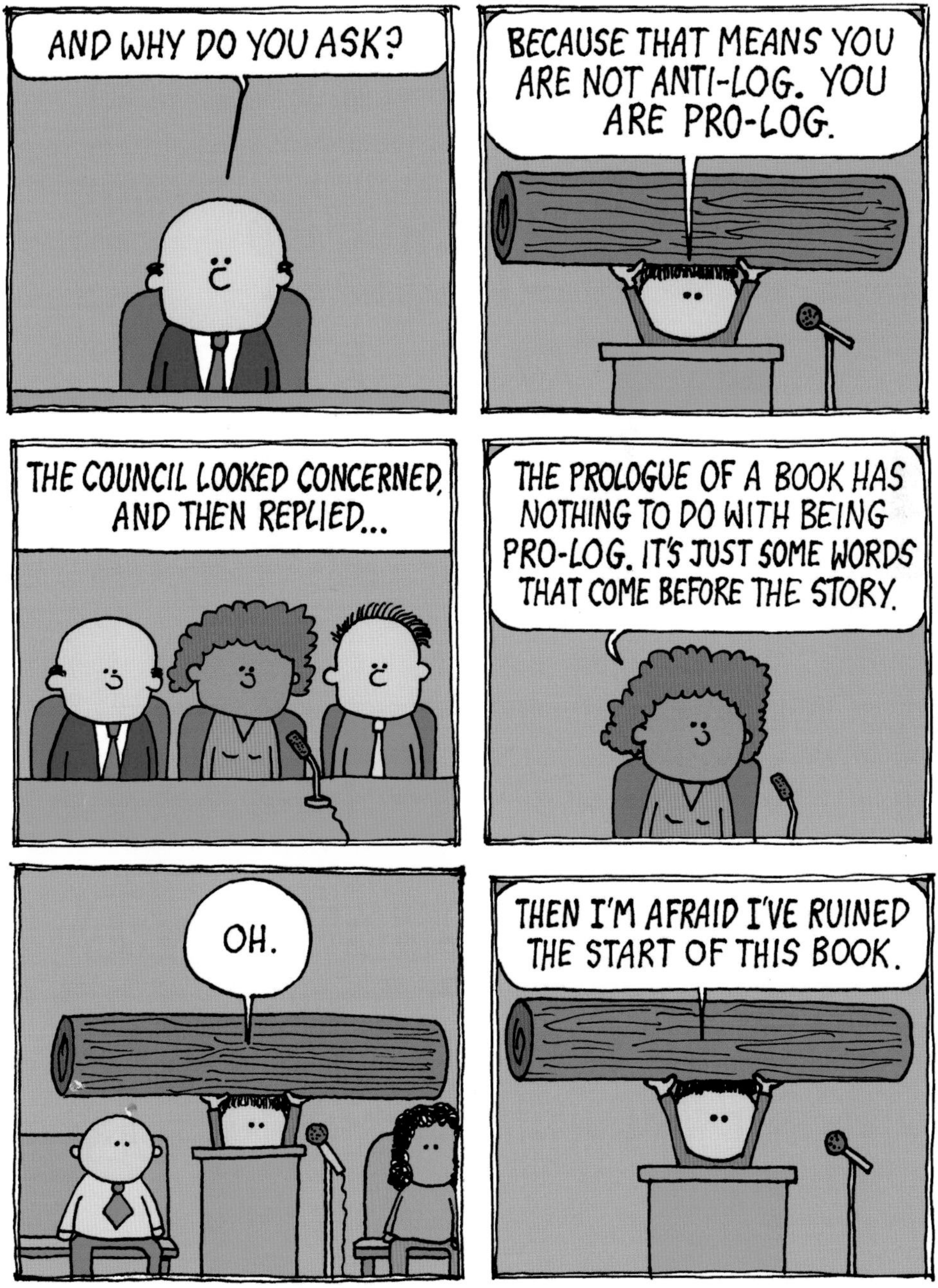
AND WHY DO YOU ASK?
BECAUSE THAT MEANS YOU ARE NOT ANTI-LOG. YOU ARE PRO-LOG.
THE COUNCIL LOOKED CONCERNED, AND THEN REPLIED...
THE PROLOGUE OF A BOOK HAS NOTHING TO DO WITH BEING PRO-LOG. IT'S JUST SOME WORDS THAT COME BEFORE THE STORY.
OH.
THEN I'M AFRAID I'VE RUINED THE START OF THIS BOOK.

CHAPTER
WON

BY THE END OF WHICH...

WE HOPE TO HAVE WON BACK THE READERS WE LOST IN THE PROLOGUE

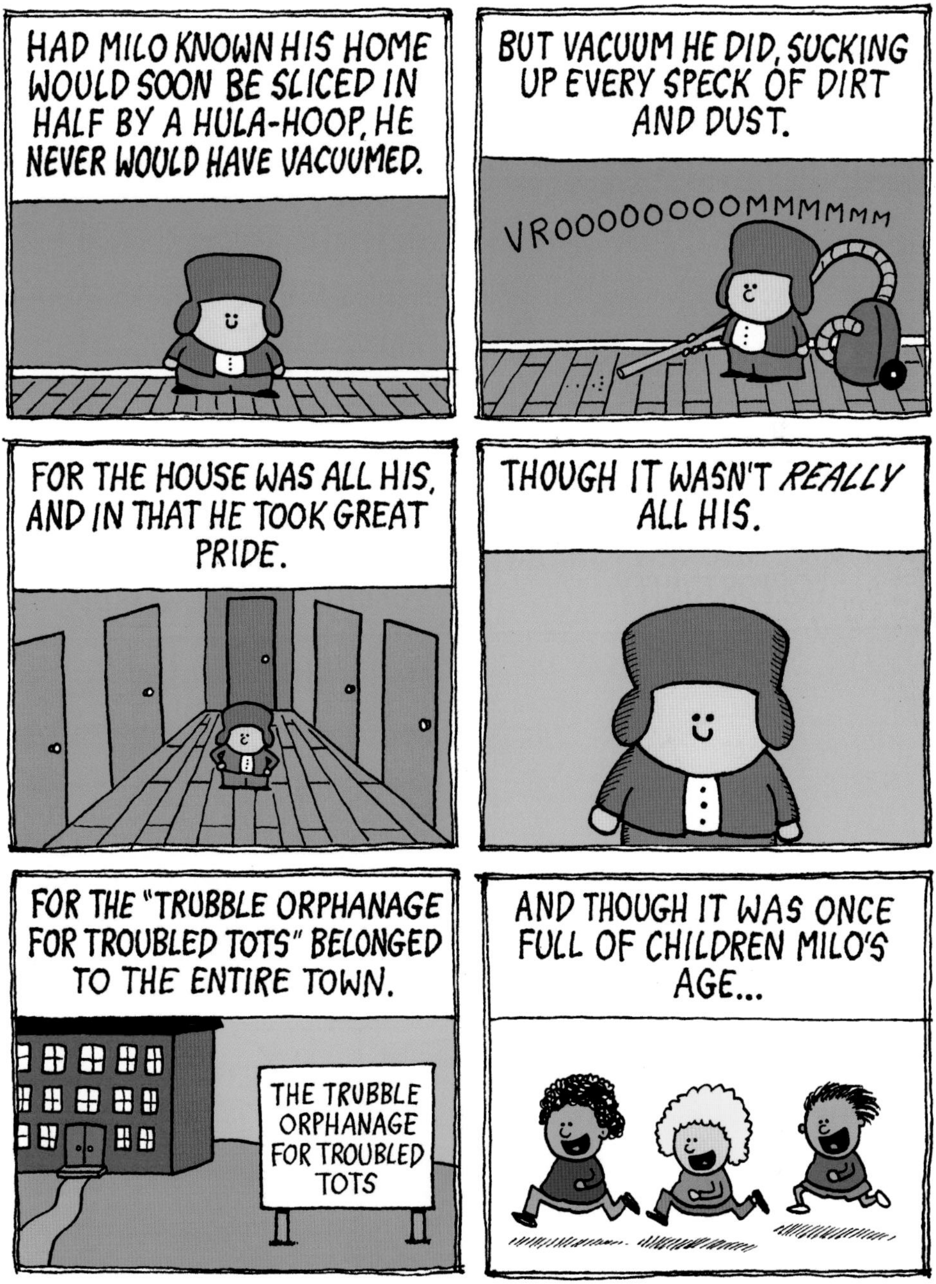
HAD MILO KNOWN HIS HOME WOULD SOON BE SLICED IN HALF BY A HULA-HOOP, HE NEVER WOULD HAVE VACUUMED.
BUT VACUUM HE DID, SUCKING UP EVERY SPECK OF DIRT AND DUST.
VROOOOOOOOOMMMMMM
FOR THE HOUSE WAS ALL HIS, AND IN THAT HE TOOK GREAT PRIDE.
THOUGH IT WASN'T *REALLY* ALL HIS.
FOR THE "TRUBBLE ORPHANAGE FOR TROUBLED TOTS" BELONGED TO THE ENTIRE TOWN.
THE TRUBBLE ORPHANAGE FOR TROUBLED TOTS
AND THOUGH IT WAS ONCE FULL OF CHILDREN MILO'S AGE...

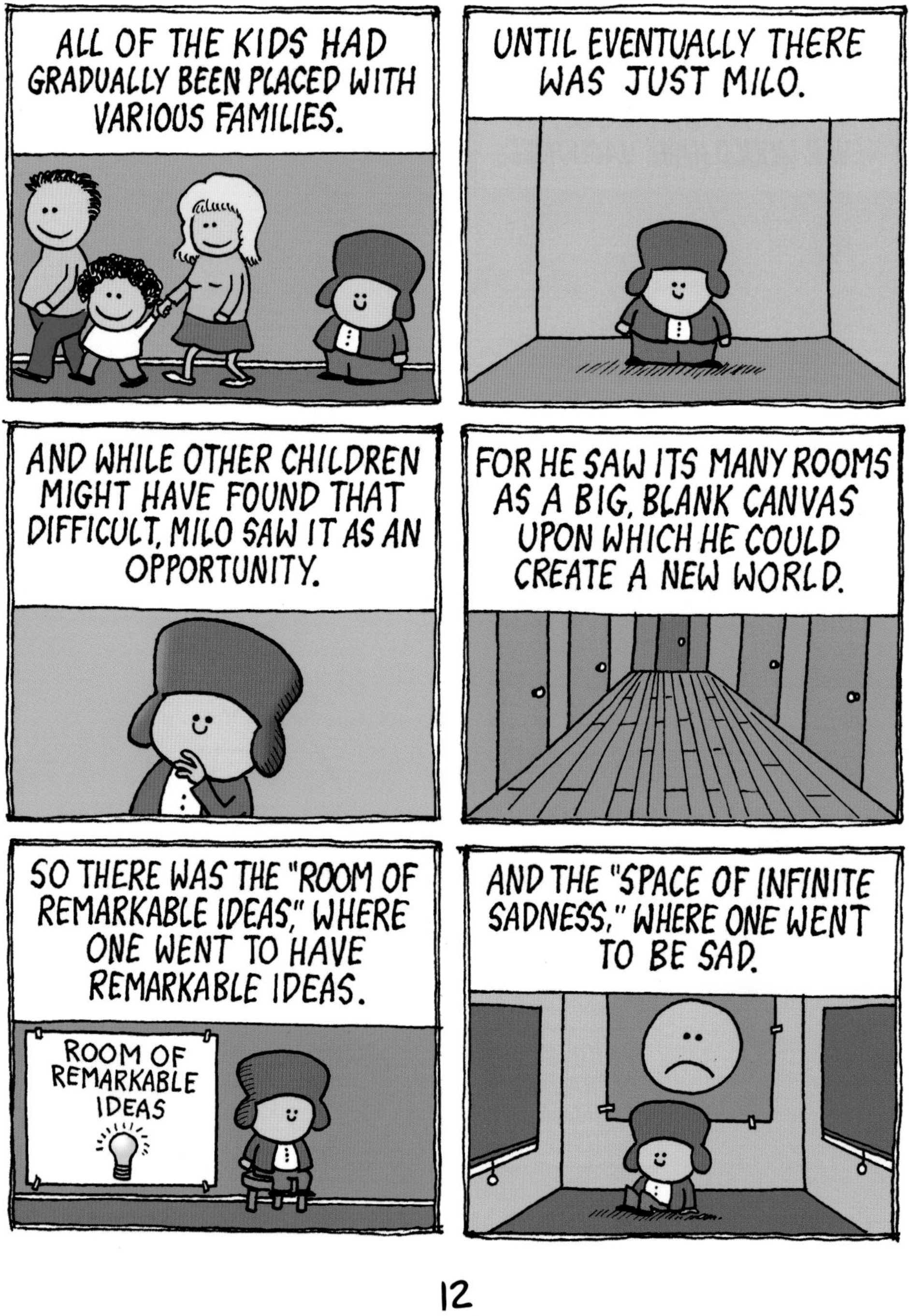
ALL OF THE KIDS HAD GRADUALLY BEEN PLACED WITH VARIOUS FAMILIES.
UNTIL EVENTUALLY THERE WAS JUST MILO.
AND WHILE OTHER CHILDREN MIGHT HAVE FOUND THAT DIFFICULT, MILO SAW IT AS AN OPPORTUNITY.
FOR HE SAW ITS MANY ROOMS AS A BIG, BLANK CANVAS UPON WHICH HE COULD CREATE A NEW WORLD.
SO THERE WAS THE "ROOM OF REMARKABLE IDEAS," WHERE ONE WENT TO HAVE REMARKABLE IDEAS.
ROOM OF REMARKABLE IDEAS
AND THE "SPACE OF INFINITE SADNESS," WHERE ONE WENT TO BE SAD.

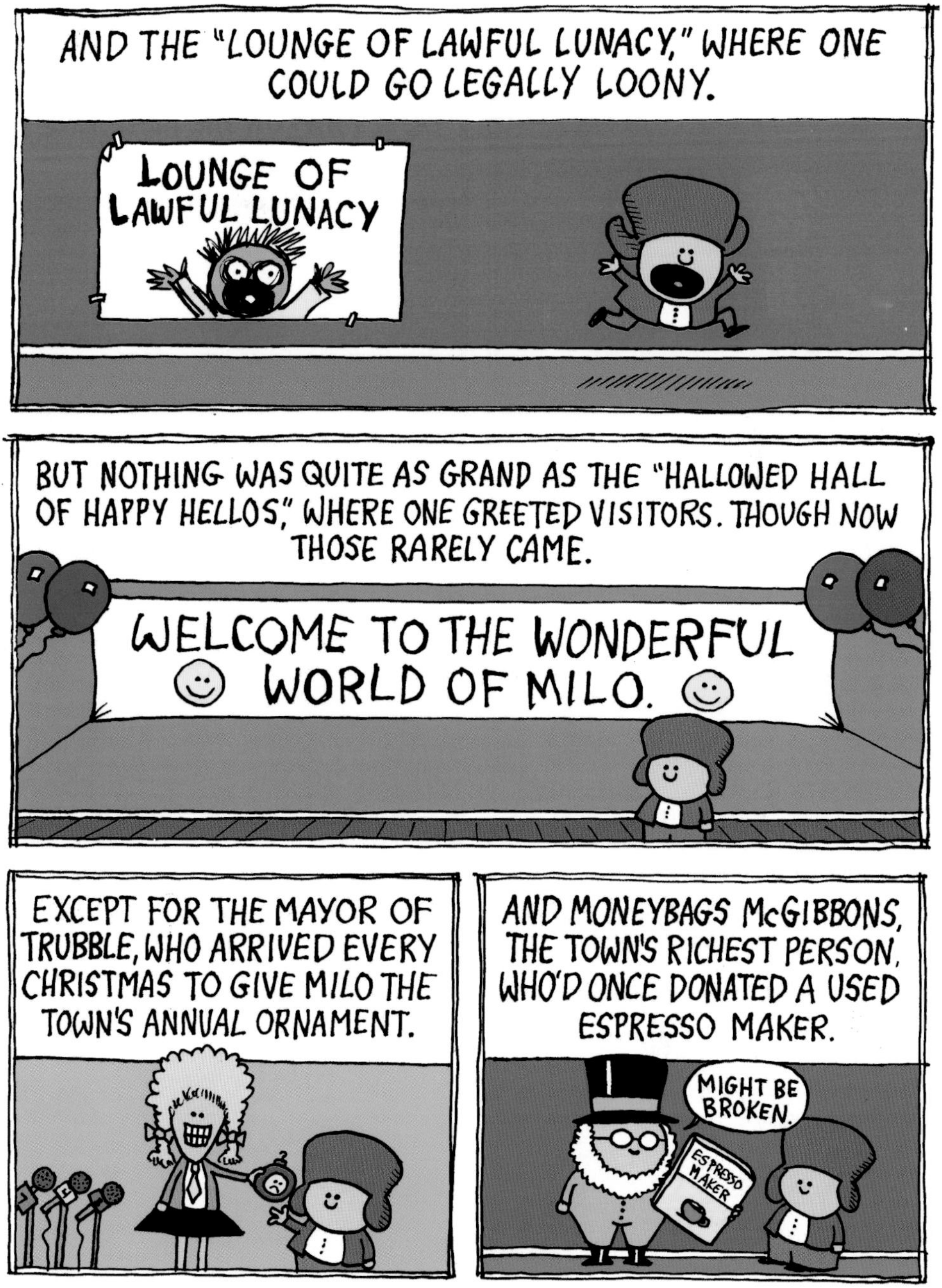
AND THE "LOUNGE OF LAWFUL LUNACY," WHERE ONE COULD GO LEGALLY LOONY.
LOUNGE OF LAWFUL LUNACY
BUT NOTHING WAS QUITE AS GRAND AS THE "HALLOWED HALL OF HAPPY HELLOS," WHERE ONE GREETED VISITORS. THOUGH NOW THOSE RARELY CAME.
WELCOME TO THE WONDERFUL WORLD OF MILO.
EXCEPT FOR THE MAYOR OF TRUBBLE, WHO ARRIVED EVERY CHRISTMAS TO GIVE MILO THE TOWN'S ANNUAL ORNAMENT.
AND MONEYBAGS McGIBBONS, THE TOWN'S RICHEST PERSON, WHO'D ONCE DONATED A USED ESPRESSO MAKER.
MIGHT BE BROKEN.
ESPRESSO MAKER

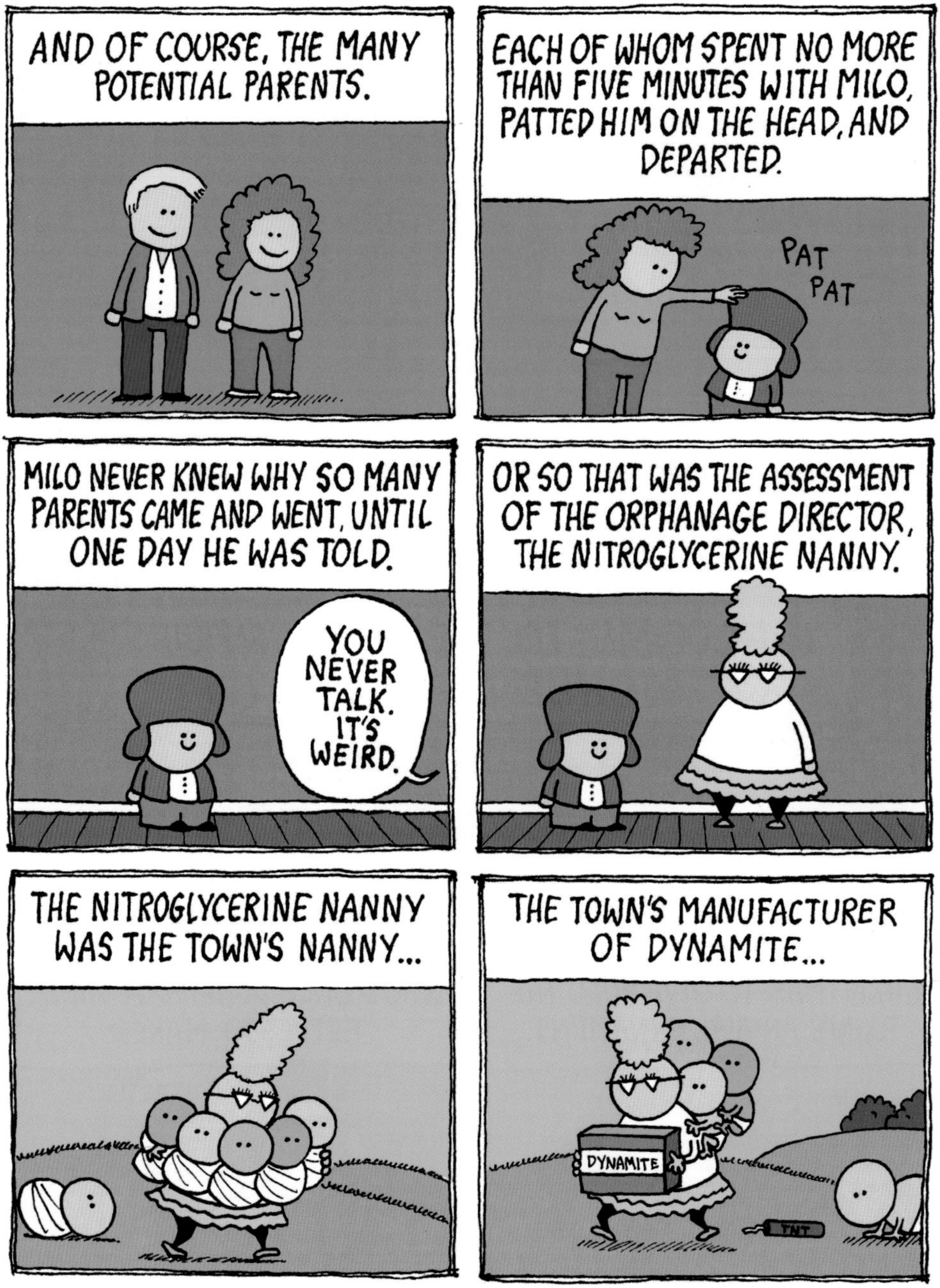
AND OF COURSE, THE MANY POTENTIAL PARENTS.
EACH OF WHOM SPENT NO MORE THAN FIVE MINUTES WITH MILO, PATTED HIM ON THE HEAD, AND DEPARTED.
PAT
PAT
MILO NEVER KNEW WHY SO MANY PARENTS CAME AND WENT, UNTIL ONE DAY HE WAS TOLD.
YOU NEVER TALK. IT'S WEIRD.
OR SO THAT WAS THE ASSESSMENT OF THE ORPHANAGE DIRECTOR, THE NITROGLYCERINE NANNY.
THE NITROGLYCERINE NANNY WAS THE TOWN'S NANNY...
THE TOWN'S MANUFACTURER OF DYNAMITE...
DYNAMITE
TNT

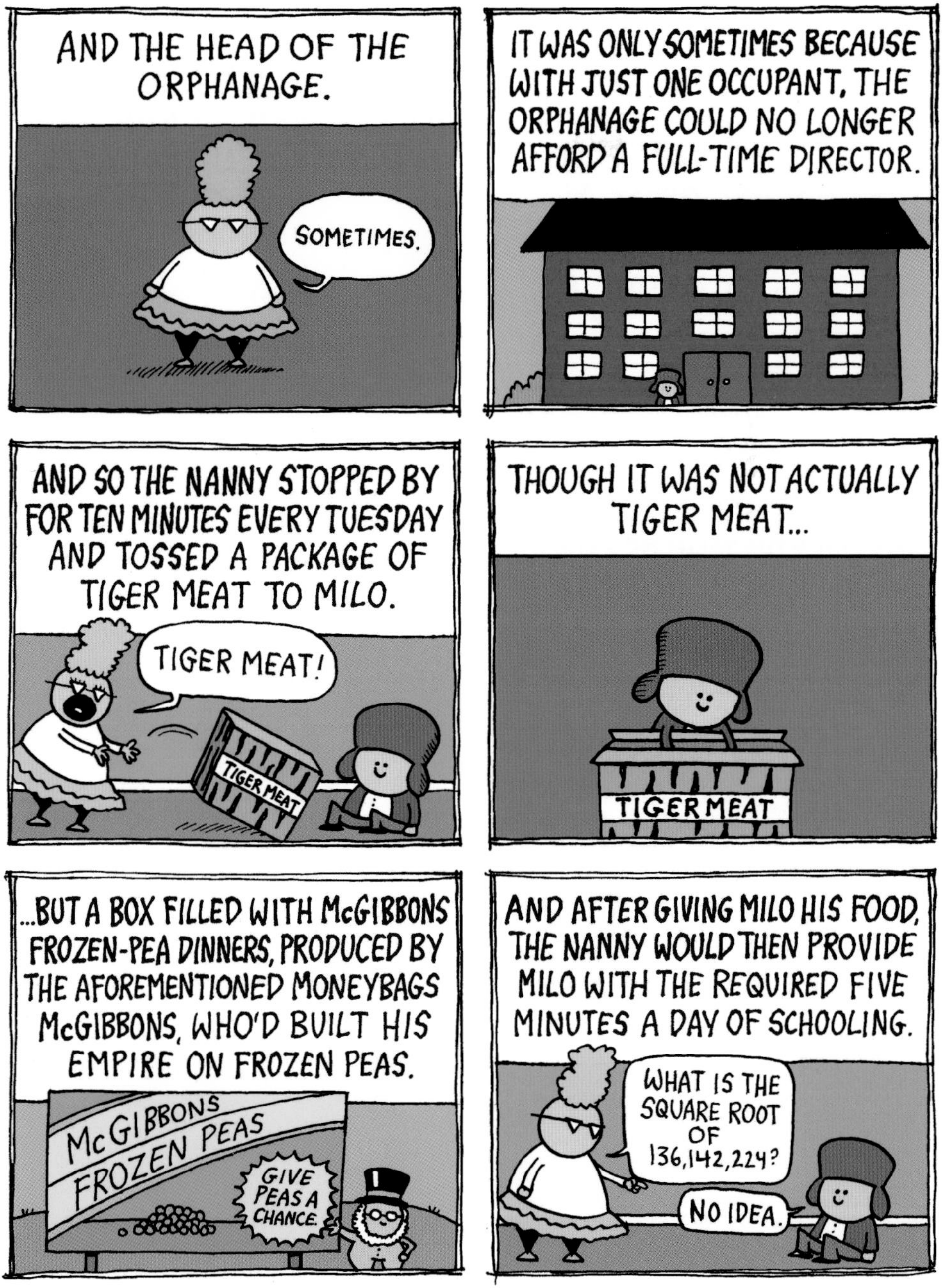
AND THE HEAD OF THE ORPHANAGE.
SOMETIMES.
IT WAS ONLY SOMETIMES BECAUSE WITH JUST ONE OCCUPANT, THE ORPHANAGE COULD NO LONGER AFFORD A FULL-TIME DIRECTOR.
AND SO THE NANNY STOPPED BY FOR TEN MINUTES EVERY TUESDAY AND TOSSED A PACKAGE OF TIGER MEAT TO MILO.
TIGER MEAT!
TIGER MEAT
THOUGH IT WAS NOT ACTUALLY TIGER MEAT...
TIGER MEAT
...BUT A BOX FILLED WITH McGIBBONS FROZEN-PEA DINNERS, PRODUCED BY THE AFOREMENTIONED MONEYBAGS McGIBBONS, WHO'D BUILT HIS EMPIRE ON FROZEN PEAS.
McGIBBONS FROZEN PEAS
GIVE PEAS A CHANCE.
AND AFTER GIVING MILO HIS FOOD, THE NANNY WOULD THEN PROVIDE MILO WITH THE REQUIRED FIVE MINUTES A DAY OF SCHOOLING.
WHAT IS THE SQUARE ROOT OF 136,142,224?
NO IDEA.

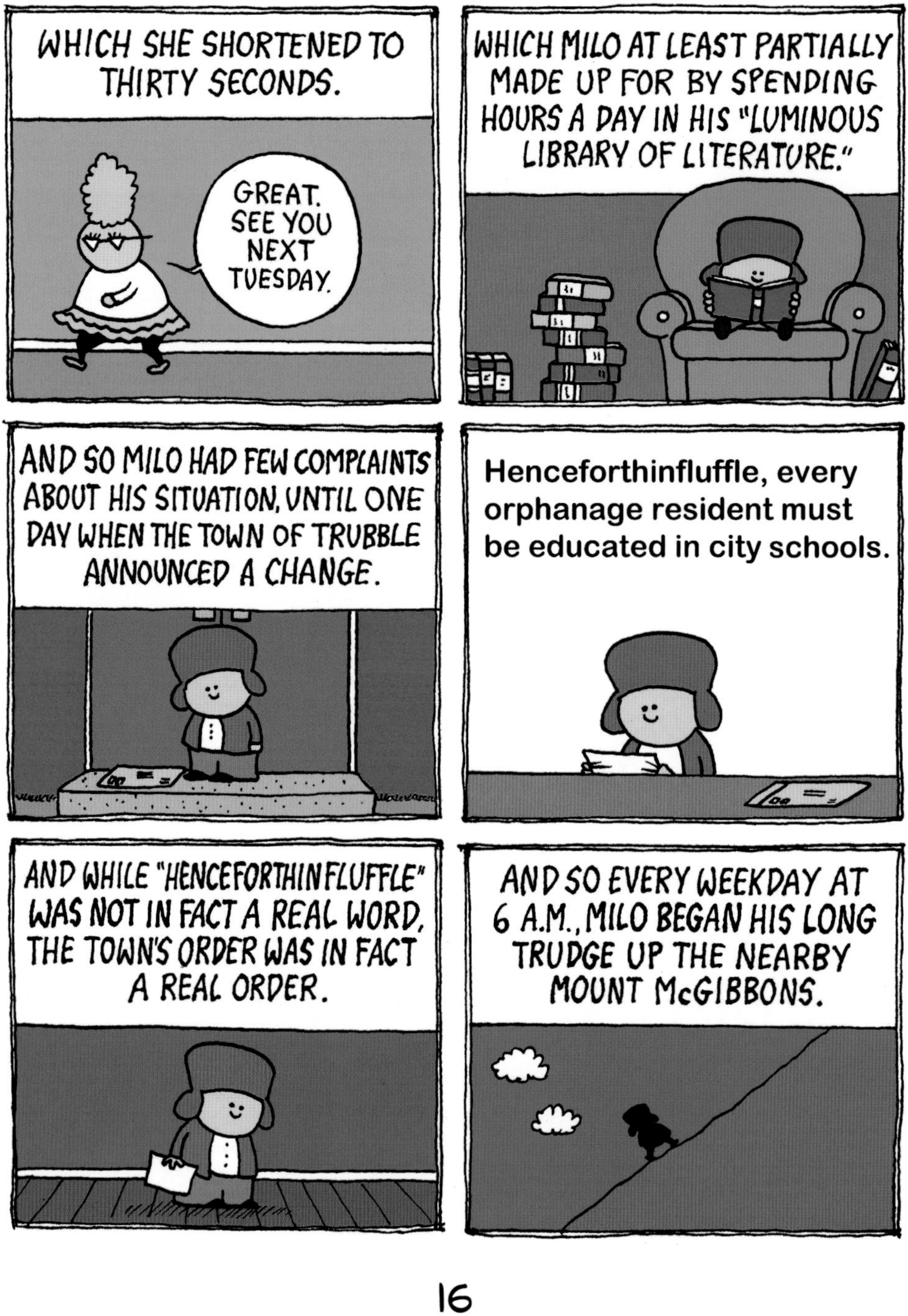
WHICH SHE SHORTENED TO THIRTY SECONDS.
GREAT. SEE YOU NEXT TUESDAY.
WHICH MILO AT LEAST PARTIALLY MADE UP FOR BY SPENDING HOURS A DAY IN HIS "LUMINOUS LIBRARY OF LITERATURE."
AND SO MILO HAD FEW COMPLAINTS ABOUT HIS SITUATION, UNTIL ONE DAY WHEN THE TOWN OF TRUBBLE ANNOUNCED A CHANGE.
Henceforthinfluffle, every orphanage resident must be educated in city schools.
AND WHILE "HENCEFORTHINFLUFFLE" WAS NOT IN FACT A REAL WORD, THE TOWN'S ORDER WAS IN FACT A REAL ORDER.
AND SO EVERY WEEKDAY AT 6 A.M., MILO BEGAN HIS LONG TRUDGE UP THE NEARBY MOUNT McGIBBONS.

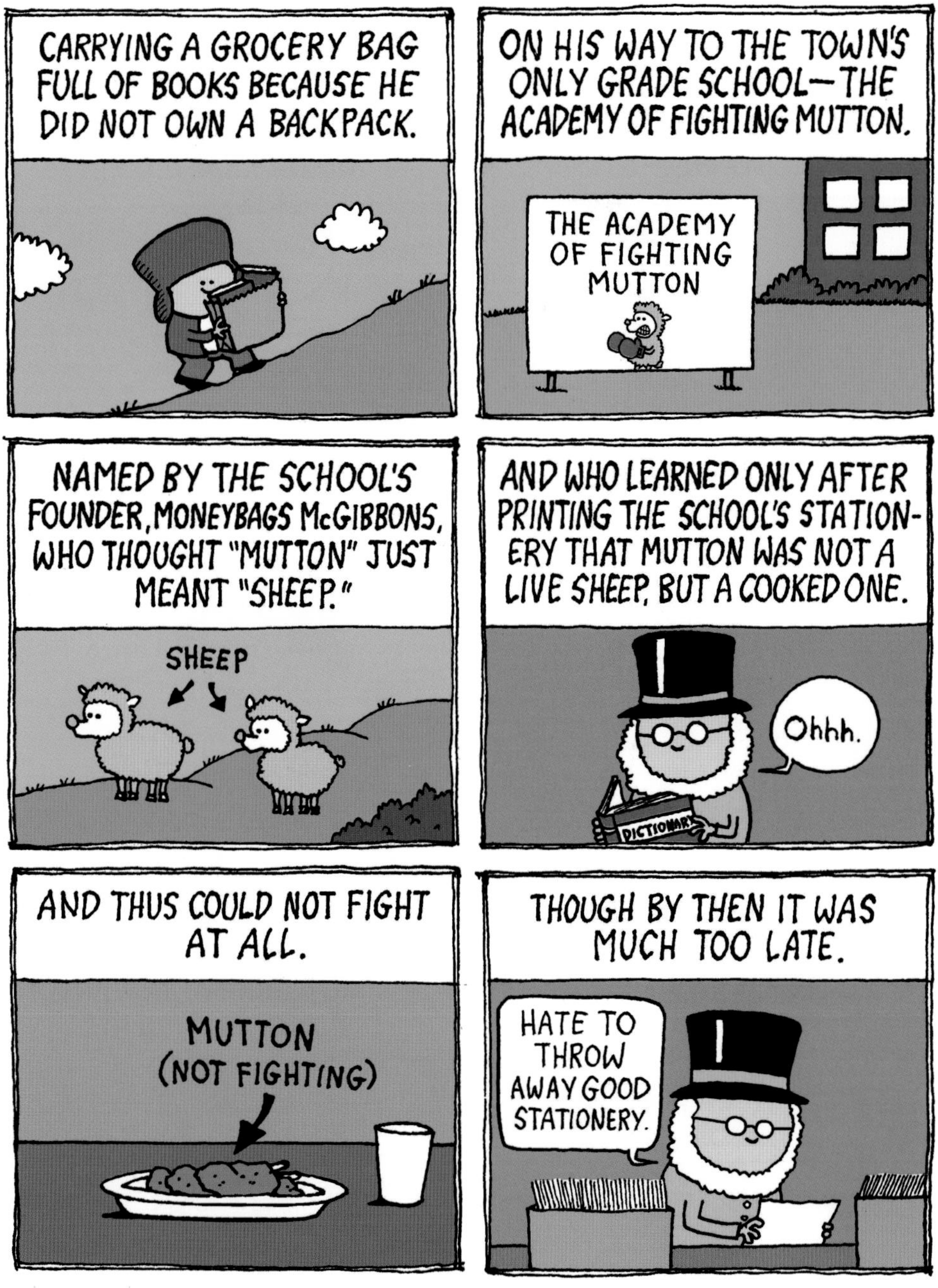
CARRYING A GROCERY BAG FULL OF BOOKS BECAUSE HE DID NOT OWN A BACKPACK.
ON HIS WAY TO THE TOWN'S ONLY GRADE SCHOOL—THE ACADEMY OF FIGHTING MUTTON.
THE ACADEMY OF FIGHTING MUTTON
NAMED BY THE SCHOOL'S FOUNDER, MONEYBAGS McGIBBONS, WHO THOUGHT "MUTTON" JUST MEANT "SHEEP."
SHEEP
AND WHO LEARNED ONLY AFTER PRINTING THE SCHOOL'S STATIONERY THAT MUTTON WAS NOT A LIVE SHEEP, BUT A COOKED ONE.
Ohhh.
DICTIONARY
AND THUS COULD NOT FIGHT AT ALL.
MUTTON (NOT FIGHTING)
THOUGH BY THEN IT WAS MUCH TOO LATE.
HATE TO THROW AWAY GOOD STATIONERY.

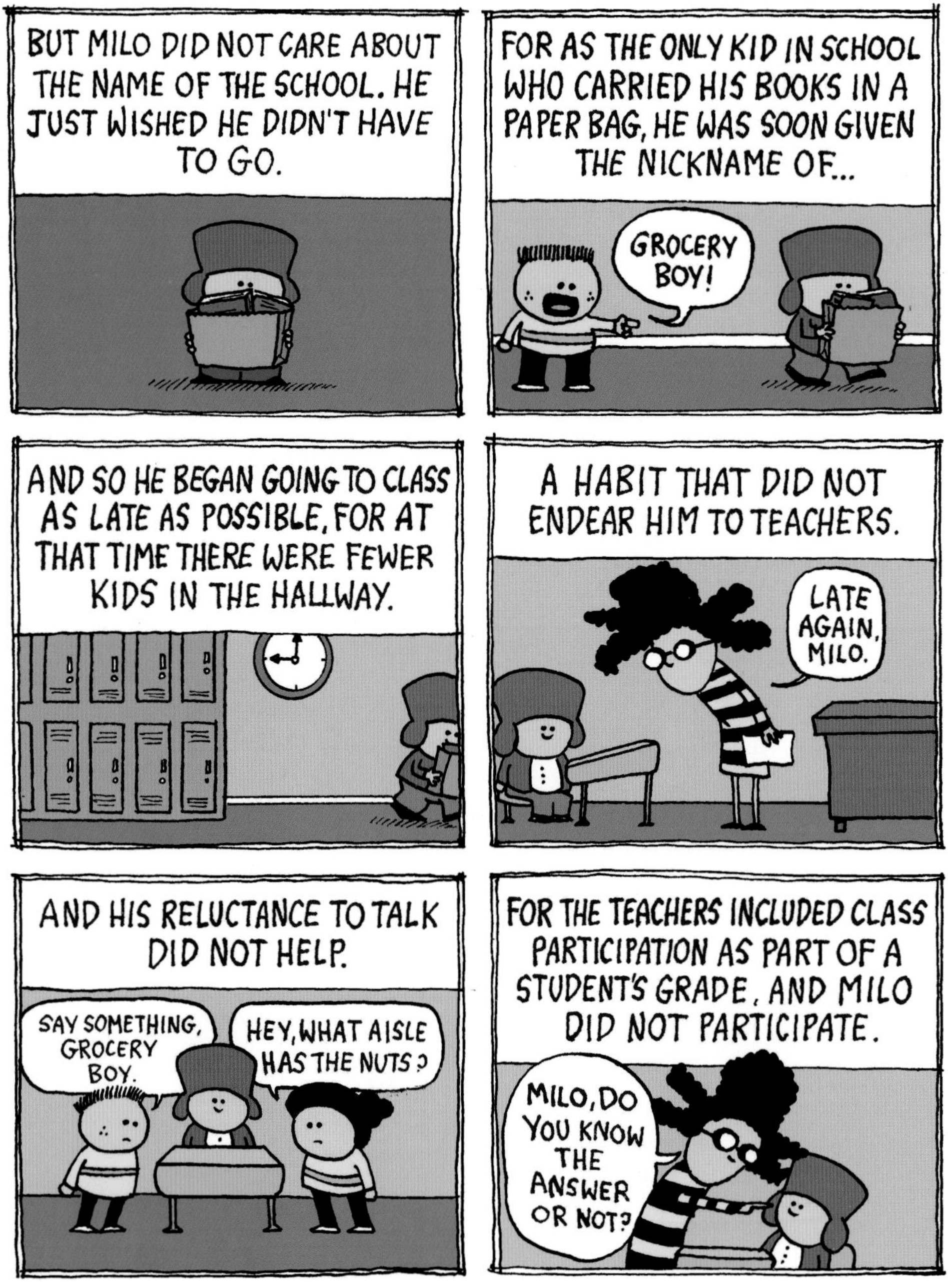
BUT MILO DID NOT CARE ABOUT THE NAME OF THE SCHOOL. HE JUST WISHED HE DIDN'T HAVE TO GO.
FOR AS THE ONLY KID IN SCHOOL WHO CARRIED HIS BOOKS IN A PAPER BAG, HE WAS SOON GIVEN THE NICKNAME OF...
GROCERY BOY!
AND SO HE BEGAN GOING TO CLASS AS LATE AS POSSIBLE, FOR AT THAT TIME THERE WERE FEWER KIDS IN THE HALLWAY.
A HABIT THAT DID NOT ENDEAR HIM TO TEACHERS.
LATE AGAIN, MILO.
AND HIS RELUCTANCE TO TALK DID NOT HELP.
SAY SOMETHING, GROCERY BOY.
HEY, WHAT AISLE HAS THE NUTS?
FOR THE TEACHERS INCLUDED CLASS PARTICIPATION AS PART OF A STUDENT'S GRADE, AND MILO DID NOT PARTICIPATE.
MILO, DO YOU KNOW THE ANSWER OR NOT?

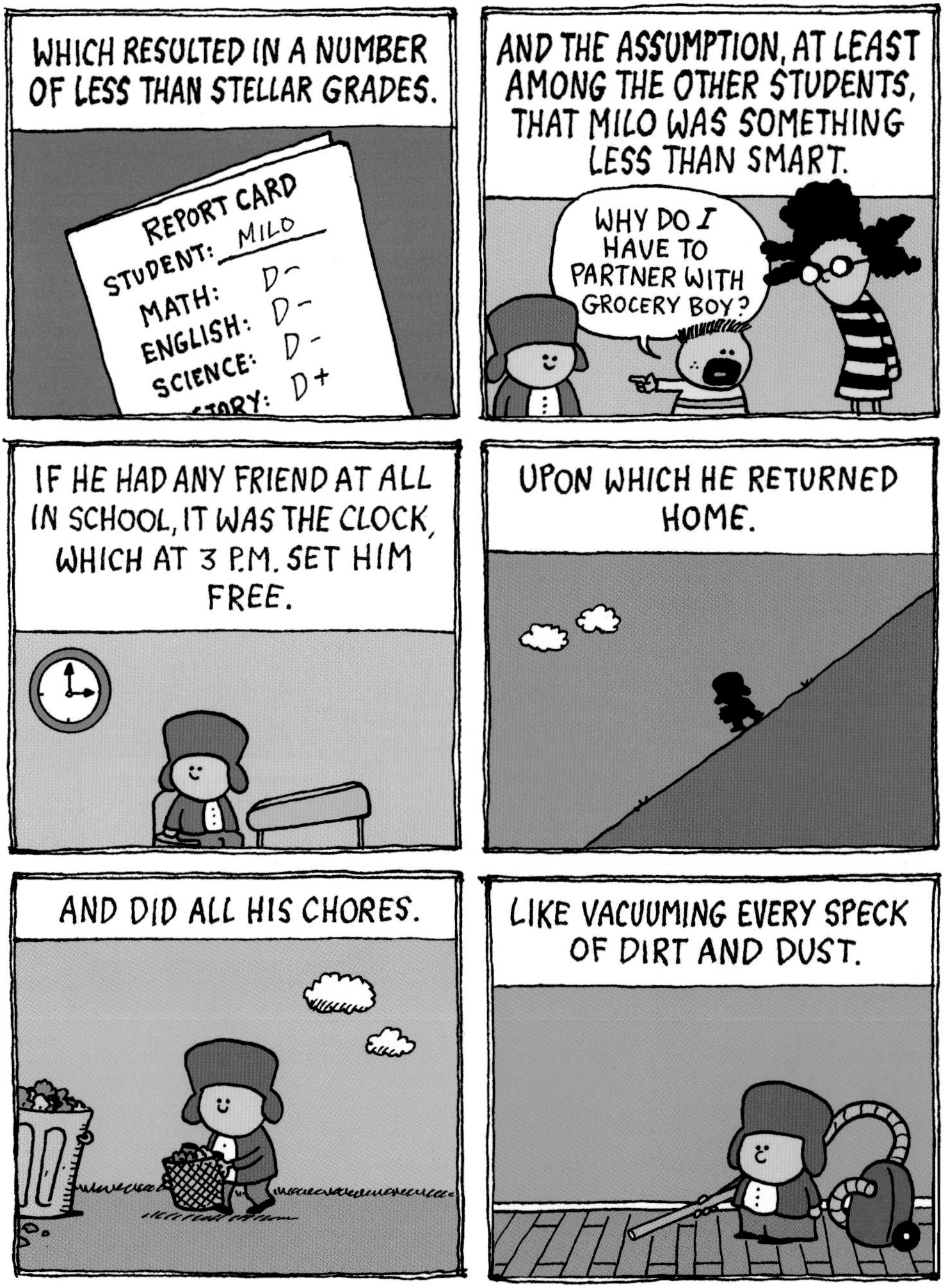
WHICH RESULTED IN A NUMBER OF LESS THAN STELLAR GRADES.
REPORT CARD
STUDENT: MILO
MATH: D-
ENGLISH: D-
SCIENCE: D-
D+
AND THE ASSUMPTION, AT LEAST AMONG THE OTHER STUDENTS, THAT MILO WAS SOMETHING LESS THAN SMART.
WHY DO I HAVE TO PARTNER WITH GROCERY BOY?
IF HE HAD ANY FRIEND AT ALL IN SCHOOL, IT WAS THE CLOCK, WHICH AT 3 P.M. SET HIM FREE.
UPON WHICH HE RETURNED HOME.
AND DID ALL HIS CHORES.
LIKE VACUUMING EVERY SPECK OF DIRT AND DUST.

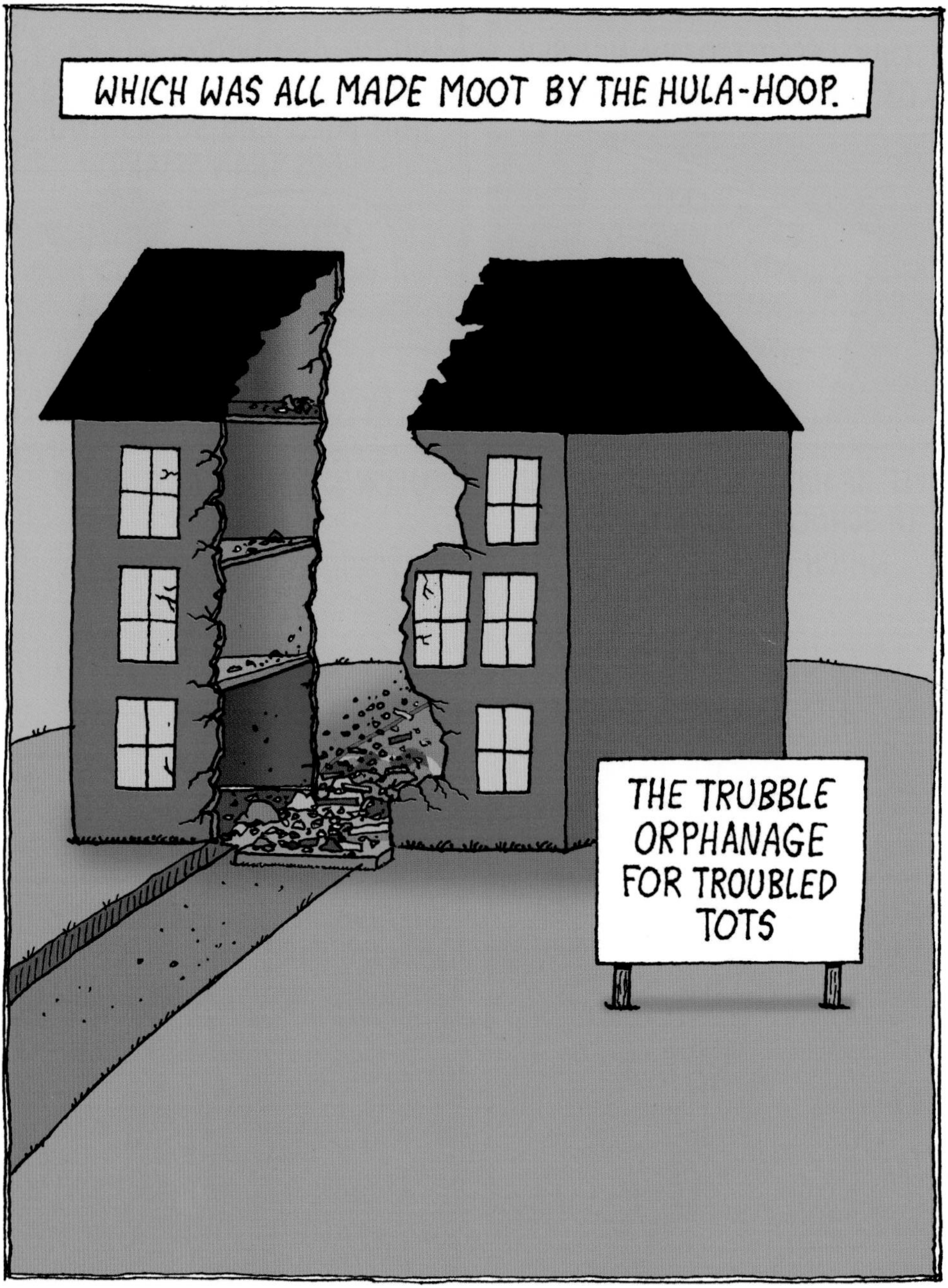
WHICH WAS ALL MADE MOOT BY THE HULA-HOOP.
THE TRUBBLE ORPHANAGE FOR TROUBLED TOTS

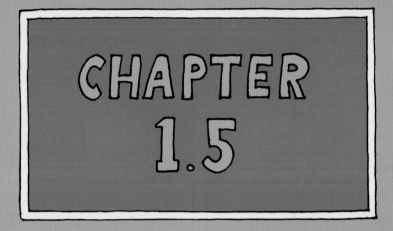

CHAPTER 1.5

BECAUSE CHAPTERS SHOULDN'T HAVE TO BE WHOLE NUMBERS

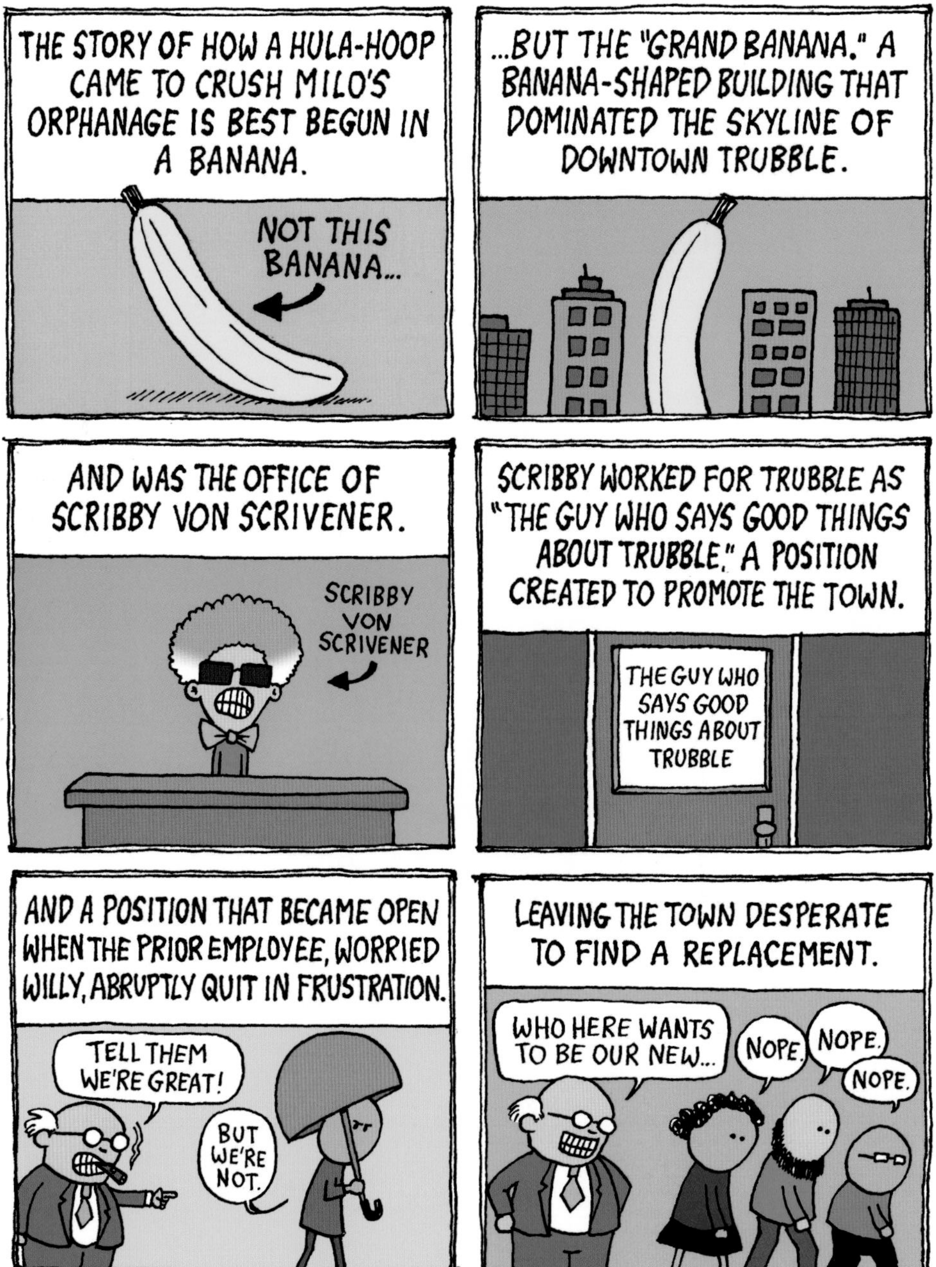
THE STORY OF HOW A HULA-HOOP CAME TO CRUSH MILO'S ORPHANAGE IS BEST BEGUN IN A BANANA.
NOT THIS BANANA...
...BUT THE "GRAND BANANA." A BANANA-SHAPED BUILDING THAT DOMINATED THE SKYLINE OF DOWNTOWN TRUBBLE.
AND WAS THE OFFICE OF SCRIBBY VON SCRIVENER.
SCRIBBY VON SCRIVENER
SCRIBBY WORKED FOR TRUBBLE AS "THE GUY WHO SAYS GOOD THINGS ABOUT TRUBBLE," A POSITION CREATED TO PROMOTE THE TOWN.
THE GUY WHO SAYS GOOD THINGS ABOUT TRUBBLE
AND A POSITION THAT BECAME OPEN WHEN THE PRIOR EMPLOYEE, WORRIED WILLY, ABRUPTLY QUIT IN FRUSTRATION.
TELL THEM WE'RE GREAT!
BUT WE'RE NOT.
LEAVING THE TOWN DESPERATE TO FIND A REPLACEMENT.
WHO HERE WANTS TO BE OUR NEW...
NOPE.
NOPE.
NOPE.

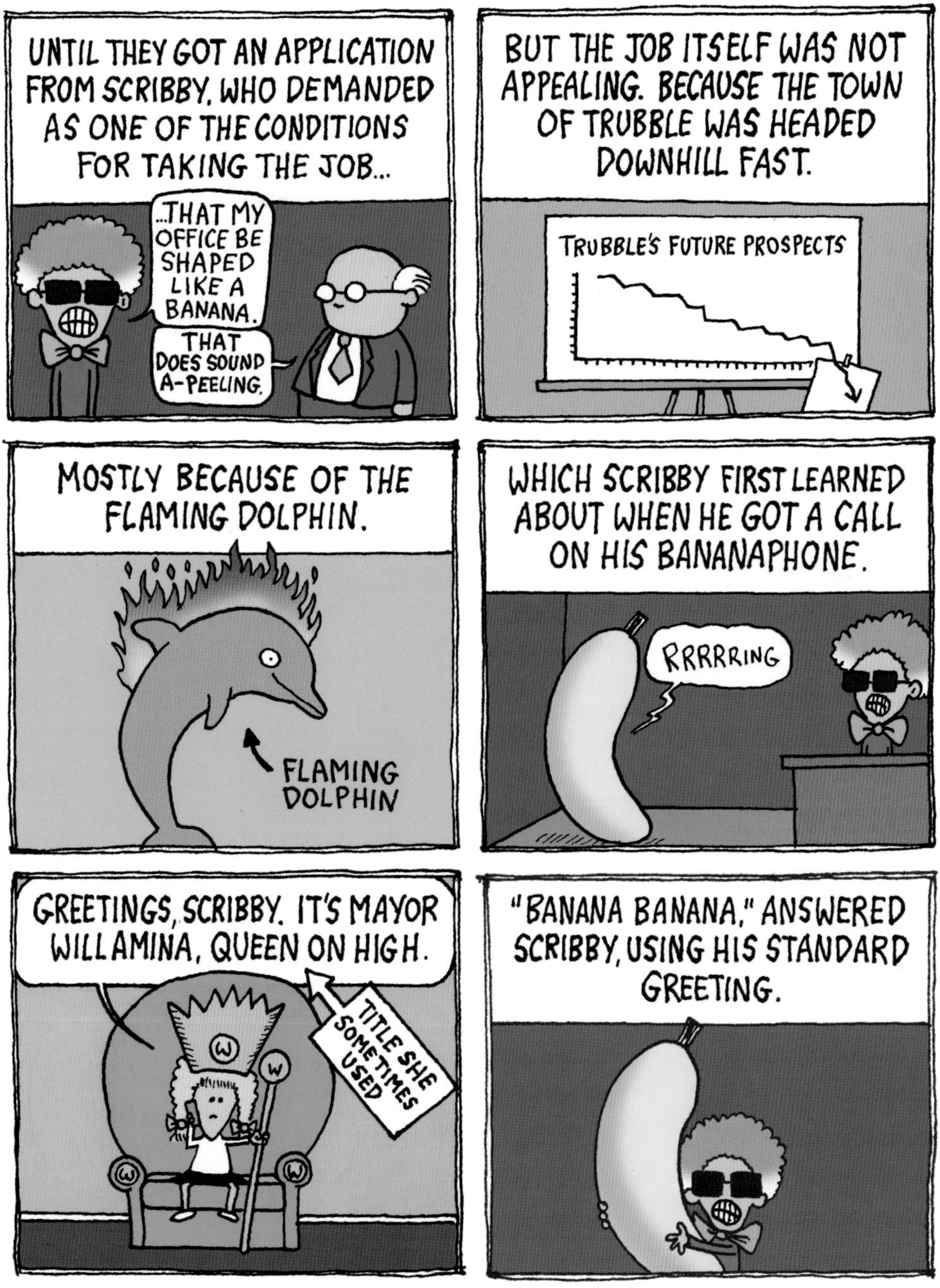
UNTIL THEY GOT AN APPLICATION FROM SCRIBBY, WHO DEMANDED AS ONE OF THE CONDITIONS FOR TAKING THE JOB...
...THAT MY OFFICE BE SHAPED LIKE A BANANA.
THAT DOES SOUND A-PEELING.
BUT THE JOB ITSELF WAS NOT APPEALING. BECAUSE THE TOWN OF TRUBBLE WAS HEADED DOWNHILL FAST.
TRUBBLE'S FUTURE PROSPECTS
MOSTLY BECAUSE OF THE FLAMING DOLPHIN.
FLAMING DOLPHIN
WHICH SCRIBBY FIRST LEARNED ABOUT WHEN HE GOT A CALL ON HIS BANANAPHONE.
RRRRRING
GREETINGS, SCRIBBY. IT'S MAYOR WILLAMINA, QUEEN ON HIGH.
TITLE SHE SOMETIMES USED
"BANANA BANANA," ANSWERED SCRIBBY, USING HIS STANDARD GREETING.

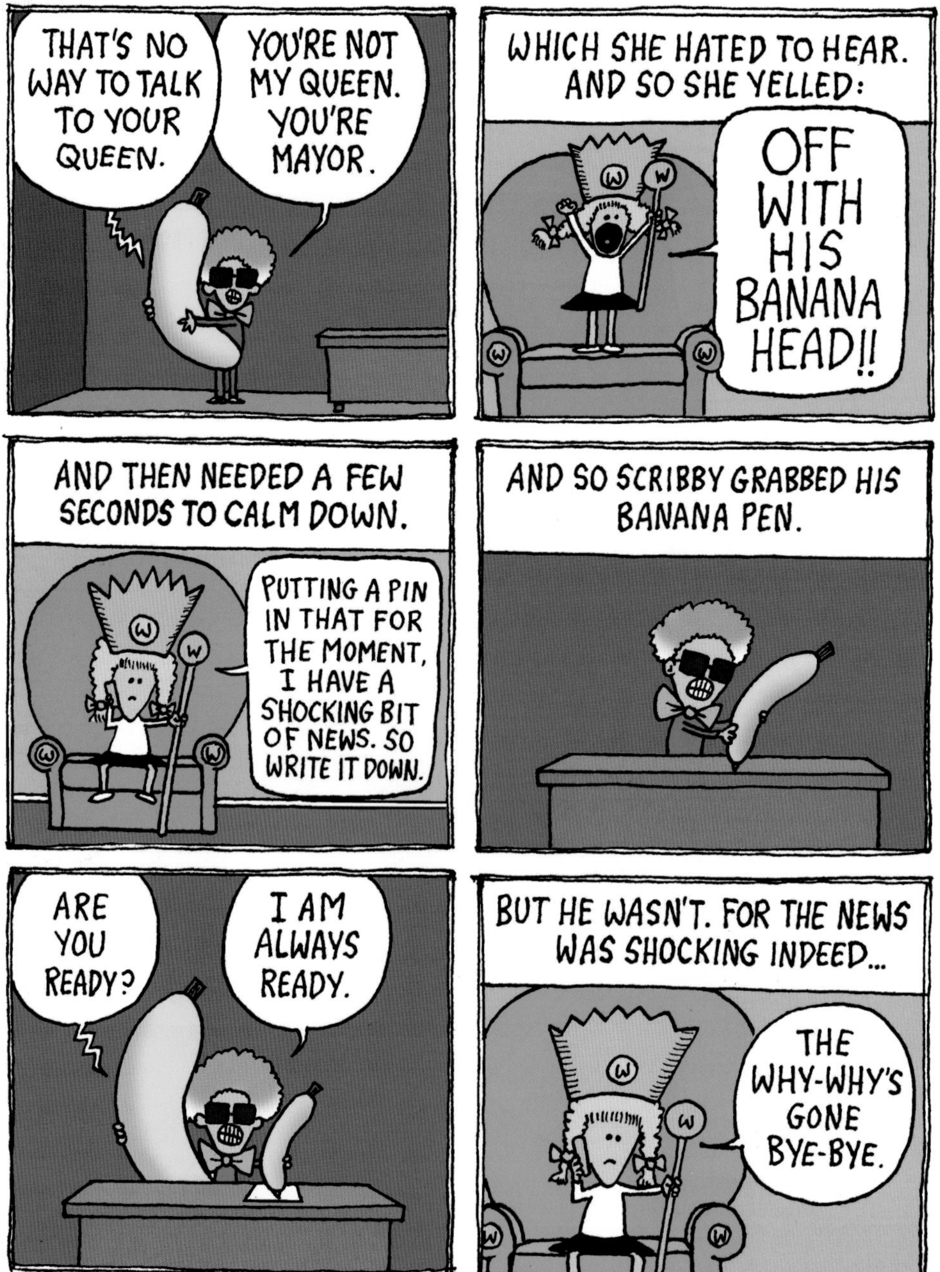
THAT'S NO WAY TO TALK TO YOUR QUEEN.
YOU'RE NOT MY QUEEN. YOU'RE MAYOR.
WHICH SHE HATED TO HEAR. AND SO SHE YELLED:
OFF WITH HIS BANANA HEAD!!
AND THEN NEEDED A FEW SECONDS TO CALM DOWN.
PUTTING A PIN IN THAT FOR THE MOMENT, I HAVE A SHOCKING BIT OF NEWS. SO WRITE IT DOWN.
AND SO SCRIBBY GRABBED HIS BANANA PEN.
ARE YOU READY?
I AM ALWAYS READY.
BUT HE WASN'T. FOR THE NEWS WAS SHOCKING INDEED...
THE WHY-WHY'S GONE BYE-BYE.

CHAPTER TOO

AS IN...

TOO SHOCKING TO BE BELIEVED

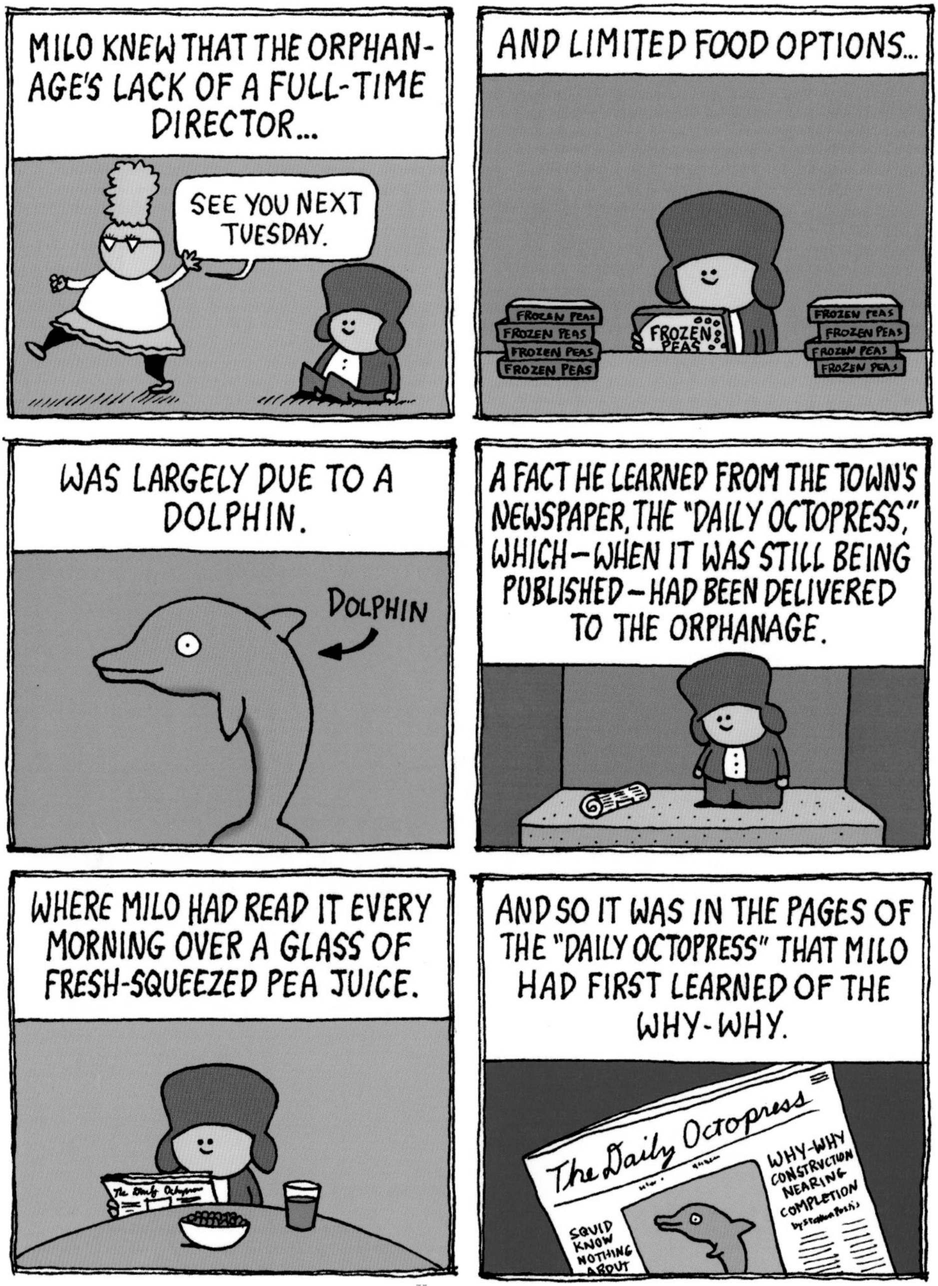
MILO KNEW THAT THE ORPHANAGE'S LACK OF A FULL-TIME DIRECTOR...
SEE YOU NEXT TUESDAY.
AND LIMITED FOOD OPTIONS...
FROZEN PEAS
FROZEN PEAS
FROZEN PEAS
FROZEN PEAS
FROZEN PEAS
FROZEN PEAS
FROZEN PEAS
FROZEN PEAS
FROZEN PEAS
WAS LARGELY DUE TO A DOLPHIN.
DOLPHIN
A FACT HE LEARNED FROM THE TOWN'S NEWSPAPER, THE "DAILY OCTOPRESS," WHICH—WHEN IT WAS STILL BEING PUBLISHED—HAD BEEN DELIVERED TO THE ORPHANAGE.
WHERE MILO HAD READ IT EVERY MORNING OVER A GLASS OF FRESH-SQUEEZED PEA JUICE.
AND SO IT WAS IN THE PAGES OF THE "DAILY OCTOPRESS" THAT MILO HAD FIRST LEARNED OF THE WHY-WHY.
The Daily Octopress
WHY-WHY CONSTRUCTION NEARING COMPLETION
SQUID KNOW NOTHING ABOUT

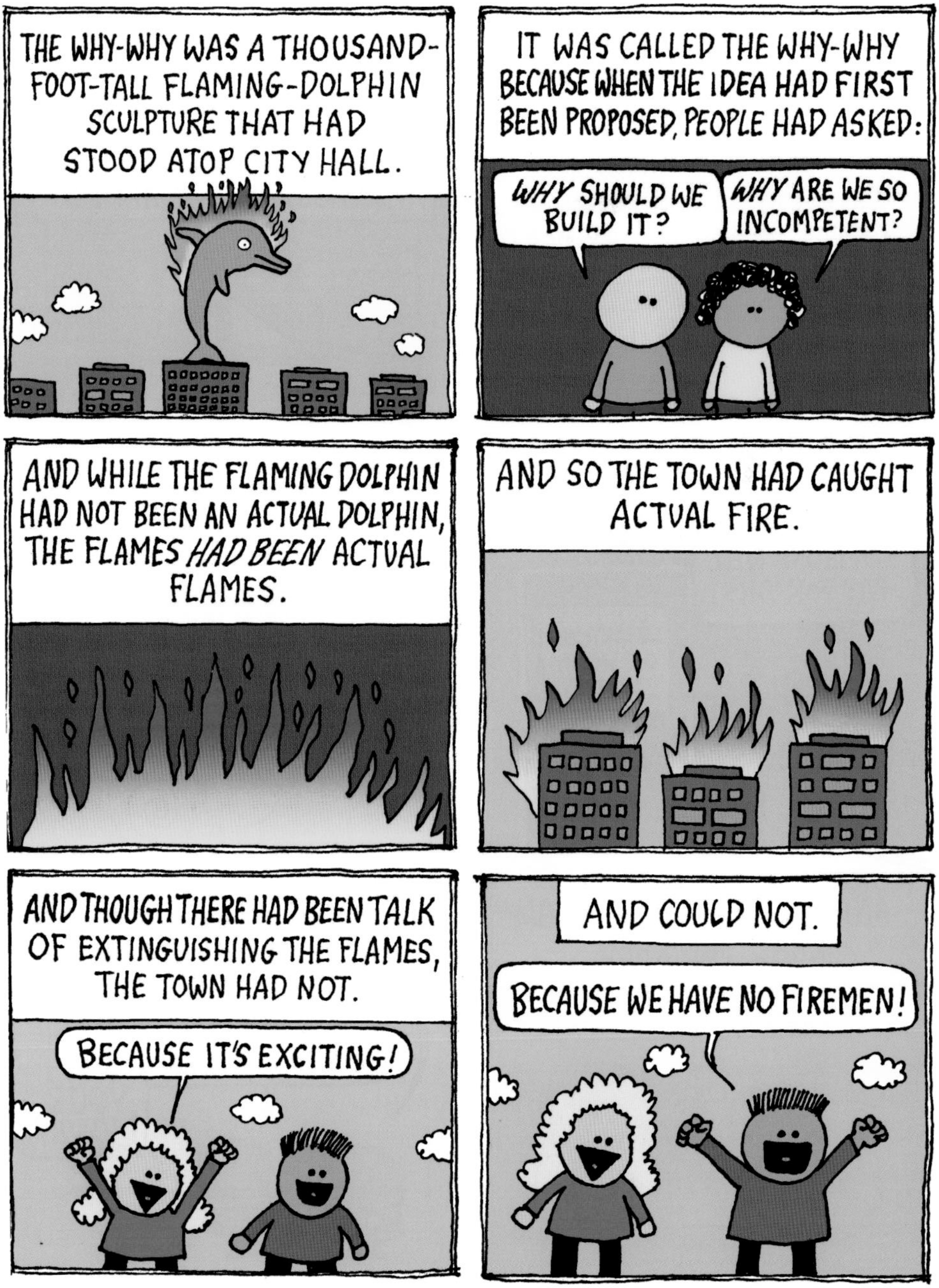
THE WHY-WHY WAS A THOUSAND-FOOT-TALL FLAMING-DOLPHIN SCULPTURE THAT HAD STOOD ATOP CITY HALL.
IT WAS CALLED THE WHY-WHY BECAUSE WHEN THE IDEA HAD FIRST BEEN PROPOSED, PEOPLE HAD ASKED:
WHY SHOULD WE BUILD IT?
WHY ARE WE SO INCOMPETENT?
AND WHILE THE FLAMING DOLPHIN HAD NOT BEEN AN ACTUAL DOLPHIN, THE FLAMES HAD BEEN ACTUAL FLAMES.
AND SO THE TOWN HAD CAUGHT ACTUAL FIRE.
AND THOUGH THERE HAD BEEN TALK OF EXTINGUISHING THE FLAMES, THE TOWN HAD NOT.
BECAUSE IT'S EXCITING!
AND COULD NOT.
BECAUSE WE HAVE NO FIREMEN!

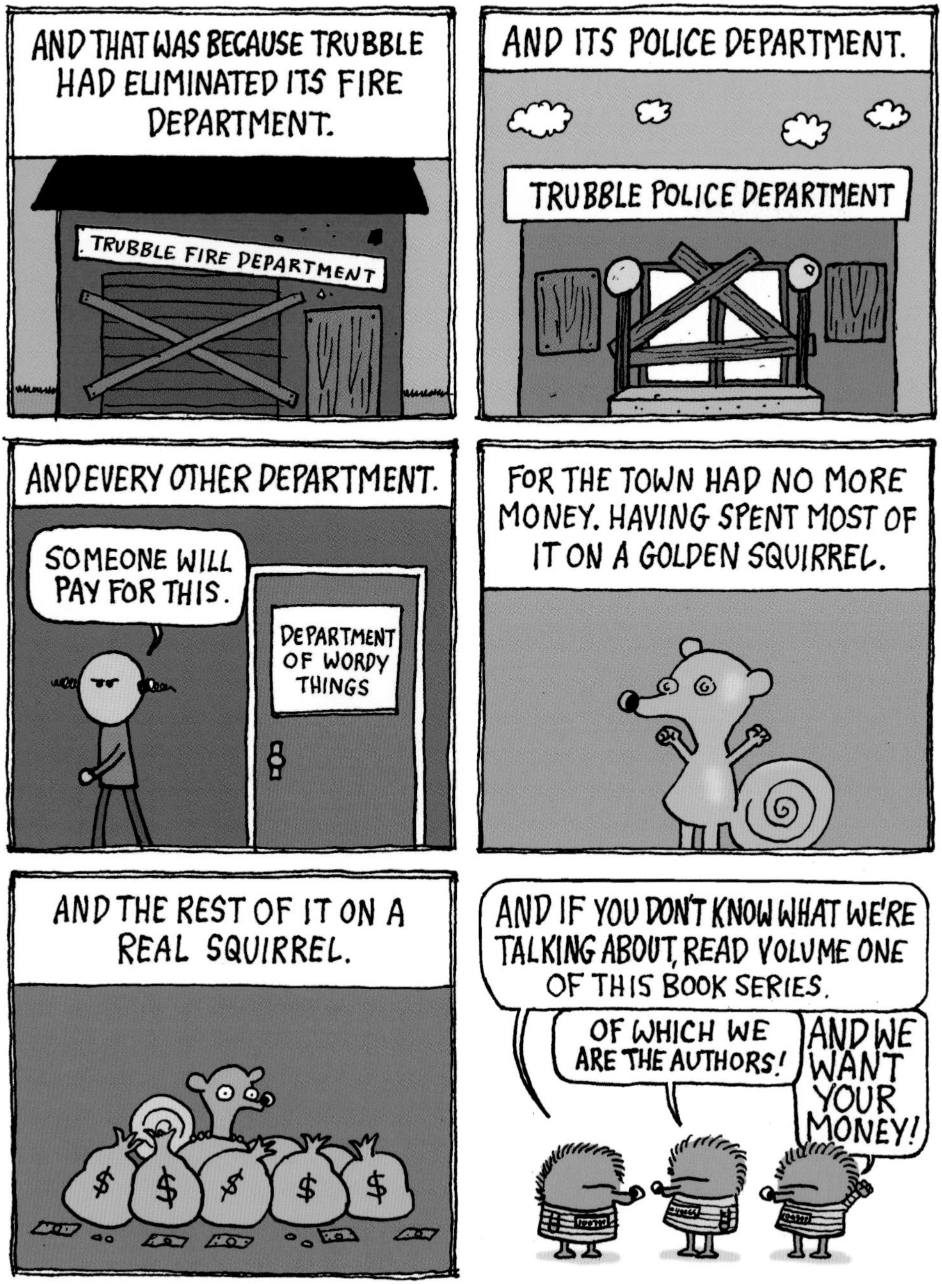
AND THAT WAS BECAUSE TRUBBLE HAD ELIMINATED ITS FIRE DEPARTMENT.
TRUBBLE FIRE DEPARTMENT
AND ITS POLICE DEPARTMENT.
TRUBBLE POLICE DEPARTMENT
AND EVERY OTHER DEPARTMENT.
SOMEONE WILL PAY FOR THIS.
DEPARTMENT OF WORDY THINGS
FOR THE TOWN HAD NO MORE MONEY. HAVING SPENT MOST OF IT ON A GOLDEN SQUIRREL.
AND THE REST OF IT ON A REAL SQUIRREL.
AND IF YOU DON'T KNOW WHAT WE'RE TALKING ABOUT, READ VOLUME ONE OF THIS BOOK SERIES.
OF WHICH WE ARE THE AUTHORS!
AND WE WANT YOUR MONEY!

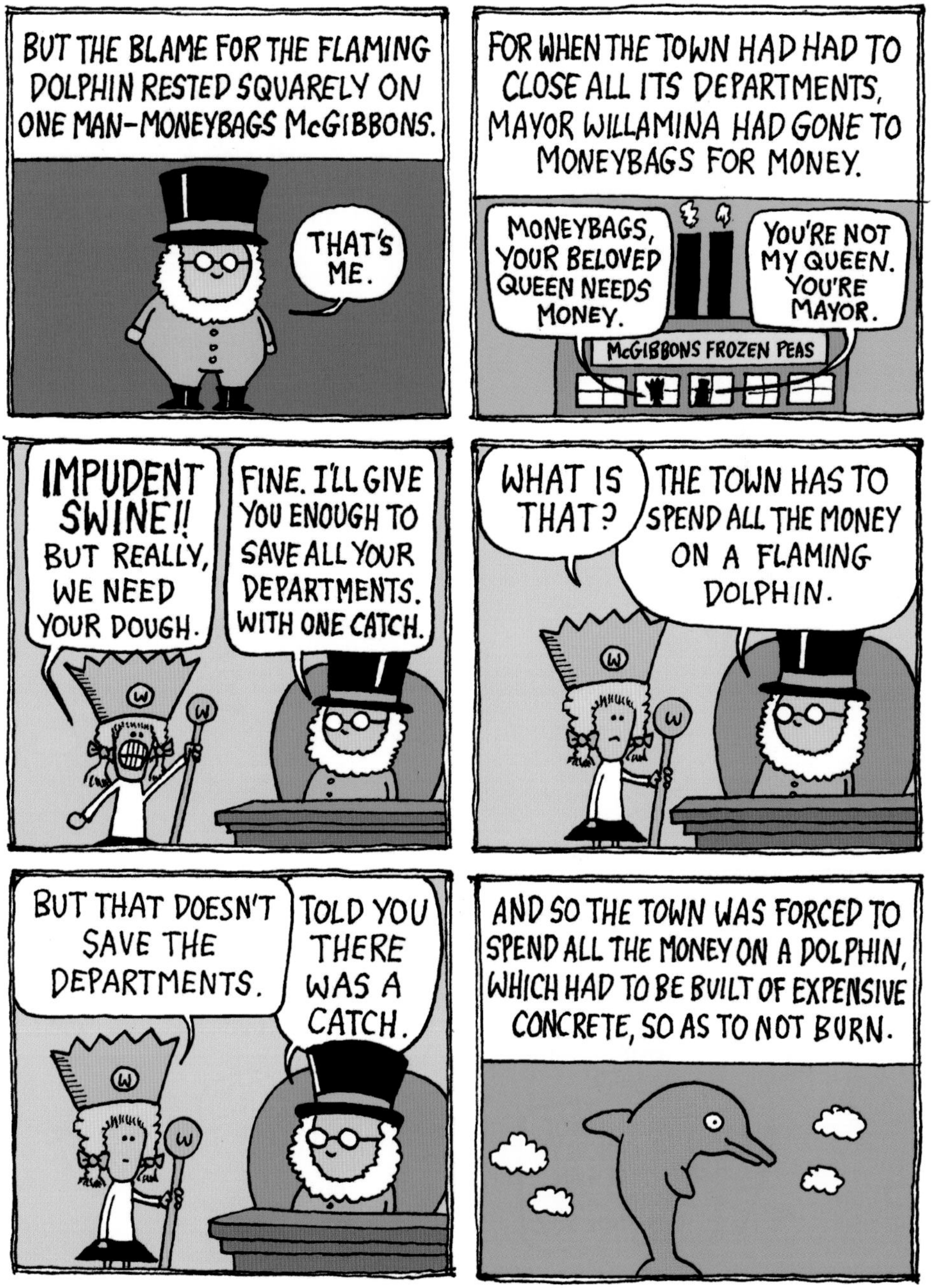
BUT THE BLAME FOR THE FLAMING DOLPHIN RESTED SQUARELY ON ONE MAN—MONEYBAGS McGIBBONS.
THAT'S ME.
FOR WHEN THE TOWN HAD HAD TO CLOSE ALL ITS DEPARTMENTS, MAYOR WILLAMINA HAD GONE TO MONEYBAGS FOR MONEY.
MONEYBAGS, YOUR BELOVED QUEEN NEEDS MONEY.
YOU'RE NOT MY QUEEN. YOU'RE MAYOR.
McGIBBONS FROZEN PEAS
IMPUDENT SWINE!! BUT REALLY, WE NEED YOUR DOUGH.
FINE. I'LL GIVE YOU ENOUGH TO SAVE ALL YOUR DEPARTMENTS. WITH ONE CATCH.
WHAT IS THAT?
THE TOWN HAS TO SPEND ALL THE MONEY ON A FLAMING DOLPHIN.
BUT THAT DOESN'T SAVE THE DEPARTMENTS.
TOLD YOU THERE WAS A CATCH.
AND SO THE TOWN WAS FORCED TO SPEND ALL THE MONEY ON A DOLPHIN, WHICH HAD TO BE BUILT OF EXPENSIVE CONCRETE, SO AS TO NOT BURN.

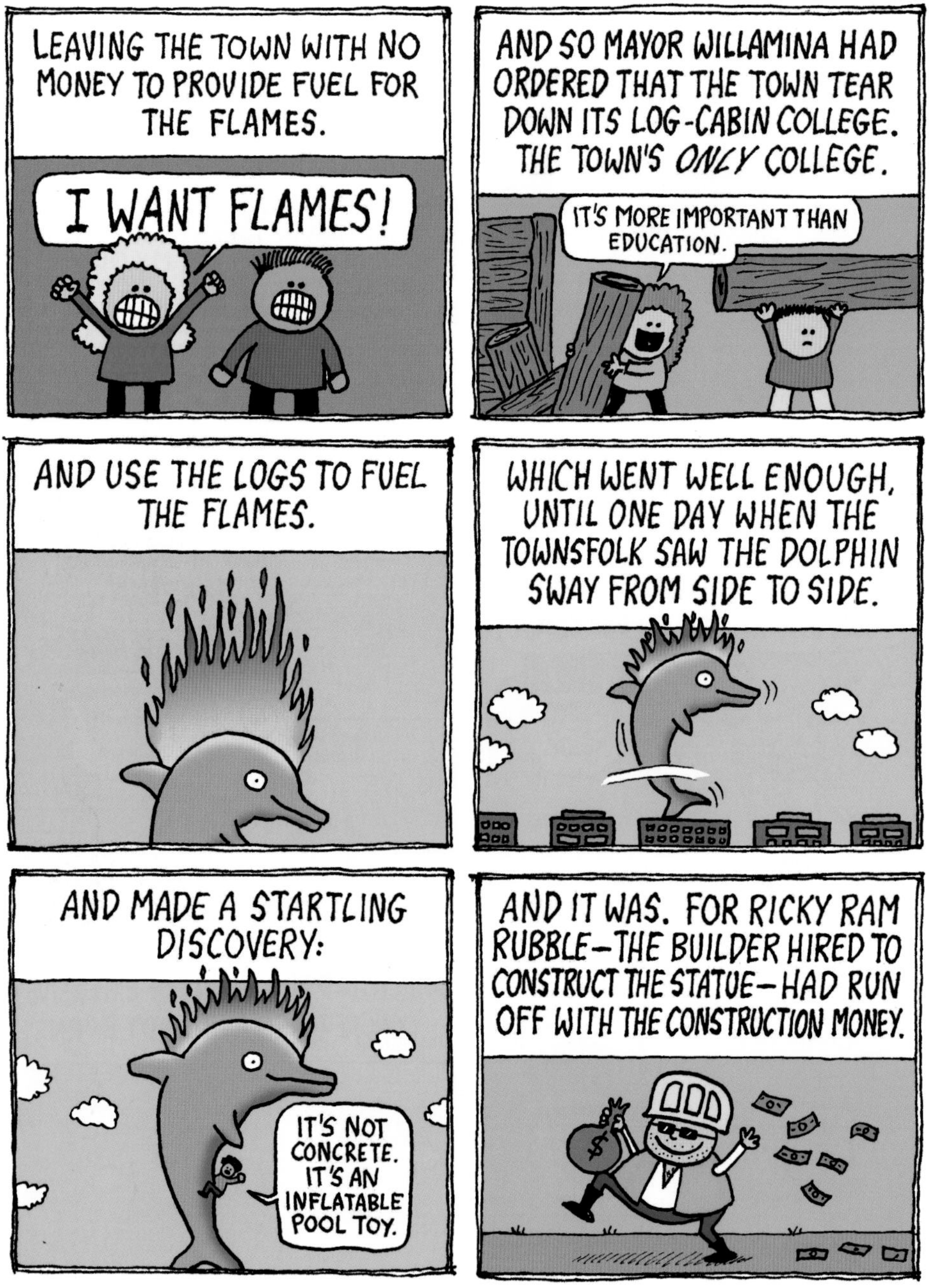
LEAVING THE TOWN WITH NO MONEY TO PROVIDE FUEL FOR THE FLAMES.
I WANT FLAMES!
AND SO MAYOR WILLAMINA HAD ORDERED THAT THE TOWN TEAR DOWN ITS LOG-CABIN COLLEGE. THE TOWN'S *ONLY* COLLEGE.
IT'S MORE IMPORTANT THAN EDUCATION.
AND USE THE LOGS TO FUEL THE FLAMES.
WHICH WENT WELL ENOUGH, UNTIL ONE DAY WHEN THE TOWNSFOLK SAW THE DOLPHIN SWAY FROM SIDE TO SIDE.
AND MADE A STARTLING DISCOVERY:
IT'S NOT CONCRETE. IT'S AN INFLATABLE POOL TOY.
AND IT WAS. FOR RICKY RAM RUBBLE—THE BUILDER HIRED TO CONSTRUCT THE STATUE—HAD RUN OFF WITH THE CONSTRUCTION MONEY.

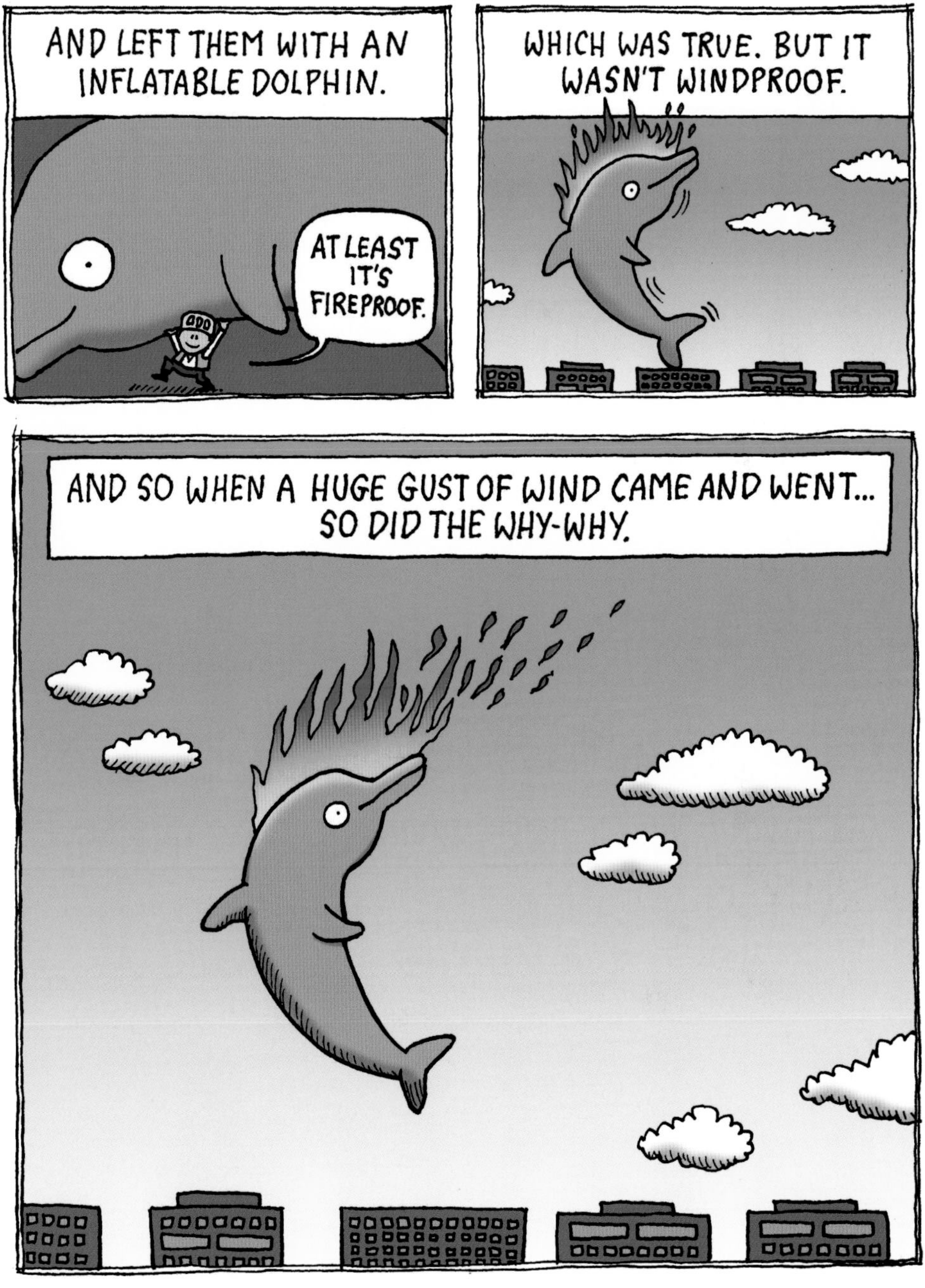
AND LEFT THEM WITH AN INFLATABLE DOLPHIN.
AT LEAST IT'S FIREPROOF.
WHICH WAS TRUE. BUT IT WASN'T WINDPROOF.
AND SO WHEN A HUGE GUST OF WIND CAME AND WENT... SO DID THE WHY-WHY.

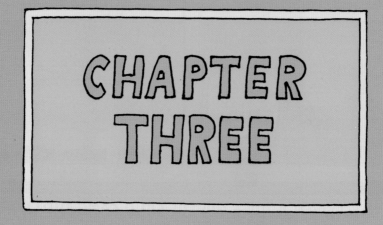

CHAPTER THREE

WHICH IS...

THREE TIMES BETTER THAN ALL THE PREVIOUS CHAPTERS COMBINED, WHICH MAY NOT BE SAYING MUCH

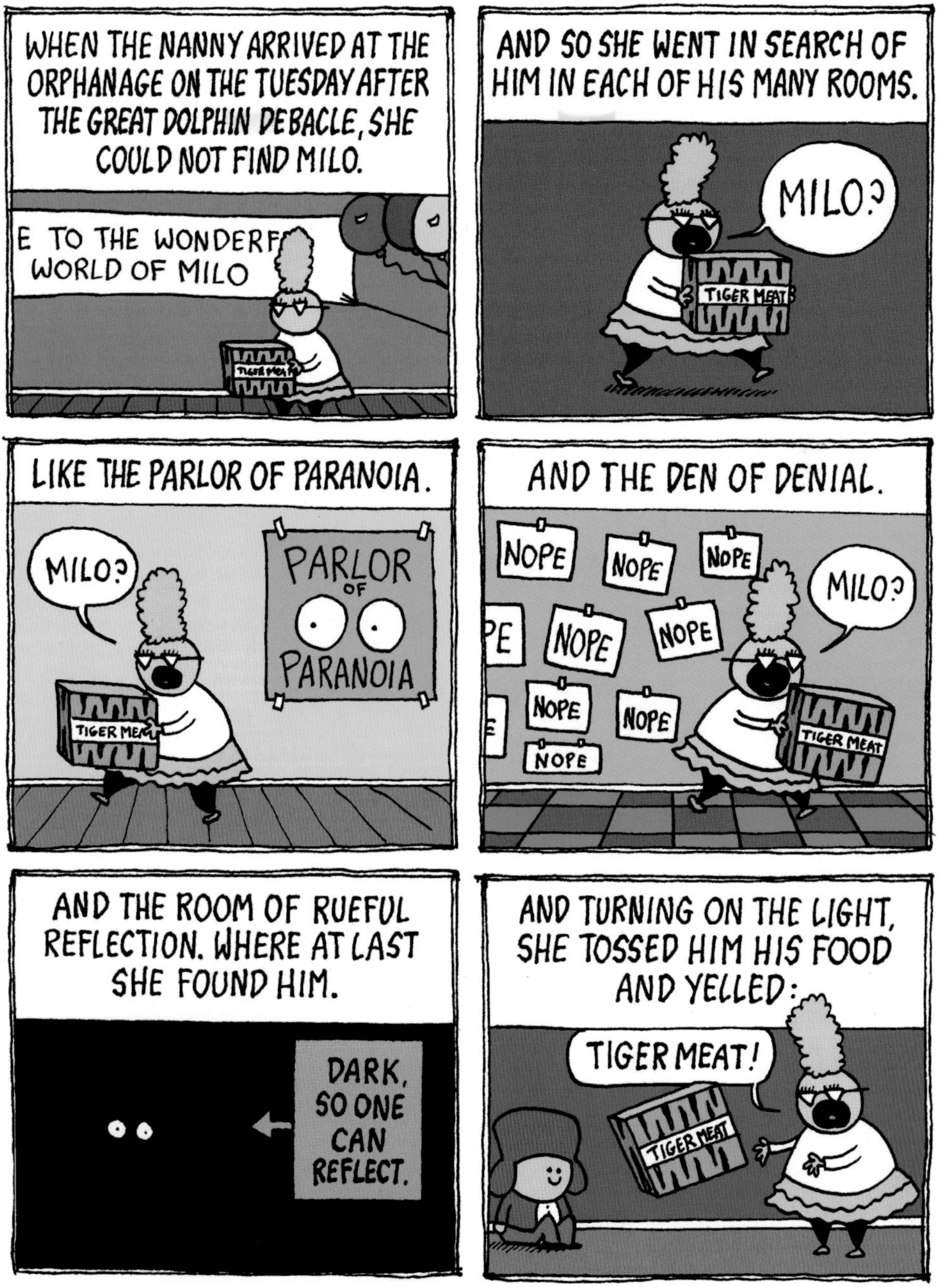
WHEN THE NANNY ARRIVED AT THE ORPHANAGE ON THE TUESDAY AFTER THE GREAT DOLPHIN DEBACLE, SHE COULD NOT FIND MILO.
E TO THE WONDERF
WORLD OF MILO
TIGER MEAT
AND SO SHE WENT IN SEARCH OF HIM IN EACH OF HIS MANY ROOMS.
MILO?
TIGER MEAT
LIKE THE PARLOR OF PARANOIA.
MILO?
PARLOR OF PARANOIA
AND THE DEN OF DENIAL.
NOPE
NOPE
NOPE
NOPE
NOPE
NOPE
NOPE
NOPE
MILO?
TIGER MEAT
AND THE ROOM OF RUEFUL REFLECTION. WHERE AT LAST SHE FOUND HIM.
DARK, SO ONE CAN REFLECT.
AND TURNING ON THE LIGHT, SHE TOSSED HIM HIS FOOD AND YELLED:
TIGER MEAT!
TIGER MEAT

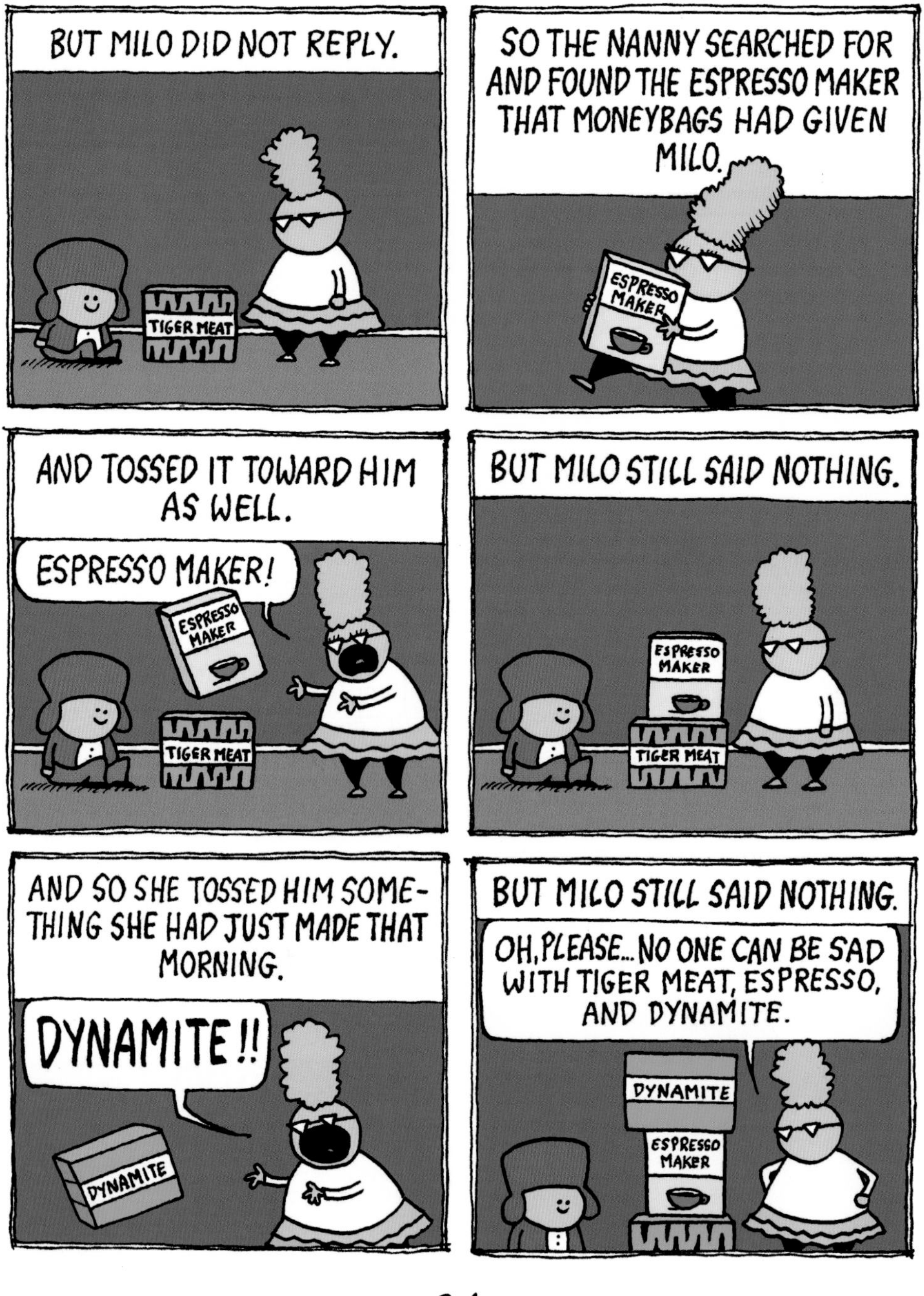
BUT MILO DID NOT REPLY.
TIGER MEAT
SO THE NANNY SEARCHED FOR AND FOUND THE ESPRESSO MAKER THAT MONEYBAGS HAD GIVEN MILO.
ESPRESSO MAKER
AND TOSSED IT TOWARD HIM AS WELL.
ESPRESSO MAKER!
ESPRESSO MAKER
TIGER MEAT
BUT MILO STILL SAID NOTHING.
ESPRESSO MAKER
TIGER MEAT
AND SO SHE TOSSED HIM SOME-THING SHE HAD JUST MADE THAT MORNING.
DYNAMITE!!
DYNAMITE
BUT MILO STILL SAID NOTHING.
OH, PLEASE... NO ONE CAN BE SAD WITH TIGER MEAT, ESPRESSO, AND DYNAMITE.
DYNAMITE
ESPRESSO MAKER

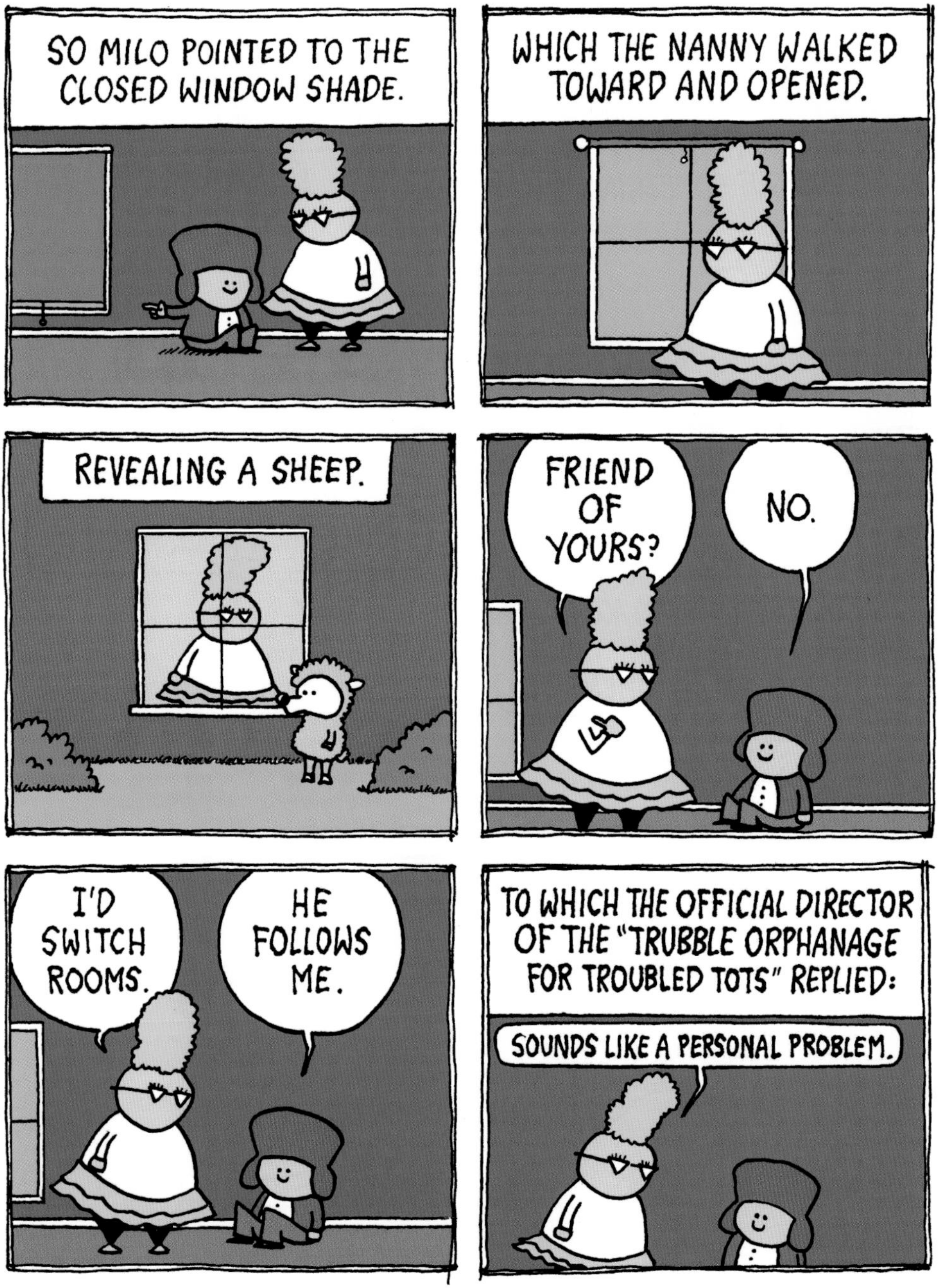
SO MILO POINTED TO THE CLOSED WINDOW SHADE.
WHICH THE NANNY WALKED TOWARD AND OPENED.
REVEALING A SHEEP.
FRIEND OF YOURS?
NO.
I'D SWITCH ROOMS.
HE FOLLOWS ME.
TO WHICH THE OFFICIAL DIRECTOR OF THE "TRUBBLE ORPHANAGE FOR TROUBLED TOTS" REPLIED:
SOUNDS LIKE A PERSONAL PROBLEM.

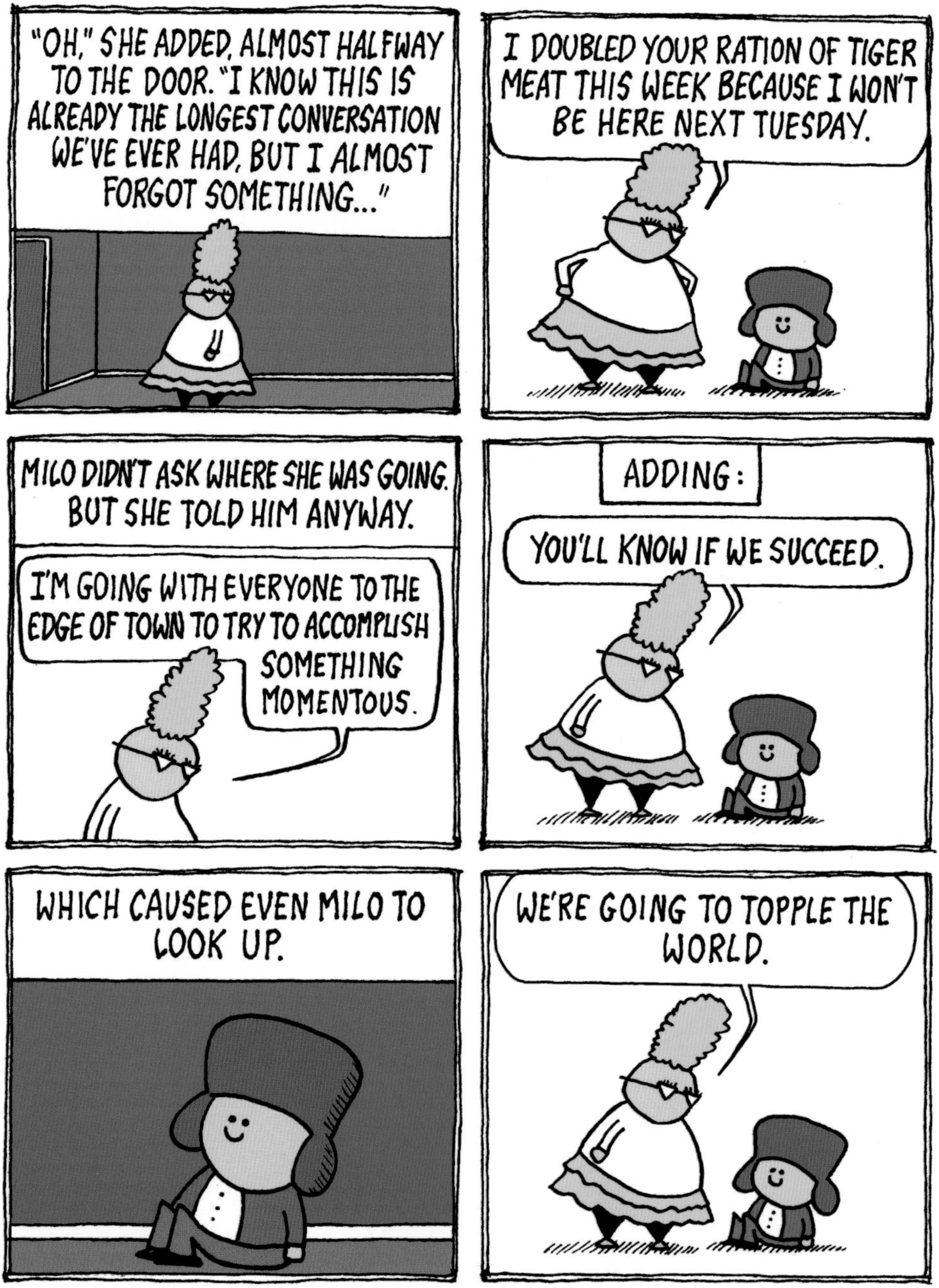
"OH," SHE ADDED, ALMOST HALFWAY TO THE DOOR. "I KNOW THIS IS ALREADY THE LONGEST CONVERSATION WE'VE EVER HAD, BUT I ALMOST FORGOT SOMETHING..."
I DOUBLED YOUR RATION OF TIGER MEAT THIS WEEK BECAUSE I WON'T BE HERE NEXT TUESDAY.
MILO DIDN'T ASK WHERE SHE WAS GOING. BUT SHE TOLD HIM ANYWAY.
I'M GOING WITH EVERYONE TO THE EDGE OF TOWN TO TRY TO ACCOMPLISH SOMETHING MOMENTOUS.
ADDING:
YOU'LL KNOW IF WE SUCCEED.
WHICH CAUSED EVEN MILO TO LOOK UP.
WE'RE GOING TO TOPPLE THE WORLD.

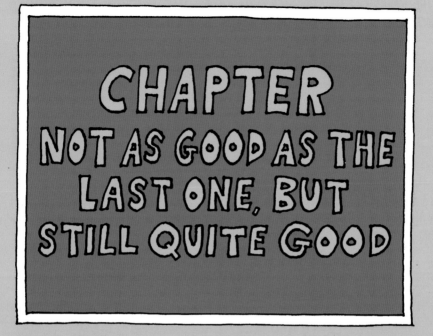

CHAPTER
NOT AS GOOD AS THE LAST ONE, BUT STILL QUITE GOOD

IN WHICH...

WE GET POINTS FOR HONESTY

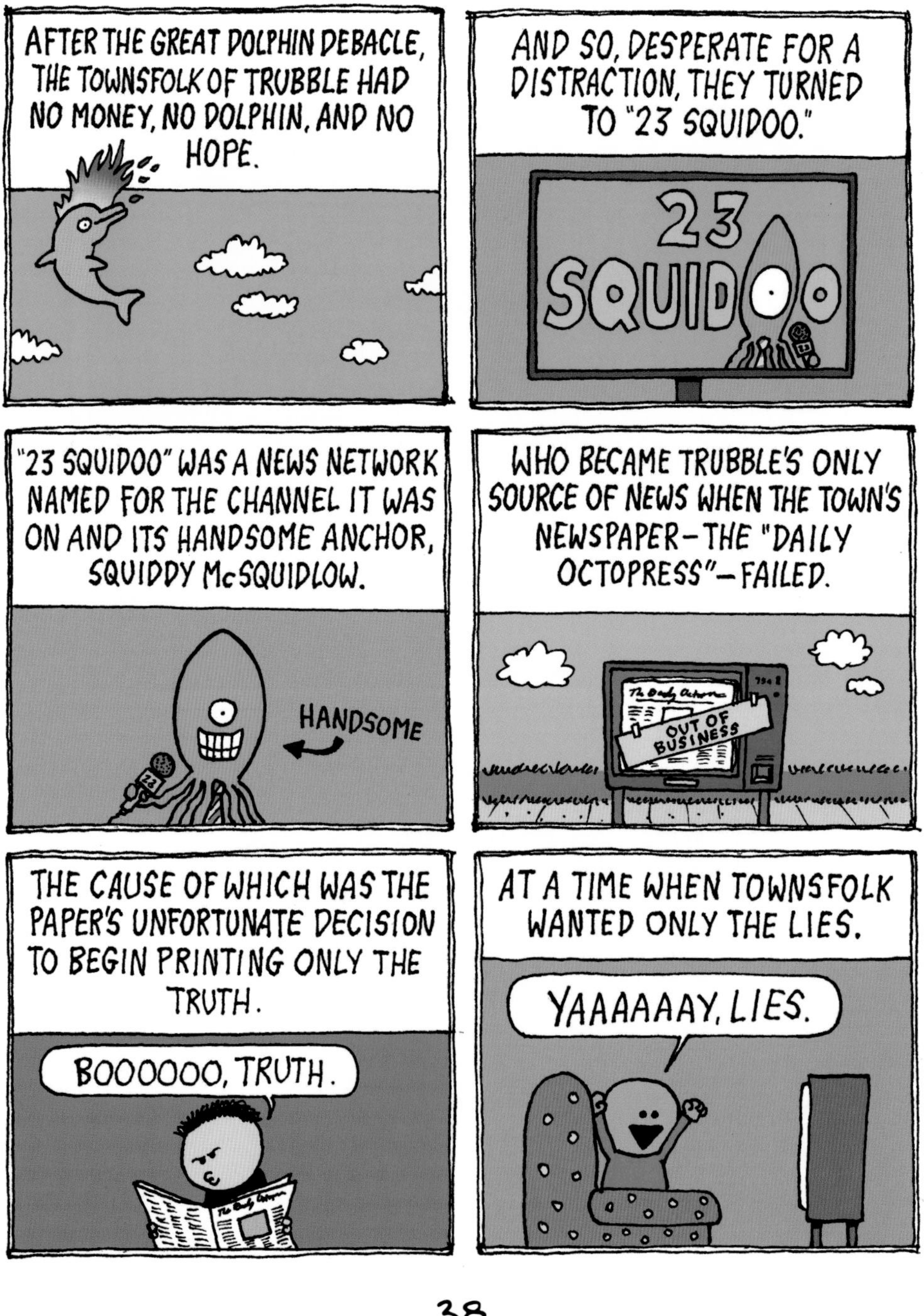
AFTER THE GREAT DOLPHIN DEBACLE, THE TOWNSFOLK OF TRUBBLE HAD NO MONEY, NO DOLPHIN, AND NO HOPE.
AND SO, DESPERATE FOR A DISTRACTION, THEY TURNED TO "23 SQUIDOO."
23 SQUIDOO
"23 SQUIDOO" WAS A NEWS NETWORK NAMED FOR THE CHANNEL IT WAS ON AND ITS HANDSOME ANCHOR, SQUIDDY McSQUIDLOW.
HANDSOME
WHO BECAME TRUBBLE'S ONLY SOURCE OF NEWS WHEN THE TOWN'S NEWSPAPER—THE "DAILY OCTOPRESS"—FAILED.
OUT OF BUSINESS
THE CAUSE OF WHICH WAS THE PAPER'S UNFORTUNATE DECISION TO BEGIN PRINTING ONLY THE TRUTH.
BOOOOOO, TRUTH.
AT A TIME WHEN TOWNSFOLK WANTED ONLY THE LIES.
YAAAAAAY, LIES.

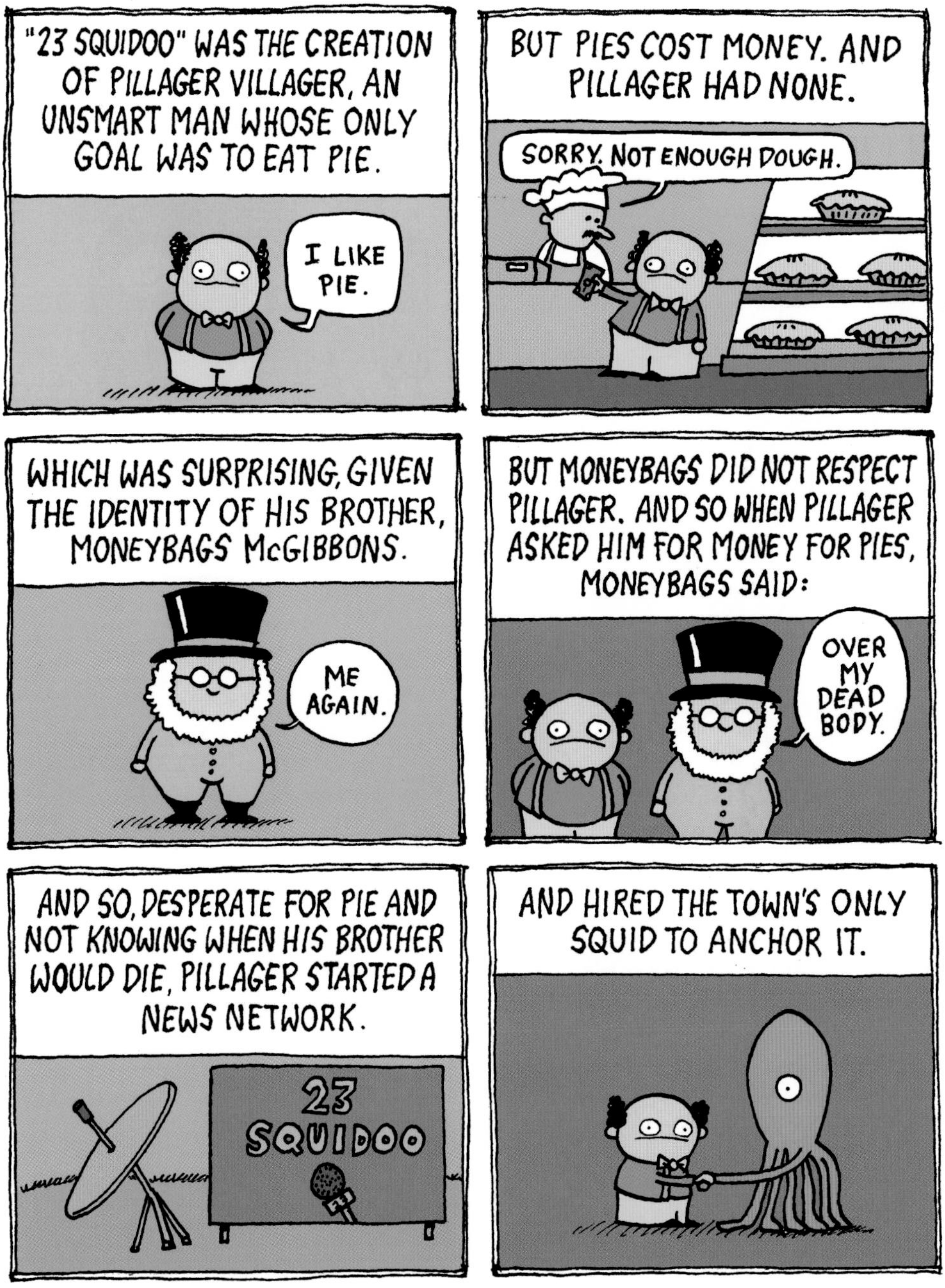
"23 SQUIDOO" WAS THE CREATION OF PILLAGER VILLAGER, AN UNSMART MAN WHOSE ONLY GOAL WAS TO EAT PIE.
I LIKE PIE.
BUT PIES COST MONEY. AND PILLAGER HAD NONE.
SORRY. NOT ENOUGH DOUGH.
WHICH WAS SURPRISING, GIVEN THE IDENTITY OF HIS BROTHER, MONEYBAGS McGIBBONS.
ME AGAIN.
BUT MONEYBAGS DID NOT RESPECT PILLAGER. AND SO WHEN PILLAGER ASKED HIM FOR MONEY FOR PIES, MONEYBAGS SAID:
OVER MY DEAD BODY.
AND SO, DESPERATE FOR PIE AND NOT KNOWING WHEN HIS BROTHER WOULD DIE, PILLAGER STARTED A NEWS NETWORK.
23 SQUIDOO
AND HIRED THE TOWN'S ONLY SQUID TO ANCHOR IT.

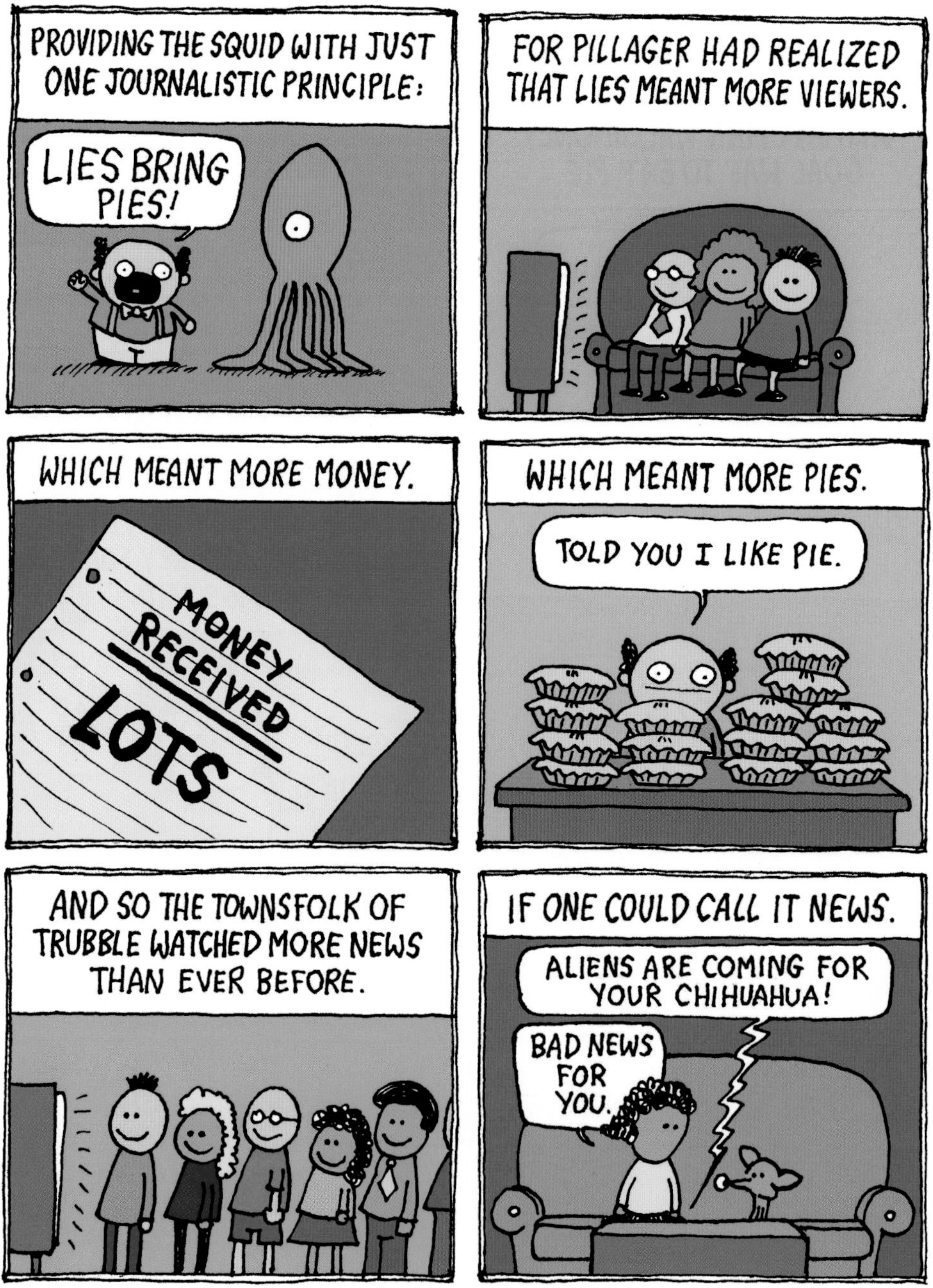
PROVIDING THE SQUID WITH JUST ONE JOURNALISTIC PRINCIPLE:
LIES BRING PIES!
FOR PILLAGER HAD REALIZED THAT LIES MEANT MORE VIEWERS.
WHICH MEANT MORE MONEY.
MONEY RECEIVED
LOTS
WHICH MEANT MORE PIES.
TOLD YOU I LIKE PIE.
AND SO THE TOWNSFOLK OF TRUBBLE WATCHED MORE NEWS THAN EVER BEFORE.
IF ONE COULD CALL IT NEWS.
ALIENS ARE COMING FOR YOUR CHIHUAHUA!
BAD NEWS FOR YOU.

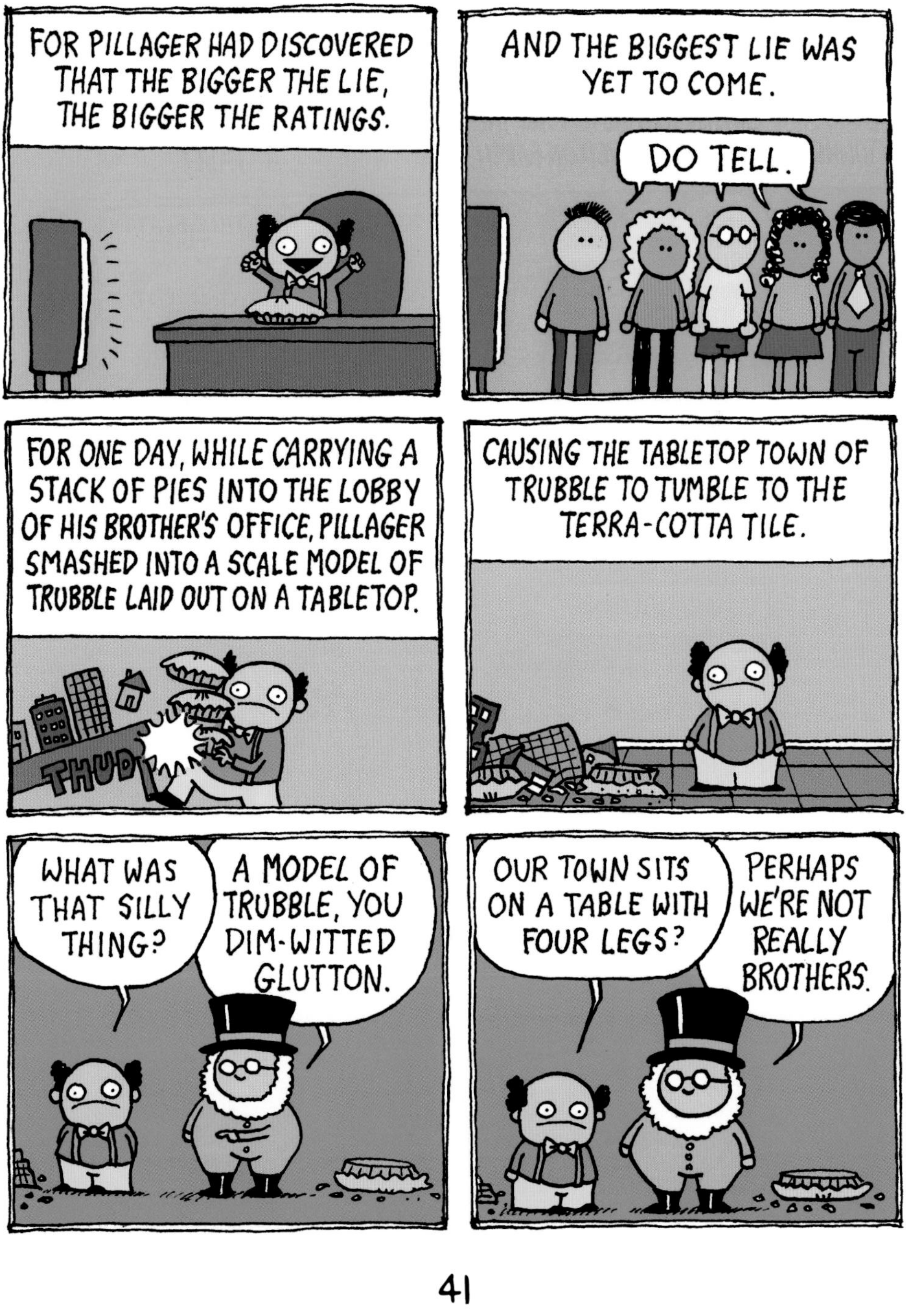

FOR PILLAGER HAD DISCOVERED THAT THE BIGGER THE LIE, THE BIGGER THE RATINGS.
AND THE BIGGEST LIE WAS YET TO COME.
DO TELL.
FOR ONE DAY, WHILE CARRYING A STACK OF PIES INTO THE LOBBY OF HIS BROTHER'S OFFICE, PILLAGER SMASHED INTO A SCALE MODEL OF TRUBBLE LAID OUT ON A TABLETOP.
THUD
CAUSING THE TABLETOP TOWN OF TRUBBLE TO TUMBLE TO THE TERRA-COTTA TILE.
WHAT WAS THAT SILLY THING?
A MODEL OF TRUBBLE, YOU DIM-WITTED GLUTTON.
OUR TOWN SITS ON A TABLE WITH FOUR LEGS?
PERHAPS WE'RE NOT REALLY BROTHERS.

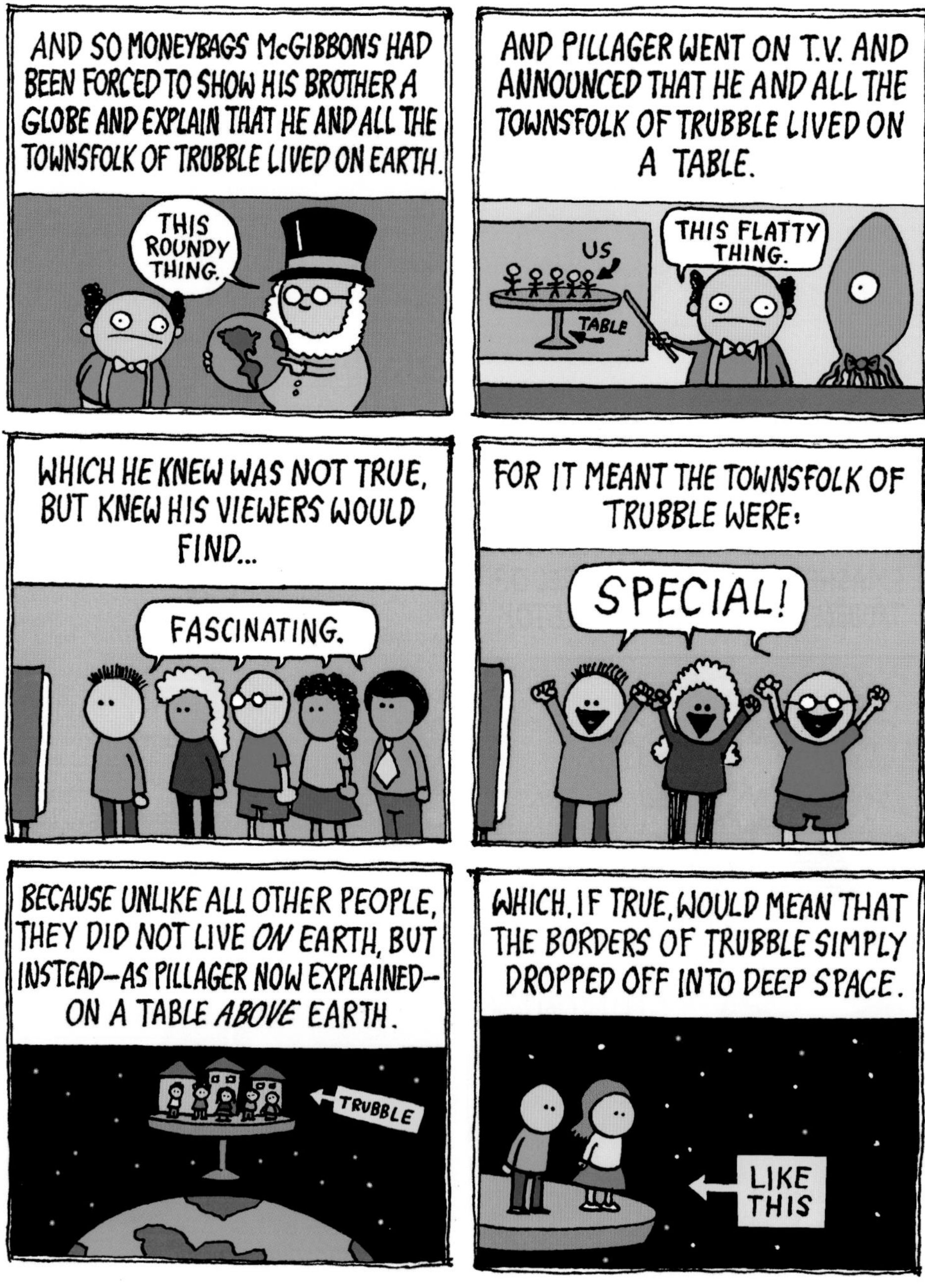
AND SO MONEYBAGS McGIBBONS HAD BEEN FORCED TO SHOW HIS BROTHER A GLOBE AND EXPLAIN THAT HE AND ALL THE TOWNSFOLK OF TRUBBLE LIVED ON EARTH.
THIS ROUNDY THING.
AND PILLAGER WENT ON T.V. AND ANNOUNCED THAT HE AND ALL THE TOWNSFOLK OF TRUBBLE LIVED ON A TABLE.
US
TABLE
THIS FLATTY THING.
WHICH HE KNEW WAS NOT TRUE, BUT KNEW HIS VIEWERS WOULD FIND...
FASCINATING.
FOR IT MEANT THE TOWNSFOLK OF TRUBBLE WERE:
SPECIAL!
BECAUSE UNLIKE ALL OTHER PEOPLE, THEY DID NOT LIVE *ON* EARTH, BUT INSTEAD—AS PILLAGER NOW EXPLAINED—ON A TABLE *ABOVE* EARTH.
TRUBBLE
WHICH, IF TRUE, WOULD MEAN THAT THE BORDERS OF TRUBBLE SIMPLY DROPPED OFF INTO DEEP SPACE.
LIKE THIS

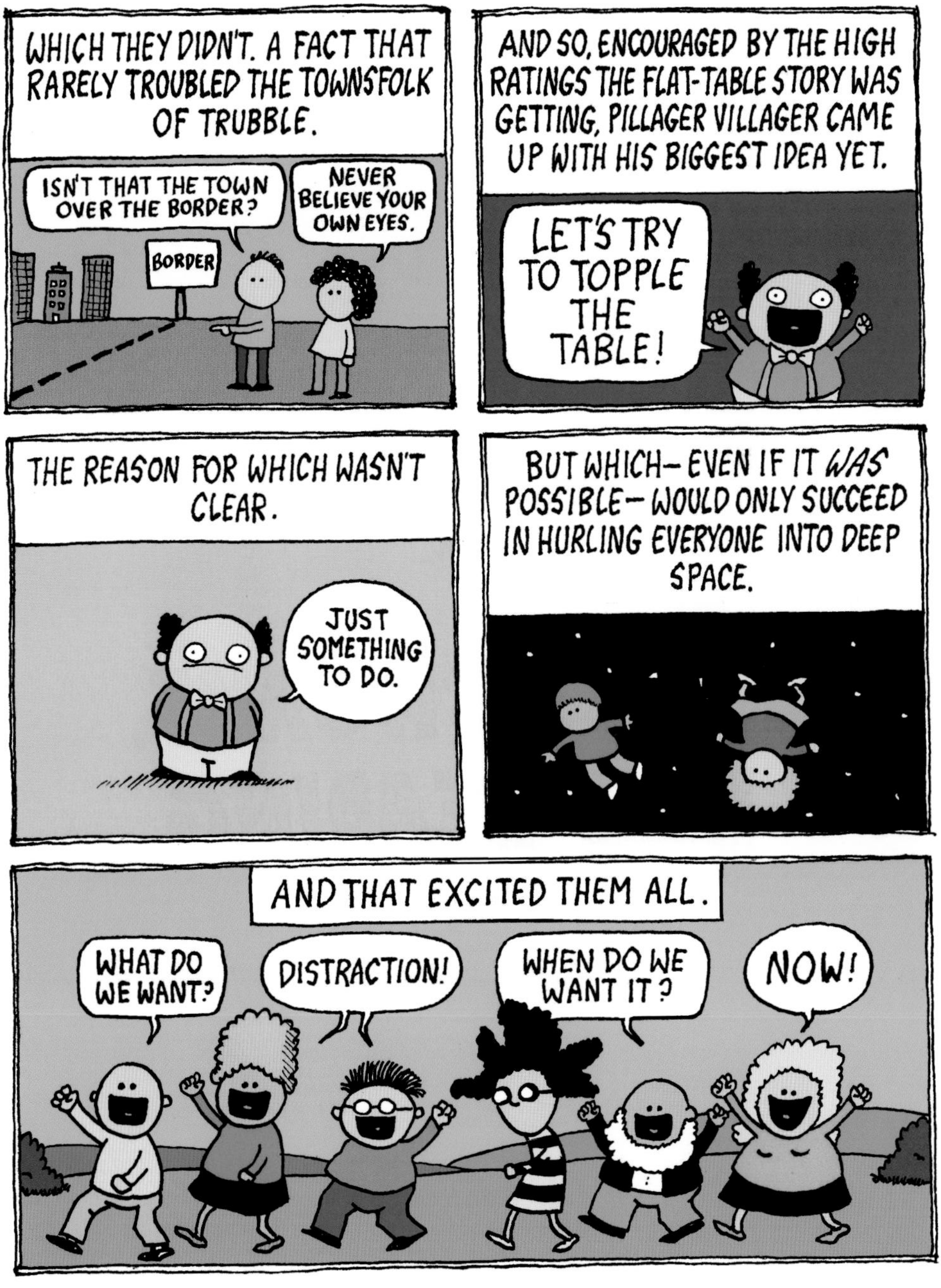
WHICH THEY DIDN'T. A FACT THAT RARELY TROUBLED THE TOWNSFOLK OF TRUBBLE.
ISN'T THAT THE TOWN OVER THE BORDER?
NEVER BELIEVE YOUR OWN EYES.
BORDER
AND SO, ENCOURAGED BY THE HIGH RATINGS THE FLAT-TABLE STORY WAS GETTING, PILLAGER VILLAGER CAME UP WITH HIS BIGGEST IDEA YET.
LET'S TRY TO TOPPLE THE TABLE!
THE REASON FOR WHICH WASN'T CLEAR.
JUST SOMETHING TO DO.
BUT WHICH—EVEN IF IT *WAS* POSSIBLE—WOULD ONLY SUCCEED IN HURLING EVERYONE INTO DEEP SPACE.
AND THAT EXCITED THEM ALL.
WHAT DO WE WANT?
DISTRACTION!
WHEN DO WE WANT IT?
NOW!

CHAPTER
FOR

AS IN...

FOR GOSH SAKE,
KEEP READING

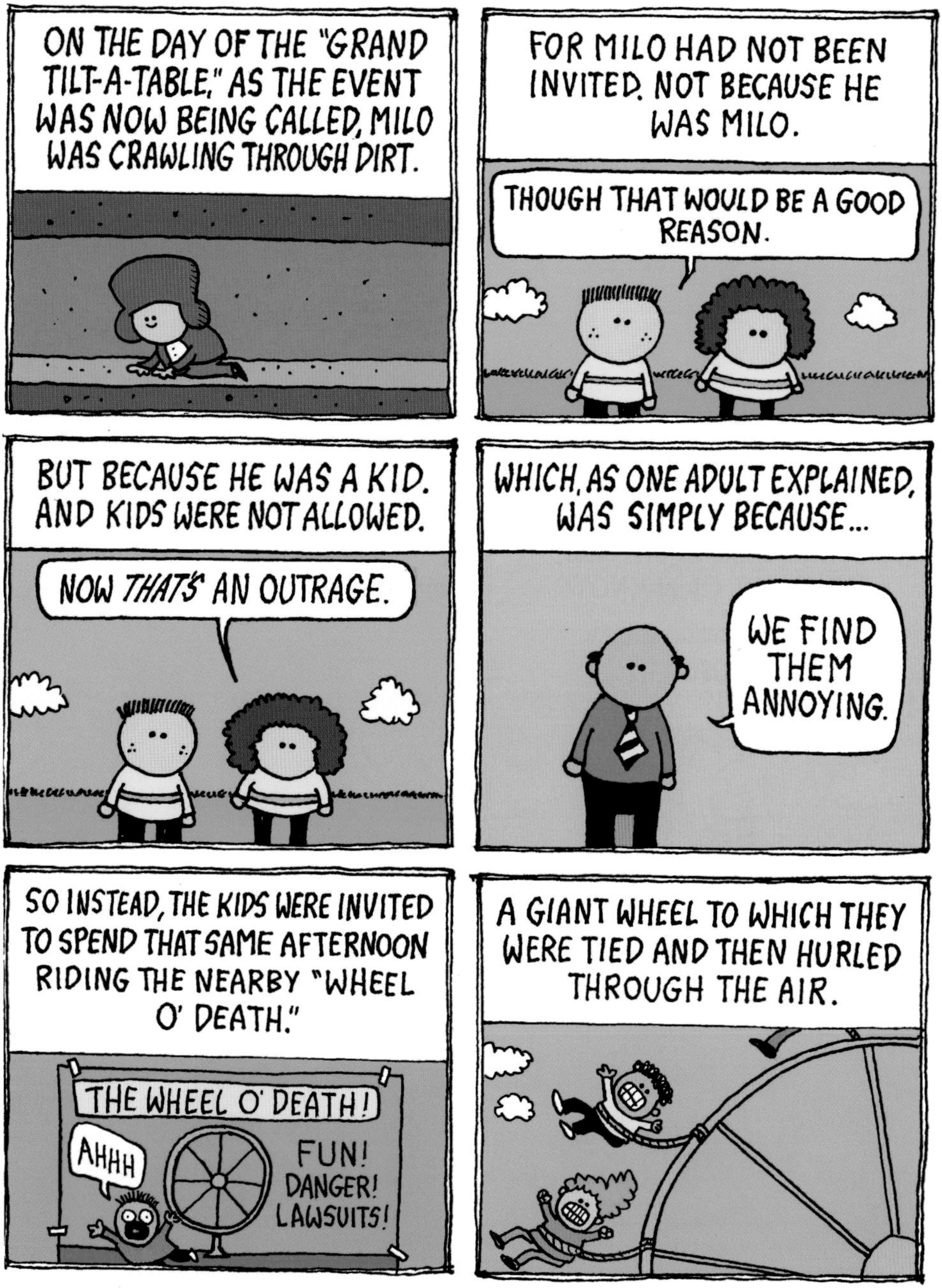
ON THE DAY OF THE "GRAND TILT-A-TABLE," AS THE EVENT WAS NOW BEING CALLED, MILO WAS CRAWLING THROUGH DIRT.
FOR MILO HAD NOT BEEN INVITED. NOT BECAUSE HE WAS MILO.
THOUGH THAT WOULD BE A GOOD REASON.
BUT BECAUSE HE WAS A KID. AND KIDS WERE NOT ALLOWED.
NOW *THAT'S* AN OUTRAGE.
WHICH, AS ONE ADULT EXPLAINED, WAS SIMPLY BECAUSE...
WE FIND THEM ANNOYING.
SO INSTEAD, THE KIDS WERE INVITED TO SPEND THAT SAME AFTERNOON RIDING THE NEARBY "WHEEL O' DEATH."
THE WHEEL O' DEATH!
AHHH
FUN! DANGER! LAWSUITS!
A GIANT WHEEL TO WHICH THEY WERE TIED AND THEN HURLED THROUGH THE AIR.

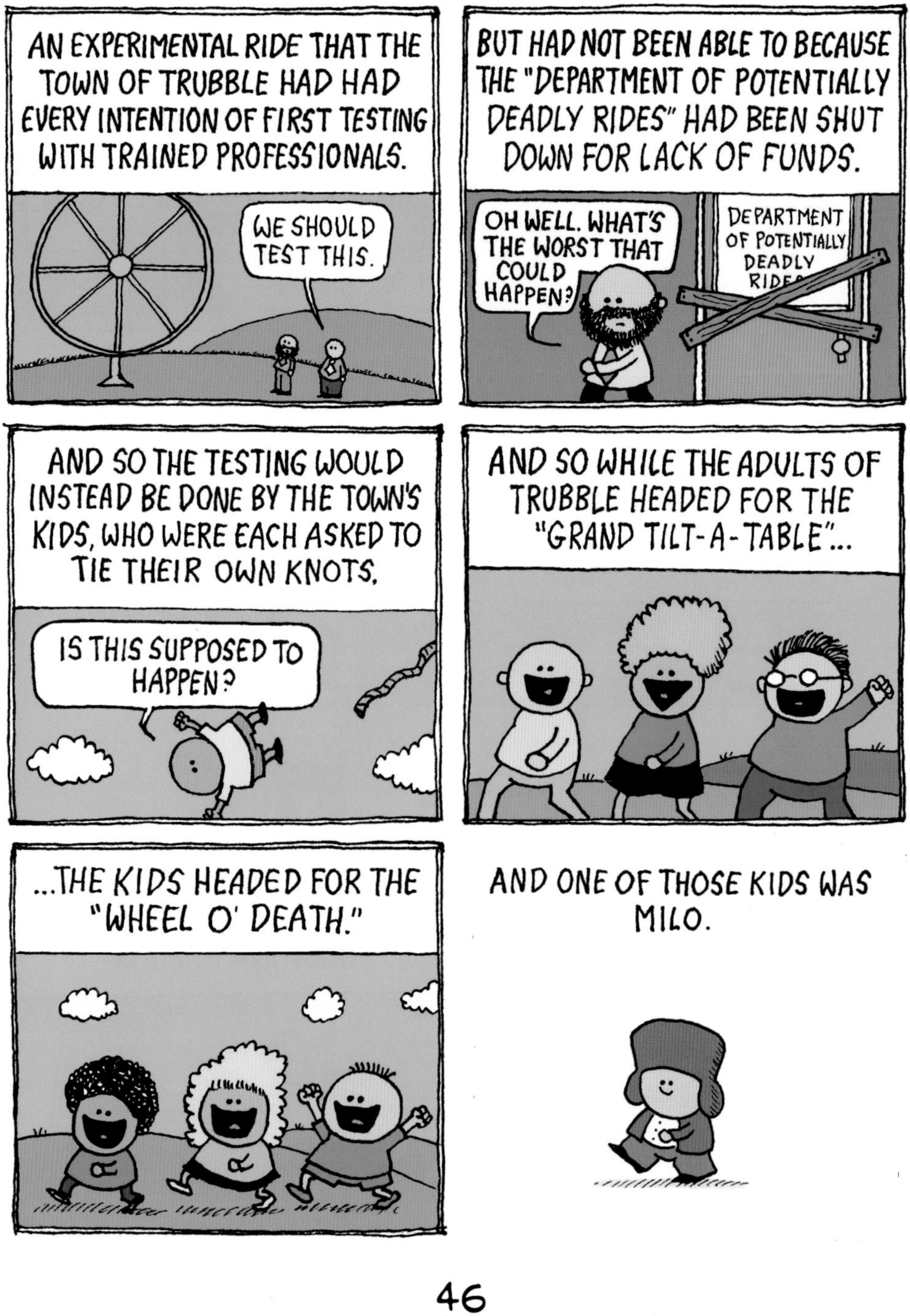
AN EXPERIMENTAL RIDE THAT THE TOWN OF TRUBBLE HAD HAD EVERY INTENTION OF FIRST TESTING WITH TRAINED PROFESSIONALS.
WE SHOULD TEST THIS.
BUT HAD NOT BEEN ABLE TO BECAUSE THE "DEPARTMENT OF POTENTIALLY DEADLY RIDES" HAD BEEN SHUT DOWN FOR LACK OF FUNDS.
OH WELL. WHAT'S THE WORST THAT COULD HAPPEN?
DEPARTMENT OF POTENTIALLY DEADLY
AND SO THE TESTING WOULD INSTEAD BE DONE BY THE TOWN'S KIDS, WHO WERE EACH ASKED TO TIE THEIR OWN KNOTS.
IS THIS SUPPOSED TO HAPPEN?
AND SO WHILE THE ADULTS OF TRUBBLE HEADED FOR THE "GRAND TILT-A-TABLE"...
...THE KIDS HEADED FOR THE "WHEEL O' DEATH."
AND ONE OF THOSE KIDS WAS MILO.

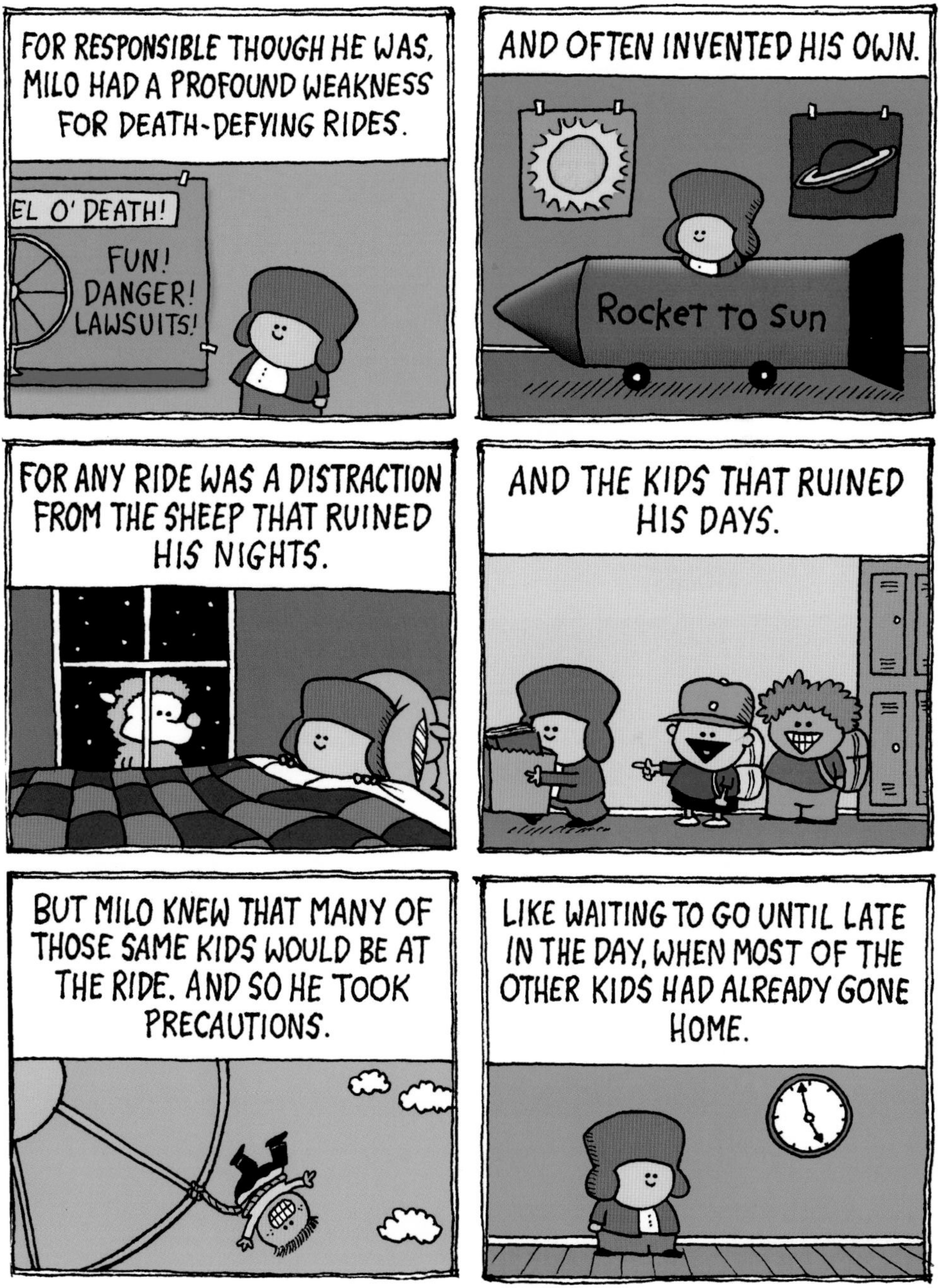
FOR RESPONSIBLE THOUGH HE WAS, MILO HAD A PROFOUND WEAKNESS FOR DEATH-DEFYING RIDES.
EL O' DEATH!
FUN! DANGER! LAWSUITS!
AND OFTEN INVENTED HIS OWN.
Rocket to sun
FOR ANY RIDE WAS A DISTRACTION FROM THE SHEEP THAT RUINED HIS NIGHTS.
AND THE KIDS THAT RUINED HIS DAYS.
BUT MILO KNEW THAT MANY OF THOSE SAME KIDS WOULD BE AT THE RIDE. AND SO HE TOOK PRECAUTIONS.
LIKE WAITING TO GO UNTIL LATE IN THE DAY, WHEN MOST OF THE OTHER KIDS HAD ALREADY GONE HOME.

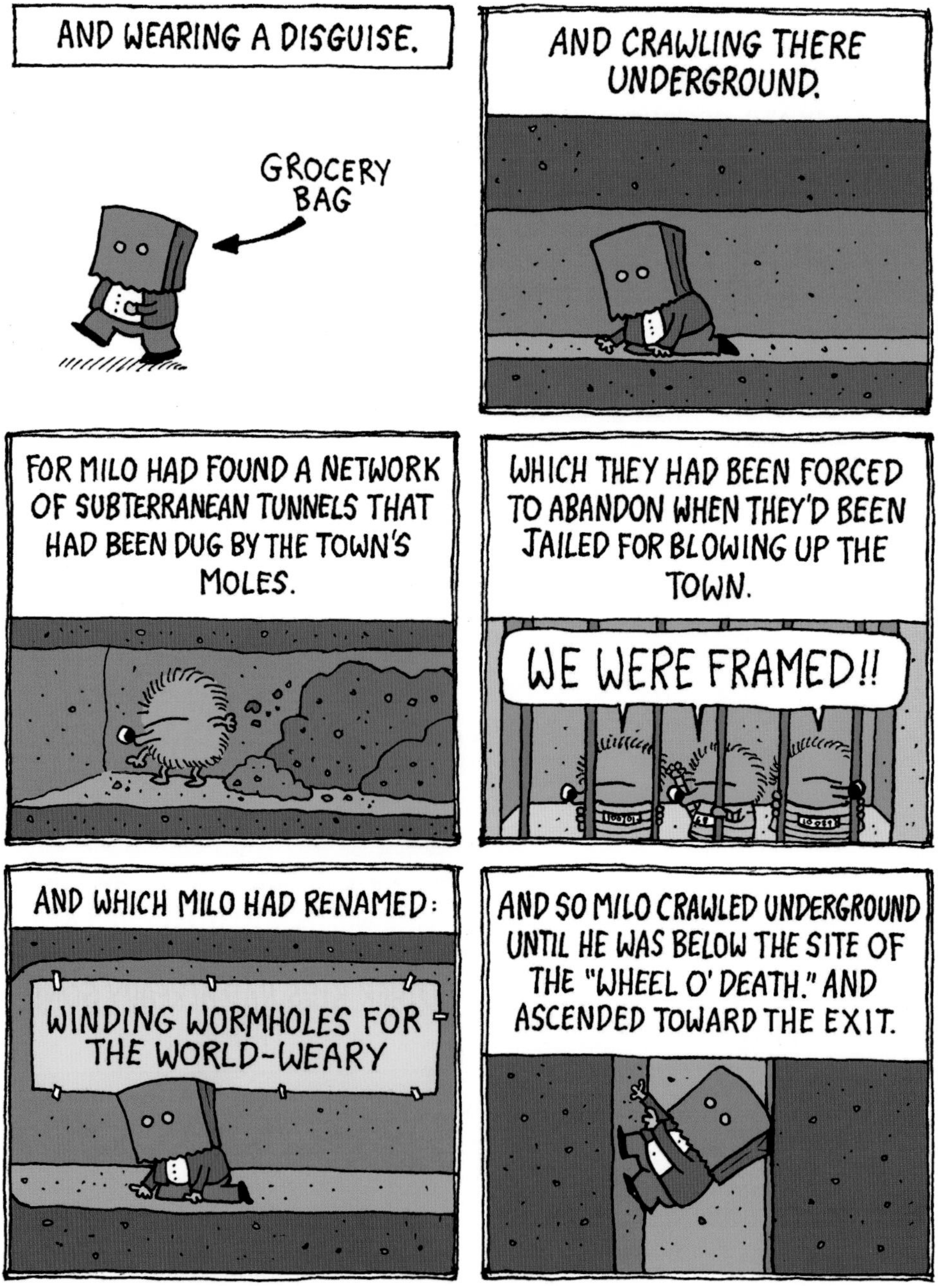
AND WEARING A DISGUISE.
GROCERY BAG
AND CRAWLING THERE UNDERGROUND.
FOR MILO HAD FOUND A NETWORK OF SUBTERRANEAN TUNNELS THAT HAD BEEN DUG BY THE TOWN'S MOLES.
WHICH THEY HAD BEEN FORCED TO ABANDON WHEN THEY'D BEEN JAILED FOR BLOWING UP THE TOWN.
WE WERE FRAMED!!
AND WHICH MILO HAD RENAMED:
WINDING WORMHOLES FOR THE WORLD-WEARY
AND SO MILO CRAWLED UNDERGROUND UNTIL HE WAS BELOW THE SITE OF THE "WHEEL O' DEATH," AND ASCENDED TOWARD THE EXIT.

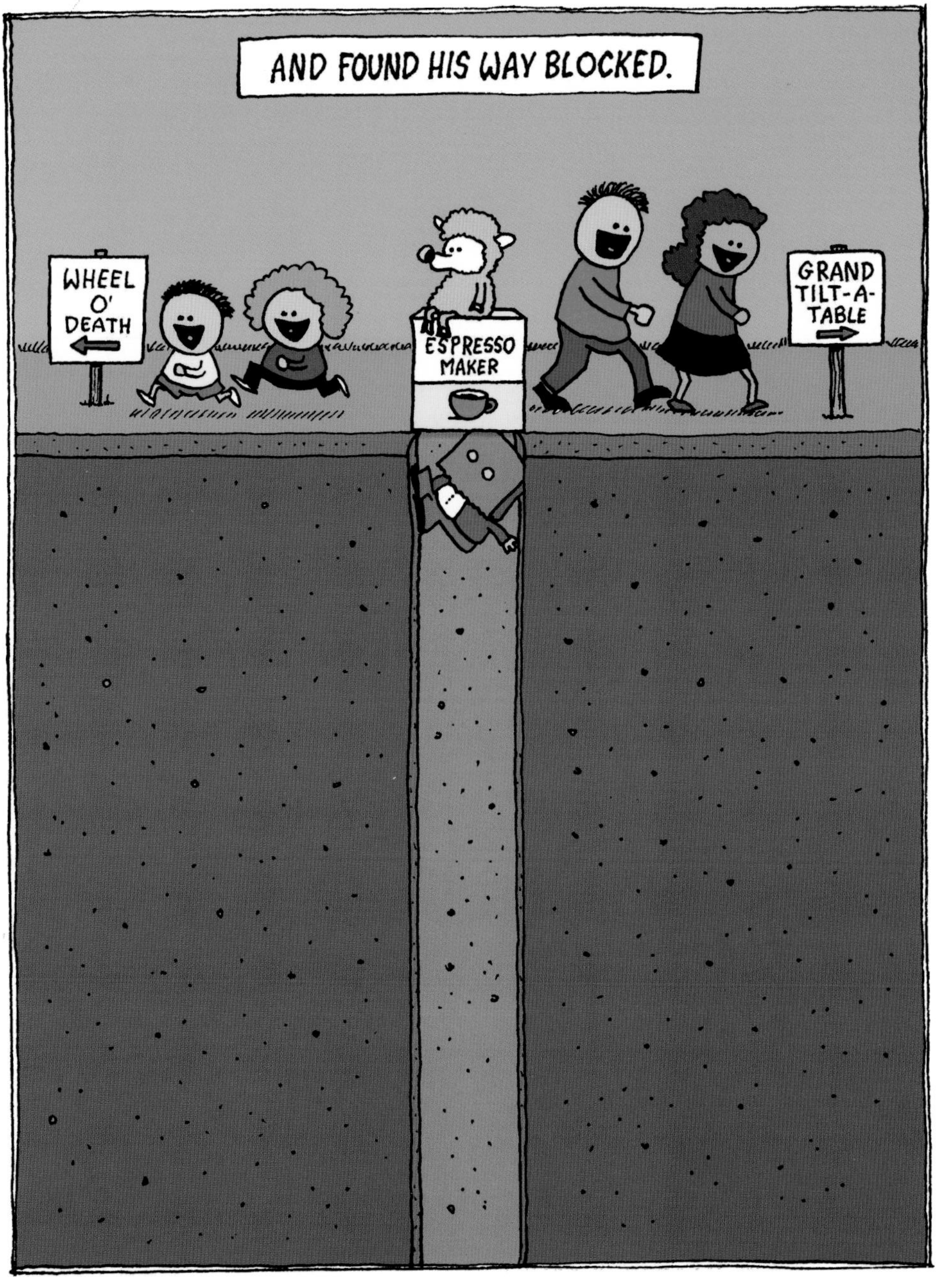
AND FOUND HIS WAY BLOCKED.
WHEEL O' DEATH
ESPRESSO MAKER
GRAND TILT-A-TABLE

CHAPTER
G

AS IN...

GEE, I DIDN'T KNOW
CHAPTERS COULD BE
LETTERED INSTEAD
OF NUMBERED, BUT
IT TURNS OUT THAT
THEY CAN

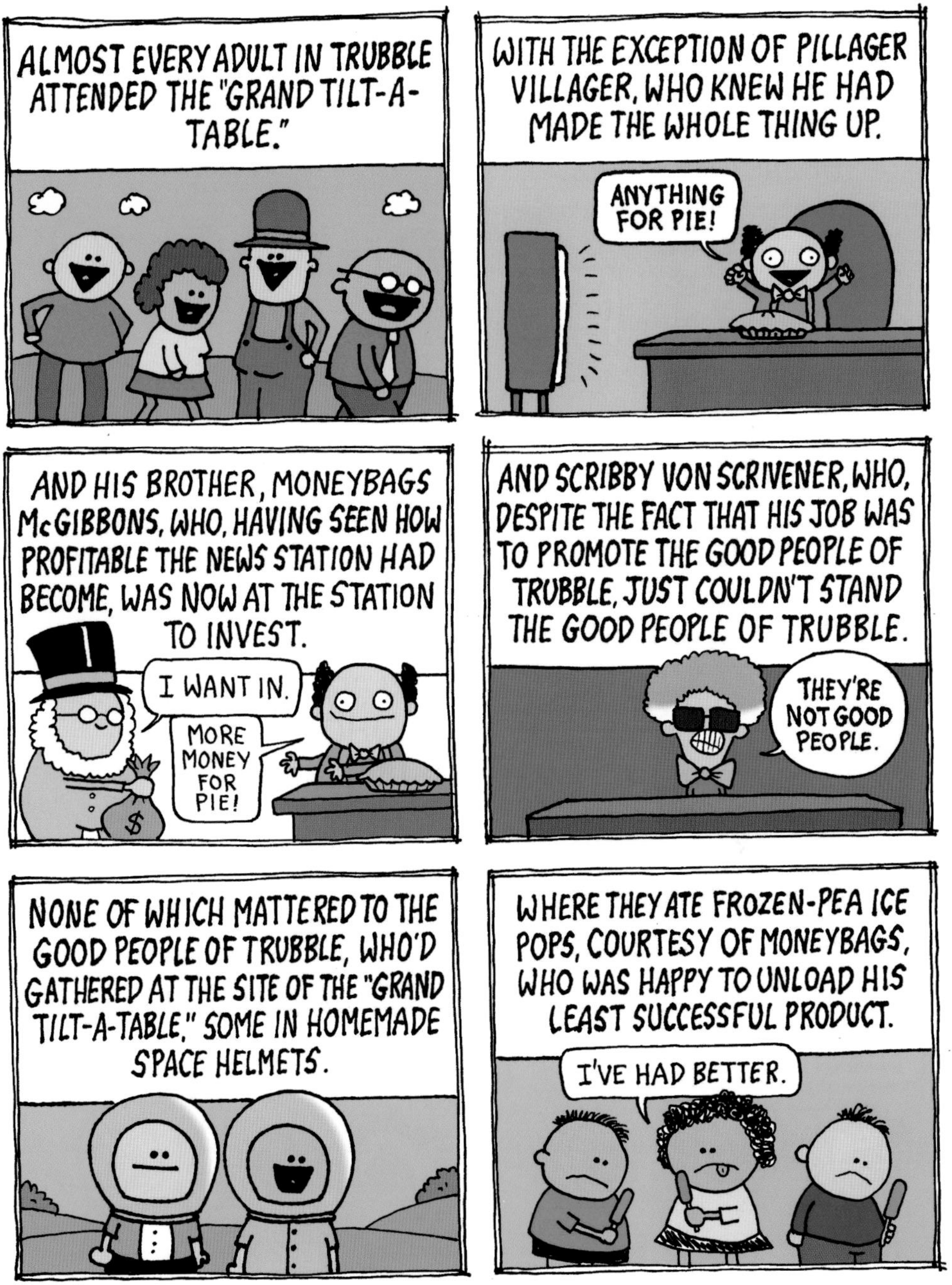
ALMOST EVERY ADULT IN TRUBBLE ATTENDED THE "GRAND TILT-A-TABLE."
WITH THE EXCEPTION OF PILLAGER VILLAGER, WHO KNEW HE HAD MADE THE WHOLE THING UP.
ANYTHING FOR PIE!
AND HIS BROTHER, MONEYBAGS McGIBBONS, WHO, HAVING SEEN HOW PROFITABLE THE NEWS STATION HAD BECOME, WAS NOW AT THE STATION TO INVEST.
I WANT IN.
MORE MONEY FOR PIE!
AND SCRIBBY VON SCRIVENER, WHO, DESPITE THE FACT THAT HIS JOB WAS TO PROMOTE THE GOOD PEOPLE OF TRUBBLE, JUST COULDN'T STAND THE GOOD PEOPLE OF TRUBBLE.
THEY'RE NOT GOOD PEOPLE.
NONE OF WHICH MATTERED TO THE GOOD PEOPLE OF TRUBBLE, WHO'D GATHERED AT THE SITE OF THE "GRAND TILT-A-TABLE," SOME IN HOMEMADE SPACE HELMETS.
WHERE THEY ATE FROZEN-PEA ICE POPS, COURTESY OF MONEYBAGS, WHO WAS HAPPY TO UNLOAD HIS LEAST SUCCESSFUL PRODUCT.
I'VE HAD BETTER.

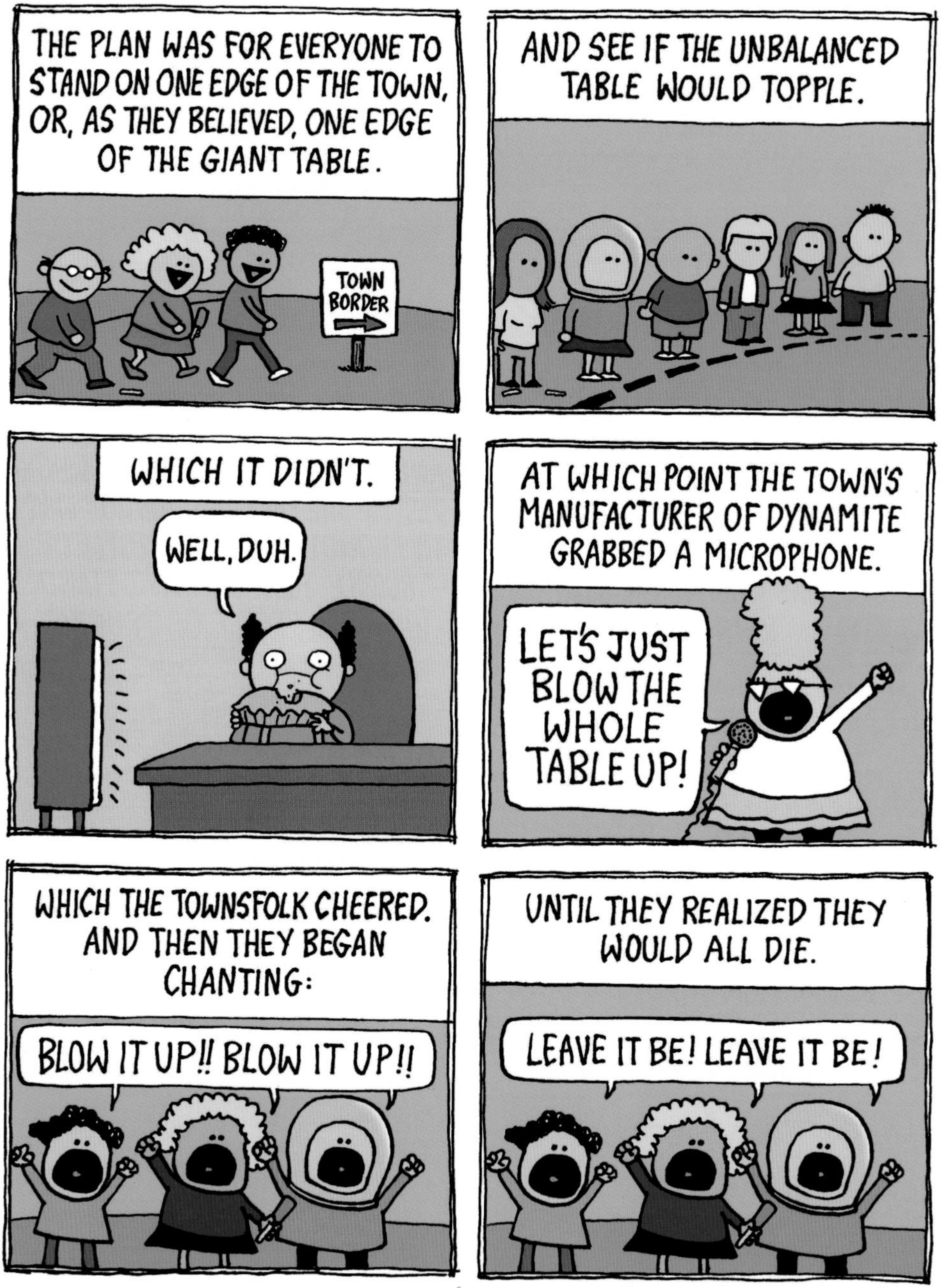
THE PLAN WAS FOR EVERYONE TO STAND ON ONE EDGE OF THE TOWN, OR, AS THEY BELIEVED, ONE EDGE OF THE GIANT TABLE.
TOWN BORDER
AND SEE IF THE UNBALANCED TABLE WOULD TOPPLE.
WHICH IT DIDN'T.
WELL, DUH.
AT WHICH POINT THE TOWN'S MANUFACTURER OF DYNAMITE GRABBED A MICROPHONE.
LET'S JUST BLOW THE WHOLE TABLE UP!
WHICH THE TOWNSFOLK CHEERED. AND THEN THEY BEGAN CHANTING:
BLOW IT UP!! BLOW IT UP!!
UNTIL THEY REALIZED THEY WOULD ALL DIE.
LEAVE IT BE! LEAVE IT BE!

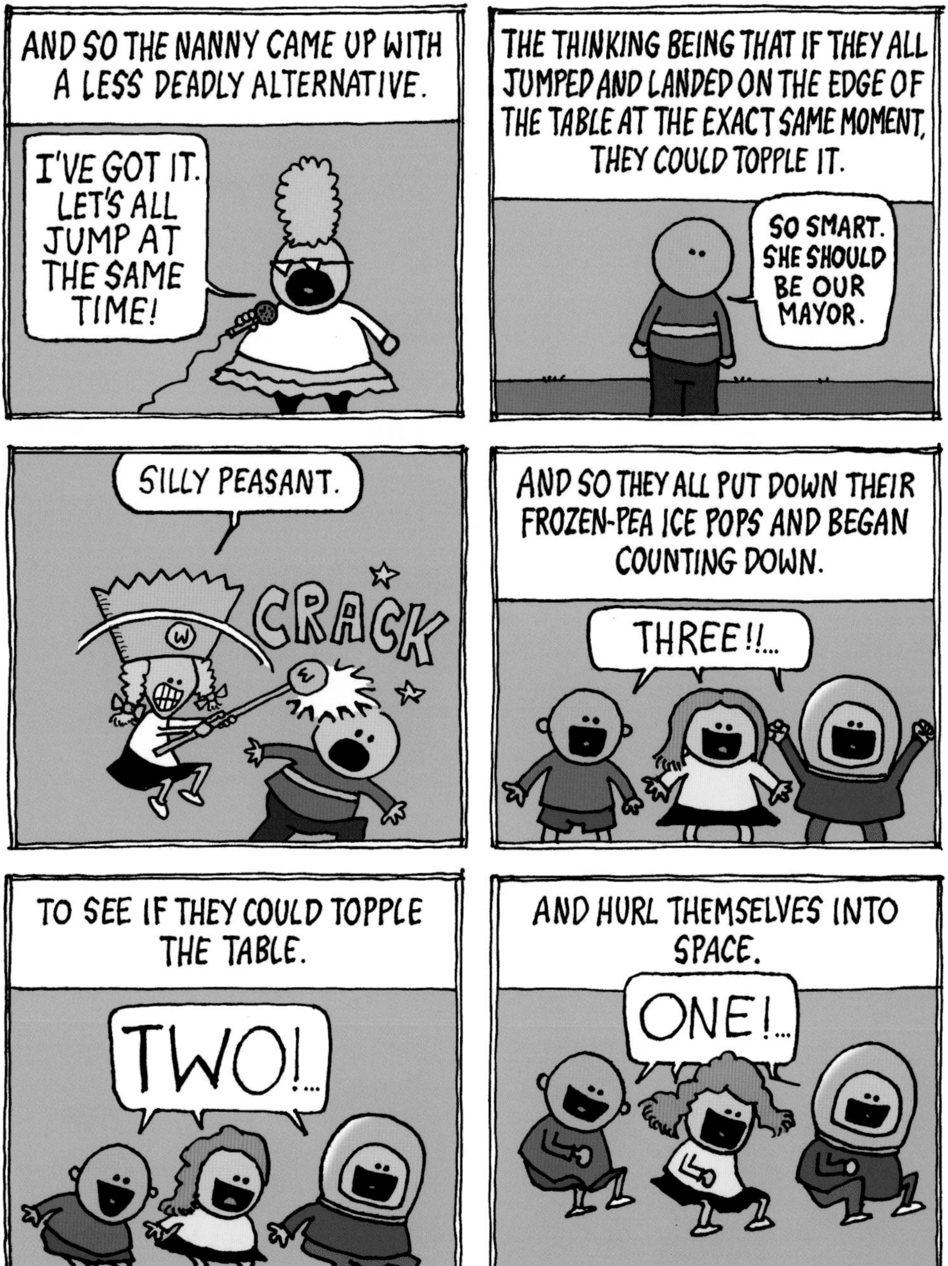
AND SO THE NANNY CAME UP WITH A LESS DEADLY ALTERNATIVE.
I'VE GOT IT. LET'S ALL JUMP AT THE SAME TIME!
THE THINKING BEING THAT IF THEY ALL JUMPED AND LANDED ON THE EDGE OF THE TABLE AT THE EXACT SAME MOMENT, THEY COULD TOPPLE IT.
SO SMART. SHE SHOULD BE OUR MAYOR.
SILLY PEASANT.
CRACK
AND SO THEY ALL PUT DOWN THEIR FROZEN-PEA ICE POPS AND BEGAN COUNTING DOWN.
THREE!!...
TO SEE IF THEY COULD TOPPLE THE TABLE.
TWO!...
AND HURL THEMSELVES INTO SPACE.
ONE!...

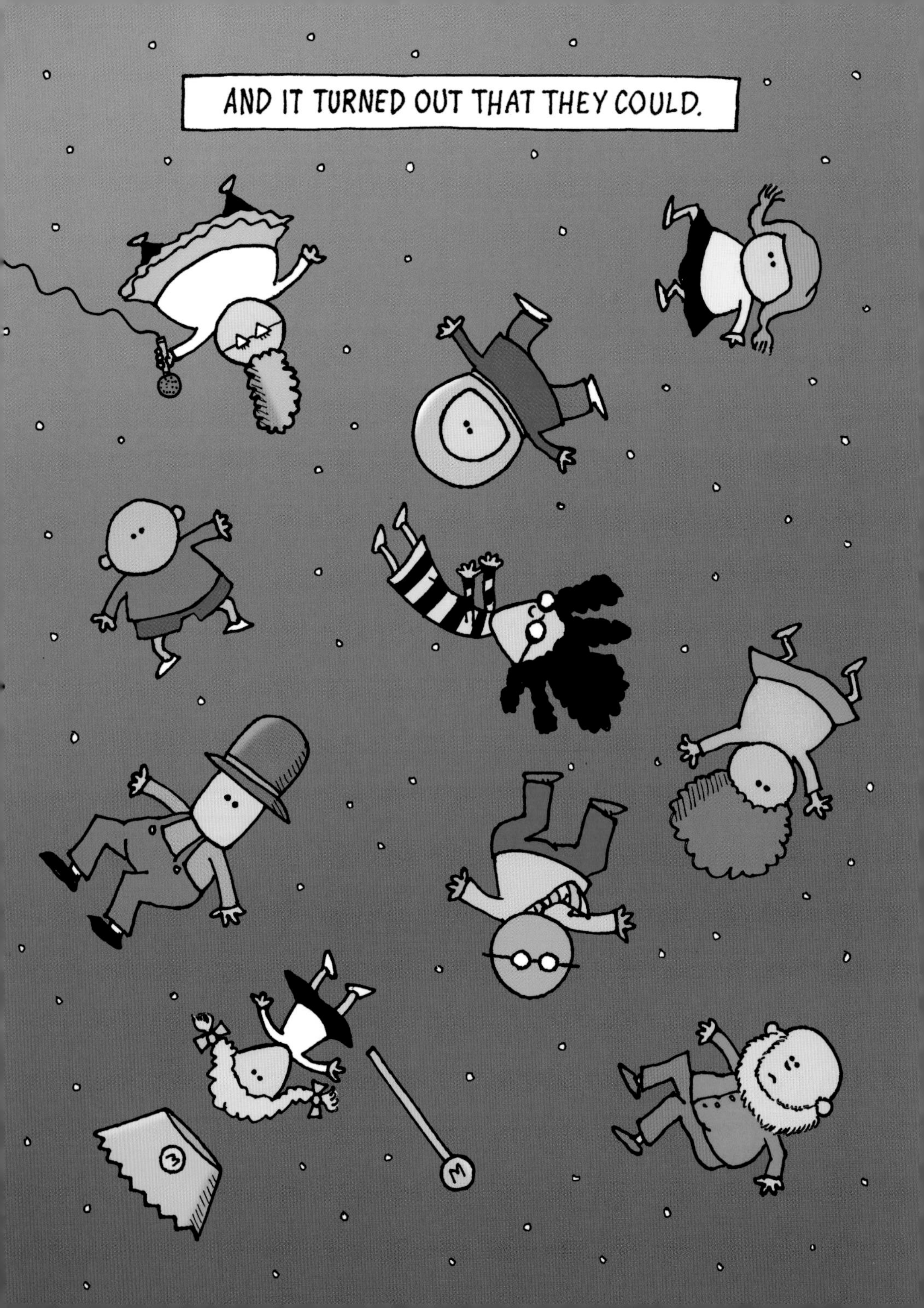
AND IT TURNED OUT THAT THEY COULD.

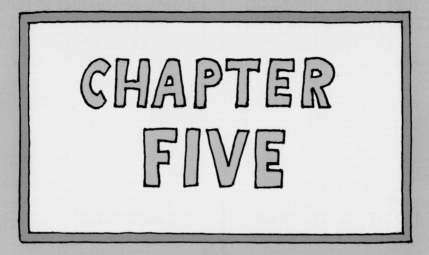

CHAPTER FIVE

AS IN...

HIGH-FIVE, WE TOPPLED THE TABLE

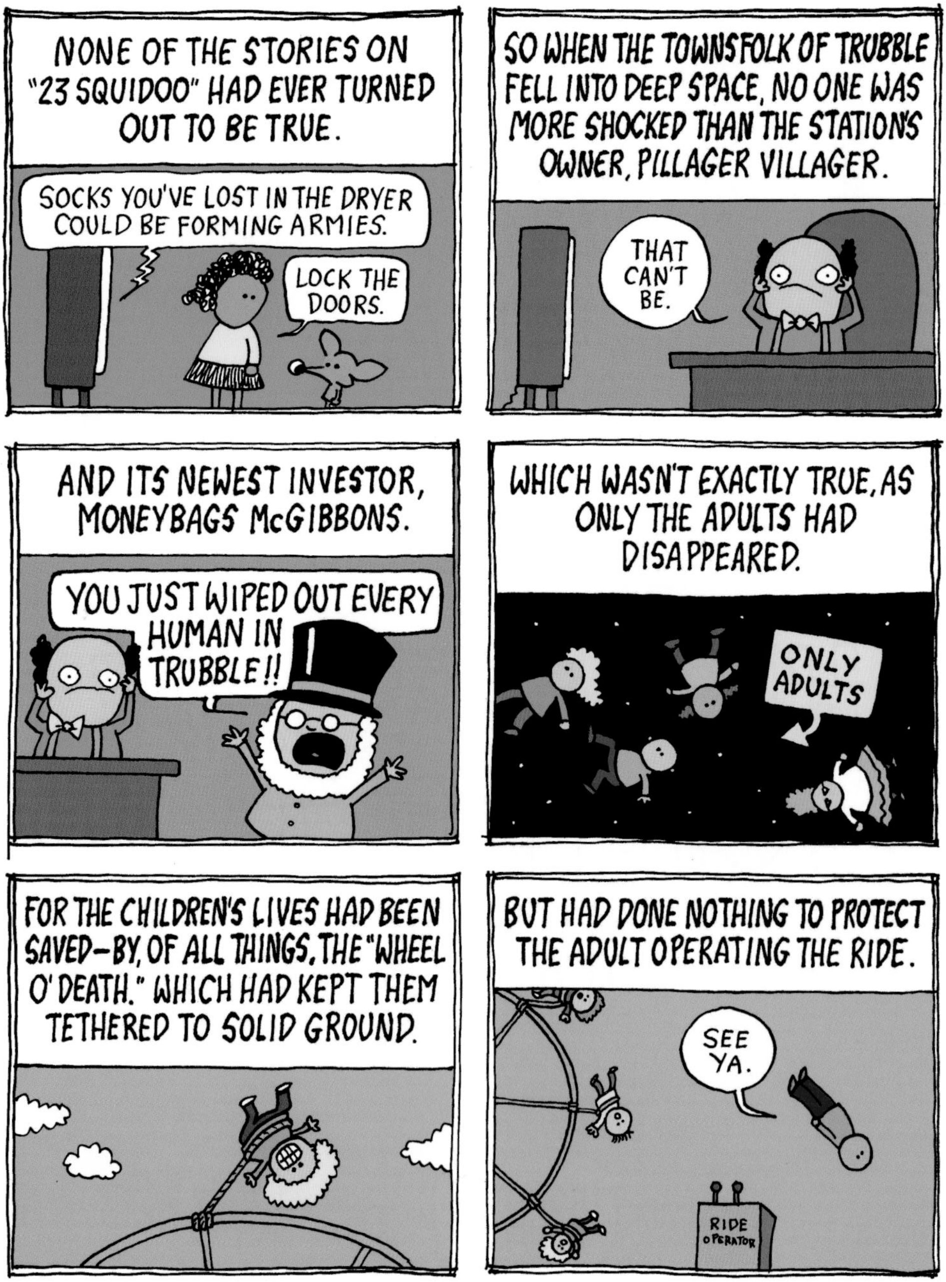
NONE OF THE STORIES ON "23 SQUIDOO" HAD EVER TURNED OUT TO BE TRUE.
SOCKS YOU'VE LOST IN THE DRYER COULD BE FORMING ARMIES.
LOCK THE DOORS.
SO WHEN THE TOWNSFOLK OF TRUBBLE FELL INTO DEEP SPACE, NO ONE WAS MORE SHOCKED THAN THE STATION'S OWNER, PILLAGER VILLAGER.
THAT CAN'T BE.
AND ITS NEWEST INVESTOR, MONEYBAGS McGIBBONS.
YOU JUST WIPED OUT EVERY HUMAN IN TRUBBLE!!
WHICH WASN'T EXACTLY TRUE, AS ONLY THE ADULTS HAD DISAPPEARED.
ONLY ADULTS
FOR THE CHILDREN'S LIVES HAD BEEN SAVED—BY, OF ALL THINGS, THE "WHEEL O' DEATH," WHICH HAD KEPT THEM TETHERED TO SOLID GROUND.
BUT HAD DONE NOTHING TO PROTECT THE ADULT OPERATING THE RIDE.
SEE YA.
RIDE OPERATOR

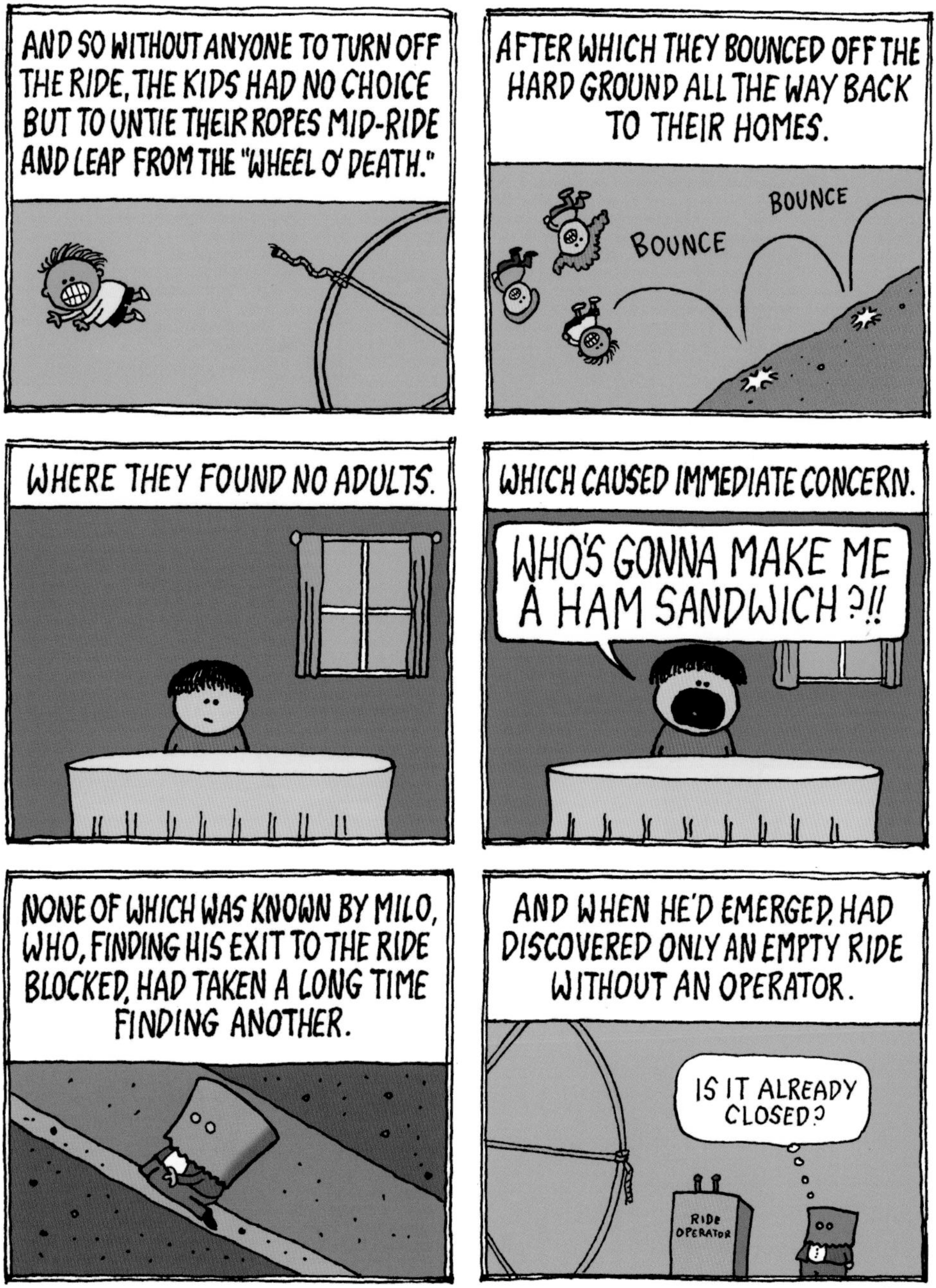
AND SO WITHOUT ANYONE TO TURN OFF THE RIDE, THE KIDS HAD NO CHOICE BUT TO UNTIE THEIR ROPES MID-RIDE AND LEAP FROM THE "WHEEL O' DEATH."
AFTER WHICH THEY BOUNCED OFF THE HARD GROUND ALL THE WAY BACK TO THEIR HOMES.
BOUNCE
BOUNCE
WHERE THEY FOUND NO ADULTS.
WHICH CAUSED IMMEDIATE CONCERN.
WHO'S GONNA MAKE ME A HAM SANDWICH?!!
NONE OF WHICH WAS KNOWN BY MILO, WHO, FINDING HIS EXIT TO THE RIDE BLOCKED, HAD TAKEN A LONG TIME FINDING ANOTHER.
AND WHEN HE'D EMERGED, HAD DISCOVERED ONLY AN EMPTY RIDE WITHOUT AN OPERATOR.
IS IT ALREADY CLOSED?
RIDE OPERATOR

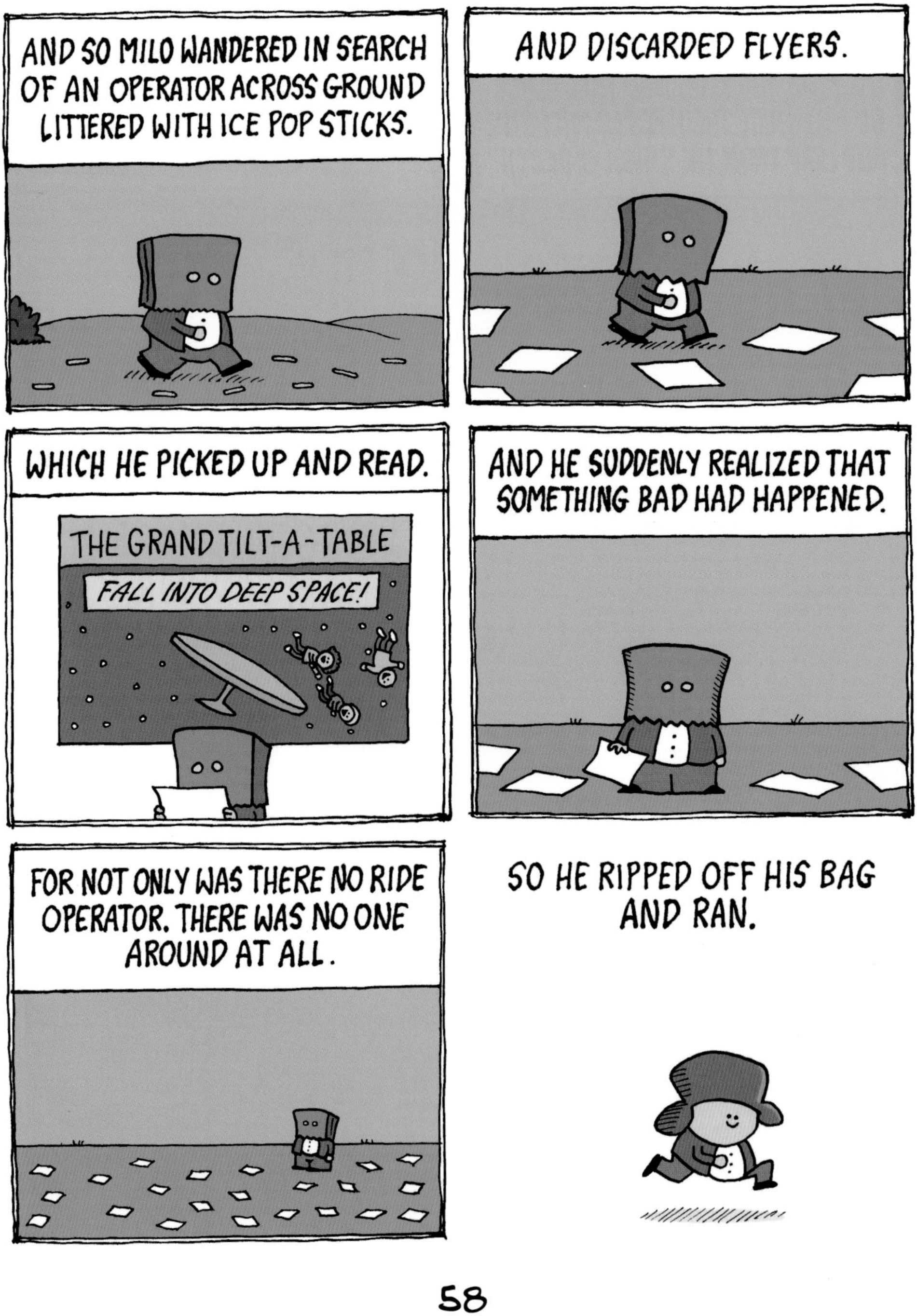
AND SO MILO WANDERED IN SEARCH OF AN OPERATOR ACROSS GROUND LITTERED WITH ICE POP STICKS.
AND DISCARDED FLYERS.
WHICH HE PICKED UP AND READ.
THE GRAND TILT-A-TABLE
FALL INTO DEEP SPACE!
AND HE SUDDENLY REALIZED THAT SOMETHING BAD HAD HAPPENED.
FOR NOT ONLY WAS THERE NO RIDE OPERATOR. THERE WAS NO ONE AROUND AT ALL.
SO HE RIPPED OFF HIS BAG AND RAN.

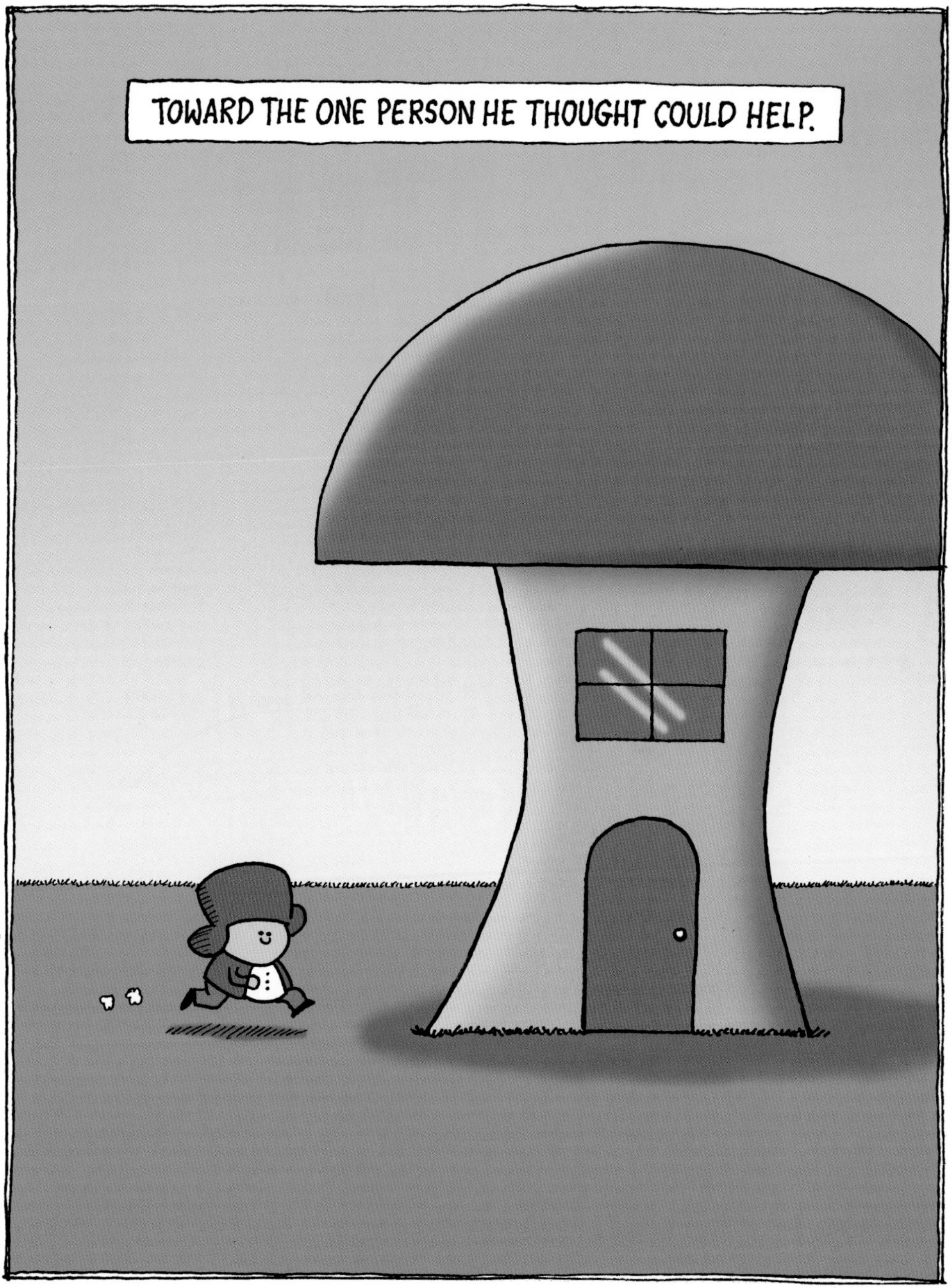
TOWARD THE ONE PERSON HE THOUGHT COULD HELP.

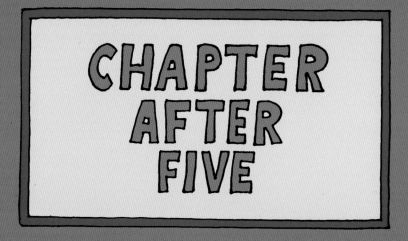

CHAPTER AFTER FIVE

WHICH...

BETTER AUTHORS MIGHT CALL "SIX"

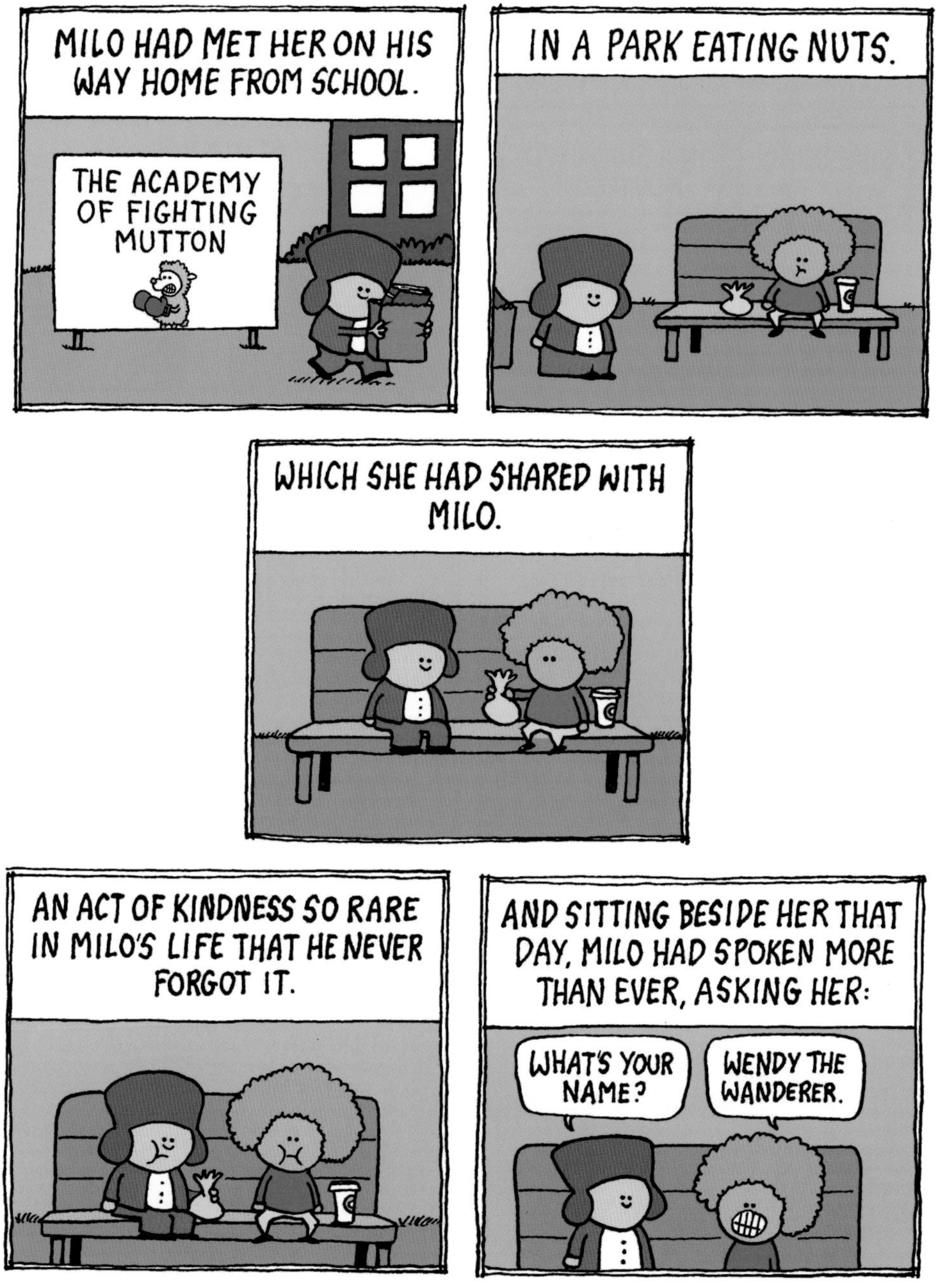
MILO HAD MET HER ON HIS WAY HOME FROM SCHOOL.
THE ACADEMY OF FIGHTING MUTTON
IN A PARK EATING NUTS.
WHICH SHE HAD SHARED WITH MILO.
AN ACT OF KINDNESS SO RARE IN MILO'S LIFE THAT HE NEVER FORGOT IT.
AND SITTING BESIDE HER THAT DAY, MILO HAD SPOKEN MORE THAN EVER, ASKING HER:
WHAT'S YOUR NAME?
WENDY THE WANDERER.

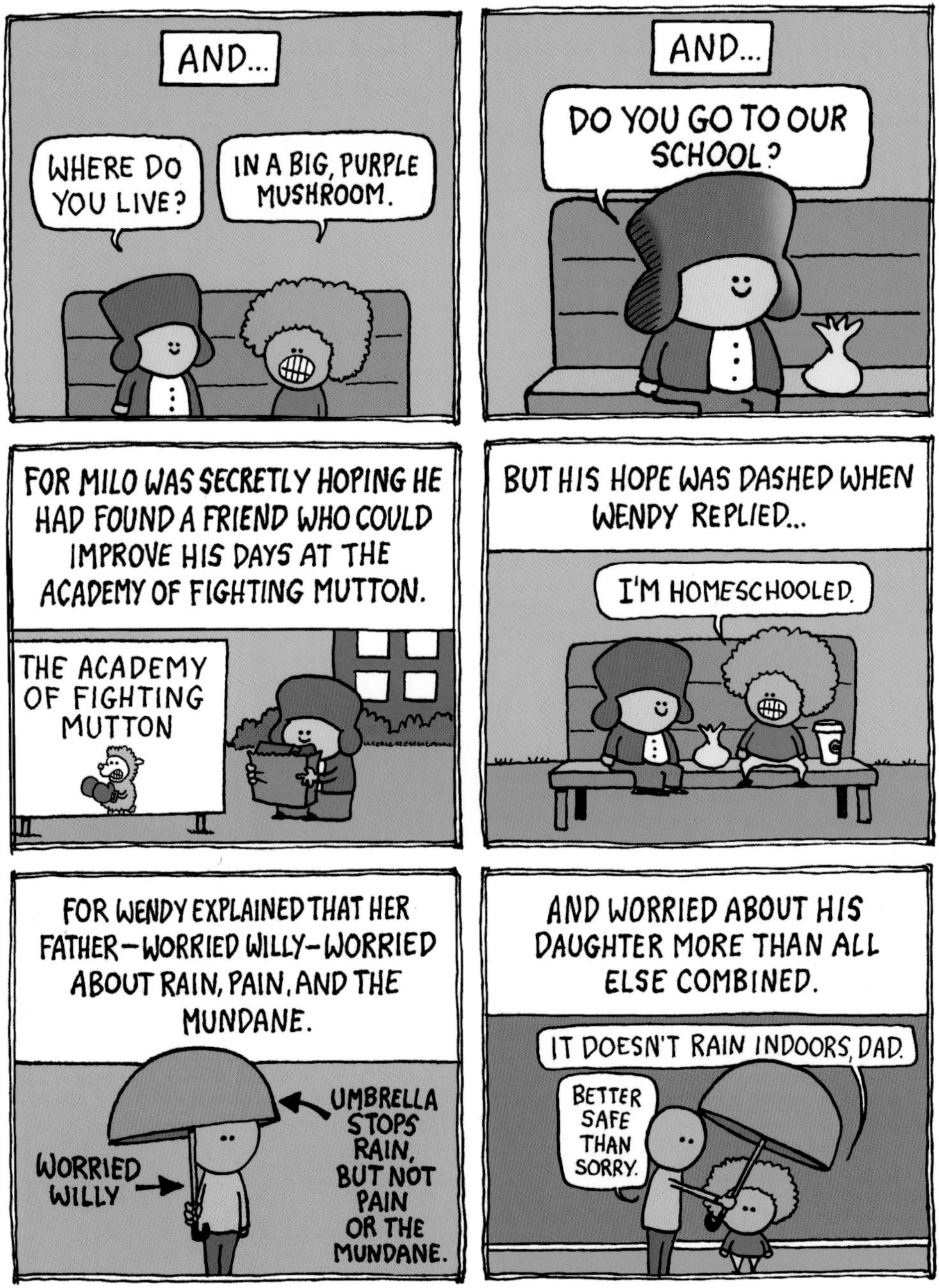
AND...
WHERE DO YOU LIVE?
IN A BIG, PURPLE MUSHROOM.
AND...
DO YOU GO TO OUR SCHOOL?
FOR MILO WAS SECRETLY HOPING HE HAD FOUND A FRIEND WHO COULD IMPROVE HIS DAYS AT THE ACADEMY OF FIGHTING MUTTON.
THE ACADEMY OF FIGHTING MUTTON
BUT HIS HOPE WAS DASHED WHEN WENDY REPLIED...
I'M HOMESCHOOLED.
FOR WENDY EXPLAINED THAT HER FATHER—WORRIED WILLY—WORRIED ABOUT RAIN, PAIN, AND THE MUNDANE.
UMBRELLA STOPS RAIN, BUT NOT PAIN OR THE MUNDANE.
WORRIED WILLY
AND WORRIED ABOUT HIS DAUGHTER MORE THAN ALL ELSE COMBINED.
IT DOESN'T RAIN INDOORS, DAD.
BETTER SAFE THAN SORRY.

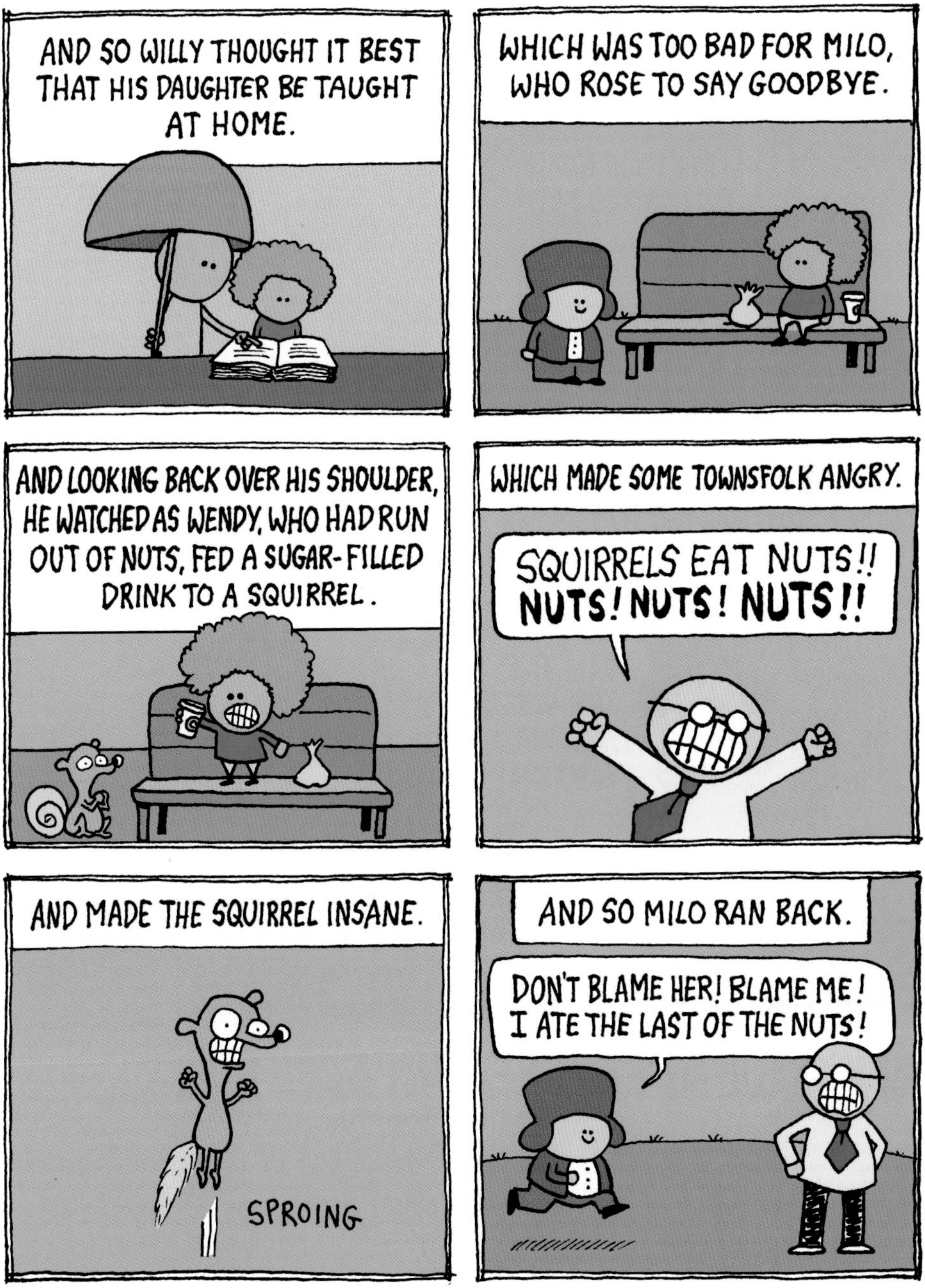
AND SO WILLY THOUGHT IT BEST THAT HIS DAUGHTER BE TAUGHT AT HOME.
WHICH WAS TOO BAD FOR MILO, WHO ROSE TO SAY GOODBYE.
AND LOOKING BACK OVER HIS SHOULDER, HE WATCHED AS WENDY, WHO HAD RUN OUT OF NUTS, FED A SUGAR-FILLED DRINK TO A SQUIRREL.
WHICH MADE SOME TOWNSFOLK ANGRY.
SQUIRRELS EAT NUTS!! NUTS! NUTS! NUTS!!
AND MADE THE SQUIRREL INSANE.
SPROING
AND SO MILO RAN BACK.
DON'T BLAME HER! BLAME ME! I ATE THE LAST OF THE NUTS!

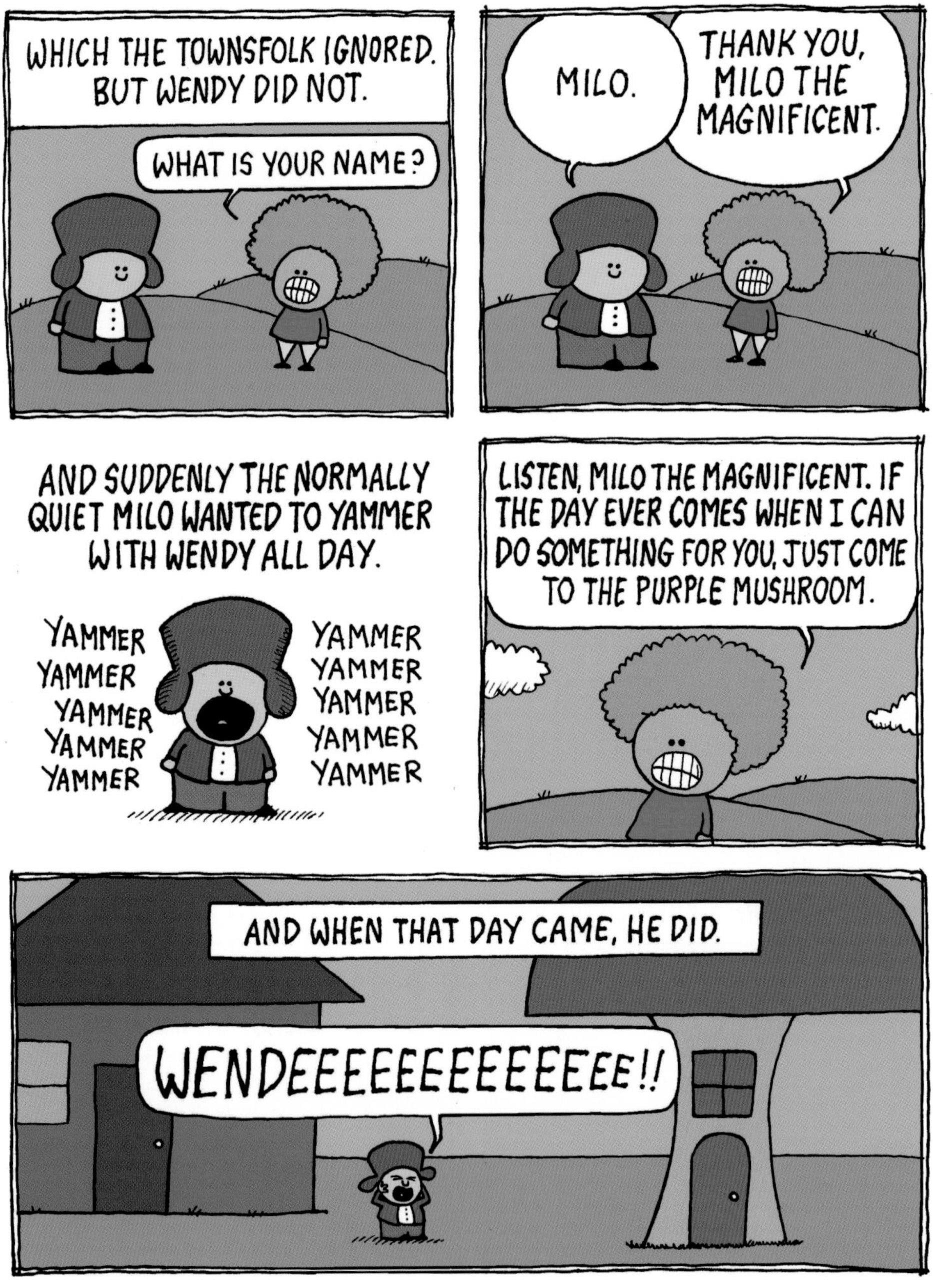
WHICH THE TOWNSFOLK IGNORED. BUT WENDY DID NOT.
WHAT IS YOUR NAME?
MILO.
THANK YOU, MILO THE MAGNIFICENT.
AND SUDDENLY THE NORMALLY QUIET MILO WANTED TO YAMMER WITH WENDY ALL DAY.
YAMMER YAMMER YAMMER YAMMER YAMMER
YAMMER YAMMER YAMMER YAMMER YAMMER
LISTEN, MILO THE MAGNIFICENT. IF THE DAY EVER COMES WHEN I CAN DO SOMETHING FOR YOU, JUST COME TO THE PURPLE MUSHROOM.
AND WHEN THAT DAY CAME, HE DID.
WENDEEEEEEEEEEEEEE!!

CHAPTER 711

NAMED NOT FOR THE
CONVENIENCE STORE
BUT JUST BECAUSE IT'S A
BIG NUMBER WE LIKE. THOUGH
WE HAVE NOTHING AGAINST
THE CONVENIENCE STORE.

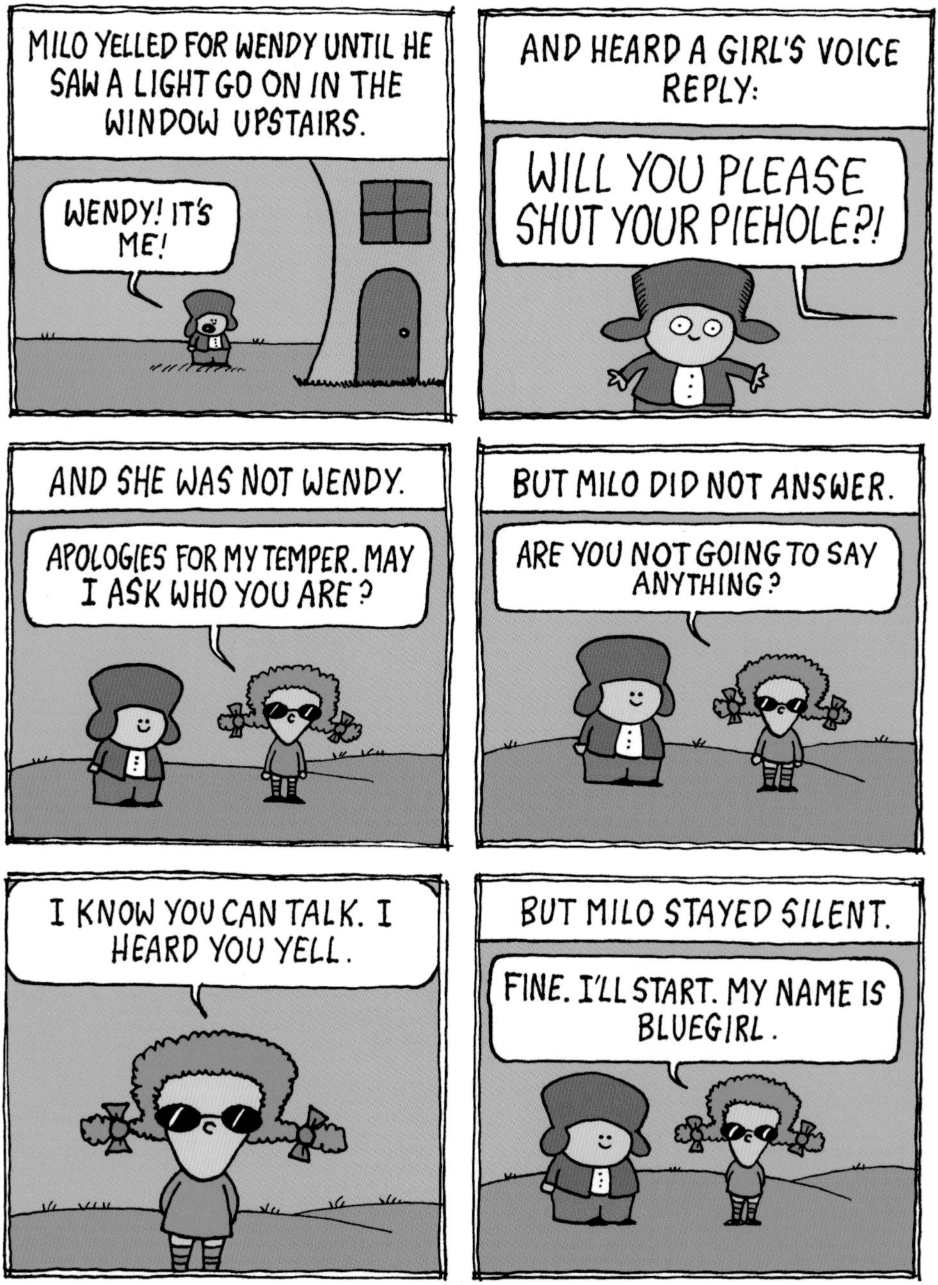
MILO YELLED FOR WENDY UNTIL HE SAW A LIGHT GO ON IN THE WINDOW UPSTAIRS.
WENDY! IT'S ME!
AND HEARD A GIRL'S VOICE REPLY:
WILL YOU PLEASE SHUT YOUR PIEHOLE?!
AND SHE WAS NOT WENDY.
APOLOGIES FOR MY TEMPER. MAY I ASK WHO YOU ARE?
BUT MILO DID NOT ANSWER.
ARE YOU NOT GOING TO SAY ANYTHING?
I KNOW YOU CAN TALK. I HEARD YOU YELL.
BUT MILO STAYED SILENT.
FINE. I'LL START. MY NAME IS BLUEGIRL.

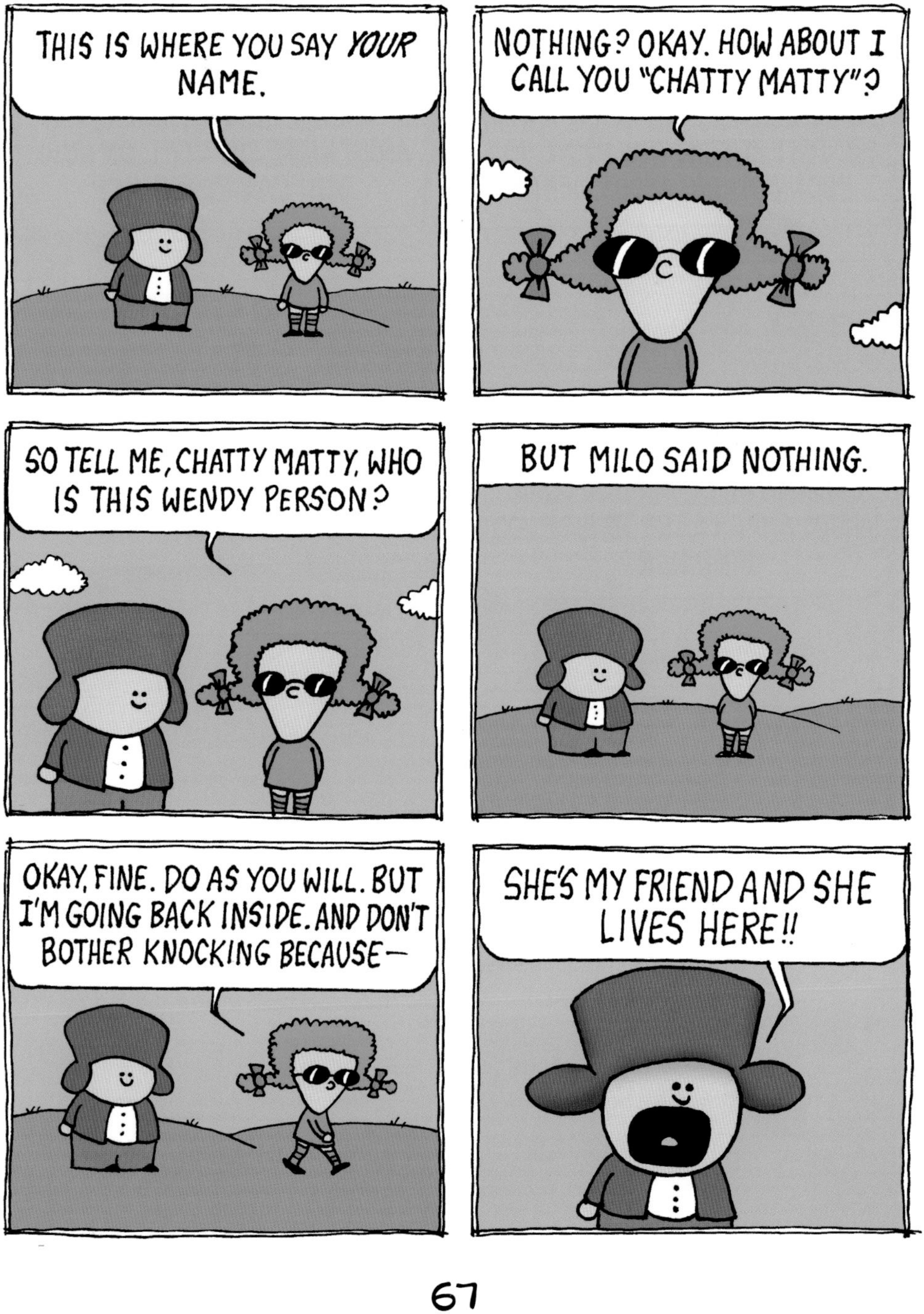
THIS IS WHERE YOU SAY *YOUR* NAME.
NOTHING? OKAY. HOW ABOUT I CALL YOU "CHATTY MATTY"?
SO TELL ME, CHATTY MATTY, WHO IS THIS WENDY PERSON?
BUT MILO SAID NOTHING.
OKAY, FINE. DO AS YOU WILL. BUT I'M GOING BACK INSIDE. AND DON'T BOTHER KNOCKING BECAUSE—
SHE'S MY FRIEND AND SHE LIVES HERE!!

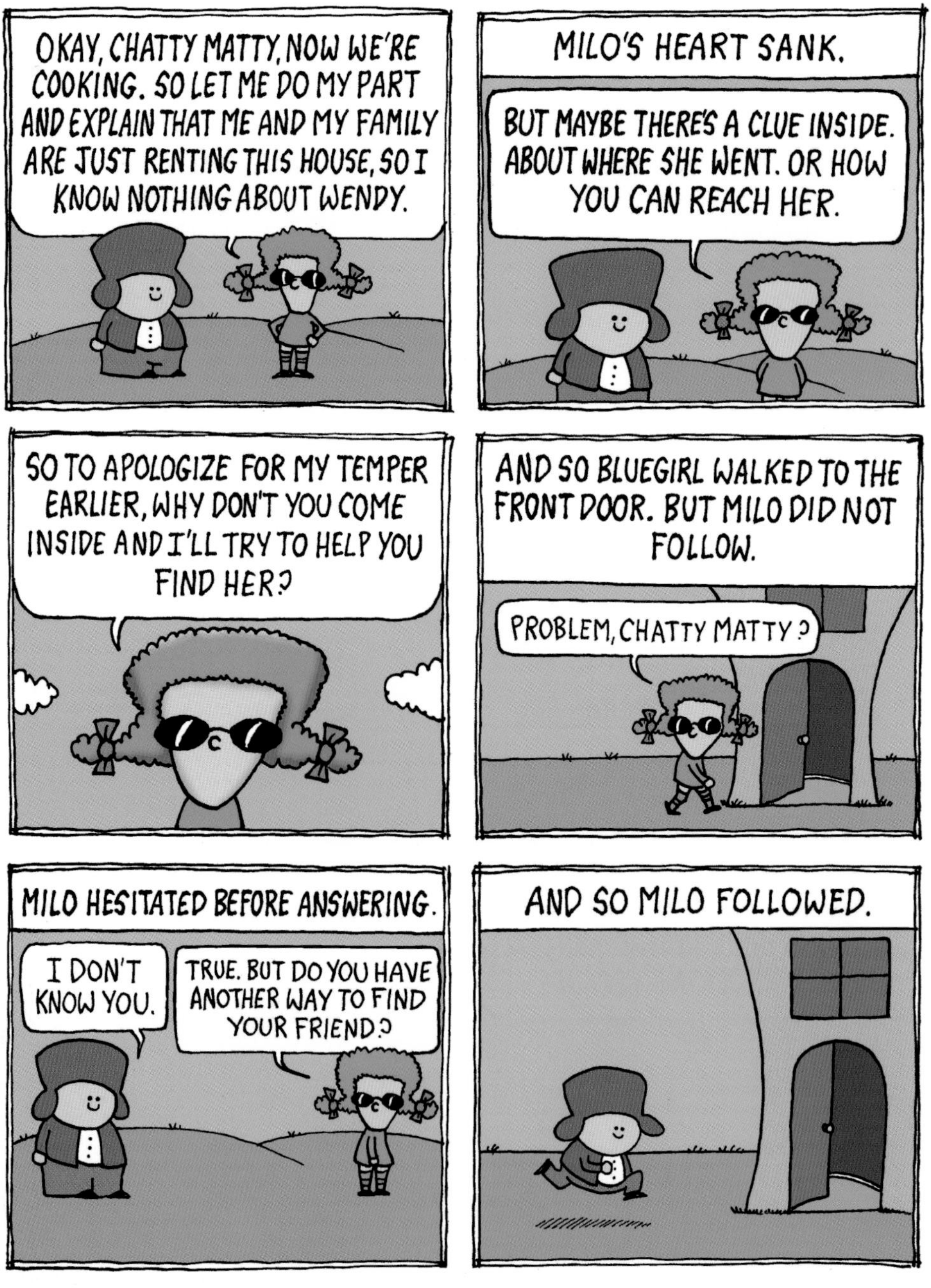
OKAY, CHATTY MATTY, NOW WE'RE COOKING. SO LET ME DO MY PART AND EXPLAIN THAT ME AND MY FAMILY ARE JUST RENTING THIS HOUSE, SO I KNOW NOTHING ABOUT WENDY.
MILO'S HEART SANK.
BUT MAYBE THERE'S A CLUE INSIDE. ABOUT WHERE SHE WENT. OR HOW YOU CAN REACH HER.
SO TO APOLOGIZE FOR MY TEMPER EARLIER, WHY DON'T YOU COME INSIDE AND I'LL TRY TO HELP YOU FIND HER?
AND SO BLUEGIRL WALKED TO THE FRONT DOOR. BUT MILO DID NOT FOLLOW.
PROBLEM, CHATTY MATTY?
MILO HESITATED BEFORE ANSWERING.
I DON'T KNOW YOU.
TRUE. BUT DO YOU HAVE ANOTHER WAY TO FIND YOUR FRIEND?
AND SO MILO FOLLOWED.

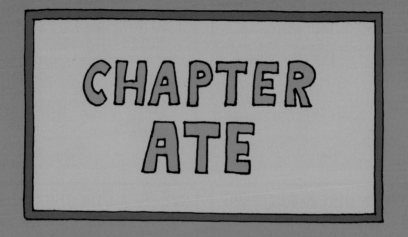

CHAPTER ATE

AS IN...

MILO ATE A DONUT, WHICH DOES NOT IN FACT HAPPEN UNTIL THE *NEXT* CHAPTER, BUT WE REALLY LIKE THE PUN

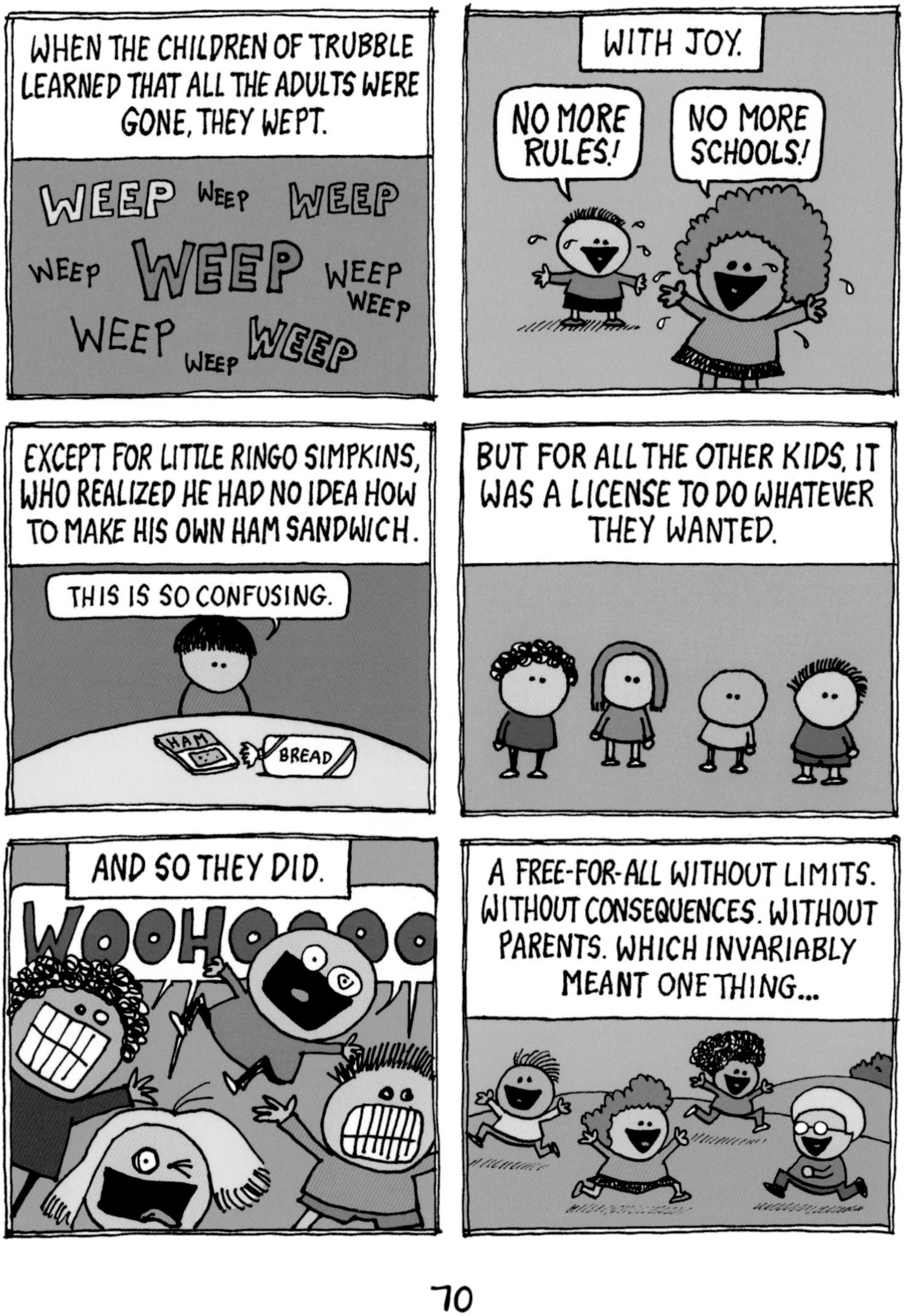
WHEN THE CHILDREN OF TRUBBLE LEARNED THAT ALL THE ADULTS WERE GONE, THEY WEPT.
WEEP WEEP WEEP
WEEP WEEP WEEP WEEP
WEEP WEEP WEEP
WITH JOY.
NO MORE RULES!
NO MORE SCHOOLS!
EXCEPT FOR LITTLE RINGO SIMPKINS, WHO REALIZED HE HAD NO IDEA HOW TO MAKE HIS OWN HAM SANDWICH.
THIS IS SO CONFUSING.
HAM
BREAD
BUT FOR ALL THE OTHER KIDS, IT WAS A LICENSE TO DO WHATEVER THEY WANTED.
AND SO THEY DID.
WOOHOOOOO
A FREE-FOR-ALL WITHOUT LIMITS. WITHOUT CONSEQUENCES. WITHOUT PARENTS. WHICH INVARIABLY MEANT ONE THING...

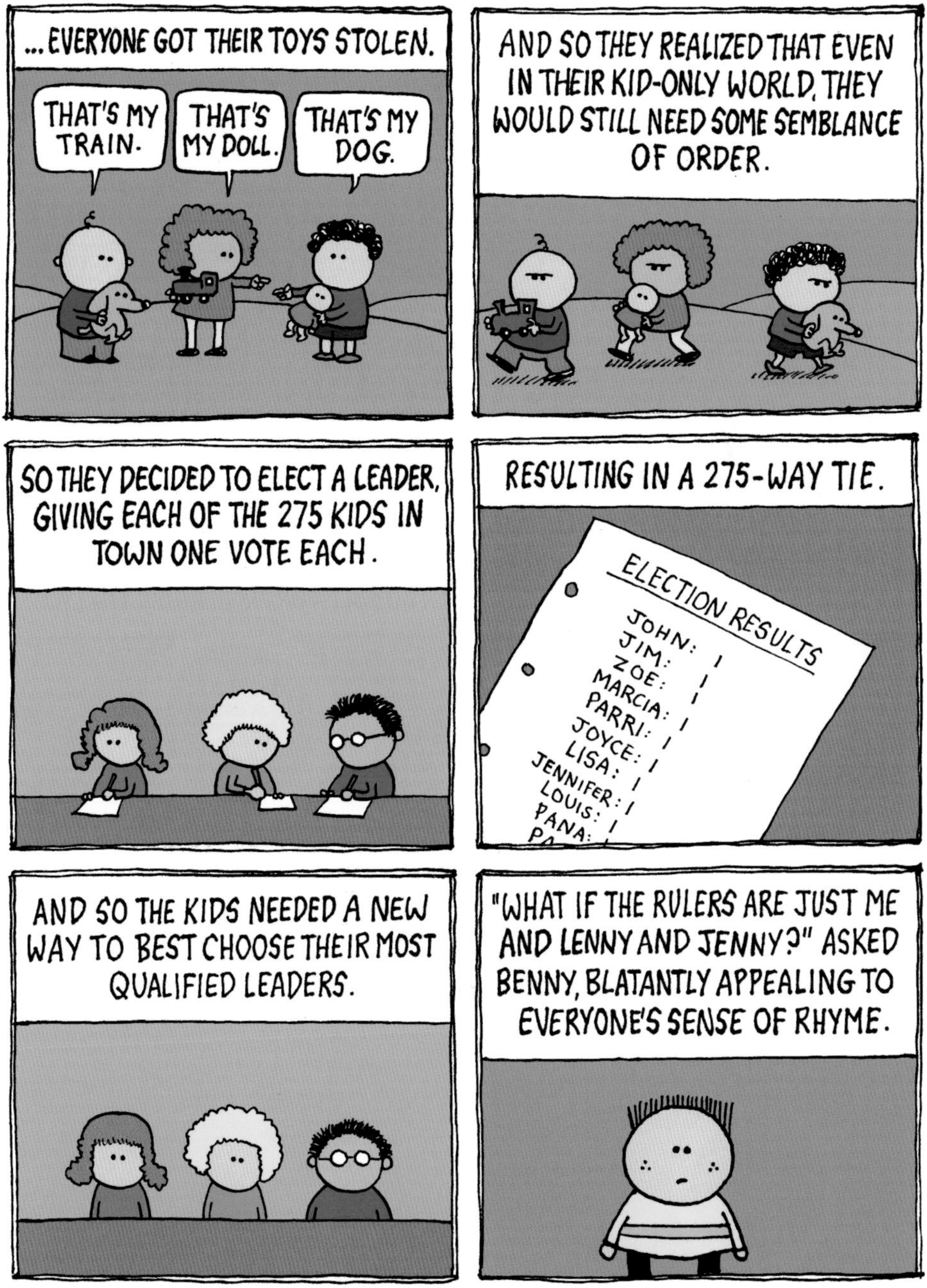
...EVERYONE GOT THEIR TOYS STOLEN.
THAT'S MY TRAIN.
THAT'S MY DOLL.
THAT'S MY DOG.
AND SO THEY REALIZED THAT EVEN IN THEIR KID-ONLY WORLD, THEY WOULD STILL NEED SOME SEMBLANCE OF ORDER.
SO THEY DECIDED TO ELECT A LEADER, GIVING EACH OF THE 275 KIDS IN TOWN ONE VOTE EACH.
RESULTING IN A 275-WAY TIE.
ELECTION RESULTS
JOHN: I
JIM: I
ZOE: I
MARCIA: I
PARRI: I
JOYCE: I
LISA: I
JENNIFER: I
LOUIS: I
PANA: I
AND SO THE KIDS NEEDED A NEW WAY TO BEST CHOOSE THEIR MOST QUALIFIED LEADERS.
"WHAT IF THE RULERS ARE JUST ME AND LENNY AND JENNY?" ASKED BENNY, BLATANTLY APPEALING TO EVERYONE'S SENSE OF RHYME.

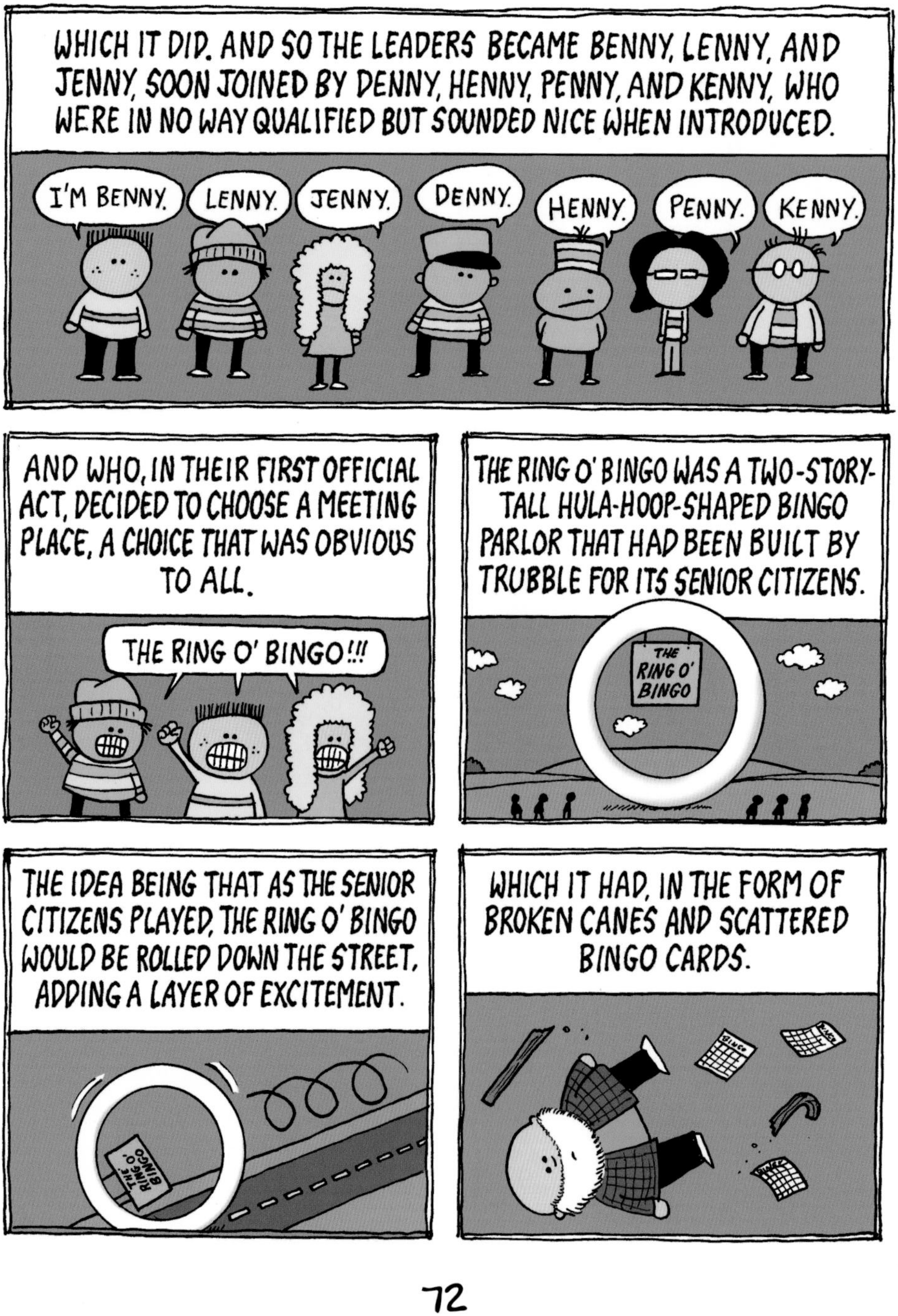
WHICH IT DID. AND SO THE LEADERS BECAME BENNY, LENNY, AND JENNY, SOON JOINED BY DENNY, HENNY, PENNY, AND KENNY, WHO WERE IN NO WAY QUALIFIED BUT SOUNDED NICE WHEN INTRODUCED.
I'M BENNY.
LENNY.
JENNY.
DENNY.
HENNY.
PENNY.
KENNY.
AND WHO, IN THEIR FIRST OFFICIAL ACT, DECIDED TO CHOOSE A MEETING PLACE, A CHOICE THAT WAS OBVIOUS TO ALL.
THE RING O' BINGO!!!
THE RING O' BINGO WAS A TWO-STORY-TALL HULA-HOOP-SHAPED BINGO PARLOR THAT HAD BEEN BUILT BY TRUBBLE FOR ITS SENIOR CITIZENS.
THE RING O' BINGO
THE IDEA BEING THAT AS THE SENIOR CITIZENS PLAYED, THE RING O' BINGO WOULD BE ROLLED DOWN THE STREET, ADDING A LAYER OF EXCITEMENT.
THE RING O' BINGO
WHICH IT HAD, IN THE FORM OF BROKEN CANES AND SCATTERED BINGO CARDS.

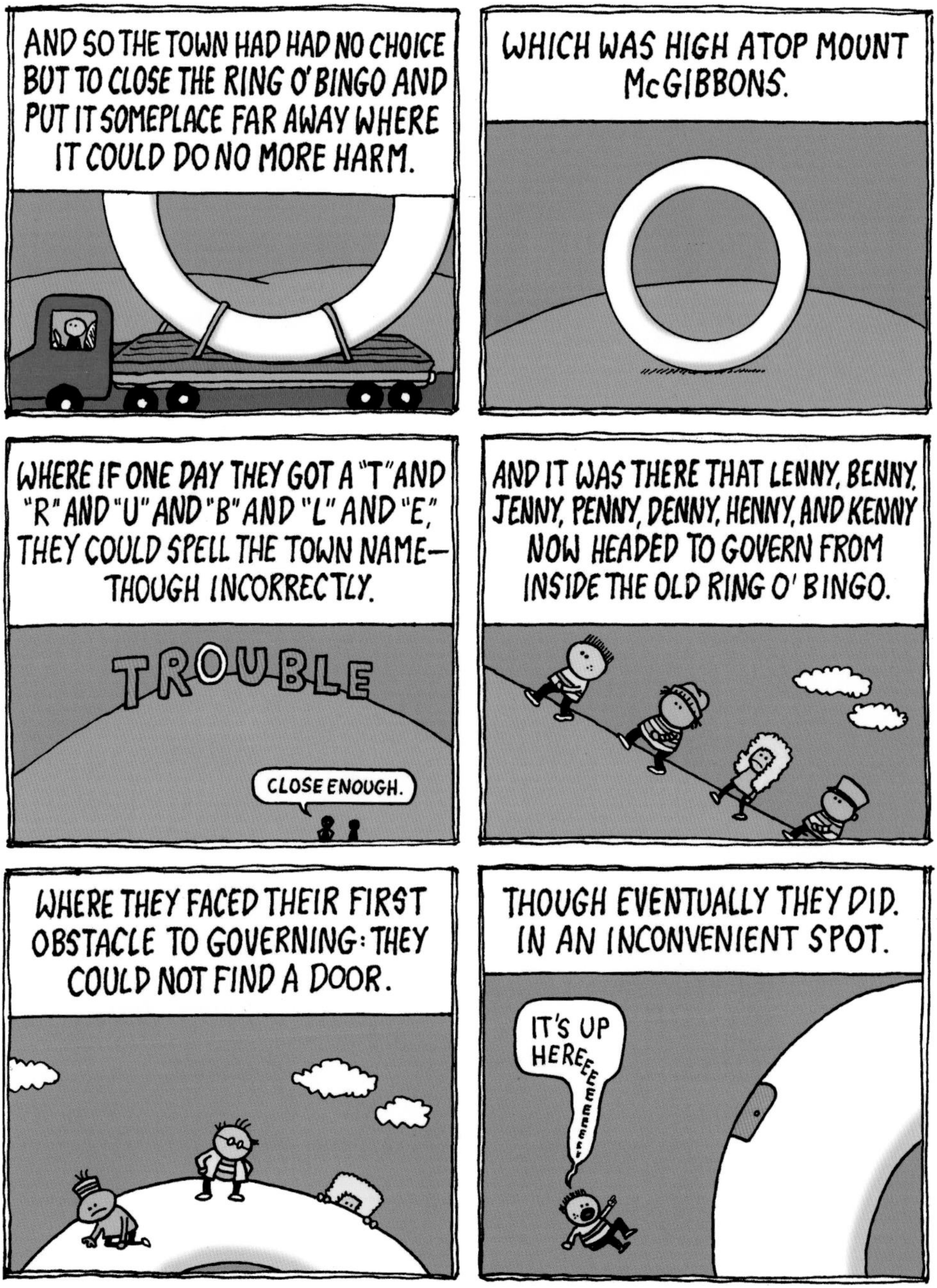
AND SO THE TOWN HAD HAD NO CHOICE BUT TO CLOSE THE RING O' BINGO AND PUT IT SOMEPLACE FAR AWAY WHERE IT COULD DO NO MORE HARM.
WHICH WAS HIGH ATOP MOUNT McGIBBONS.
WHERE IF ONE DAY THEY GOT A "T" AND "R" AND "U" AND "B" AND "L" AND "E," THEY COULD SPELL THE TOWN NAME— THOUGH INCORRECTLY.
TROUBLE
CLOSE ENOUGH.
AND IT WAS THERE THAT LENNY, BENNY, JENNY, PENNY, DENNY, HENNY, AND KENNY NOW HEADED TO GOVERN FROM INSIDE THE OLD RING O' BINGO.
WHERE THEY FACED THEIR FIRST OBSTACLE TO GOVERNING: THEY COULD NOT FIND A DOOR.
THOUGH EVENTUALLY THEY DID. IN AN INCONVENIENT SPOT.
IT'S UP HEREEEEEEEEEE

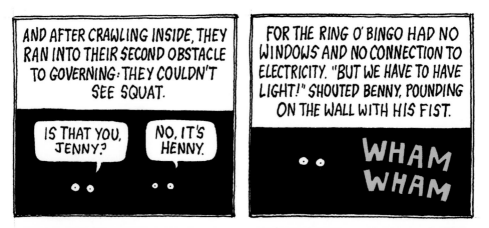

AND AFTER CRAWLING INSIDE, THEY RAN INTO THEIR SECOND OBSTACLE TO GOVERNING: THEY COULDN'T SEE SQUAT.

IS THAT YOU, JENNY?

NO, IT'S HENNY.

FOR THE RING O' BINGO HAD NO WINDOWS AND NO CONNECTION TO ELECTRICITY. "BUT WE HAVE TO HAVE LIGHT!" SHOUTED BENNY, POUNDING ON THE WALL WITH HIS FIST.

WHAM WHAM

AND SUDDENLY THEY HAD LIGHT.

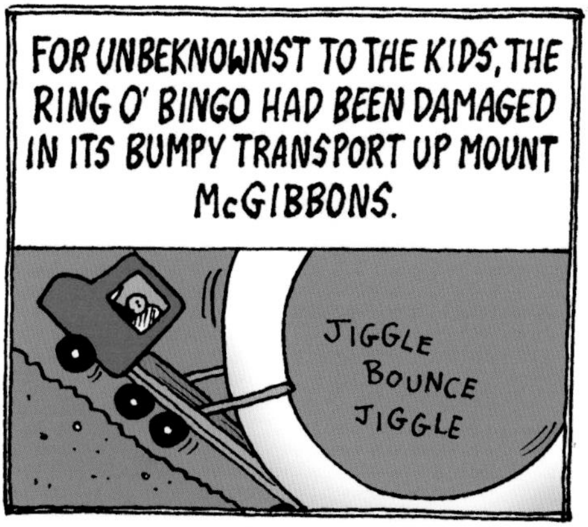
FOR UNBEKNOWNST TO THE KIDS, THE RING O' BINGO HAD BEEN DAMAGED IN ITS BUMPY TRANSPORT UP MOUNT McGIBBONS.
JIGGLE
BOUNCE
JIGGLE

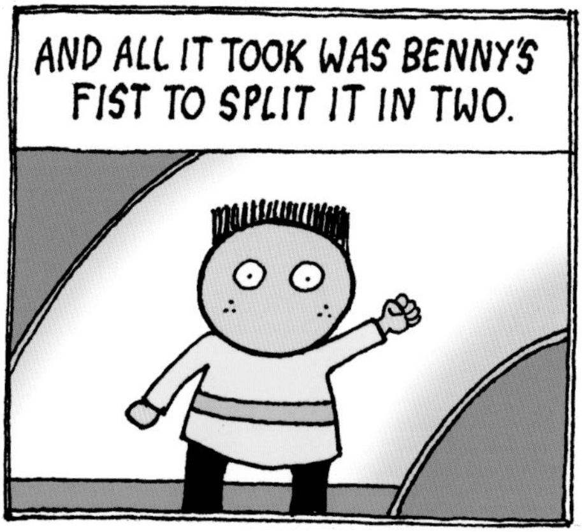
AND ALL IT TOOK WAS BENNY'S FIST TO SPLIT IT IN TWO.

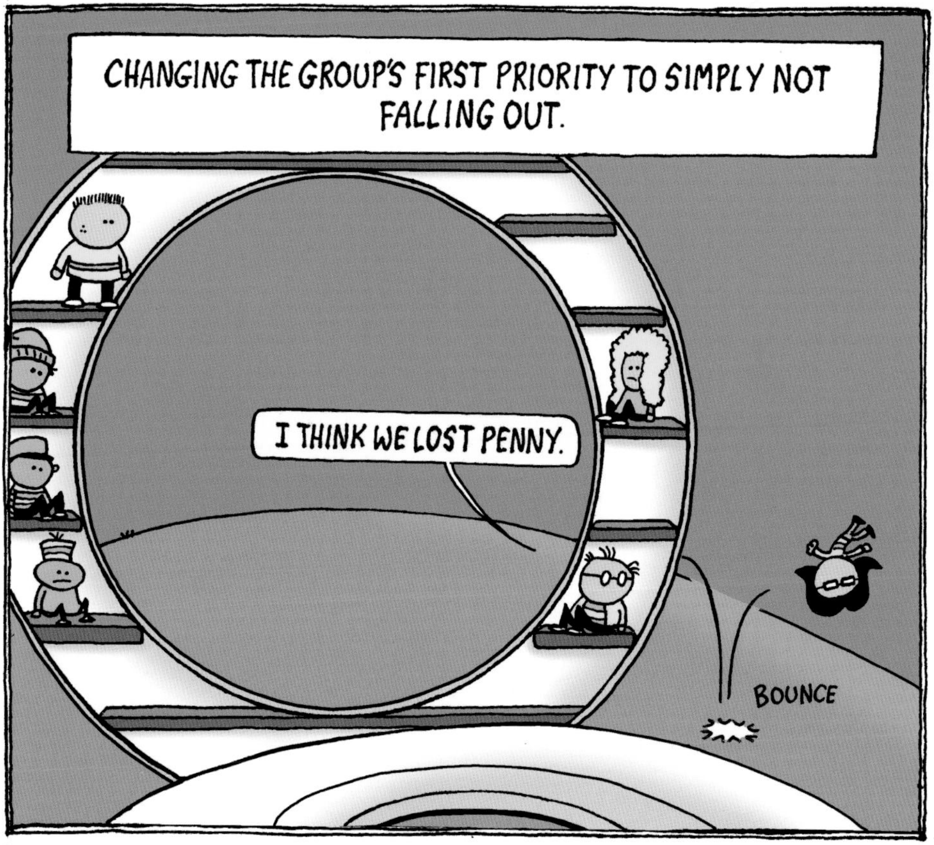
CHANGING THE GROUP'S FIRST PRIORITY TO SIMPLY NOT FALLING OUT.
I THINK WE LOST PENNY.
BOUNCE

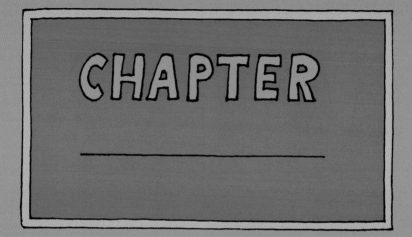

CHAPTER

_____

IN WHICH...

THERE IS NO ATTEMPT MADE TO GIVE THE CHAPTER A NUMBER

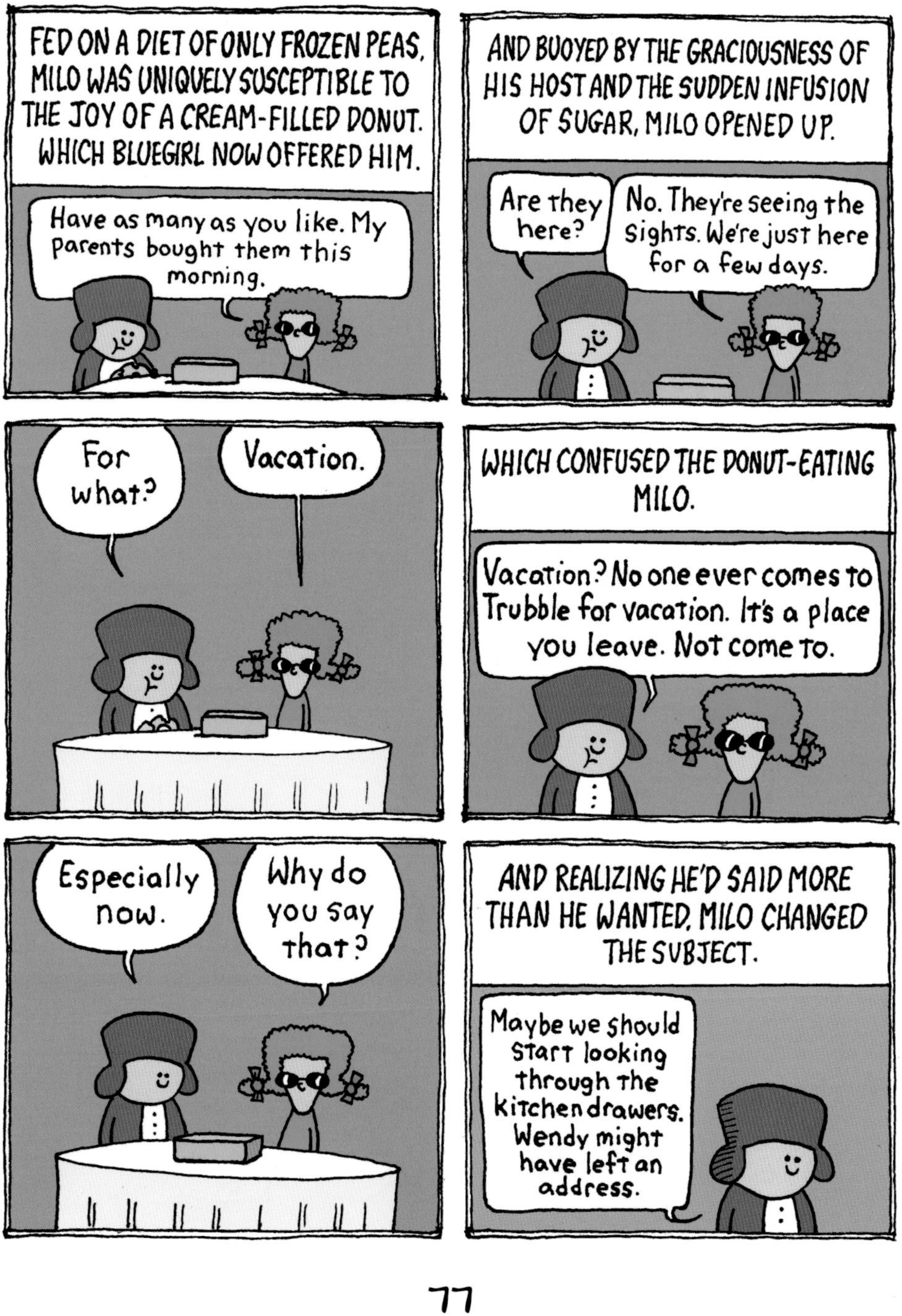
FED ON A DIET OF ONLY FROZEN PEAS, MILO WAS UNIQUELY SUSCEPTIBLE TO THE JOY OF A CREAM-FILLED DONUT. WHICH BLUEGIRL NOW OFFERED HIM.
Have as many as you like. My parents bought them this morning.
AND BUOYED BY THE GRACIOUSNESS OF HIS HOST AND THE SUDDEN INFUSION OF SUGAR, MILO OPENED UP.
Are they here?
No. They're seeing the sights. We're just here for a few days.
For what?
Vacation.
WHICH CONFUSED THE DONUT-EATING MILO.
Vacation? No one ever comes to Trubble for vacation. It's a place you leave. Not come to.
Especially now.
Why do you say that?
AND REALIZING HE'D SAID MORE THAN HE WANTED, MILO CHANGED THE SUBJECT.
Maybe we should start looking through the kitchen drawers. Wendy might have left an address.

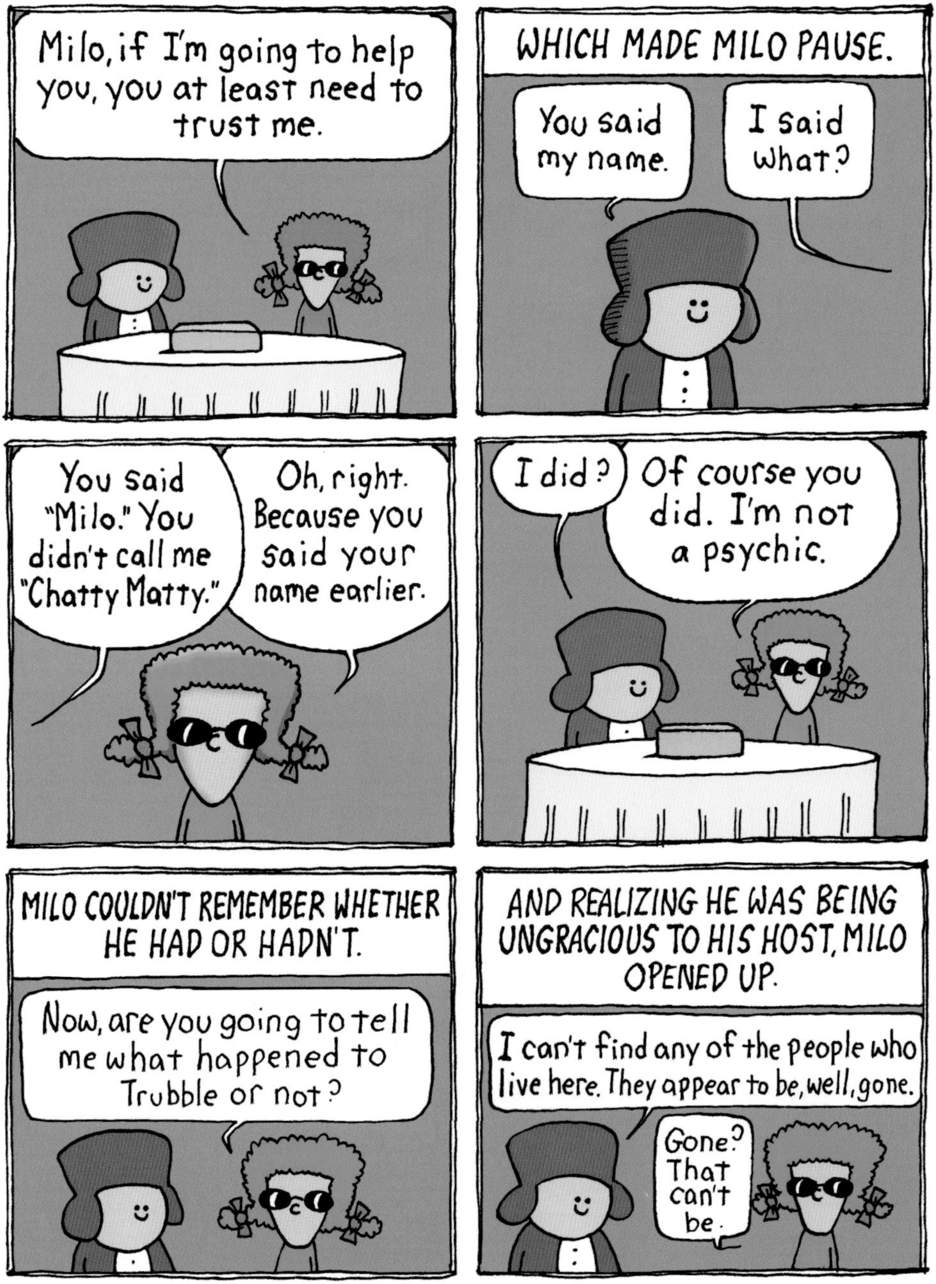

Milo, if I'm going to help you, you at least need to trust me.
WHICH MADE MILO PAUSE.
You said my name.
I said what?
You said "Milo." You didn't call me "Chatty Matty."
Oh, right. Because you said your name earlier.
I did?
Of course you did. I'm not a psychic.
MILO COULDN'T REMEMBER WHETHER HE HAD OR HADN'T.
Now, are you going to tell me what happened to Trubble or not?
AND REALIZING HE WAS BEING UNGRACIOUS TO HIS HOST, MILO OPENED UP.
I can't find any of the people who live here. They appear to be, well, gone.
Gone? That can't be.

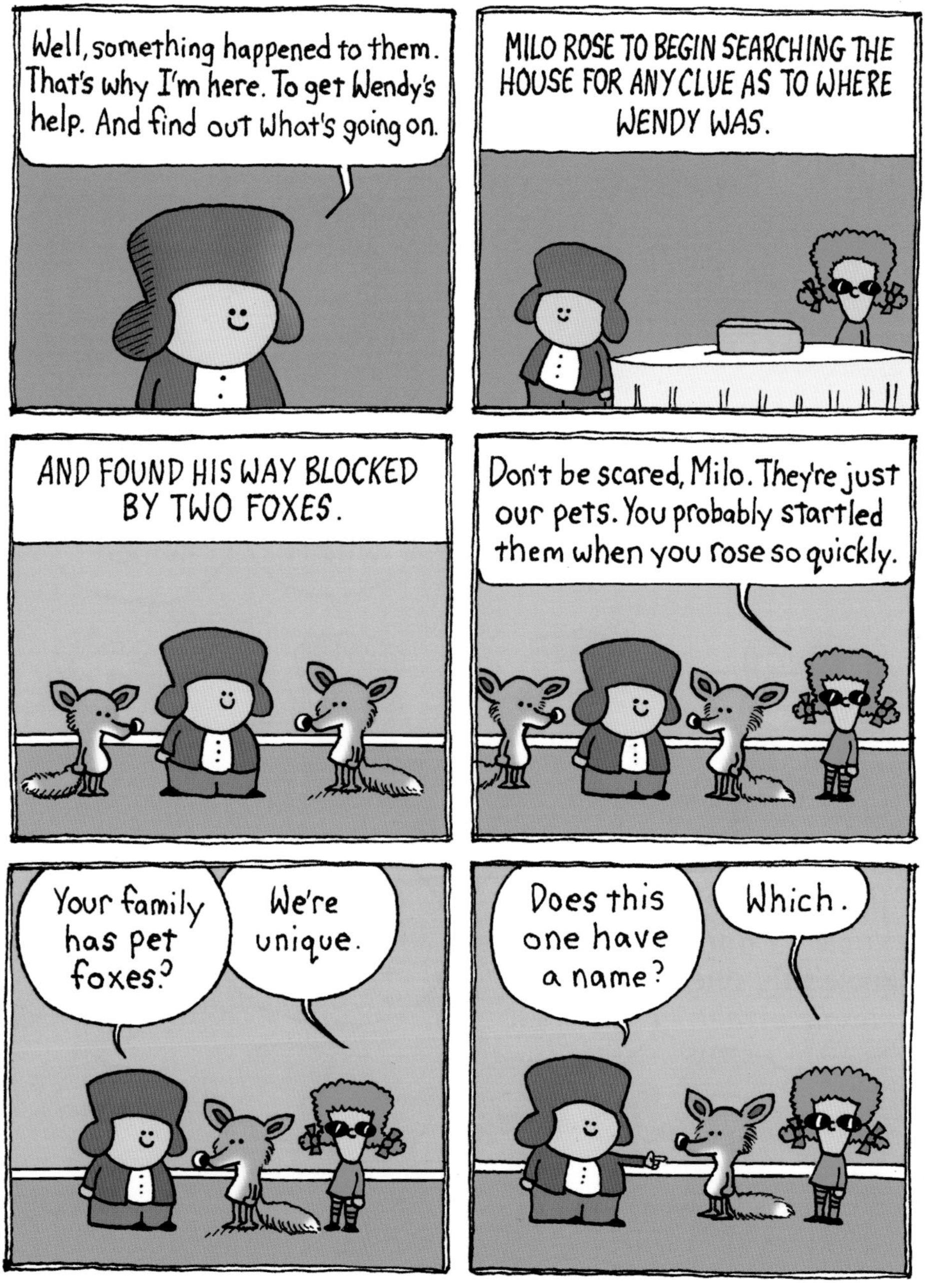
Well, something happened to them. That's why I'm here. To get Wendy's help. And find out what's going on.
MILO ROSE TO BEGIN SEARCHING THE HOUSE FOR ANY CLUE AS TO WHERE WENDY WAS.
AND FOUND HIS WAY BLOCKED BY TWO FOXES.
Don't be scared, Milo. They're just our pets. You probably startled them when you rose so quickly.
Your family has pet foxes?
We're unique.
Does this one have a name?
Which.

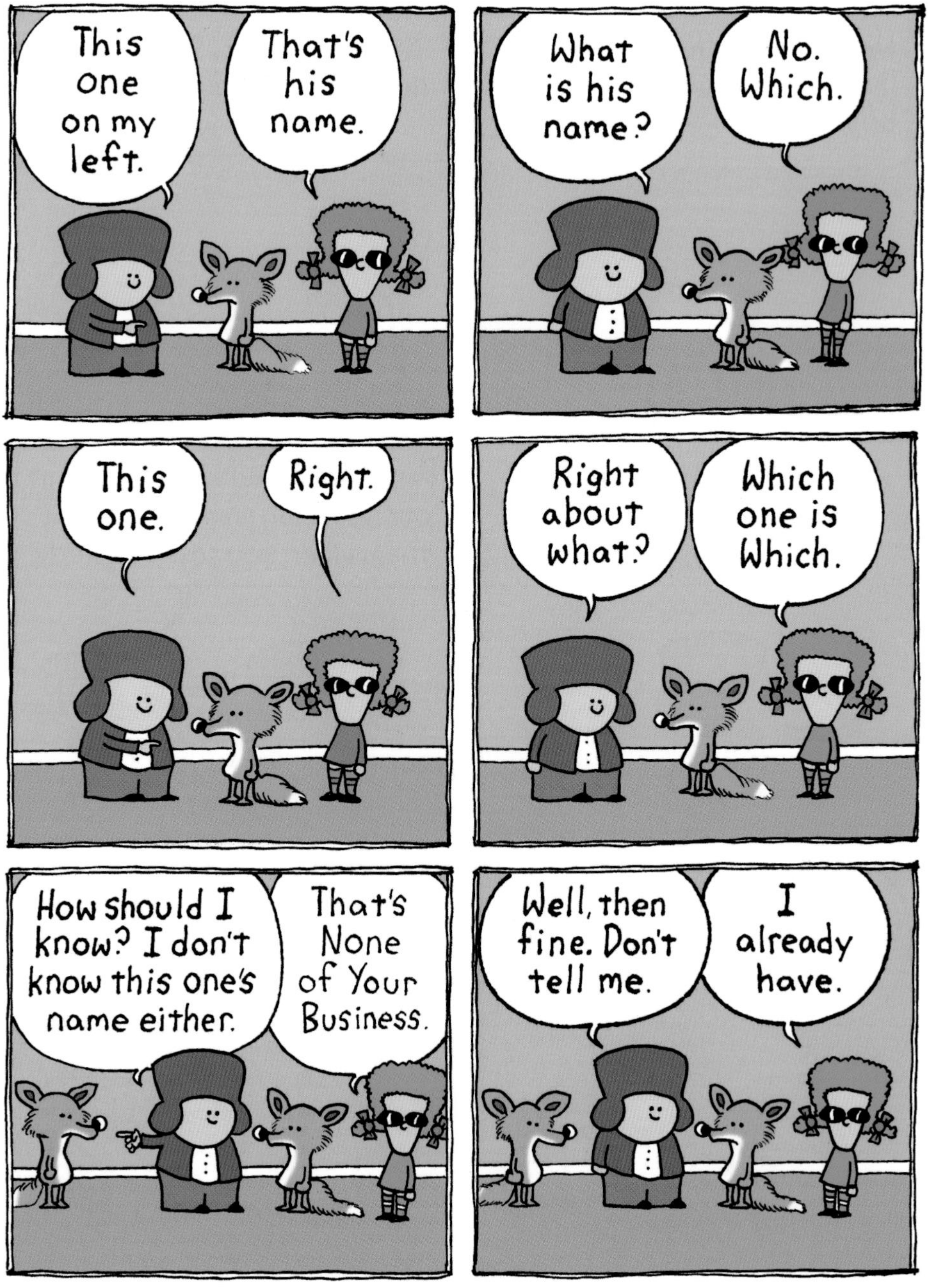
This one on my left.
That's his name.
What is his name?
No. Which.
This one.
Right.
Right about what?
Which one is Which.
How should I know? I don't know this one's name either.
That's None of Your Business.
Well, then fine. Don't tell me.
I already have.

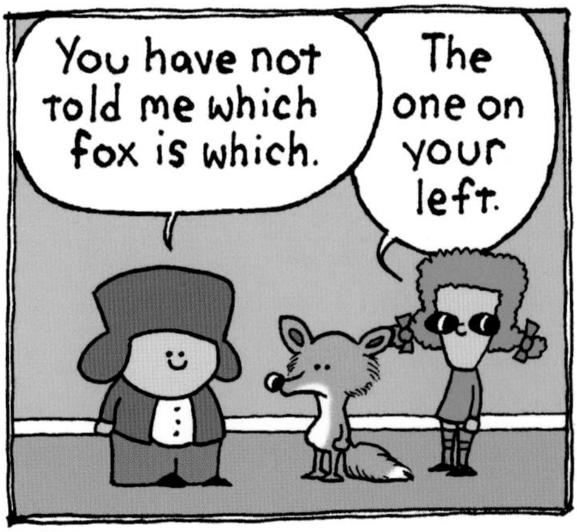
You have not told me which fox is which.
The one on your left.

IT WAS THE MOST MILO HAD EVER SPOKEN IN HIS LIFE. AND IT HAD GOTTEN HIM NOWHERE.

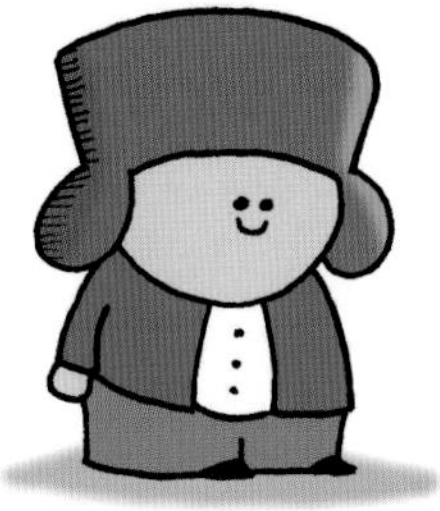

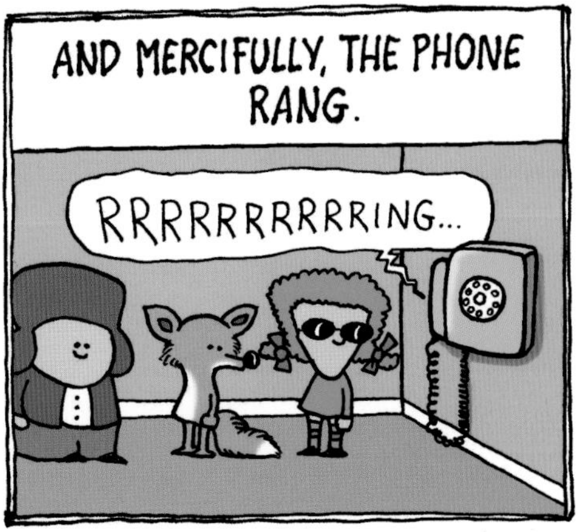
AND MERCIFULLY, THE PHONE RANG.
RRRRRRRRRRING...

CHAPTER
SORRY

IN WHICH...

WE APOLOGIZE FOR THE
HEADACHE WE CAUSED
YOU IN THE LAST
CHAPTER AND PROMISE
TO DO BETTER

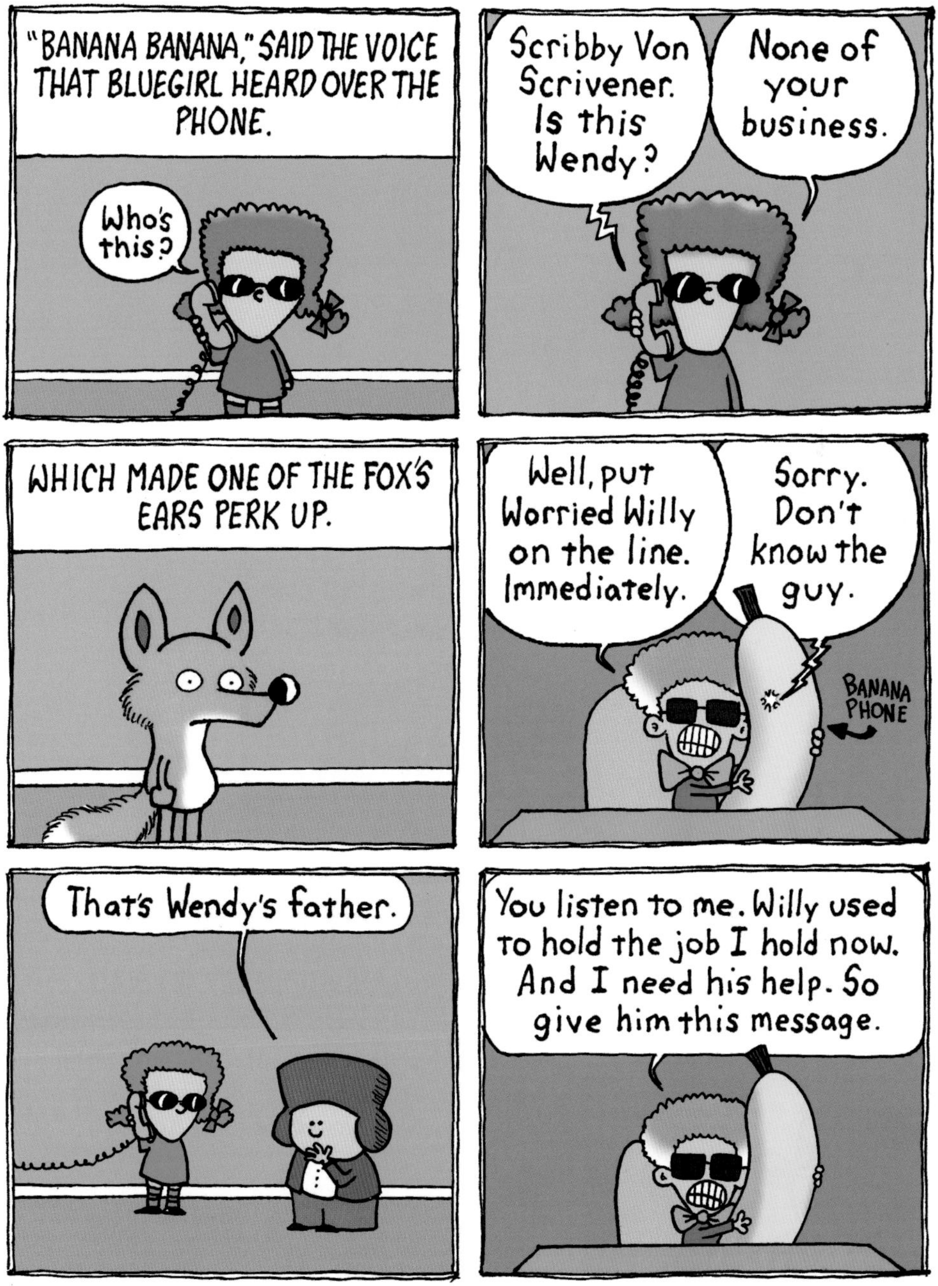
"BANANA BANANA," SAID THE VOICE THAT BLUEGIRL HEARD OVER THE PHONE.
Who's this?
Scribby Von Scrivener. Is this Wendy?
None of your business.
WHICH MADE ONE OF THE FOX'S EARS PERK UP.
Well, put Worried Willy on the line. Immediately.
Sorry. Don't know the guy.
BANANA PHONE
That's Wendy's father.
You listen to me. Willy used to hold the job I hold now. And I need his help. So give him this message.

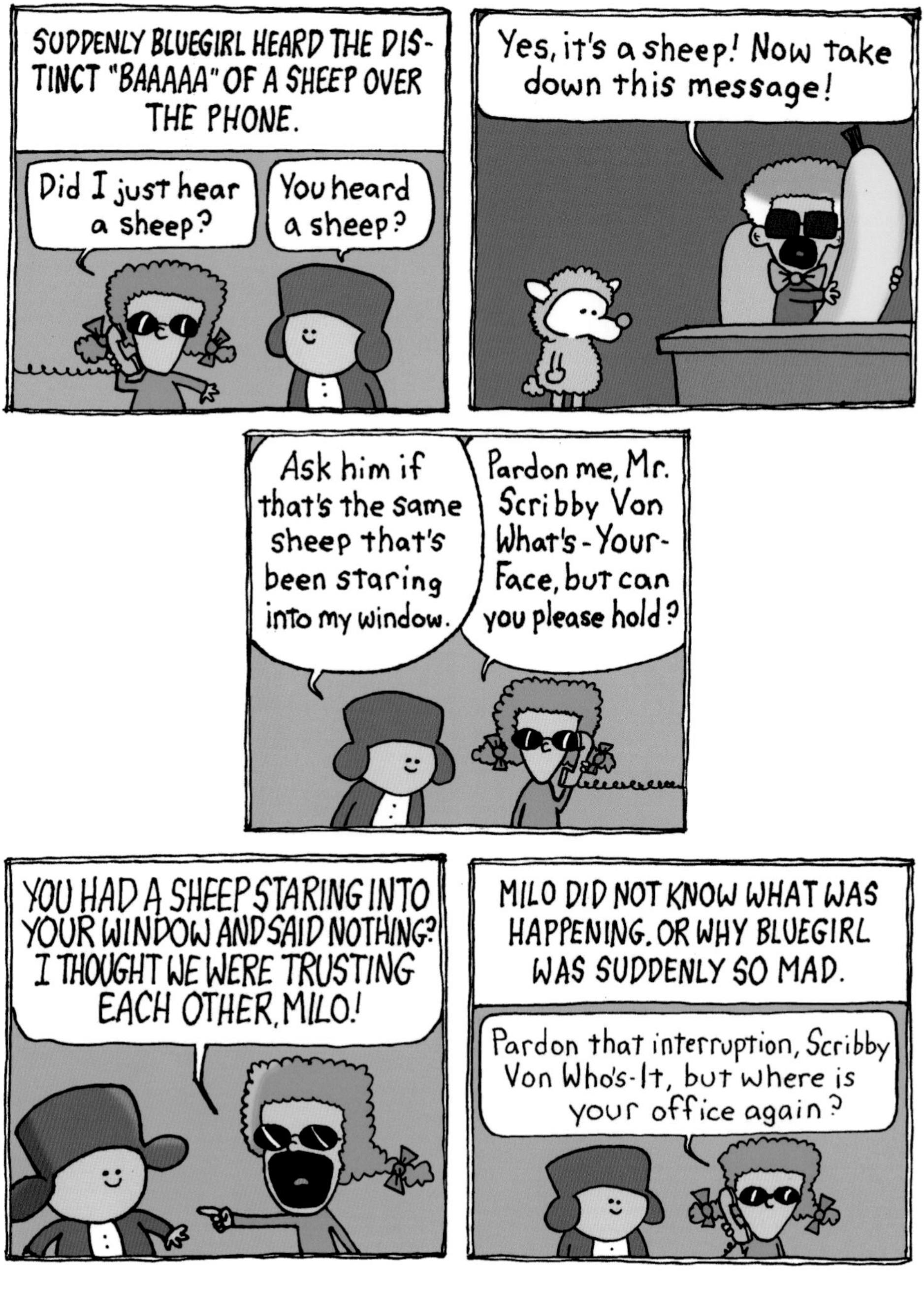
SUDDENLY BLUEGIRL HEARD THE DISTINCT "BAAAAA" OF A SHEEP OVER THE PHONE.
Did I just hear a sheep?
You heard a sheep?
Yes, it's a sheep! Now take down this message!
Ask him if that's the same sheep that's been staring into my window.
Pardon me, Mr. Scribby Von What's-Your-Face, but can you please hold?
YOU HAD A SHEEP STARING INTO YOUR WINDOW AND SAID NOTHING? I THOUGHT WE WERE TRUSTING EACH OTHER, MILO!
MILO DID NOT KNOW WHAT WAS HAPPENING. OR WHY BLUEGIRL WAS SUDDENLY SO MAD.
Pardon that interruption, Scribby Von Who's-It, but where is your office again?

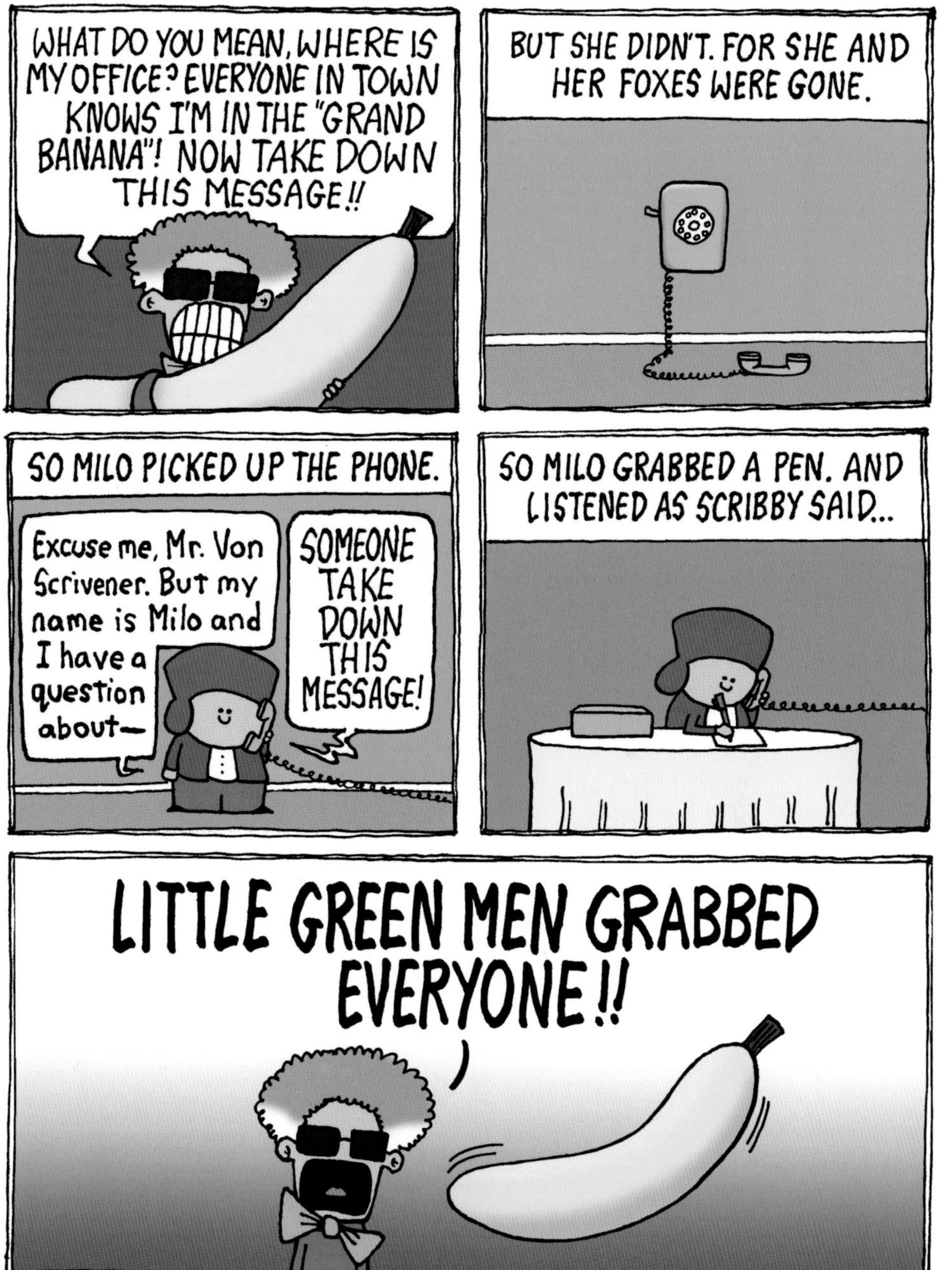
WHAT DO YOU MEAN, WHERE IS MY OFFICE? EVERYONE IN TOWN KNOWS I'M IN THE "GRAND BANANA"! NOW TAKE DOWN THIS MESSAGE!!
BUT SHE DIDN'T. FOR SHE AND HER FOXES WERE GONE.
SO MILO PICKED UP THE PHONE.
Excuse me, Mr. Von Scrivener. But my name is Milo and I have a question about—
SOMEONE TAKE DOWN THIS MESSAGE!
SO MILO GRABBED A PEN. AND LISTENED AS SCRIBBY SAID...
LITTLE GREEN MEN GRABBED EVERYONE!!

CHAPTER RAPTOR

IN WHICH...

THERE ARE NO RAPTORS, BUT NOT MUCH RHYMES WITH "CHAPTER"

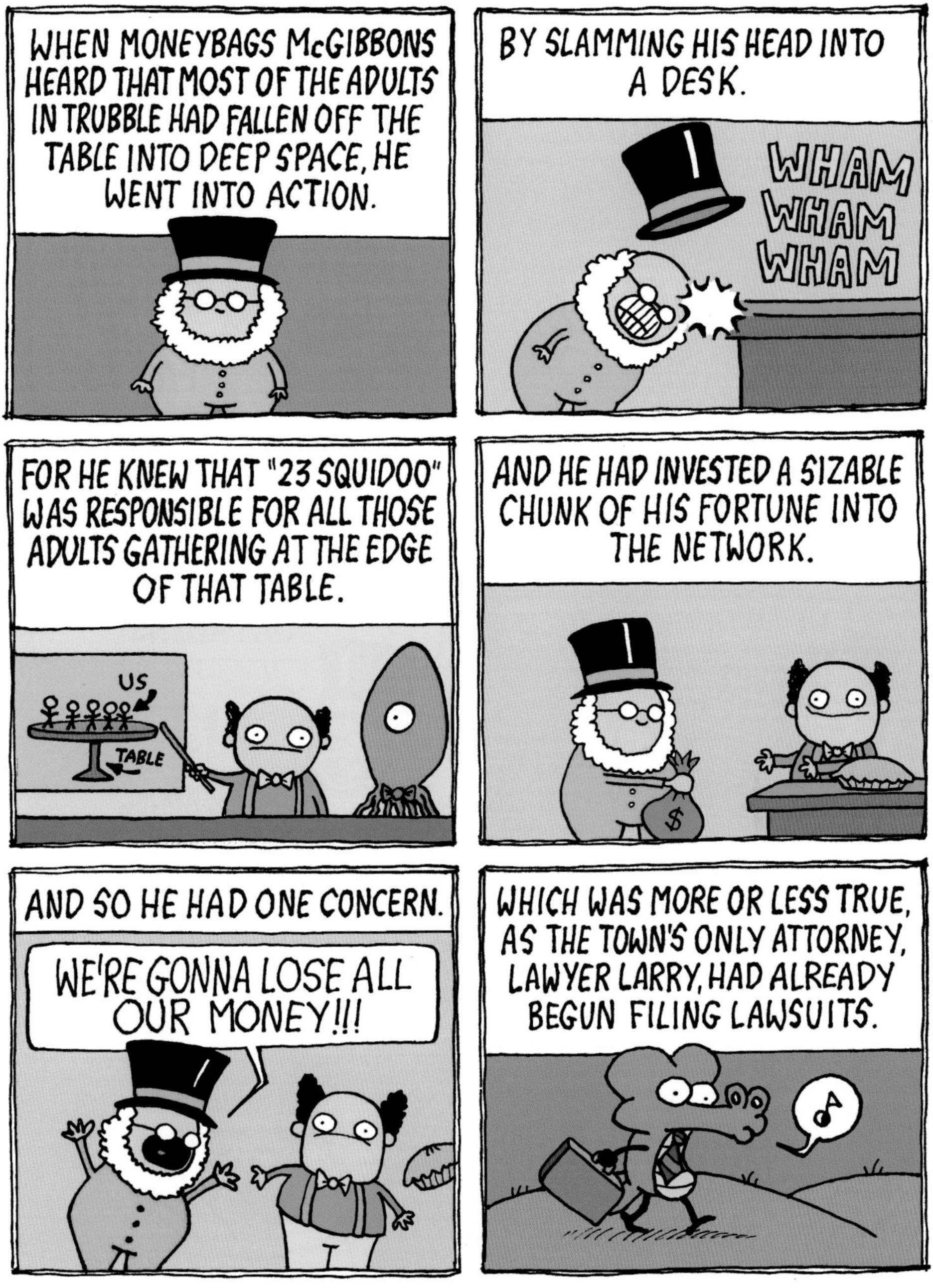
WHEN MONEYBAGS McGIBBONS HEARD THAT MOST OF THE ADULTS IN TRUBBLE HAD FALLEN OFF THE TABLE INTO DEEP SPACE, HE WENT INTO ACTION.
BY SLAMMING HIS HEAD INTO A DESK.
WHAM
WHAM
WHAM
FOR HE KNEW THAT "23 SQUIDOO" WAS RESPONSIBLE FOR ALL THOSE ADULTS GATHERING AT THE EDGE OF THAT TABLE.
US
TABLE
AND HE HAD INVESTED A SIZABLE CHUNK OF HIS FORTUNE INTO THE NETWORK.
$
AND SO HE HAD ONE CONCERN.
WE'RE GONNA LOSE ALL OUR MONEY!!!
WHICH WAS MORE OR LESS TRUE, AS THE TOWN'S ONLY ATTORNEY, LAWYER LARRY, HAD ALREADY BEGUN FILING LAWSUITS.

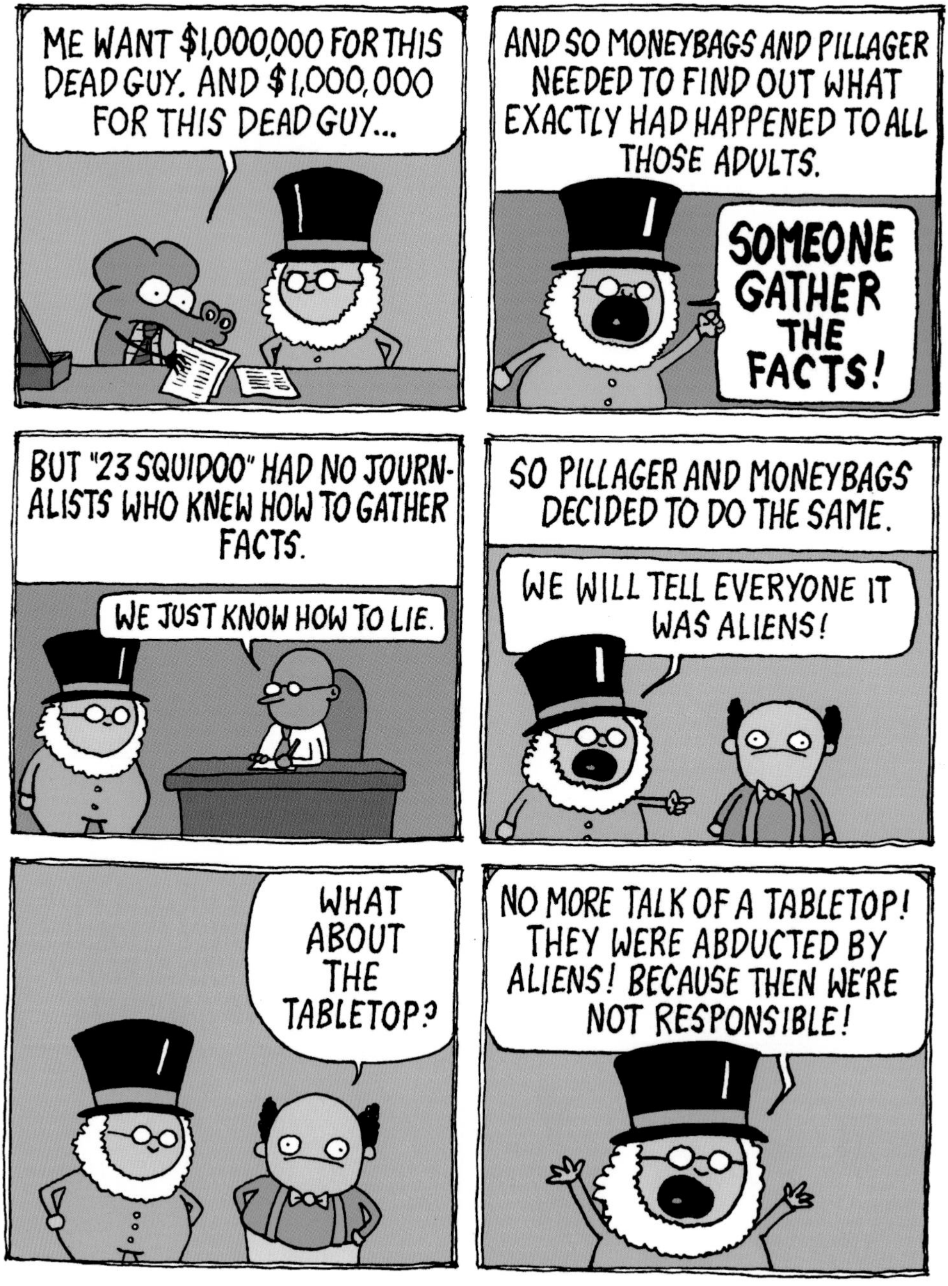
ME WANT $1,000,000 FOR THIS DEAD GUY. AND $1,000,000 FOR THIS DEAD GUY...
AND SO MONEYBAGS AND PILLAGER NEEDED TO FIND OUT WHAT EXACTLY HAD HAPPENED TO ALL THOSE ADULTS.
SOMEONE GATHER THE FACTS!
BUT "23 SQUIDOO" HAD NO JOURNALISTS WHO KNEW HOW TO GATHER FACTS.
WE JUST KNOW HOW TO LIE.
SO PILLAGER AND MONEYBAGS DECIDED TO DO THE SAME.
WE WILL TELL EVERYONE IT WAS ALIENS!
WHAT ABOUT THE TABLETOP?
NO MORE TALK OF A TABLETOP! THEY WERE ABDUCTED BY ALIENS! BECAUSE THEN WE'RE NOT RESPONSIBLE!

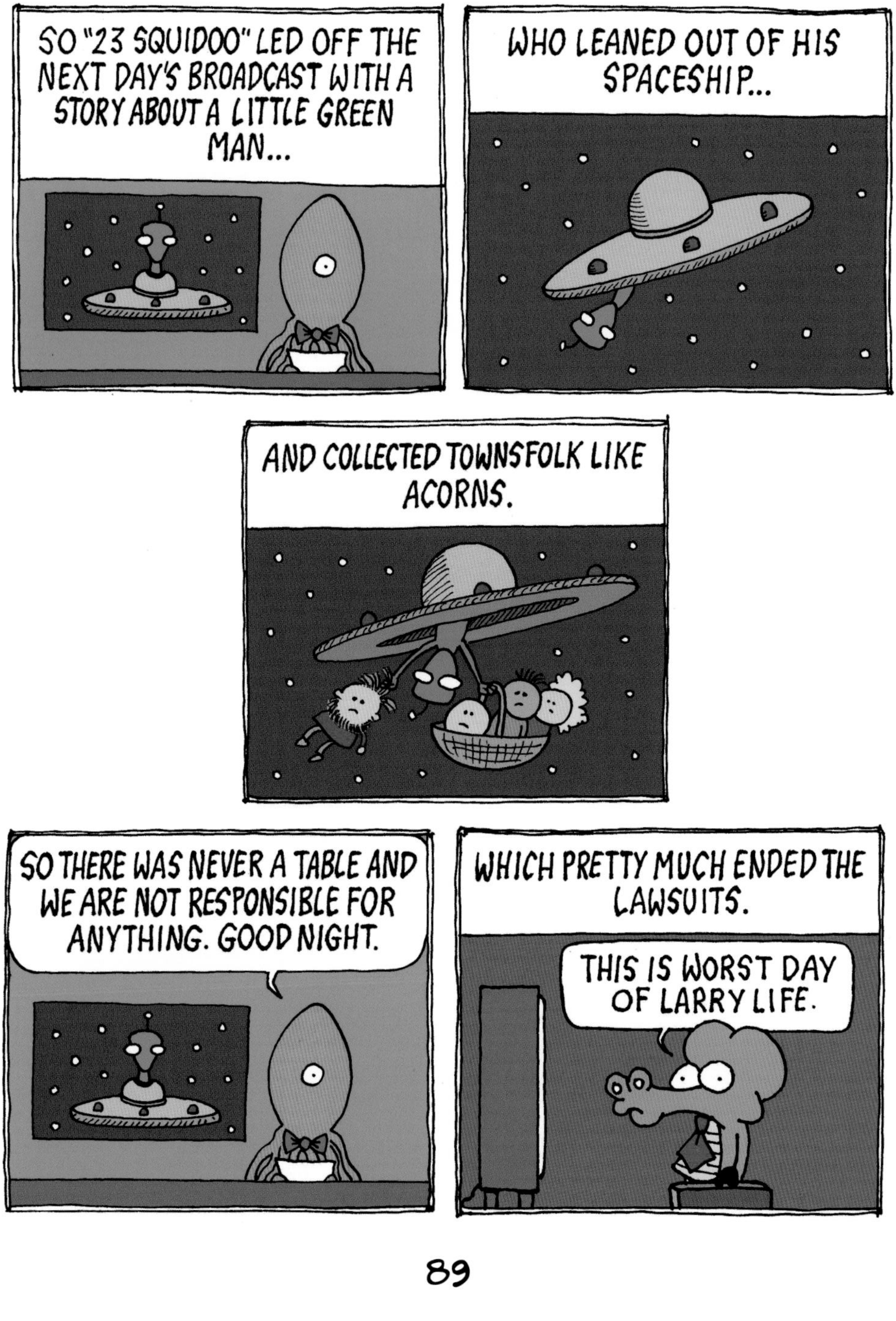
SO "23 SQUIDOO" LED OFF THE NEXT DAY'S BROADCAST WITH A STORY ABOUT A LITTLE GREEN MAN...
WHO LEANED OUT OF HIS SPACESHIP...
AND COLLECTED TOWNSFOLK LIKE ACORNS.
SO THERE WAS NEVER A TABLE AND WE ARE NOT RESPONSIBLE FOR ANYTHING. GOOD NIGHT.
WHICH PRETTY MUCH ENDED THE LAWSUITS.
THIS IS WORST DAY OF LARRY LIFE.

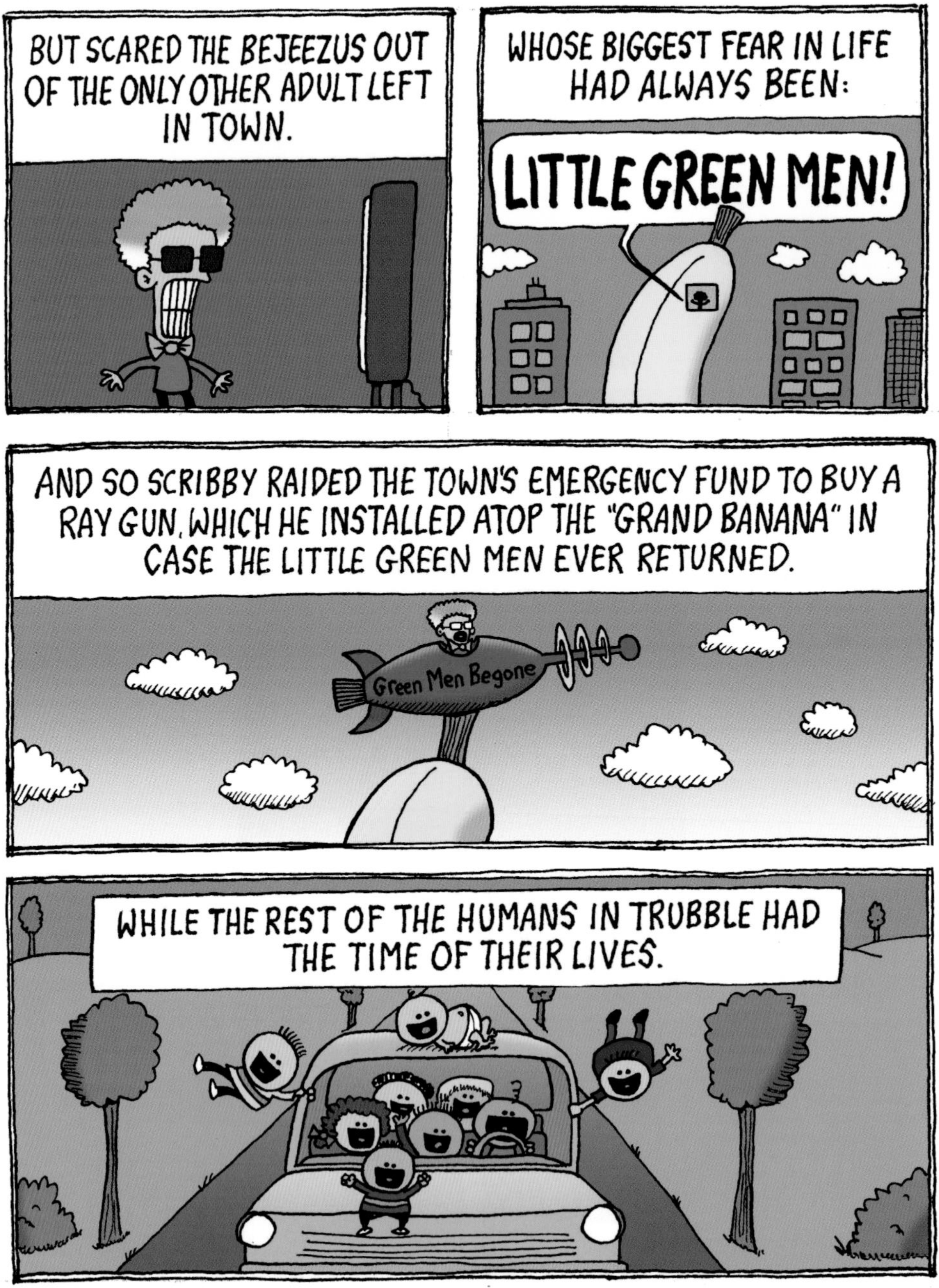
BUT SCARED THE BEJEEZUS OUT OF THE ONLY OTHER ADULT LEFT IN TOWN.
WHOSE BIGGEST FEAR IN LIFE HAD ALWAYS BEEN:
LITTLE GREEN MEN!
AND SO SCRIBBY RAIDED THE TOWN'S EMERGENCY FUND TO BUY A RAY GUN, WHICH HE INSTALLED ATOP THE "GRAND BANANA" IN CASE THE LITTLE GREEN MEN EVER RETURNED.
Green Men Begone
WHILE THE REST OF THE HUMANS IN TRUBBLE HAD THE TIME OF THEIR LIVES.

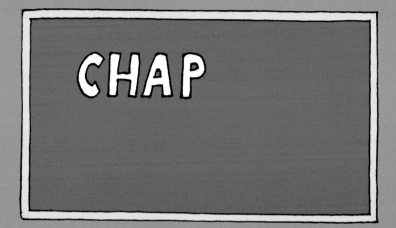

CHAP

IN WHICH...

WE GET SO LAZY WE DON'T EVEN WRITE OUT THE WHOLE WORD

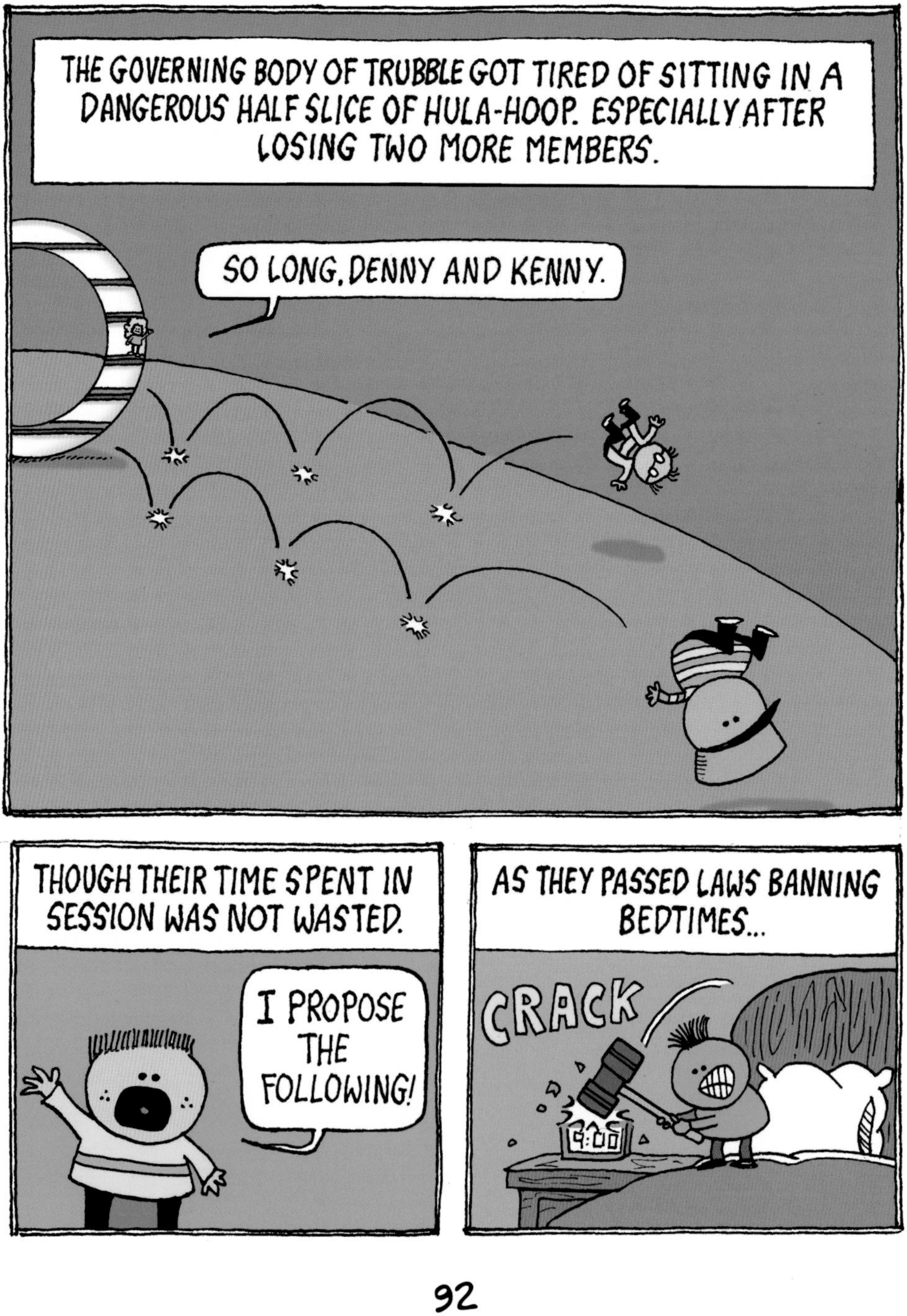
THE GOVERNING BODY OF TRUBBLE GOT TIRED OF SITTING IN A DANGEROUS HALF SLICE OF HULA-HOOP. ESPECIALLY AFTER LOSING TWO MORE MEMBERS.
SO LONG, DENNY AND KENNY.
THOUGH THEIR TIME SPENT IN SESSION WAS NOT WASTED.
I PROPOSE THE FOLLOWING!
AS THEY PASSED LAWS BANNING BEDTIMES...
CRACK
9:00

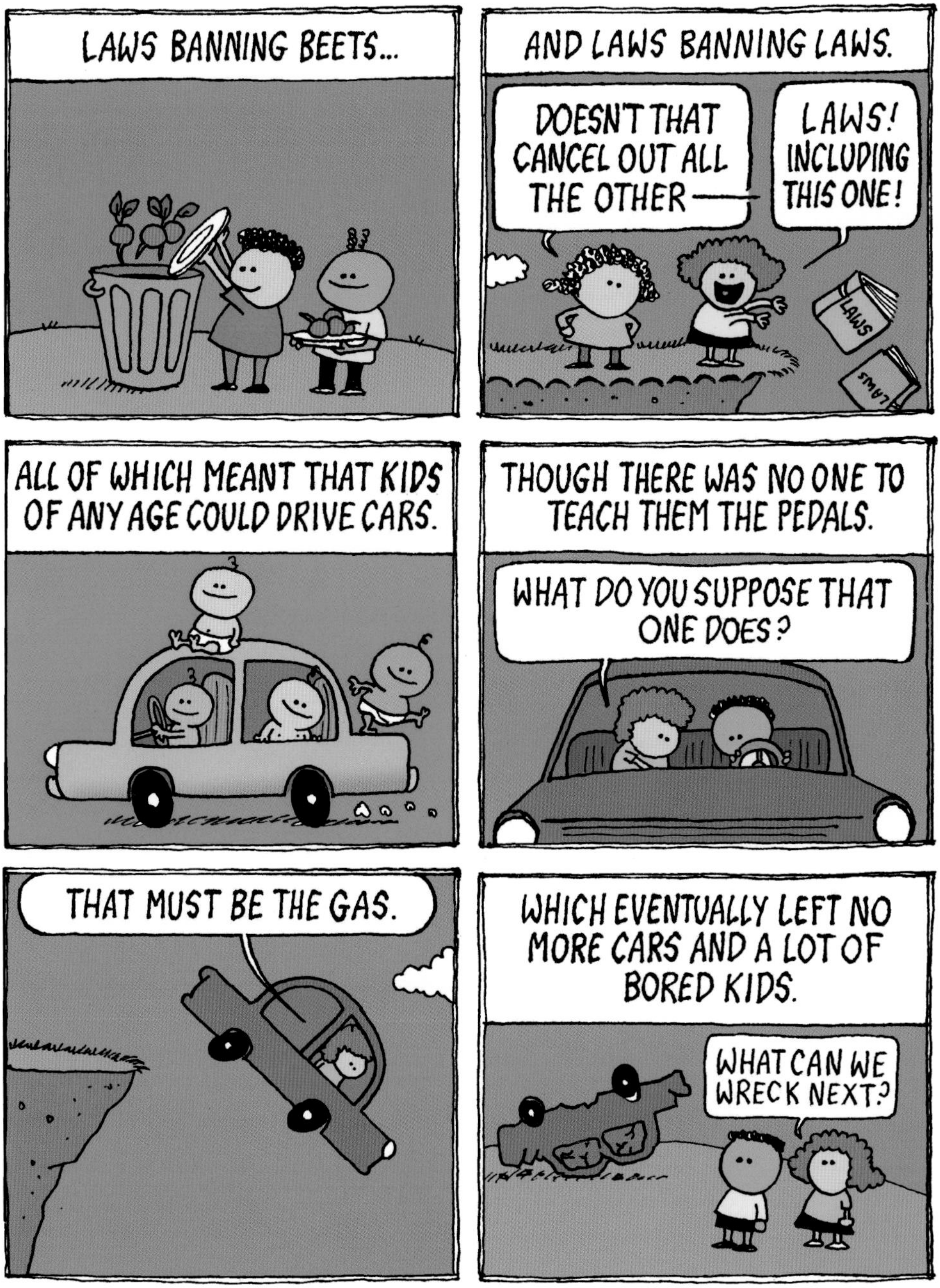
LAWS BANNING BEETS...
AND LAWS BANNING LAWS.
DOESN'T THAT CANCEL OUT ALL THE OTHER—
LAWS! INCLUDING THIS ONE!
LAWS
LAWS
ALL OF WHICH MEANT THAT KIDS OF ANY AGE COULD DRIVE CARS.
THOUGH THERE WAS NO ONE TO TEACH THEM THE PEDALS.
WHAT DO YOU SUPPOSE THAT ONE DOES?
THAT MUST BE THE GAS.
WHICH EVENTUALLY LEFT NO MORE CARS AND A LOT OF BORED KIDS.
WHAT CAN WE WRECK NEXT?

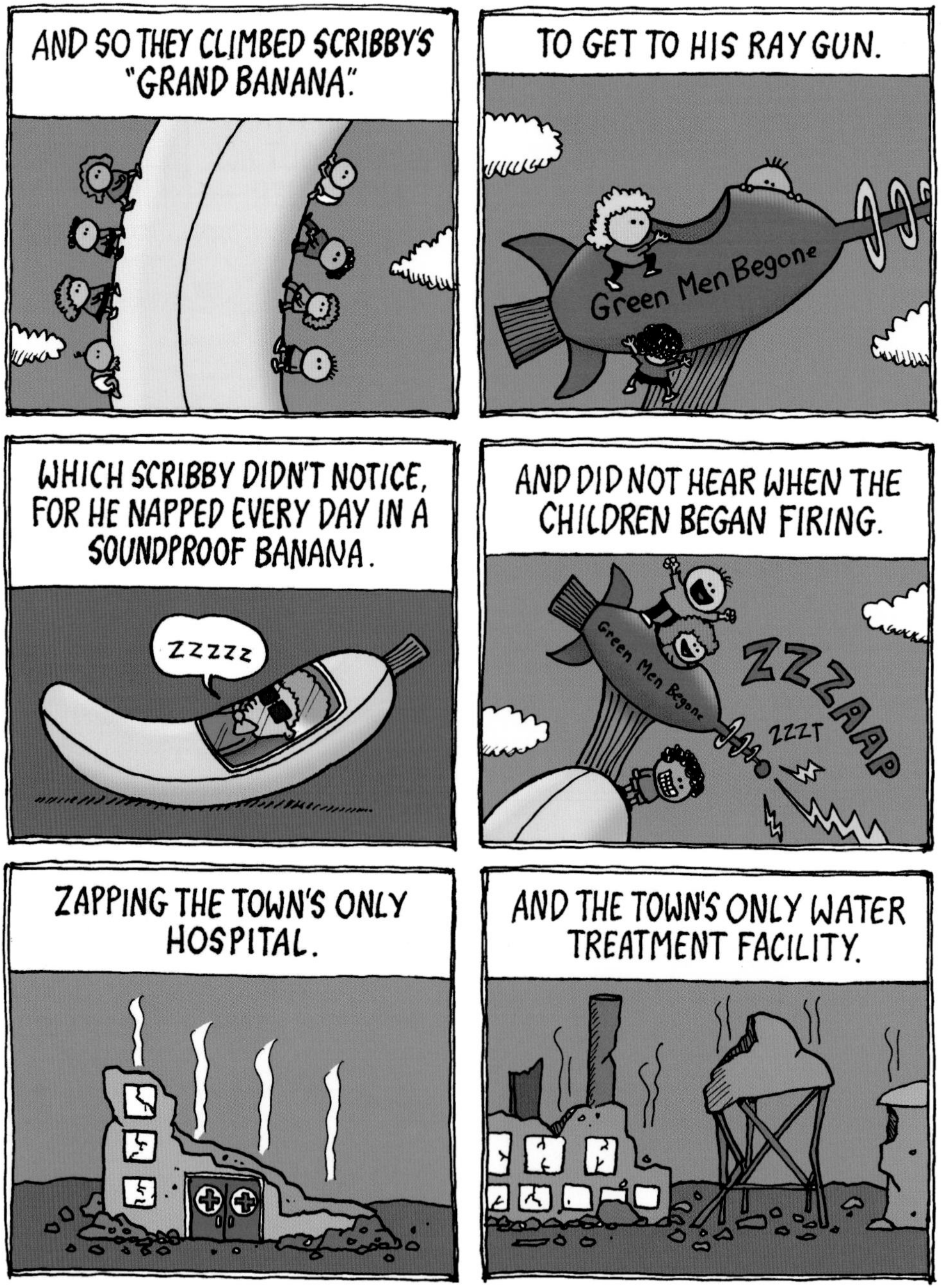
AND SO THEY CLIMBED SCRIBBY'S "GRAND BANANA."
TO GET TO HIS RAY GUN.
Green Men Begone
WHICH SCRIBBY DIDN'T NOTICE, FOR HE NAPPED EVERY DAY IN A SOUNDPROOF BANANA.
ZZZZZ
AND DID NOT HEAR WHEN THE CHILDREN BEGAN FIRING.
Green Men Begone
ZZZAAP
ZZZT
ZAPPING THE TOWN'S ONLY HOSPITAL.
AND THE TOWN'S ONLY WATER TREATMENT FACILITY.

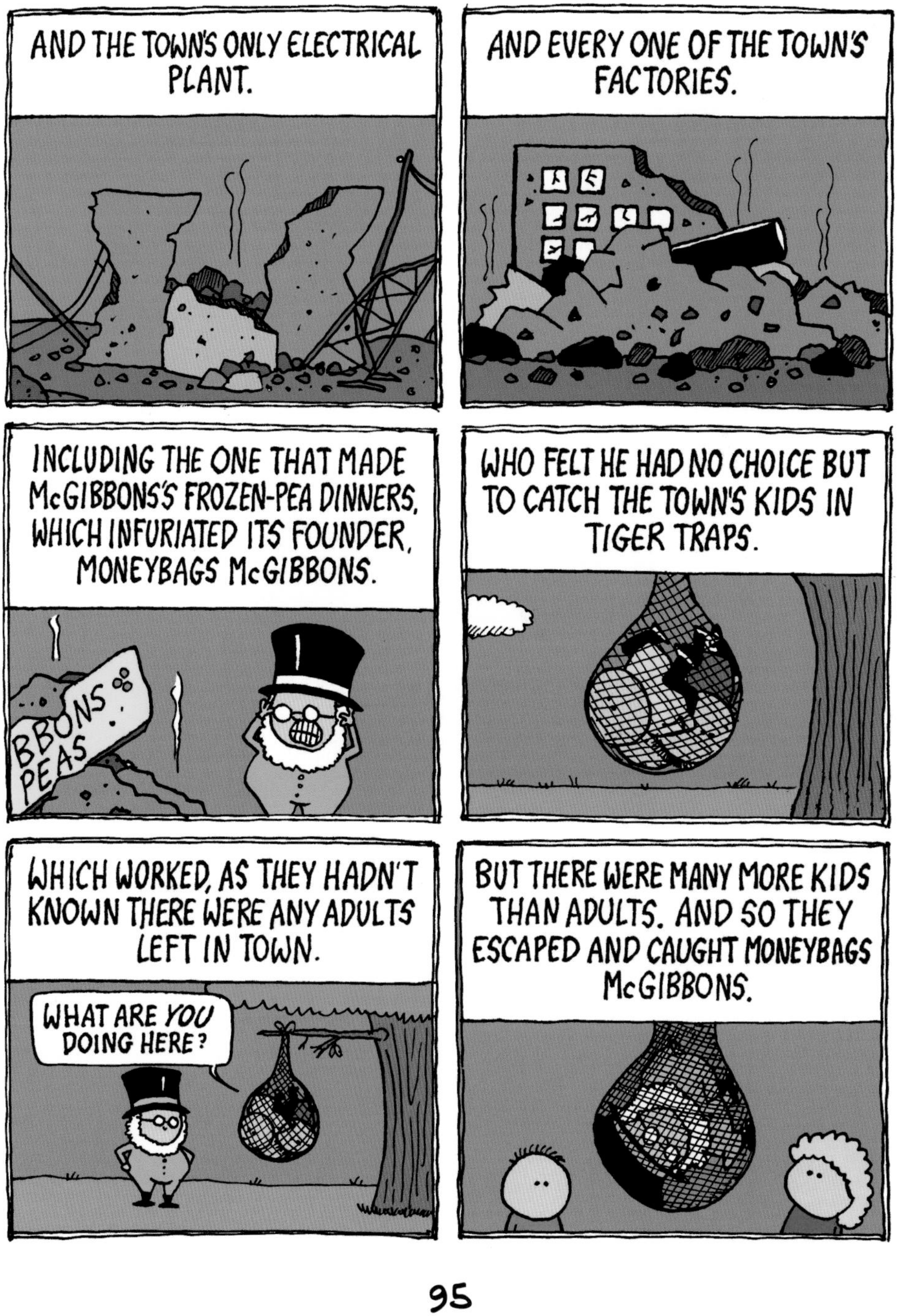
AND THE TOWN'S ONLY ELECTRICAL PLANT.
AND EVERY ONE OF THE TOWN'S FACTORIES.
INCLUDING THE ONE THAT MADE McGIBBONS'S FROZEN-PEA DINNERS, WHICH INFURIATED ITS FOUNDER, MONEYBAGS McGIBBONS.
BBONS PEAS
WHO FELT HE HAD NO CHOICE BUT TO CATCH THE TOWN'S KIDS IN TIGER TRAPS.
WHICH WORKED, AS THEY HADN'T KNOWN THERE WERE ANY ADULTS LEFT IN TOWN.
WHAT ARE *YOU* DOING HERE?
BUT THERE WERE MANY MORE KIDS THAN ADULTS. AND SO THEY ESCAPED AND CAUGHT MONEYBAGS McGIBBONS.

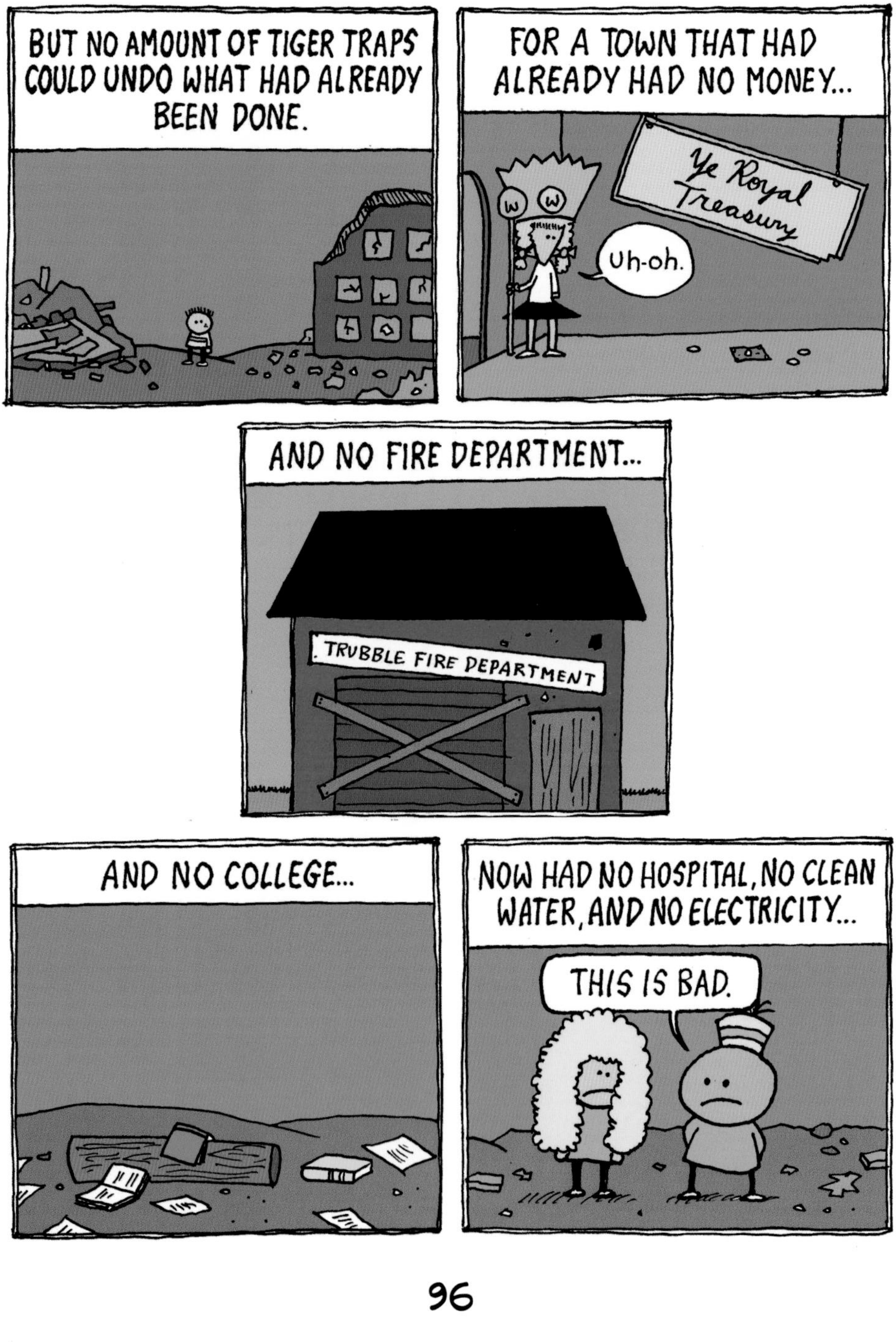
BUT NO AMOUNT OF TIGER TRAPS COULD UNDO WHAT HAD ALREADY BEEN DONE.
FOR A TOWN THAT HAD ALREADY HAD NO MONEY...
Ye Royal Treasury
Uh-oh.
AND NO FIRE DEPARTMENT...
TRUBBLE FIRE DEPARTMENT
AND NO COLLEGE...
NOW HAD NO HOSPITAL, NO CLEAN WATER, AND NO ELECTRICITY...
THIS IS BAD.

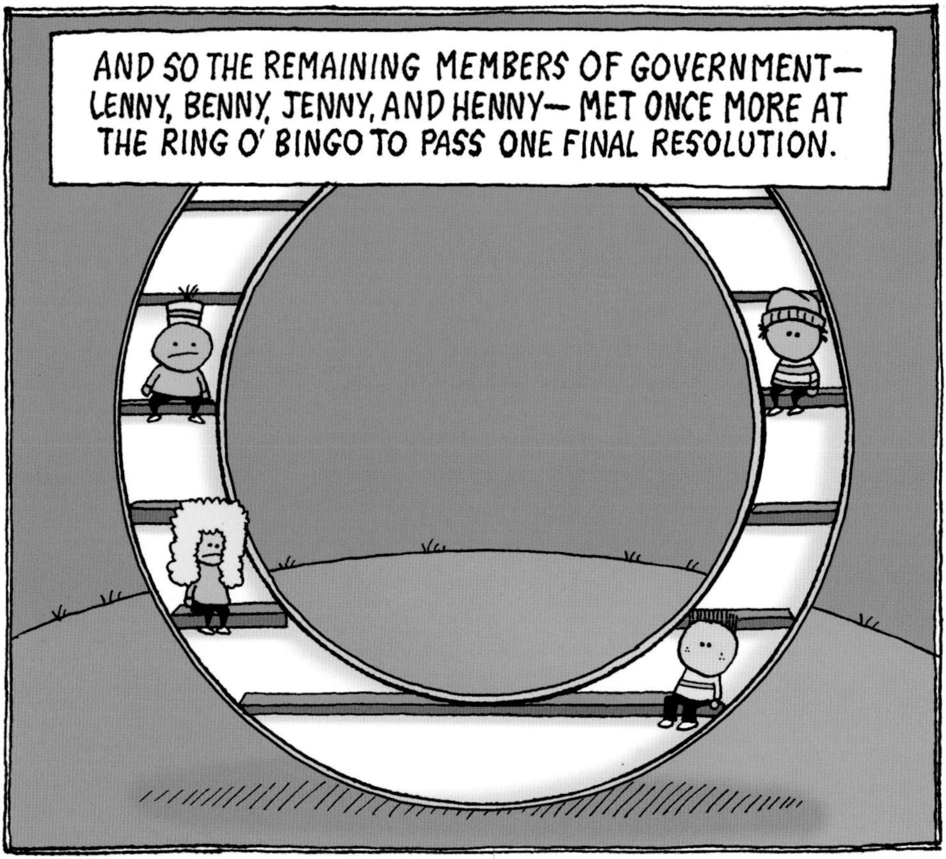
AND SO THE REMAINING MEMBERS OF GOVERNMENT—LENNY, BENNY, JENNY, AND HENNY—MET ONCE MORE AT THE RING O' BINGO TO PASS ONE FINAL RESOLUTION.

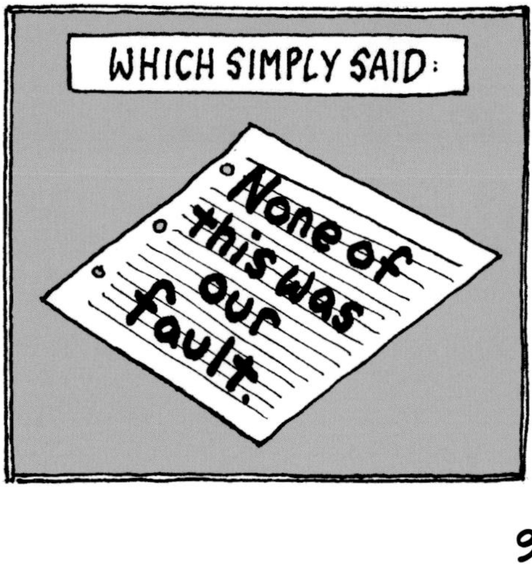
WHICH SIMPLY SAID:
None of this was our fault.

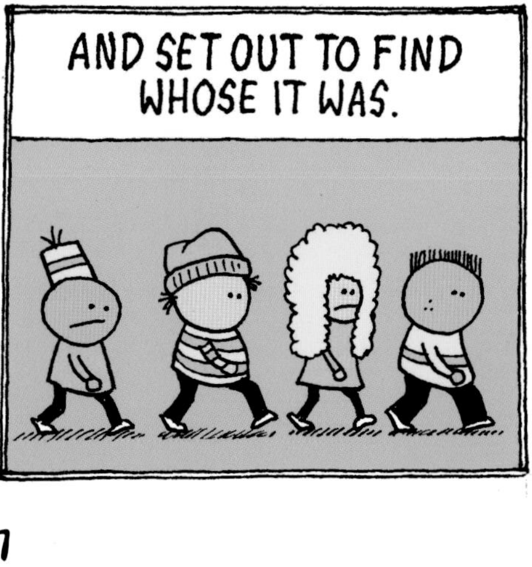
AND SET OUT TO FIND WHOSE IT WAS.

CHAPTER
SOMEWHERE
AROUND
FIFTEEN

IN WHICH...

WE GUESS WHAT
CHAPTER NUMBER
THIS MIGHT BE

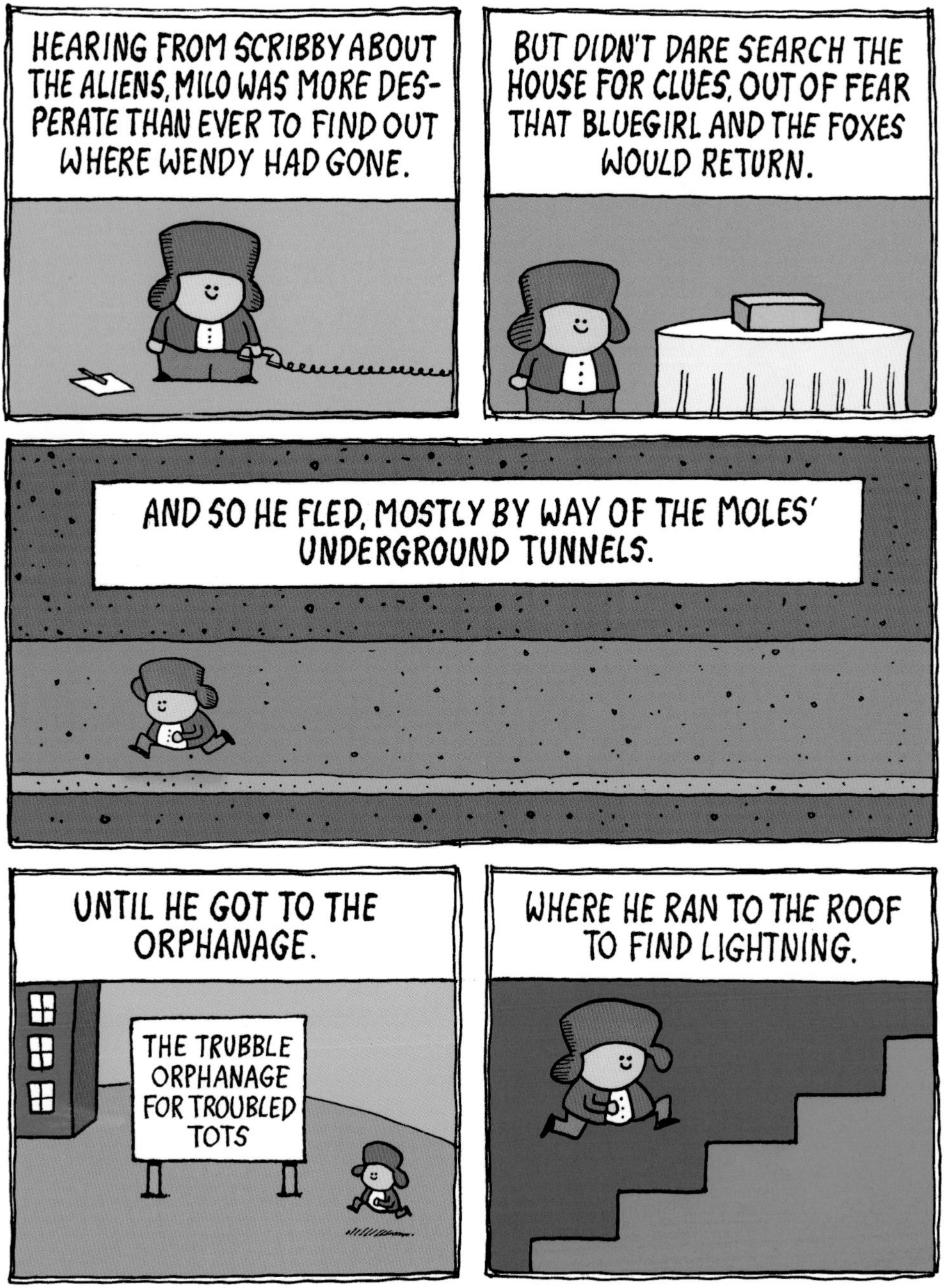
HEARING FROM SCRIBBY ABOUT THE ALIENS, MILO WAS MORE DESPERATE THAN EVER TO FIND OUT WHERE WENDY HAD GONE.
BUT DIDN'T DARE SEARCH THE HOUSE FOR CLUES, OUT OF FEAR THAT BLUEGIRL AND THE FOXES WOULD RETURN.
AND SO HE FLED, MOSTLY BY WAY OF THE MOLES' UNDERGROUND TUNNELS.
UNTIL HE GOT TO THE ORPHANAGE.
THE TRUBBLE ORPHANAGE FOR TROUBLED TOTS
WHERE HE RAN TO THE ROOF TO FIND LIGHTNING.

103

104

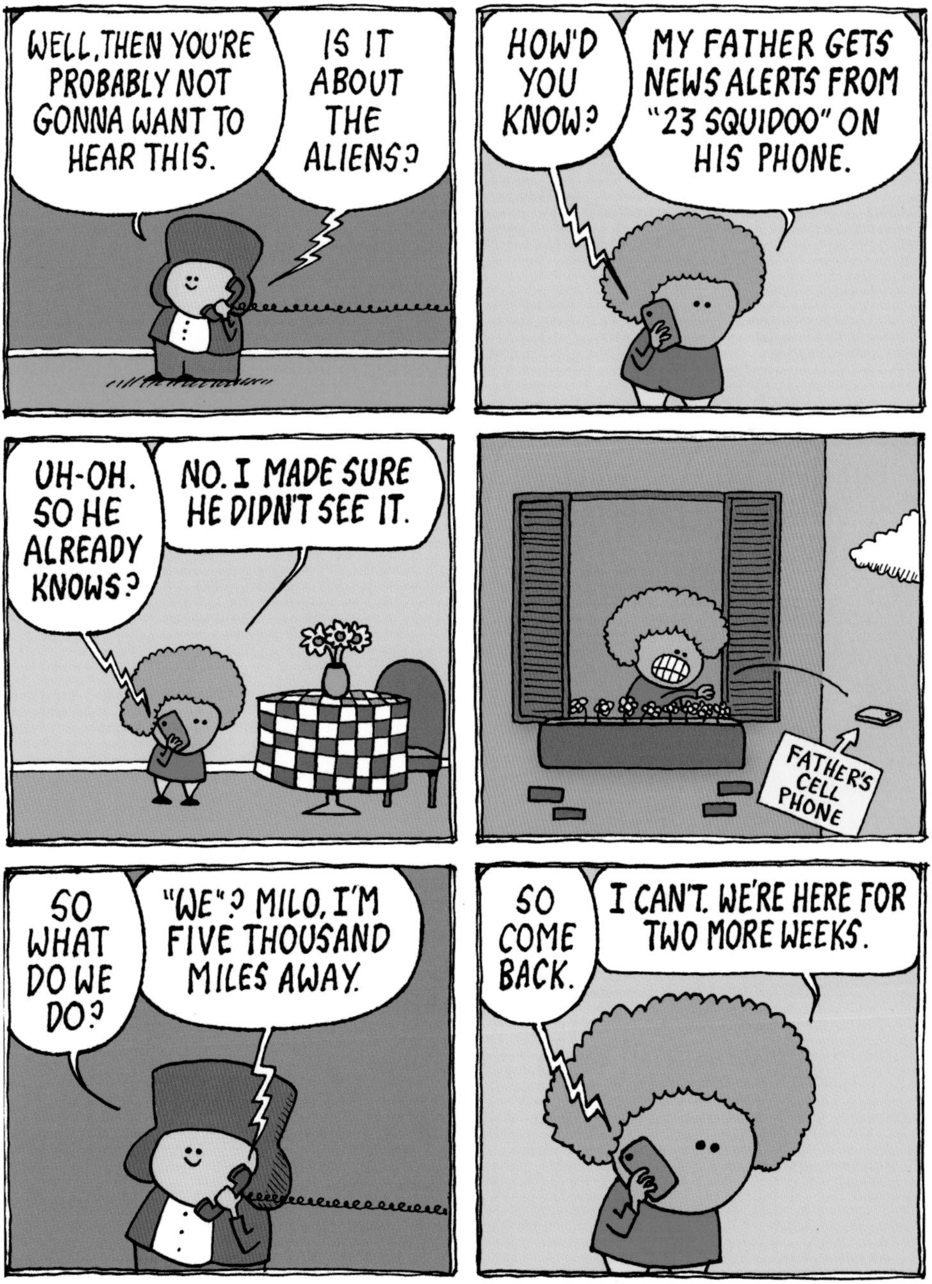
WELL, THEN YOU'RE PROBABLY NOT GONNA WANT TO HEAR THIS.
IS IT ABOUT THE ALIENS?
HOW'D YOU KNOW?
MY FATHER GETS NEWS ALERTS FROM "23 SQUIDOO" ON HIS PHONE.
UH-OH. SO HE ALREADY KNOWS?
NO. I MADE SURE HE DIDN'T SEE IT.
FATHER'S CELL PHONE
SO WHAT DO WE DO?
"WE"? MILO, I'M FIVE THOUSAND MILES AWAY.
SO COME BACK.
I CAN'T. WE'RE HERE FOR TWO MORE WEEKS.

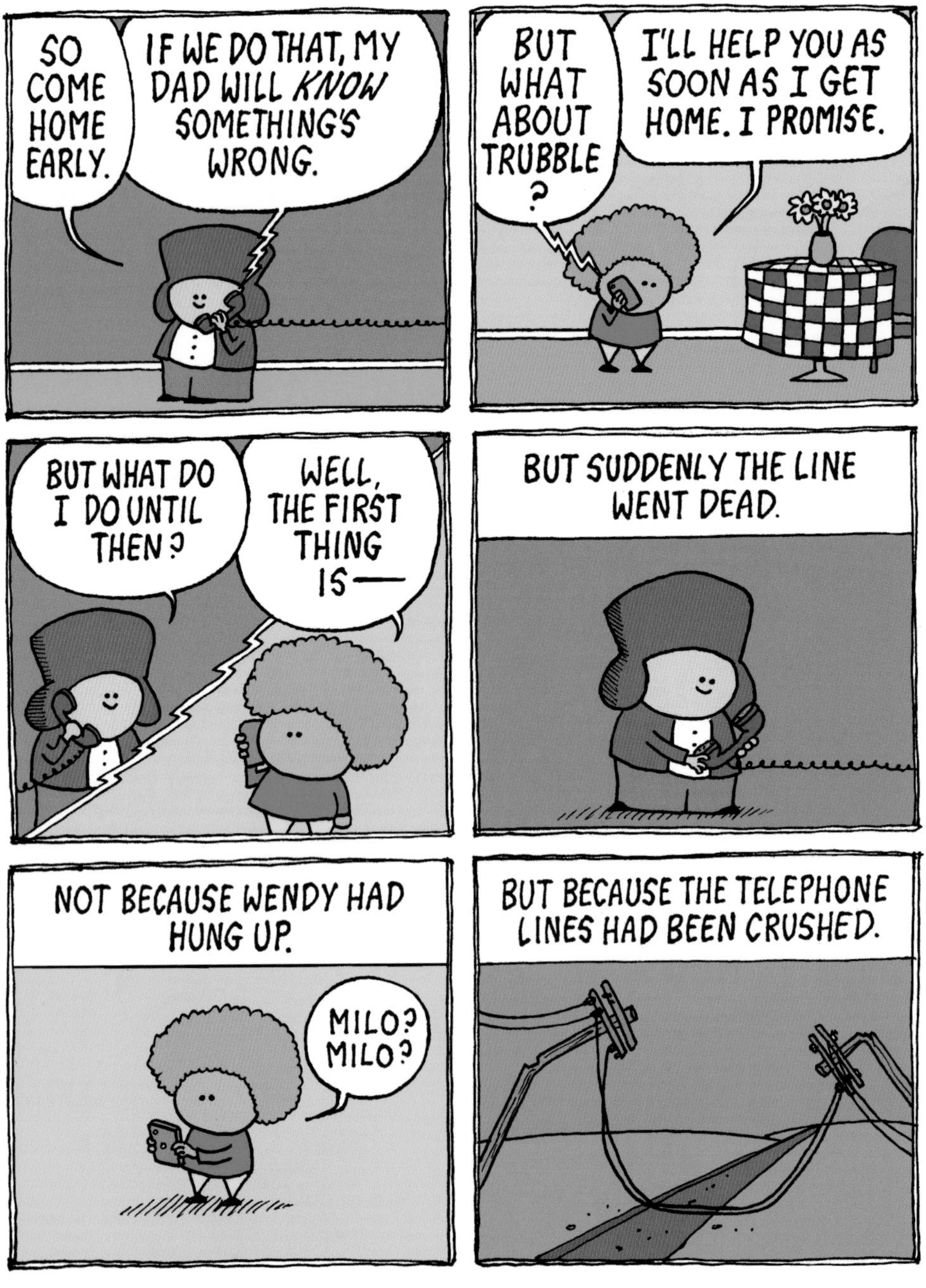

SO COME HOME EARLY.
IF WE DO THAT, MY DAD WILL KNOW SOMETHING'S WRONG.
BUT WHAT ABOUT TRUBBLE?
I'LL HELP YOU AS SOON AS I GET HOME. I PROMISE.
BUT WHAT DO I DO UNTIL THEN?
WELL, THE FIRST THING IS—
BUT SUDDENLY THE LINE WENT DEAD.
NOT BECAUSE WENDY HAD HUNG UP.
MILO? MILO?
BUT BECAUSE THE TELEPHONE LINES HAD BEEN CRUSHED.

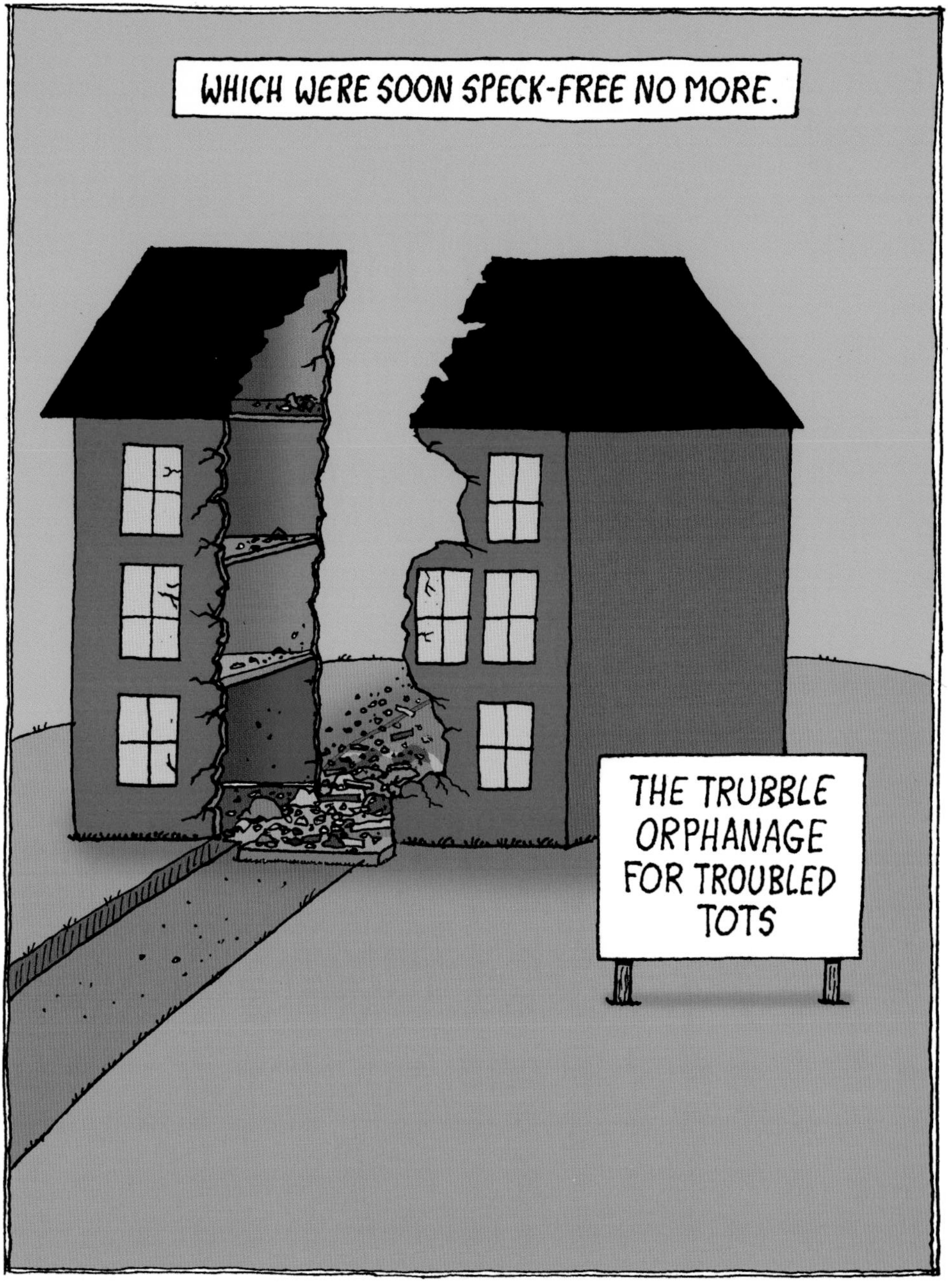
WHICH WERE SOON SPECK-FREE NO MORE.
THE TRUBBLE ORPHANAGE FOR TROUBLED TOTS

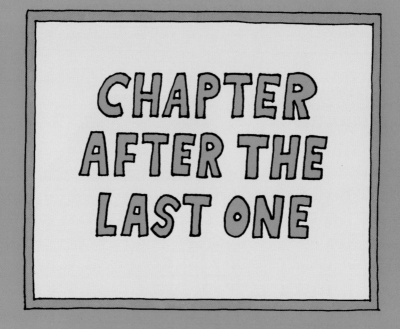

CHAPTER AFTER THE LAST ONE

WHICH IS...

AN ACCURATE DESCRIPTION OF THE PLACEMENT OF THIS CHAPTER

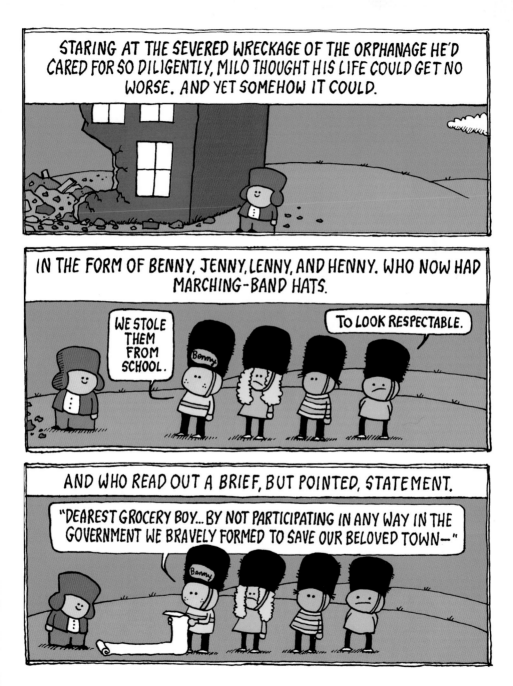

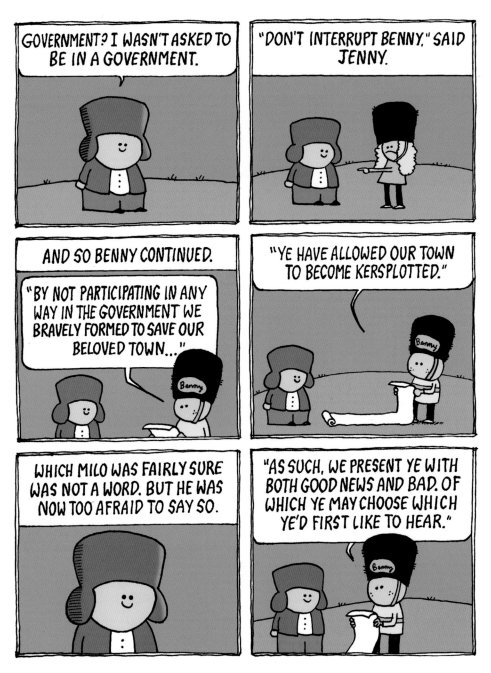

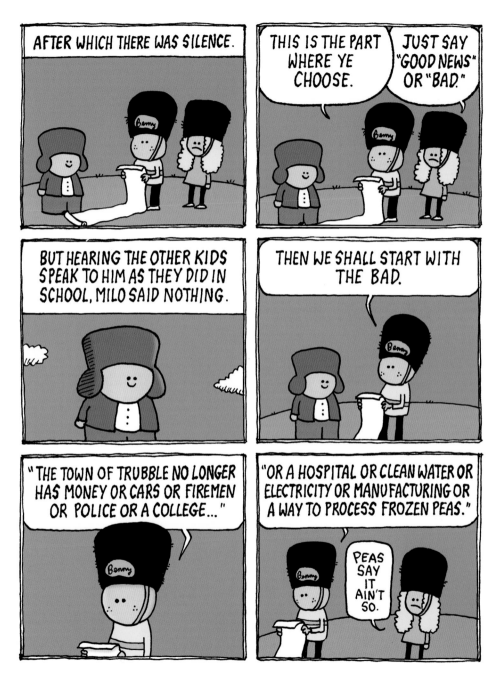

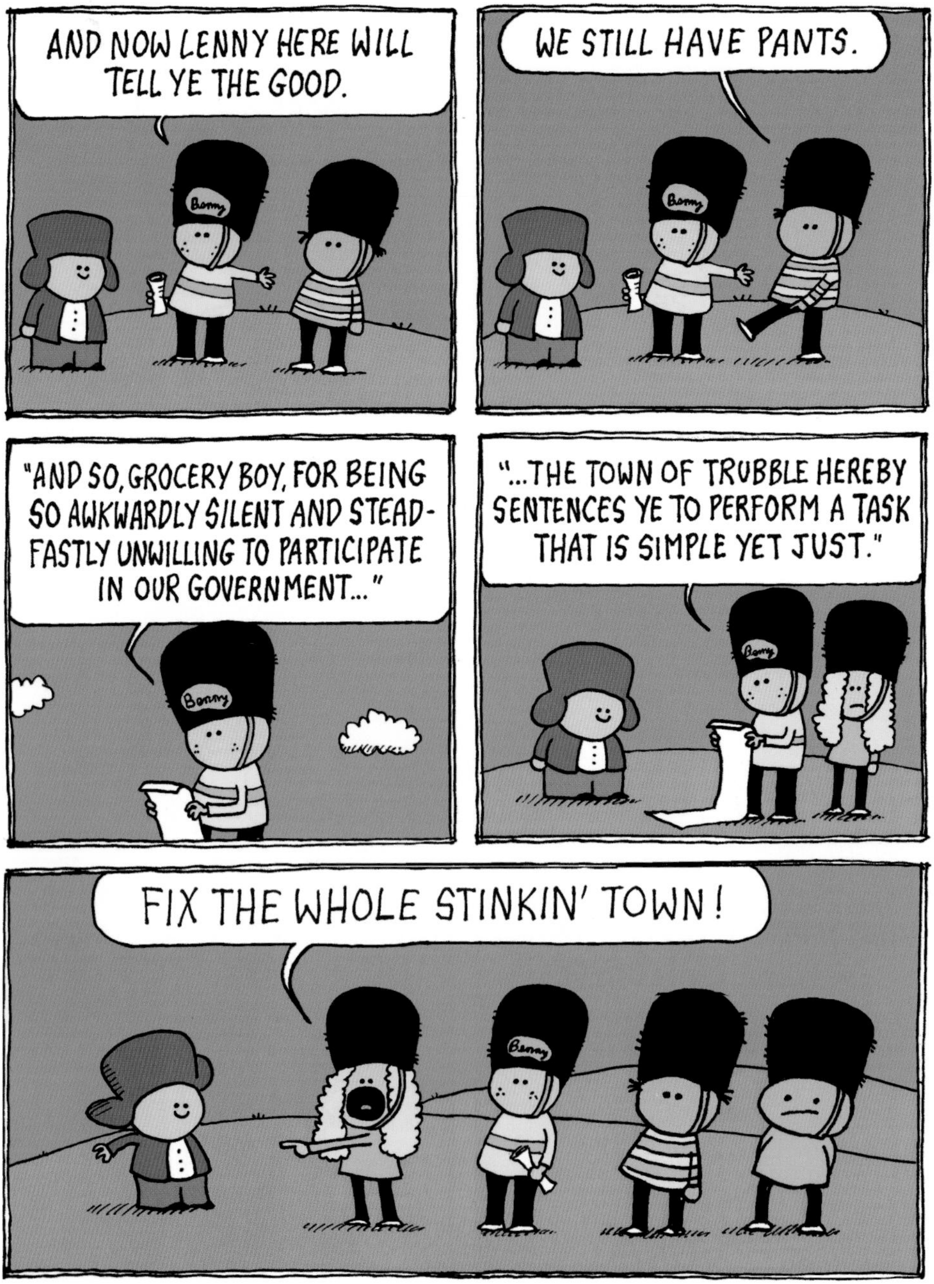
AND NOW LENNY HERE WILL TELL YE THE GOOD.
WE STILL HAVE PANTS.
"AND SO, GROCERY BOY, FOR BEING SO AWKWARDLY SILENT AND STEADFASTLY UNWILLING TO PARTICIPATE IN OUR GOVERNMENT..."
"...THE TOWN OF TRUBBLE HEREBY SENTENCES YE TO PERFORM A TASK THAT IS SIMPLE YET JUST."
FIX THE WHOLE STINKIN' TOWN!

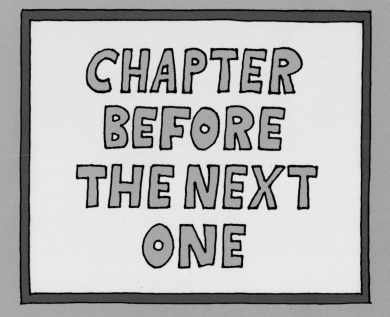

CHAPTER BEFORE THE NEXT ONE

WHICH IS...

ACCURATE IN THAT IT COMES BEFORE THE NEXT ONE

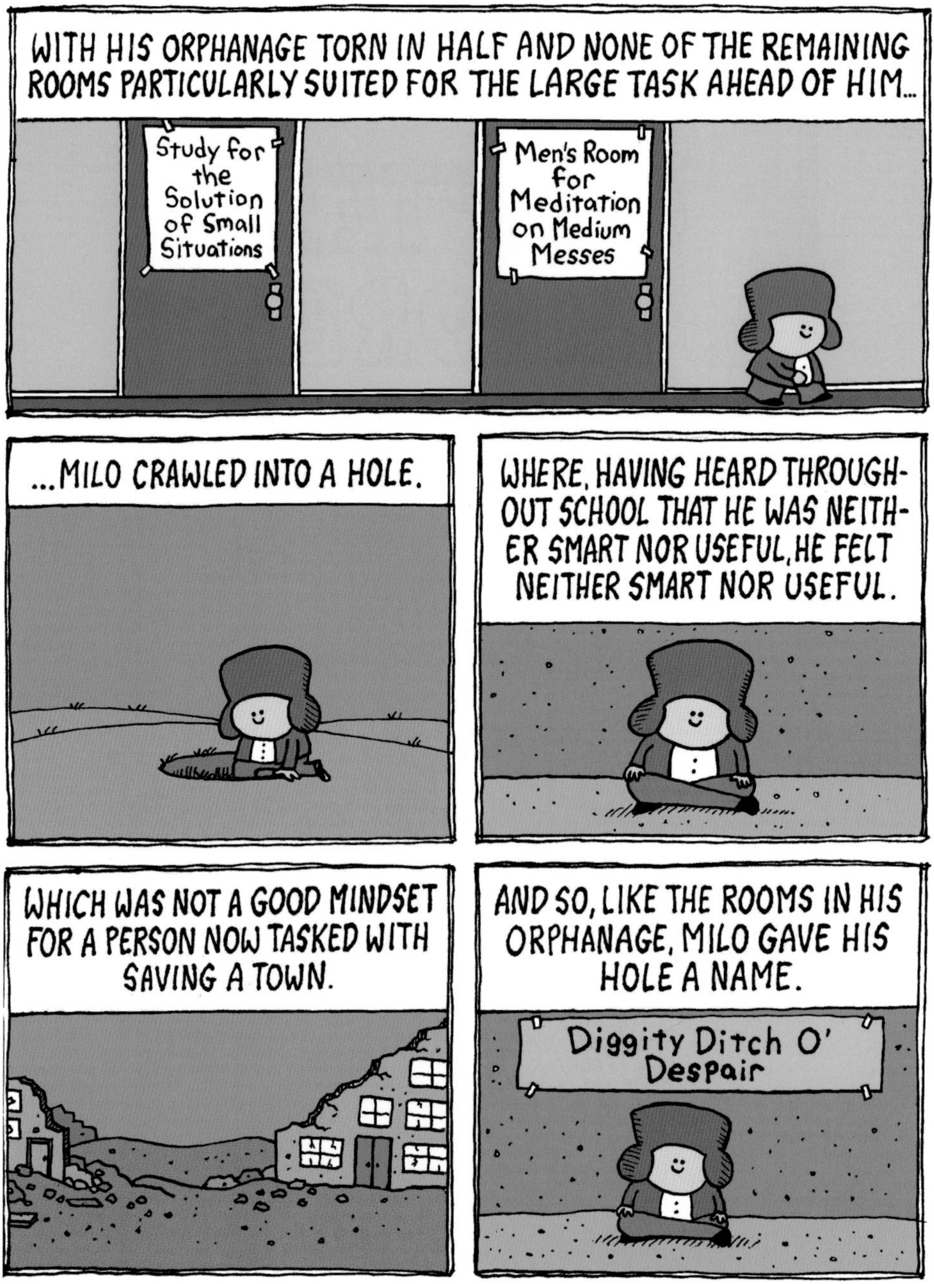
WITH HIS ORPHANAGE TORN IN HALF AND NONE OF THE REMAINING ROOMS PARTICULARLY SUITED FOR THE LARGE TASK AHEAD OF HIM...
Study for the Solution of Small Situations
Men's Room for Meditation on Medium Messes
...MILO CRAWLED INTO A HOLE.
WHERE, HAVING HEARD THROUGHOUT SCHOOL THAT HE WAS NEITHER SMART NOR USEFUL, HE FELT NEITHER SMART NOR USEFUL.
WHICH WAS NOT A GOOD MINDSET FOR A PERSON NOW TASKED WITH SAVING A TOWN.
AND SO, LIKE THE ROOMS IN HIS ORPHANAGE, MILO GAVE HIS HOLE A NAME.
Diggity Ditch O' Despair

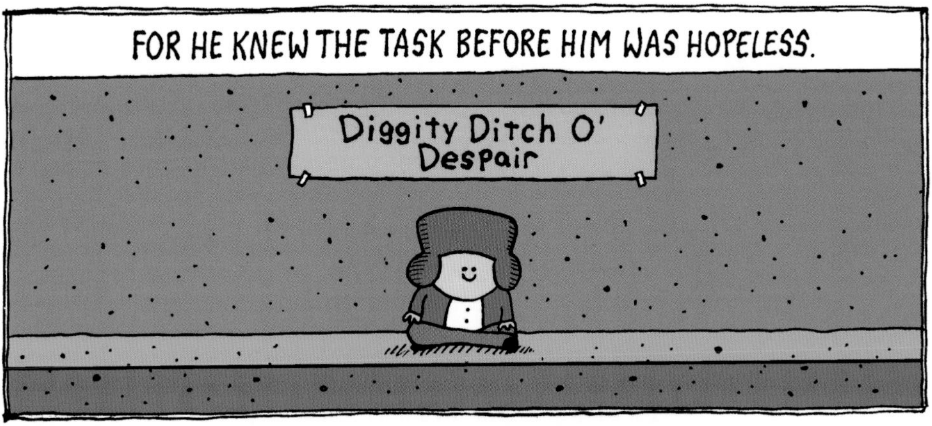
FOR HE KNEW THE TASK BEFORE HIM WAS HOPELESS.
Diggity Ditch O' Despair

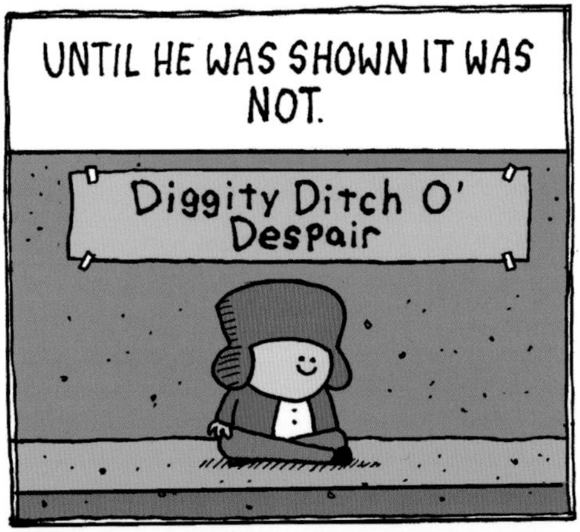
UNTIL HE WAS SHOWN IT WAS NOT.
Diggity Ditch O' Despair

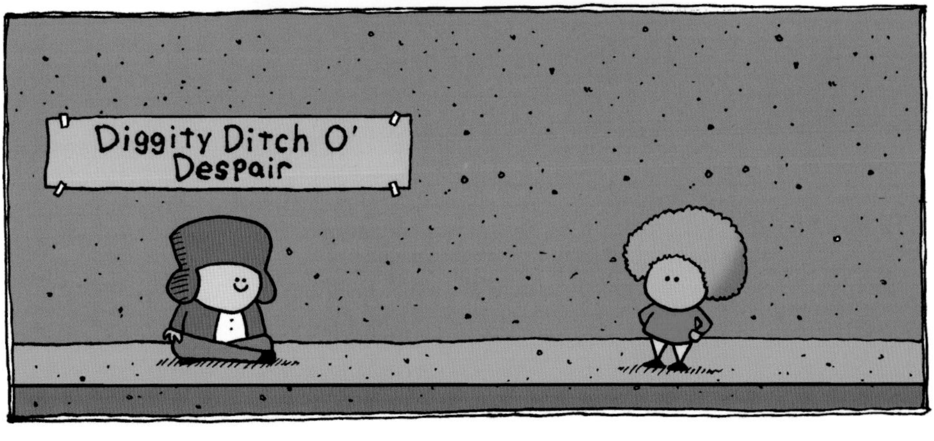
Diggity Ditch O' Despair

CHAPTER THE NEXT ONE

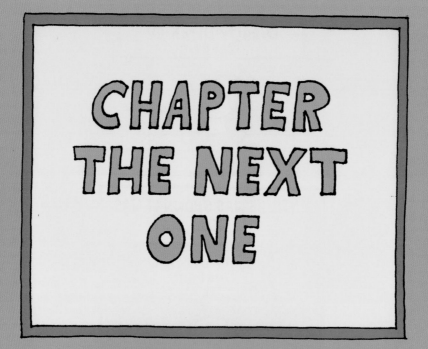

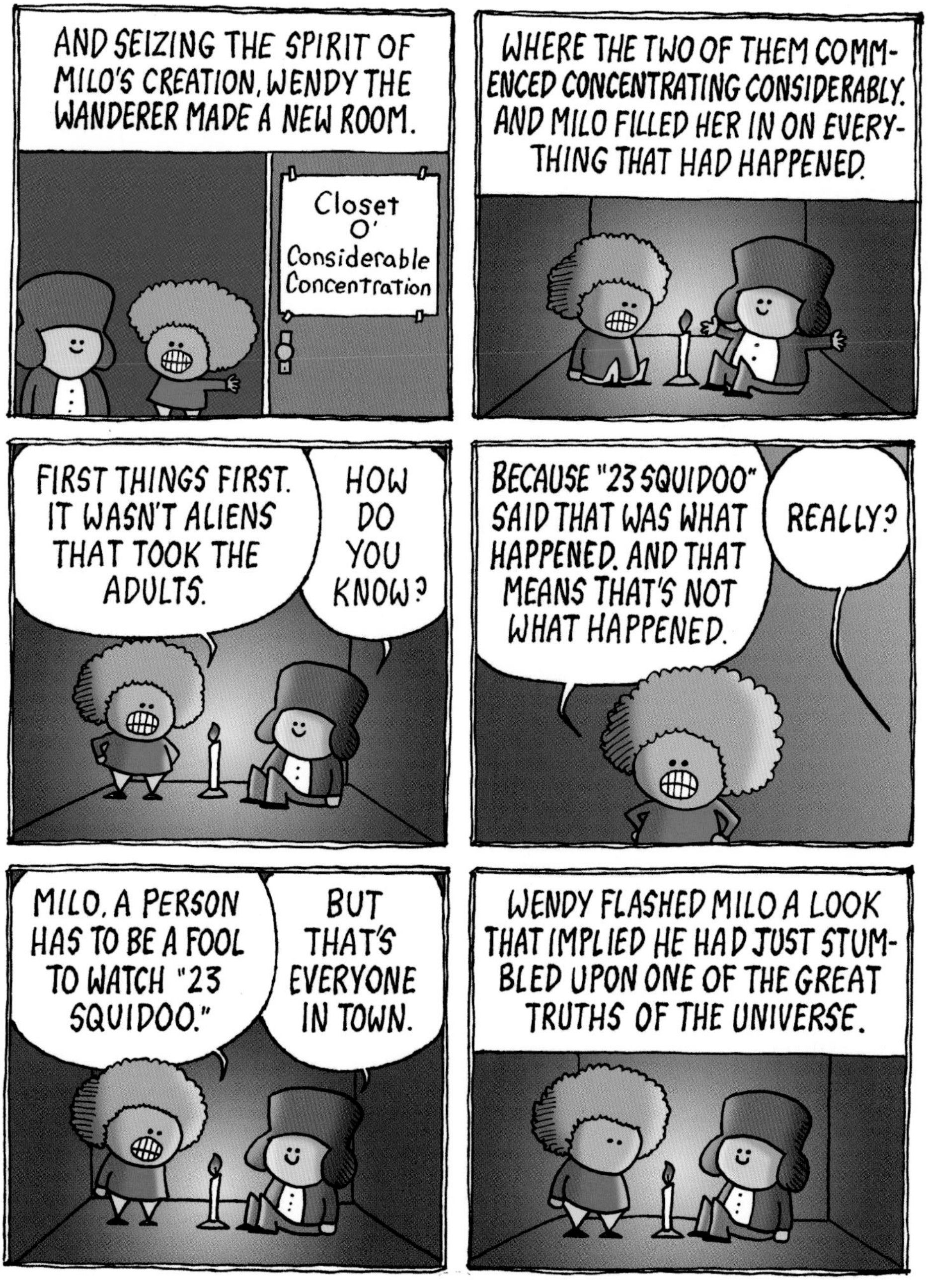
AND SEIZING THE SPIRIT OF MILO'S CREATION, WENDY THE WANDERER MADE A NEW ROOM.
Closet O' Considerable Concentration
WHERE THE TWO OF THEM COMMENCED CONCENTRATING CONSIDERABLY. AND MILO FILLED HER IN ON EVERYTHING THAT HAD HAPPENED.
FIRST THINGS FIRST. IT WASN'T ALIENS THAT TOOK THE ADULTS.
HOW DO YOU KNOW?
BECAUSE "23 SQUIDOO" SAID THAT WAS WHAT HAPPENED. AND THAT MEANS THAT'S NOT WHAT HAPPENED.
REALLY?
MILO, A PERSON HAS TO BE A FOOL TO WATCH "23 SQUIDOO."
BUT THAT'S EVERYONE IN TOWN.
WENDY FLASHED MILO A LOOK THAT IMPLIED HE HAD JUST STUMBLED UPON ONE OF THE GREAT TRUTHS OF THE UNIVERSE.

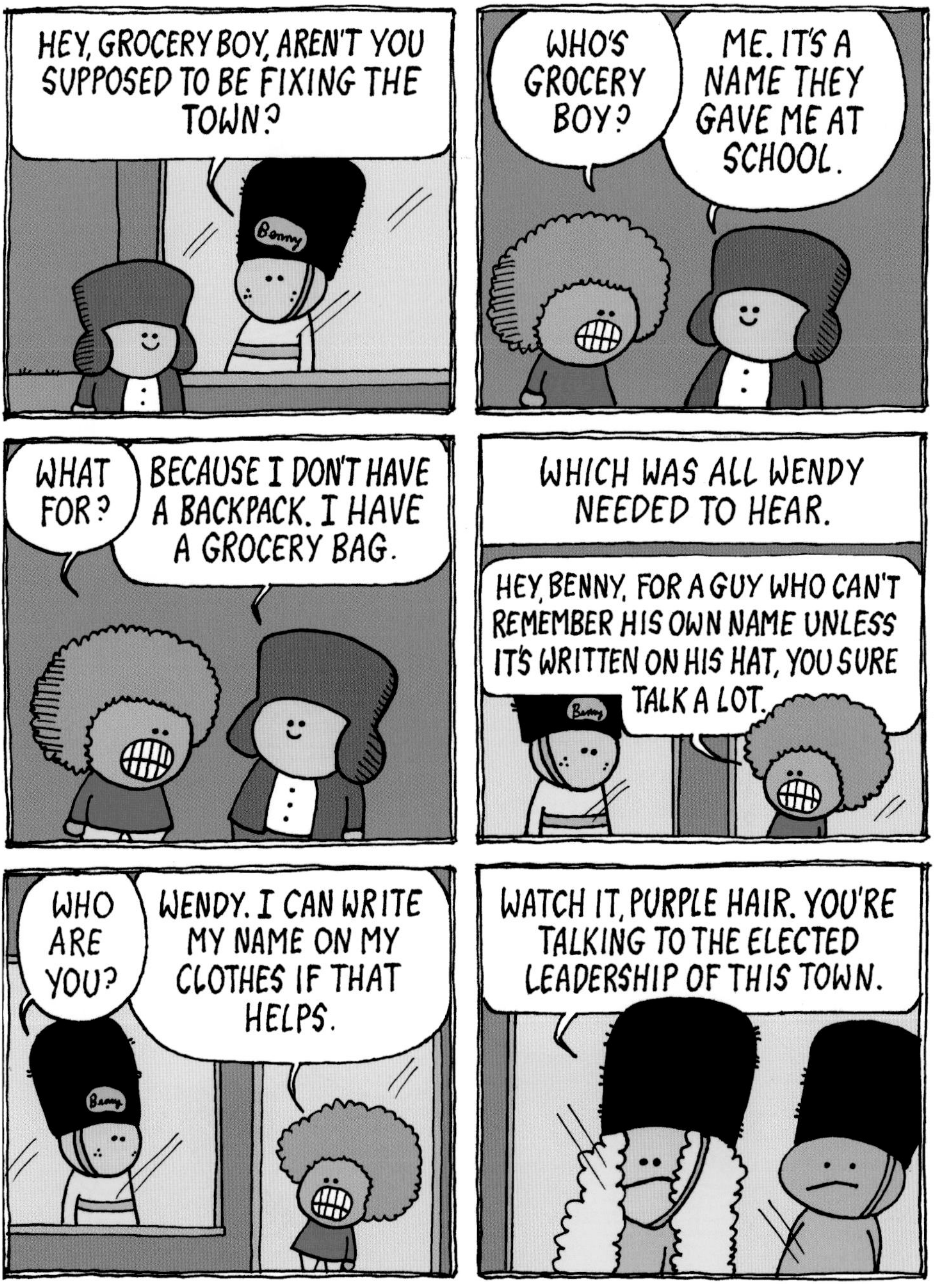
HEY, GROCERY BOY, AREN'T YOU SUPPOSED TO BE FIXING THE TOWN?
Benny
WHO'S GROCERY BOY?
ME. IT'S A NAME THEY GAVE ME AT SCHOOL.
WHAT FOR?
BECAUSE I DON'T HAVE A BACKPACK. I HAVE A GROCERY BAG.
WHICH WAS ALL WENDY NEEDED TO HEAR.
HEY, BENNY, FOR A GUY WHO CAN'T REMEMBER HIS OWN NAME UNLESS IT'S WRITTEN ON HIS HAT, YOU SURE TALK A LOT.
WHO ARE YOU?
WENDY. I CAN WRITE MY NAME ON MY CLOTHES IF THAT HELPS.
WATCH IT, PURPLE HAIR. YOU'RE TALKING TO THE ELECTED LEADERSHIP OF THIS TOWN.

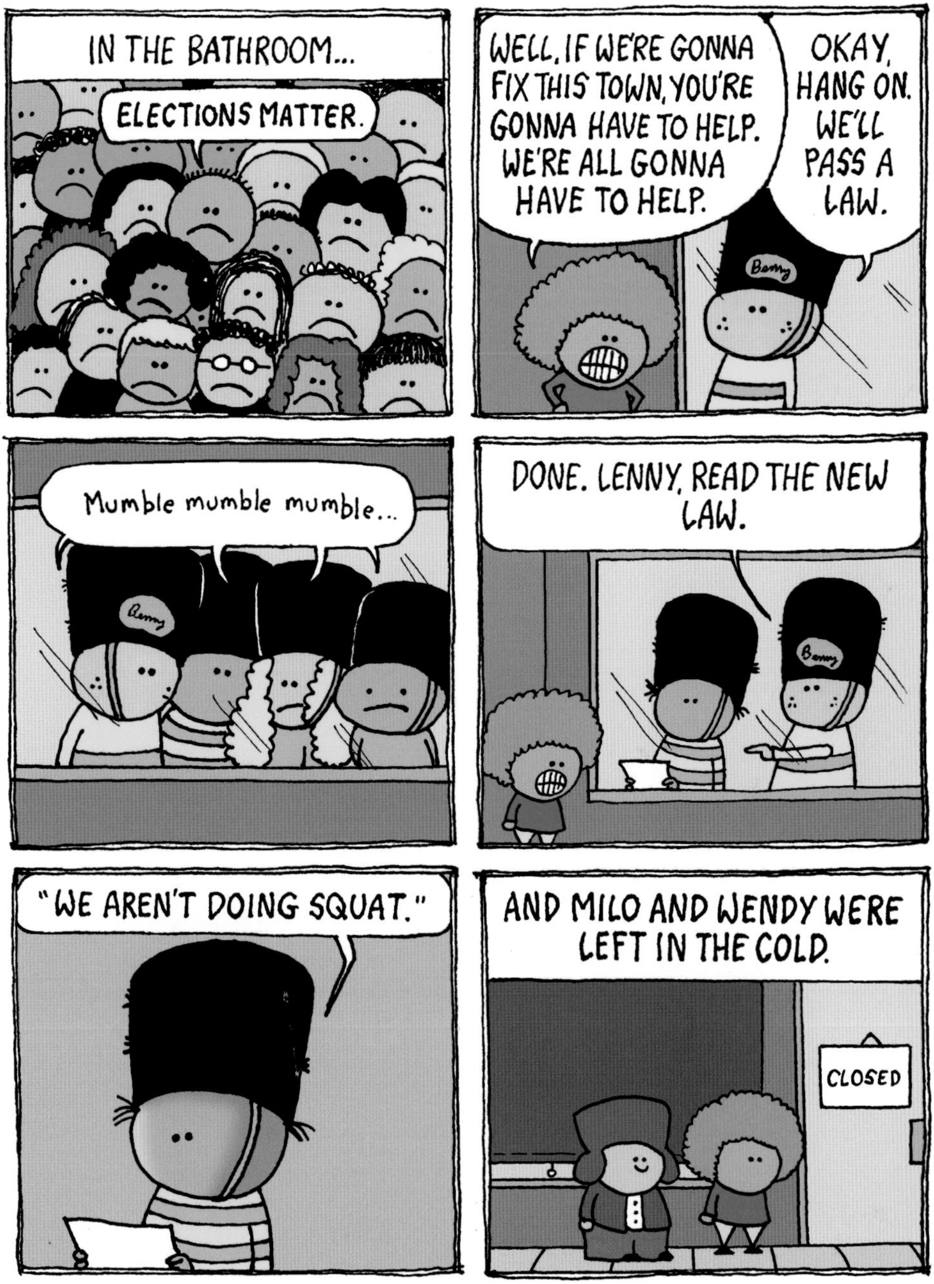
IN THE BATHROOM...
ELECTIONS MATTER.
WELL, IF WE'RE GONNA FIX THIS TOWN, YOU'RE GONNA HAVE TO HELP. WE'RE ALL GONNA HAVE TO HELP.
OKAY, HANG ON. WE'LL PASS A LAW.
Mumble mumble mumble...
DONE. LENNY, READ THE NEW LAW.
"WE AREN'T DOING SQUAT."
AND MILO AND WENDY WERE LEFT IN THE COLD.
CLOSED

CHAPTER
MUCH
BETTER

WHICH IS...

SO MUCH BETTER THAN
THE LAST CHAPTER,
IT'S NOT EVEN FUNNY

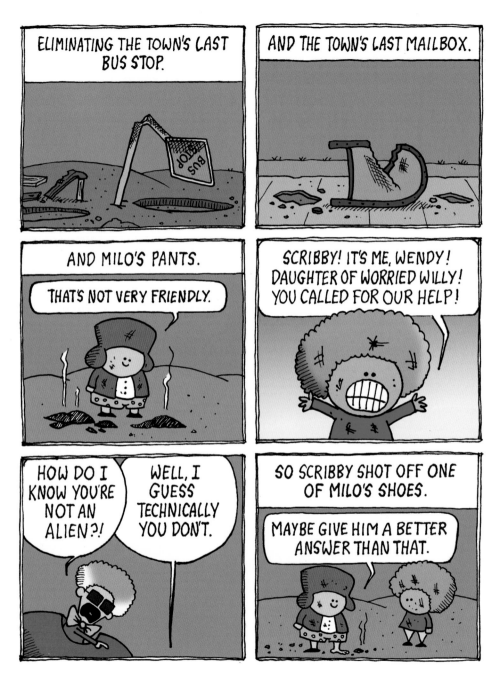

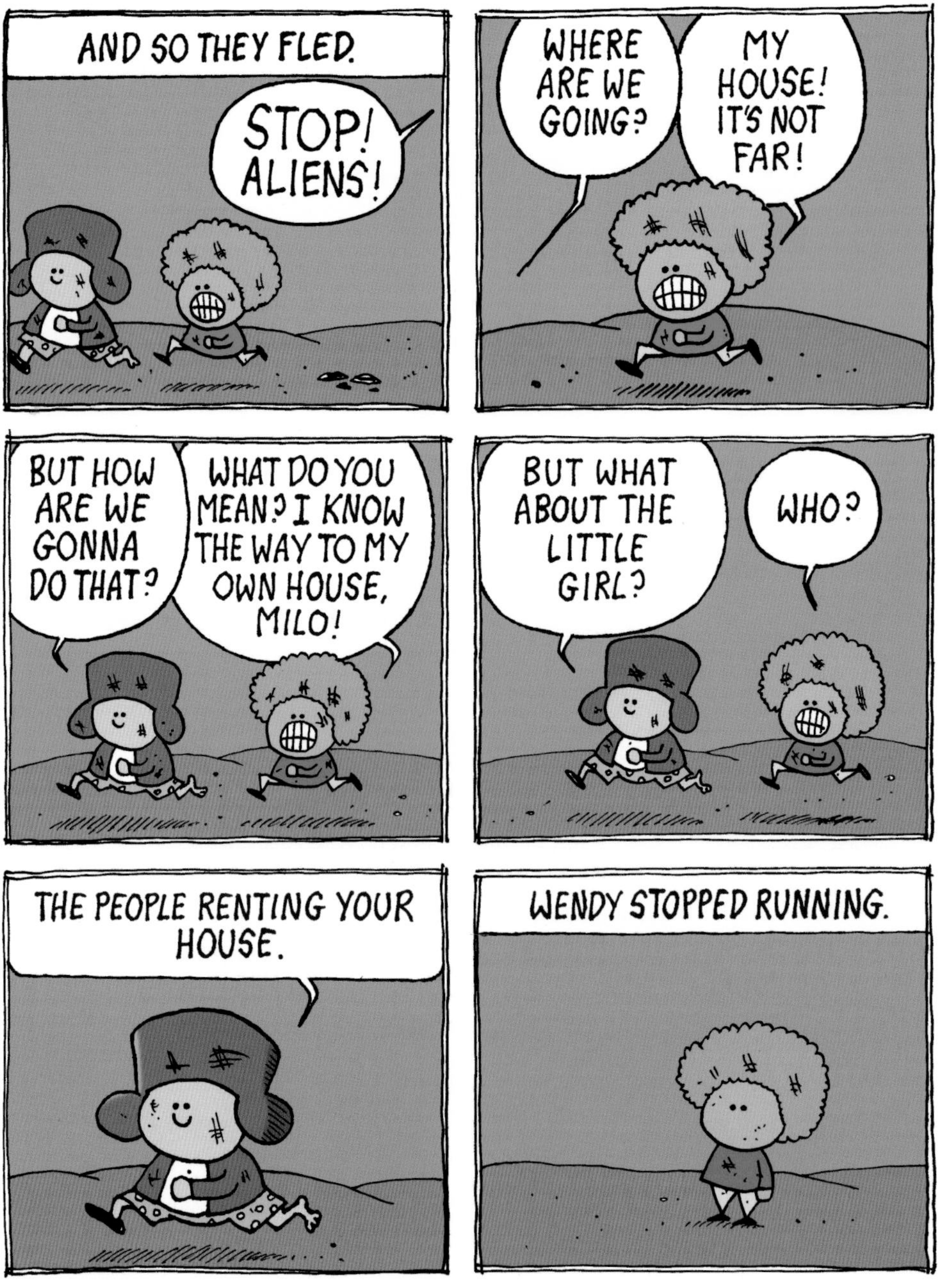
AND SO THEY FLED.
STOP! ALIENS!
WHERE ARE WE GOING?
MY HOUSE! IT'S NOT FAR!
BUT HOW ARE WE GONNA DO THAT?
WHAT DO YOU MEAN? I KNOW THE WAY TO MY OWN HOUSE, MILO!
BUT WHAT ABOUT THE LITTLE GIRL?
WHO?
THE PEOPLE RENTING YOUR HOUSE.
WENDY STOPPED RUNNING.

WE DIDN'T RENT OUR HOUSE TO ANYBODY.

CHAPTER EVEN BETTER THAN THE LAST ONE, AND THAT'S SAYING SOMETHING

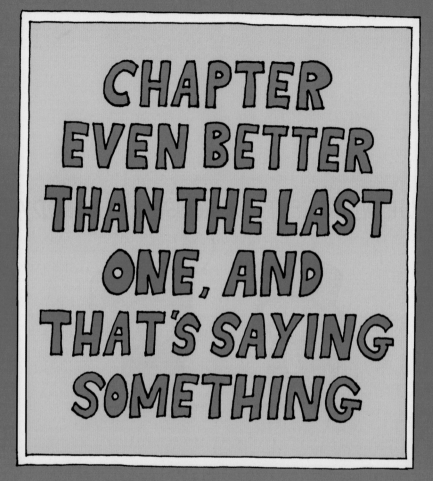

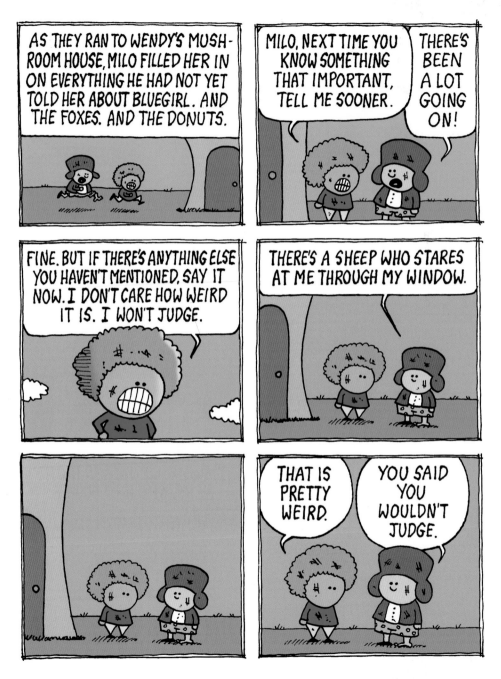

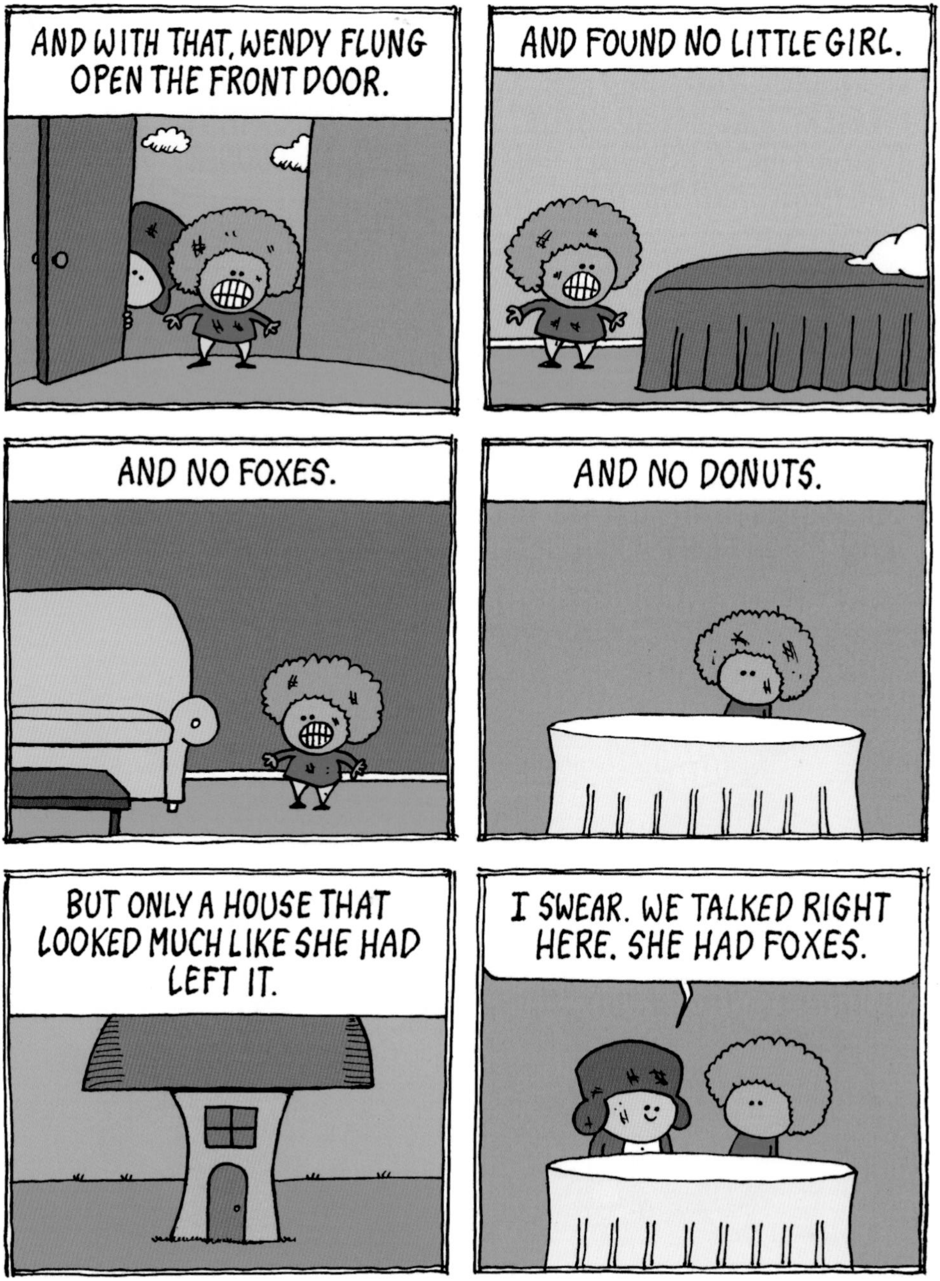
AND WITH THAT, WENDY FLUNG OPEN THE FRONT DOOR.
AND FOUND NO LITTLE GIRL.
AND NO FOXES.
AND NO DONUTS.
BUT ONLY A HOUSE THAT LOOKED MUCH LIKE SHE HAD LEFT IT.
I SWEAR. WE TALKED RIGHT HERE. SHE HAD FOXES.

138

CHAPTER 27

IN WHICH...

WE RANDOMLY ASSIGN A NUMBER TO THIS CHAPTER

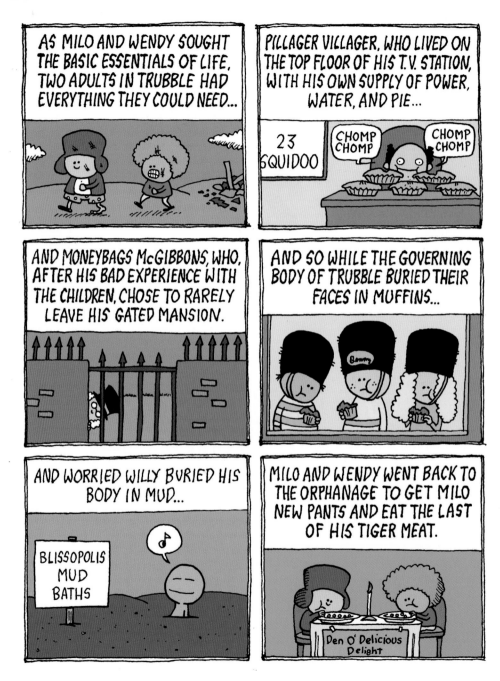

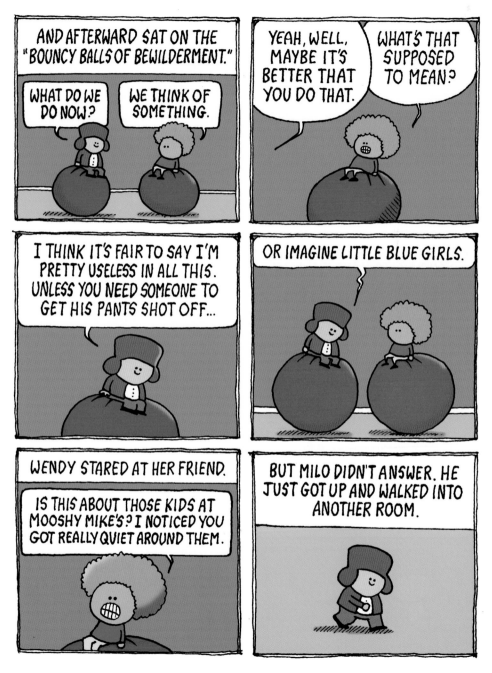

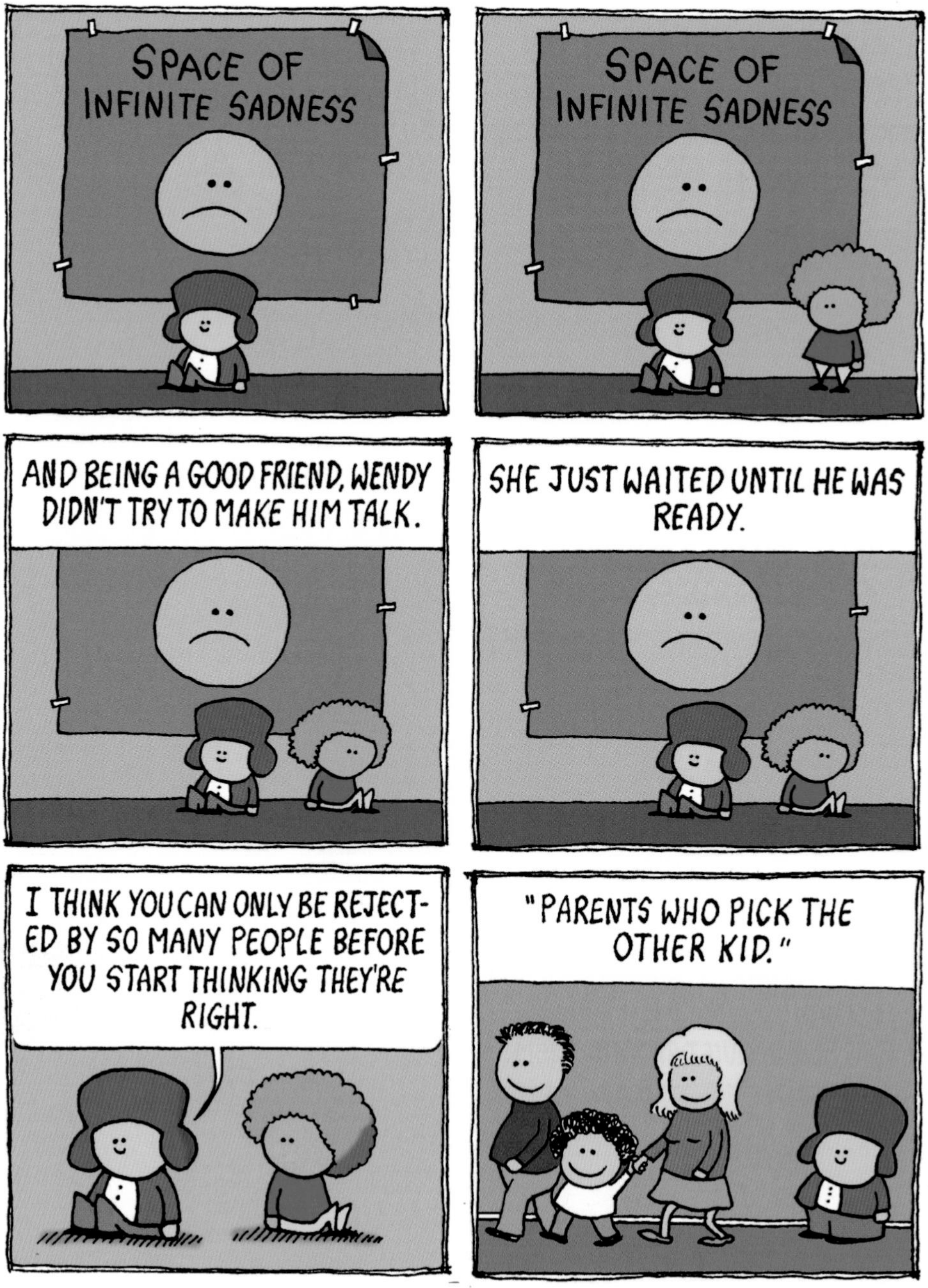
SPACE OF INFINITE SADNESS
SPACE OF INFINITE SADNESS
AND BEING A GOOD FRIEND, WENDY DIDN'T TRY TO MAKE HIM TALK.
SHE JUST WAITED UNTIL HE WAS READY.
I THINK YOU CAN ONLY BE REJECTED BY SO MANY PEOPLE BEFORE YOU START THINKING THEY'RE RIGHT.
"PARENTS WHO PICK THE OTHER KID."

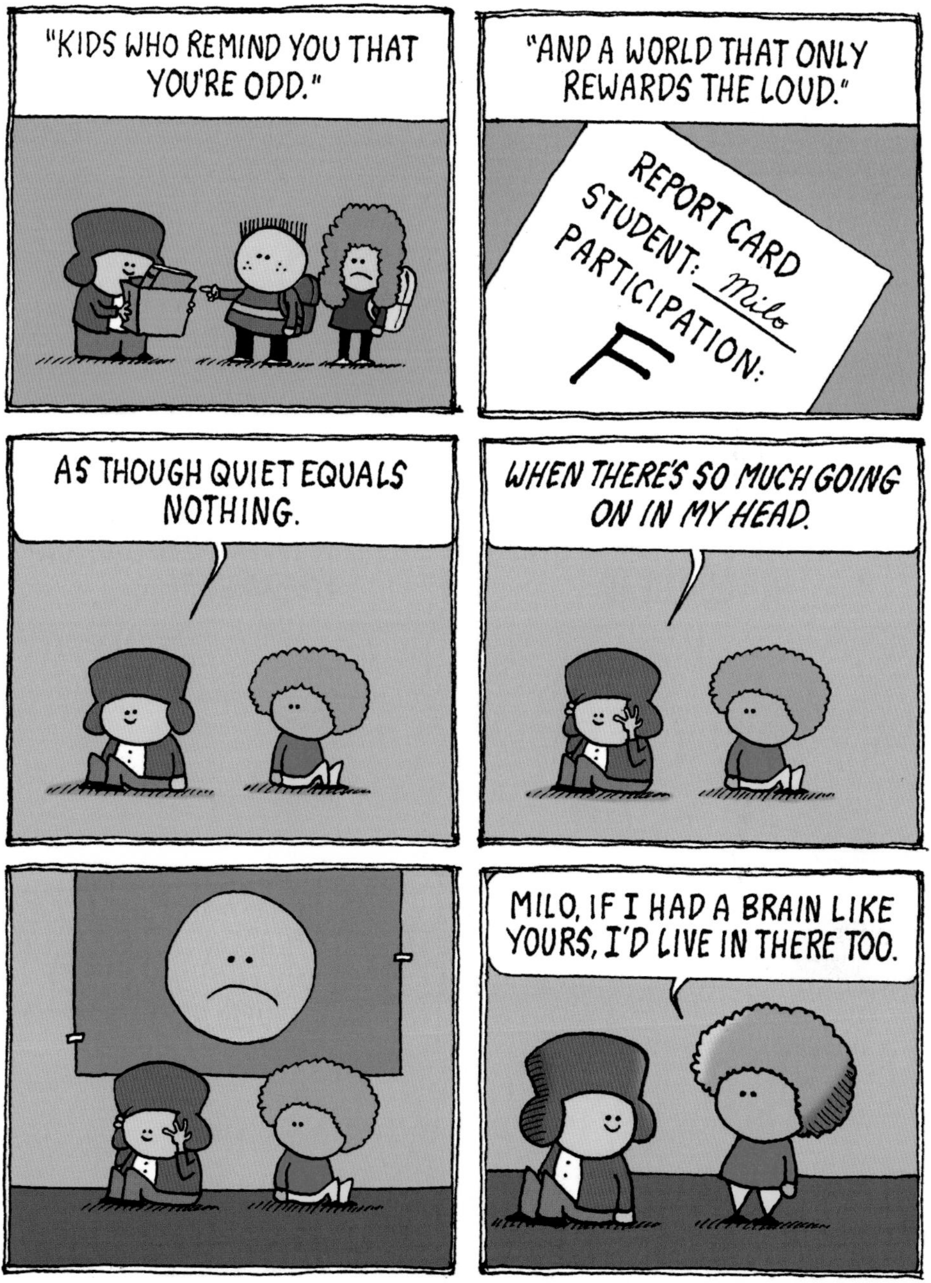
"KIDS WHO REMIND YOU THAT YOU'RE ODD."
"AND A WORLD THAT ONLY REWARDS THE LOUD."
REPORT CARD
STUDENT: Milo
PARTICIPATION:
F
AS THOUGH QUIET EQUALS NOTHING.
WHEN THERE'S SO MUCH GOING ON IN MY HEAD.
MILO, IF I HAD A BRAIN LIKE YOURS, I'D LIVE IN THERE TOO.

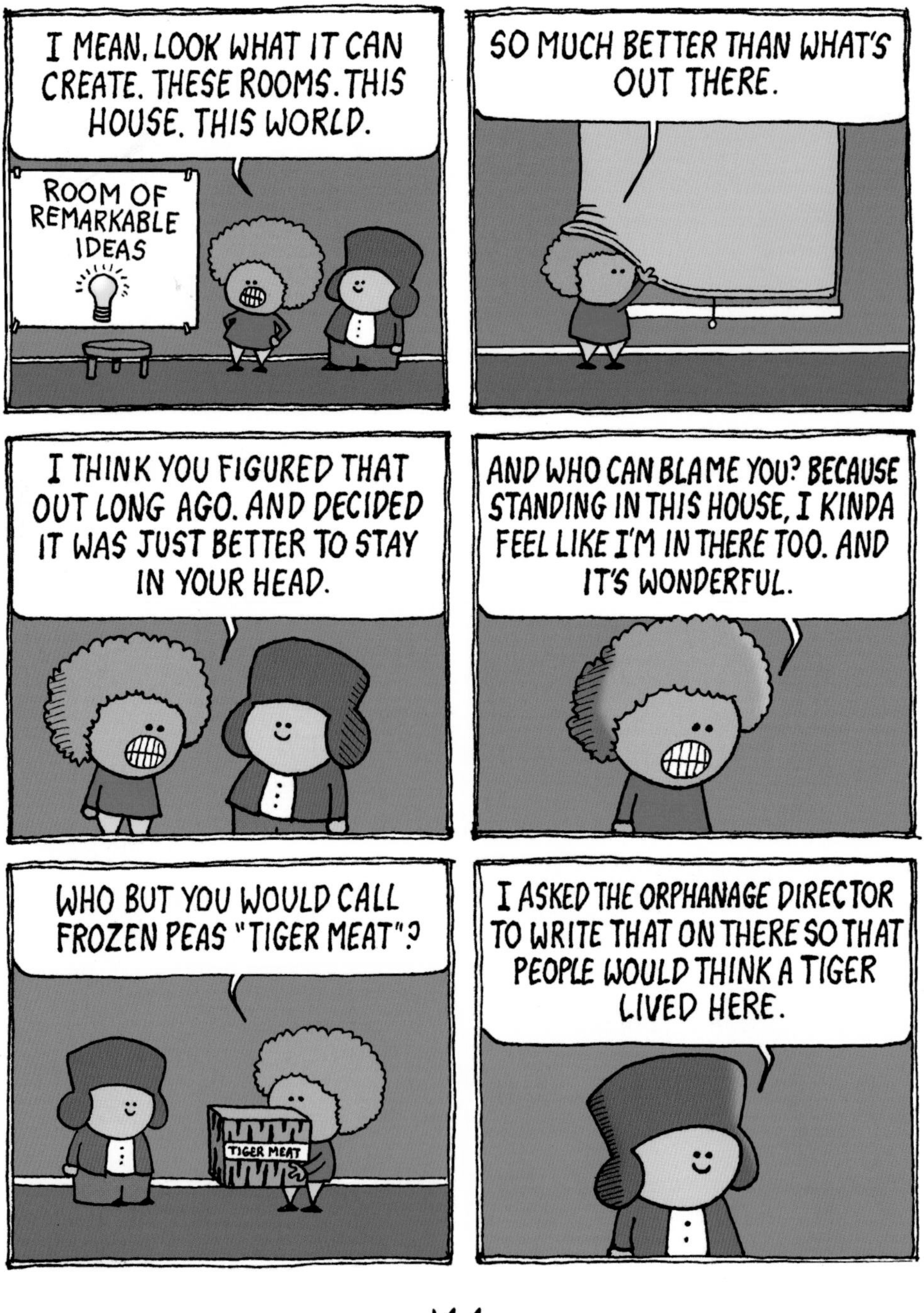
I MEAN, LOOK WHAT IT CAN CREATE. THESE ROOMS. THIS HOUSE. THIS WORLD.
ROOM OF REMARKABLE IDEAS
SO MUCH BETTER THAN WHAT'S OUT THERE.
I THINK YOU FIGURED THAT OUT LONG AGO. AND DECIDED IT WAS JUST BETTER TO STAY IN YOUR HEAD.
AND WHO CAN BLAME YOU? BECAUSE STANDING IN THIS HOUSE, I KINDA FEEL LIKE I'M IN THERE TOO. AND IT'S WONDERFUL.
WHO BUT YOU WOULD CALL FROZEN PEAS "TIGER MEAT"?
TIGER MEAT
I ASKED THE ORPHANAGE DIRECTOR TO WRITE THAT ON THERE SO THAT PEOPLE WOULD THINK A TIGER LIVED HERE.

145

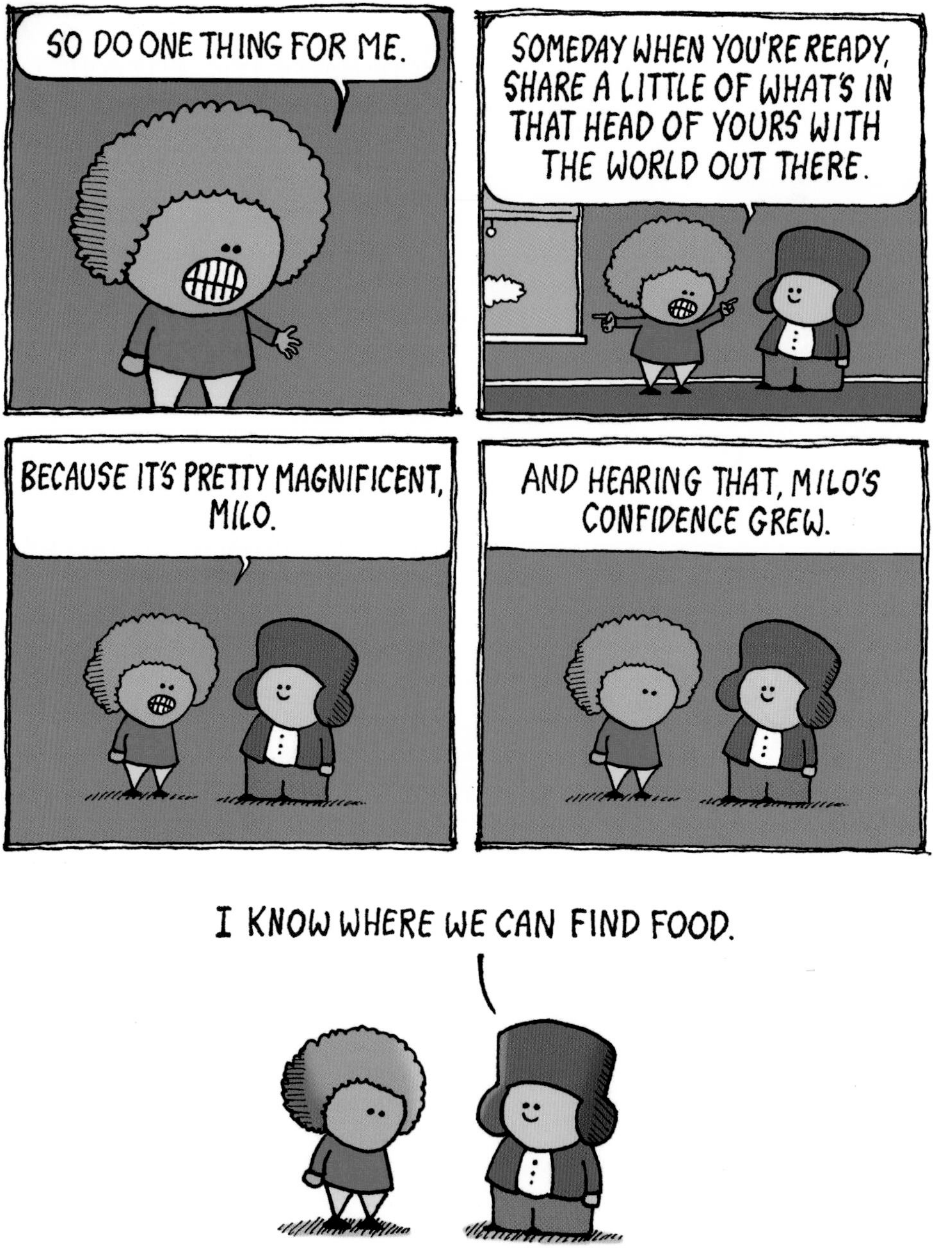
SO DO ONE THING FOR ME.
SOMEDAY WHEN YOU'RE READY, SHARE A LITTLE OF WHAT'S IN THAT HEAD OF YOURS WITH THE WORLD OUT THERE.
BECAUSE IT'S PRETTY MAGNIFICENT, MILO.
AND HEARING THAT, MILO'S CONFIDENCE GREW.
I KNOW WHERE WE CAN FIND FOOD.

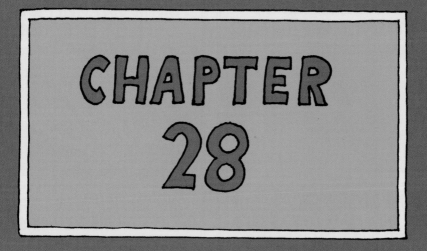

CHAPTER 28

IN WHICH...

WE NUMBER CHAPTERS LIKE NORMAL PEOPLE

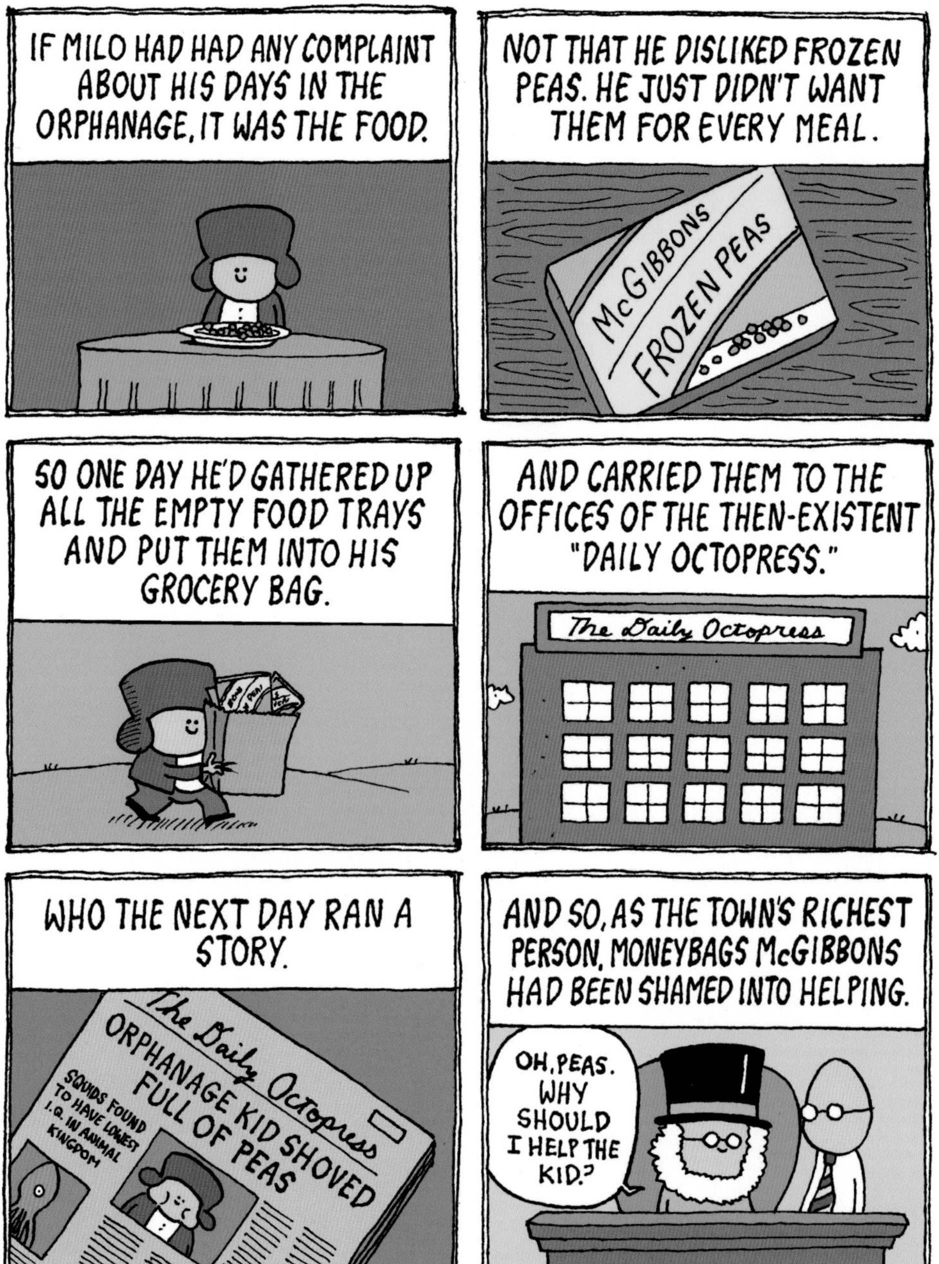
IF MILO HAD HAD ANY COMPLAINT ABOUT HIS DAYS IN THE ORPHANAGE, IT WAS THE FOOD.
NOT THAT HE DISLIKED FROZEN PEAS. HE JUST DIDN'T WANT THEM FOR EVERY MEAL.
McGIBBONS
FROZEN PEAS
SO ONE DAY HE'D GATHERED UP ALL THE EMPTY FOOD TRAYS AND PUT THEM INTO HIS GROCERY BAG.
AND CARRIED THEM TO THE OFFICES OF THE THEN-EXISTENT "DAILY OCTOPRESS."
The Daily Octopress
WHO THE NEXT DAY RAN A STORY.
The Daily Octopress
ORPHANAGE KID SHOVED FULL OF PEAS
SQUIDS FOUND TO HAVE LOWEST I.Q. IN ANIMAL KINGDOM
AND SO, AS THE TOWN'S RICHEST PERSON, MONEYBAGS McGIBBONS HAD BEEN SHAMED INTO HELPING.
OH, PEAS. WHY SHOULD I HELP THE KID?

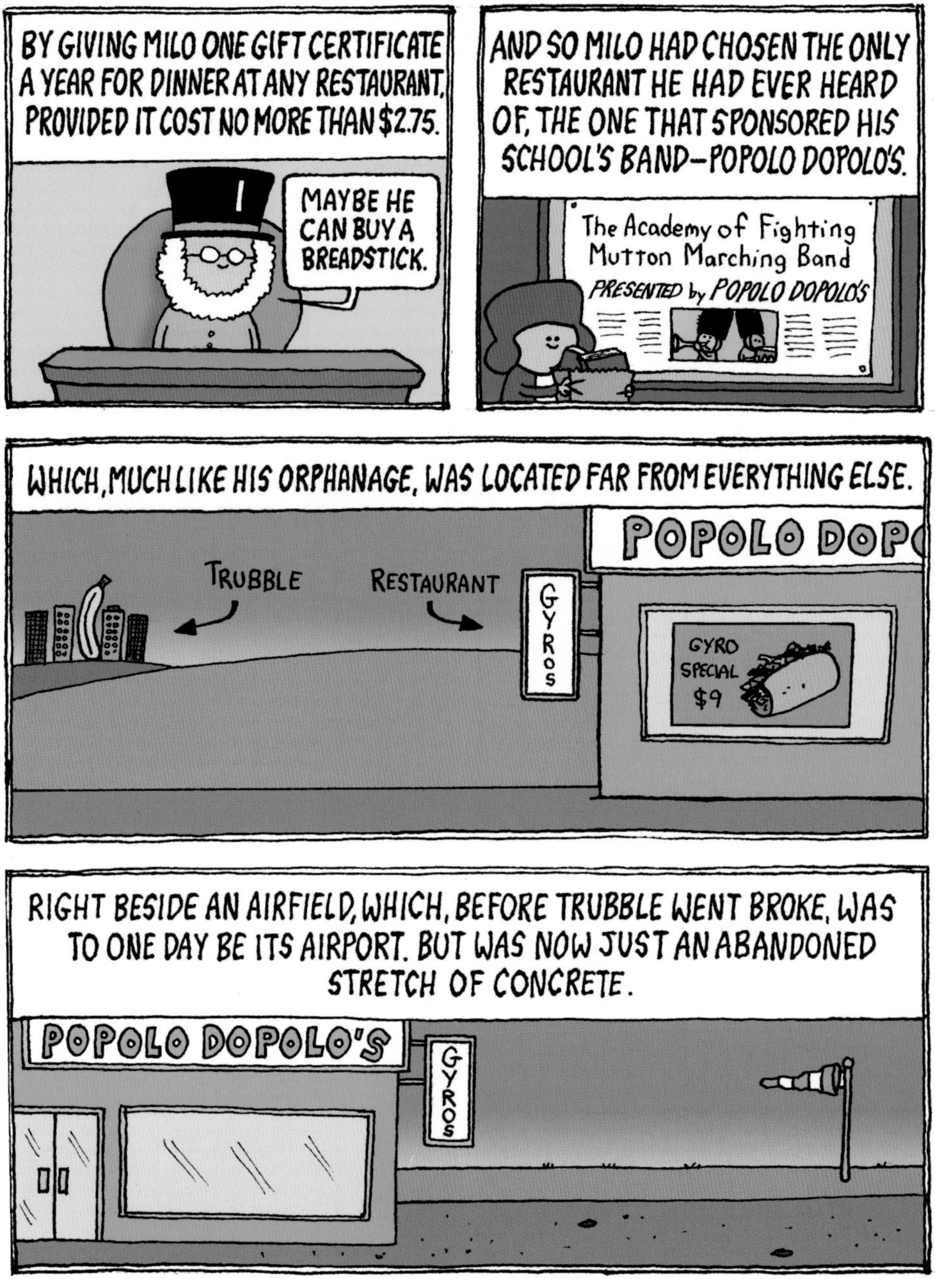
BY GIVING MILO ONE GIFT CERTIFICATE A YEAR FOR DINNER AT ANY RESTAURANT, PROVIDED IT COST NO MORE THAN $2.75.
MAYBE HE CAN BUY A BREADSTICK.
AND SO MILO HAD CHOSEN THE ONLY RESTAURANT HE HAD EVER HEARD OF, THE ONE THAT SPONSORED HIS SCHOOL'S BAND—POPOLO DOPOLO'S.
The Academy of Fighting Mutton Marching Band
PRESENTED by POPOLO DOPOLO'S
WHICH, MUCH LIKE HIS ORPHANAGE, WAS LOCATED FAR FROM EVERYTHING ELSE.
TRUBBLE
RESTAURANT
GYROS
GYRO SPECIAL $9
RIGHT BESIDE AN AIRFIELD, WHICH, BEFORE TRUBBLE WENT BROKE, WAS TO ONE DAY BE ITS AIRPORT. BUT WAS NOW JUST AN ABANDONED STRETCH OF CONCRETE.
POPOLO DOPOLO'S
GYROS

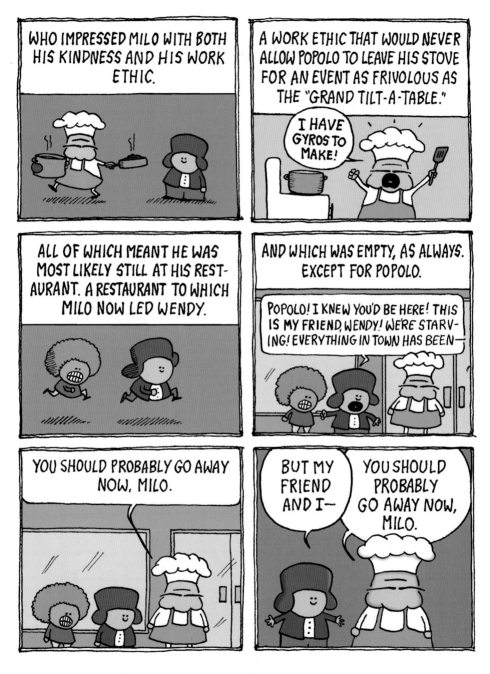

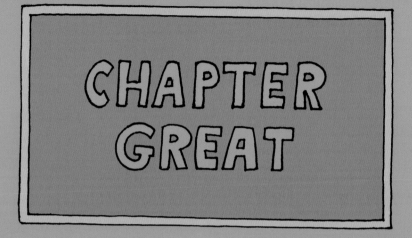

CHAPTER GREAT

IN WHICH...

WE TRY TO BE HUMBLE, BUT FAIL

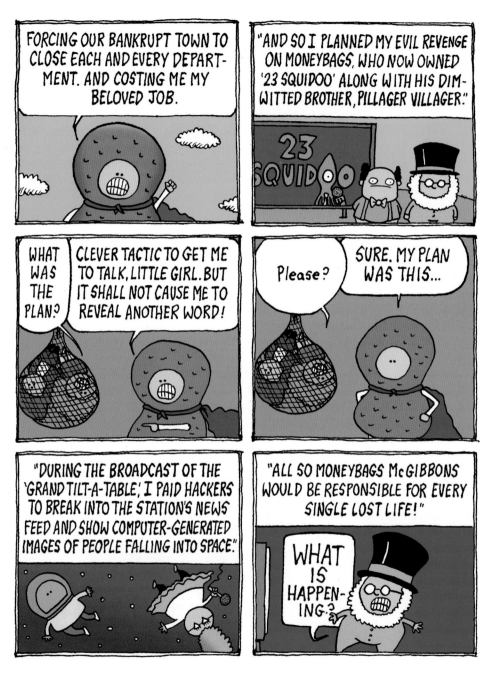

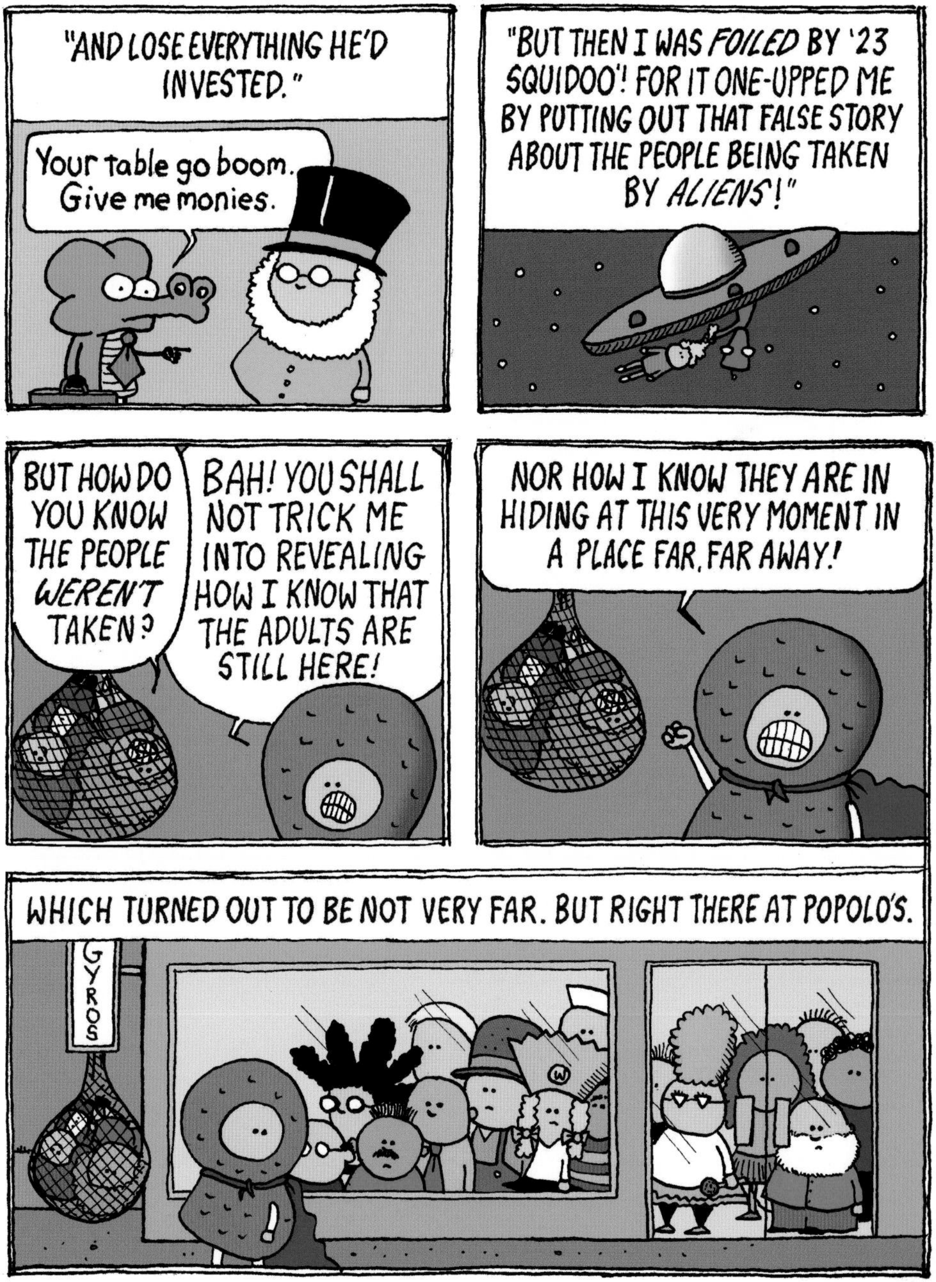
"AND LOSE EVERYTHING HE'D INVESTED."
Your table go boom. Give me monies.
"BUT THEN I WAS *FOILED* BY '23 SQUIDOO'! FOR IT ONE-UPPED ME BY PUTTING OUT THAT FALSE STORY ABOUT THE PEOPLE BEING TAKEN BY *ALIENS*!"
BUT HOW DO YOU KNOW THE PEOPLE *WEREN'T* TAKEN?
BAH! YOU SHALL NOT TRICK ME INTO REVEALING HOW I KNOW THAT THE ADULTS ARE STILL HERE!
NOR HOW I KNOW THEY ARE IN HIDING AT THIS VERY MOMENT IN A PLACE FAR, FAR AWAY!
WHICH TURNED OUT TO BE NOT VERY FAR. BUT RIGHT THERE AT POPOLO'S.
GYROS

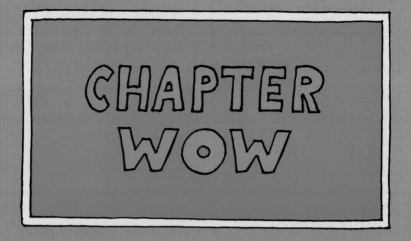

CHAPTER WOW

IN WHICH...

YOU ARE SUITABLY WOWED, OR WE GIVE YOU YOUR MONEY BACK *

* Not true. Don't try.

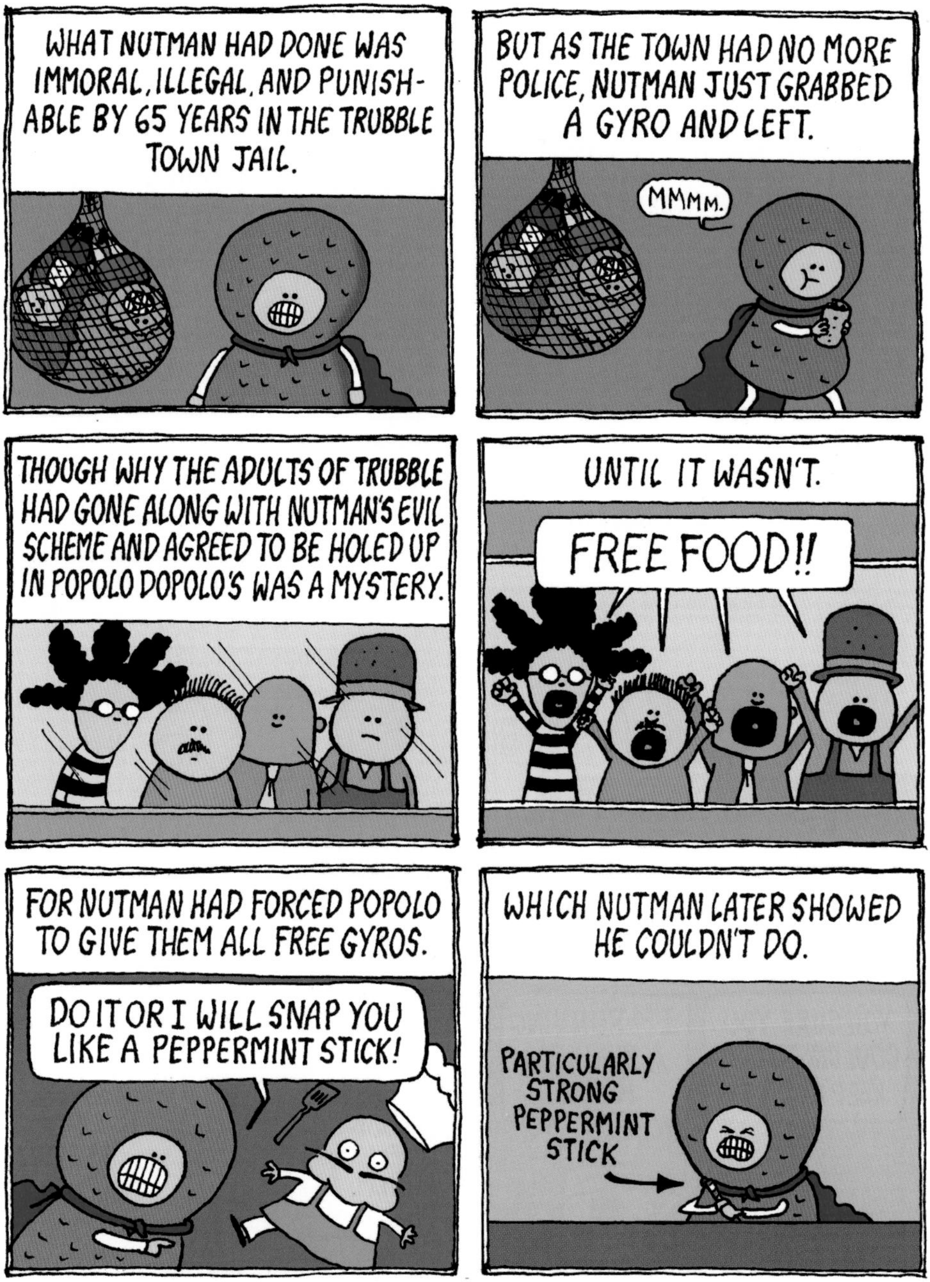
WHAT NUTMAN HAD DONE WAS IMMORAL, ILLEGAL, AND PUNISHABLE BY 65 YEARS IN THE TRUBBLE TOWN JAIL.
BUT AS THE TOWN HAD NO MORE POLICE, NUTMAN JUST GRABBED A GYRO AND LEFT.
MMMM.
THOUGH WHY THE ADULTS OF TRUBBLE HAD GONE ALONG WITH NUTMAN'S EVIL SCHEME AND AGREED TO BE HOLED UP IN POPOLO DOPOLO'S WAS A MYSTERY.
UNTIL IT WASN'T.
FREE FOOD!!
FOR NUTMAN HAD FORCED POPOLO TO GIVE THEM ALL FREE GYROS.
DO IT OR I WILL SNAP YOU LIKE A PEPPERMINT STICK!
WHICH NUTMAN LATER SHOWED HE COULDN'T DO.
PARTICULARLY STRONG PEPPERMINT STICK

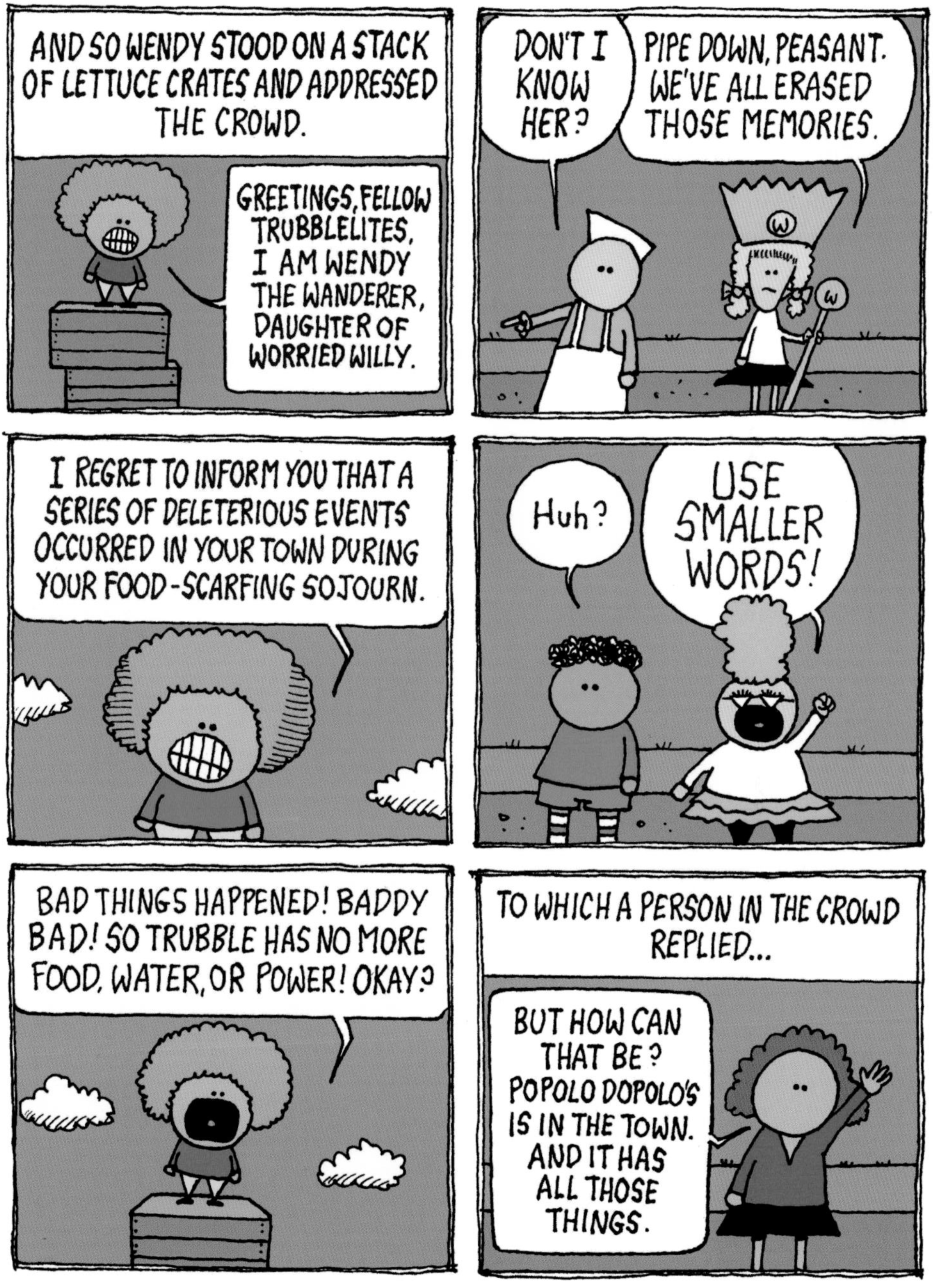
AND SO WENDY STOOD ON A STACK OF LETTUCE CRATES AND ADDRESSED THE CROWD.
GREETINGS, FELLOW TRUBBLELITES. I AM WENDY THE WANDERER, DAUGHTER OF WORRIED WILLY.
DON'T I KNOW HER?
PIPE DOWN, PEASANT. WE'VE ALL ERASED THOSE MEMORIES.
I REGRET TO INFORM YOU THAT A SERIES OF DELETERIOUS EVENTS OCCURRED IN YOUR TOWN DURING YOUR FOOD-SCARFING SOJOURN.
Huh?
USE SMALLER WORDS!
BAD THINGS HAPPENED! BADDY BAD! SO TRUBBLE HAS NO MORE FOOD, WATER, OR POWER! OKAY?
TO WHICH A PERSON IN THE CROWD REPLIED...
BUT HOW CAN THAT BE? POPOLO DOPOLO'S IS IN THE TOWN. AND IT HAS ALL THOSE THINGS.

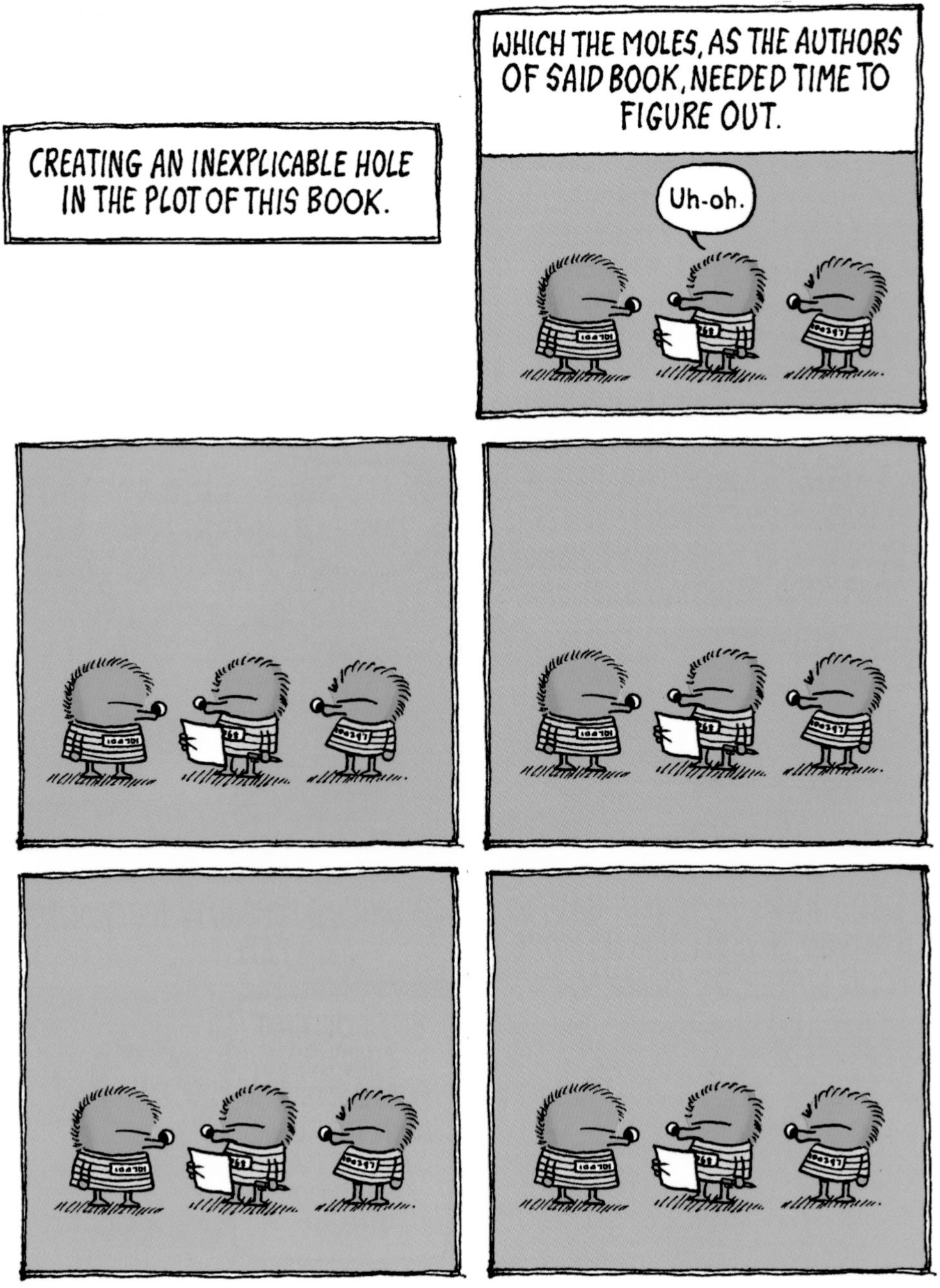
CREATING AN INEXPLICABLE HOLE IN THE PLOT OF THIS BOOK.
WHICH THE MOLES, AS THE AUTHORS OF SAID BOOK, NEEDED TIME TO FIGURE OUT.
Uh-oh.

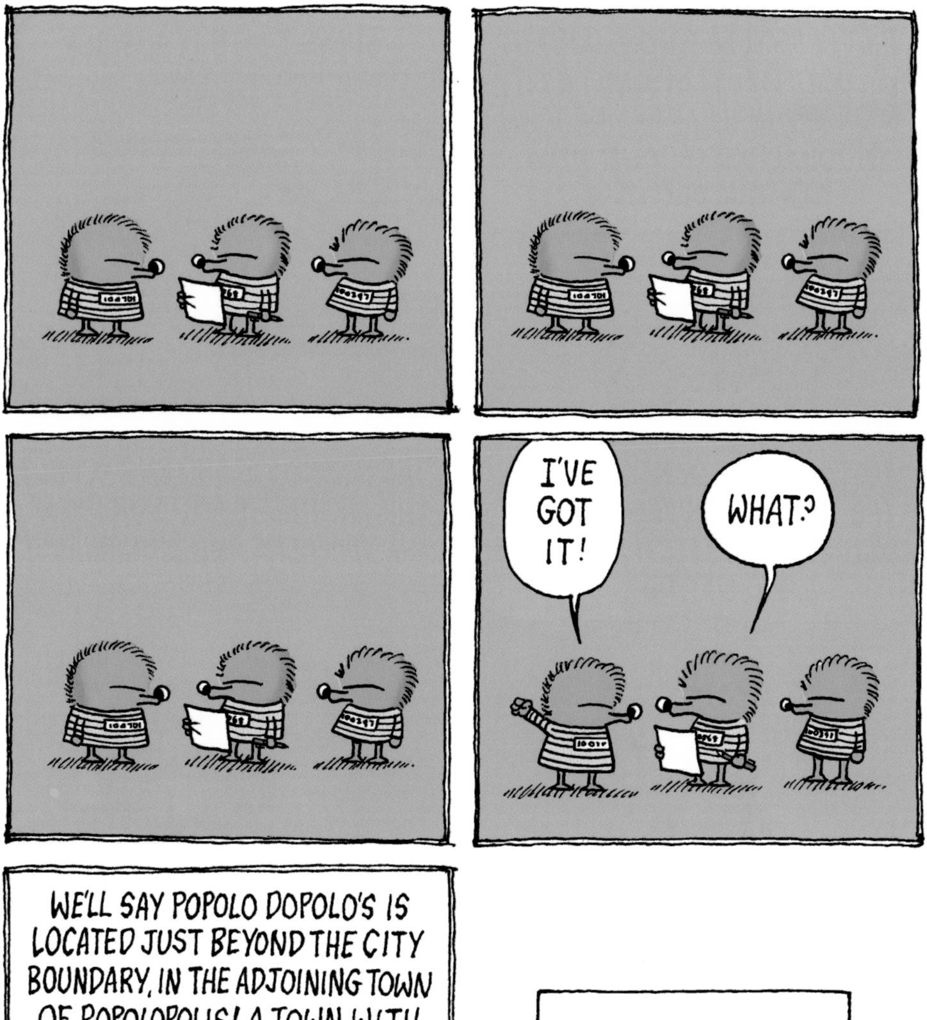
I'VE GOT IT!
WHAT?
WE'LL SAY POPOLO DOPOLO'S IS LOCATED JUST BEYOND THE CITY BOUNDARY, IN THE ADJOINING TOWN OF POPOLOPOLIS! A TOWN WITH PLENTIFUL SUPPLIES!
AND SO THE BOOK CONTINUED...

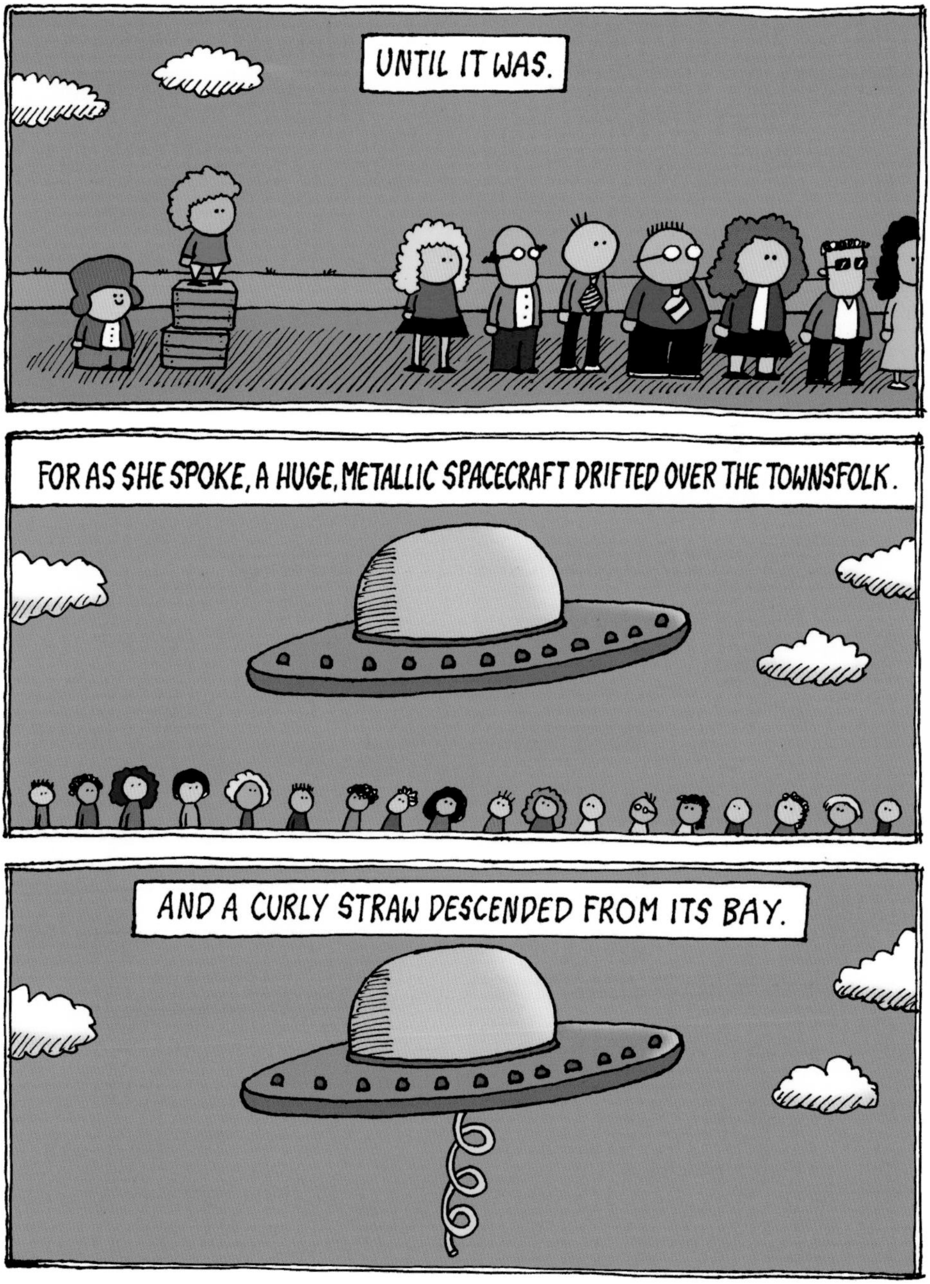
UNTIL IT WAS.
FOR AS SHE SPOKE, A HUGE, METALLIC SPACECRAFT DRIFTED OVER THE TOWNSFOLK.
AND A CURLY STRAW DESCENDED FROM ITS BAY.

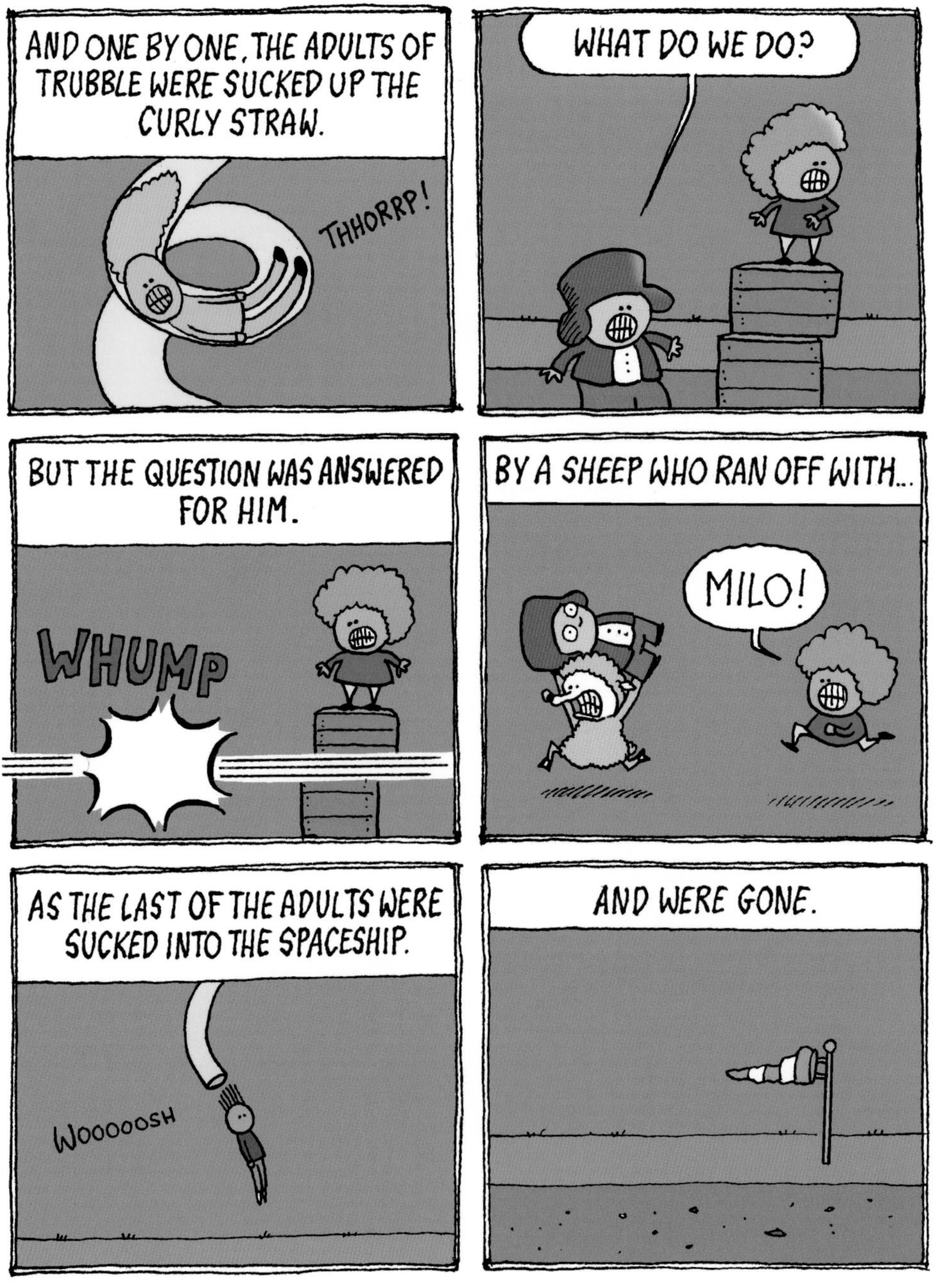
AND ONE BY ONE, THE ADULTS OF TRUBBLE WERE SUCKED UP THE CURLY STRAW.
THHORRP!
WHAT DO WE DO?
BUT THE QUESTION WAS ANSWERED FOR HIM.
WHUMP
BY A SHEEP WHO RAN OFF WITH...
MILO!
AS THE LAST OF THE ADULTS WERE SUCKED INTO THE SPACESHIP.
WOOOOOSH
AND WERE GONE.

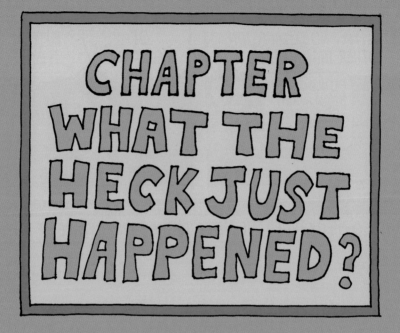

CHAPTER
WHAT THE
HECK JUST
HAPPENED?

IN WHICH...

WE HOPEFULLY
FIND THAT OUT

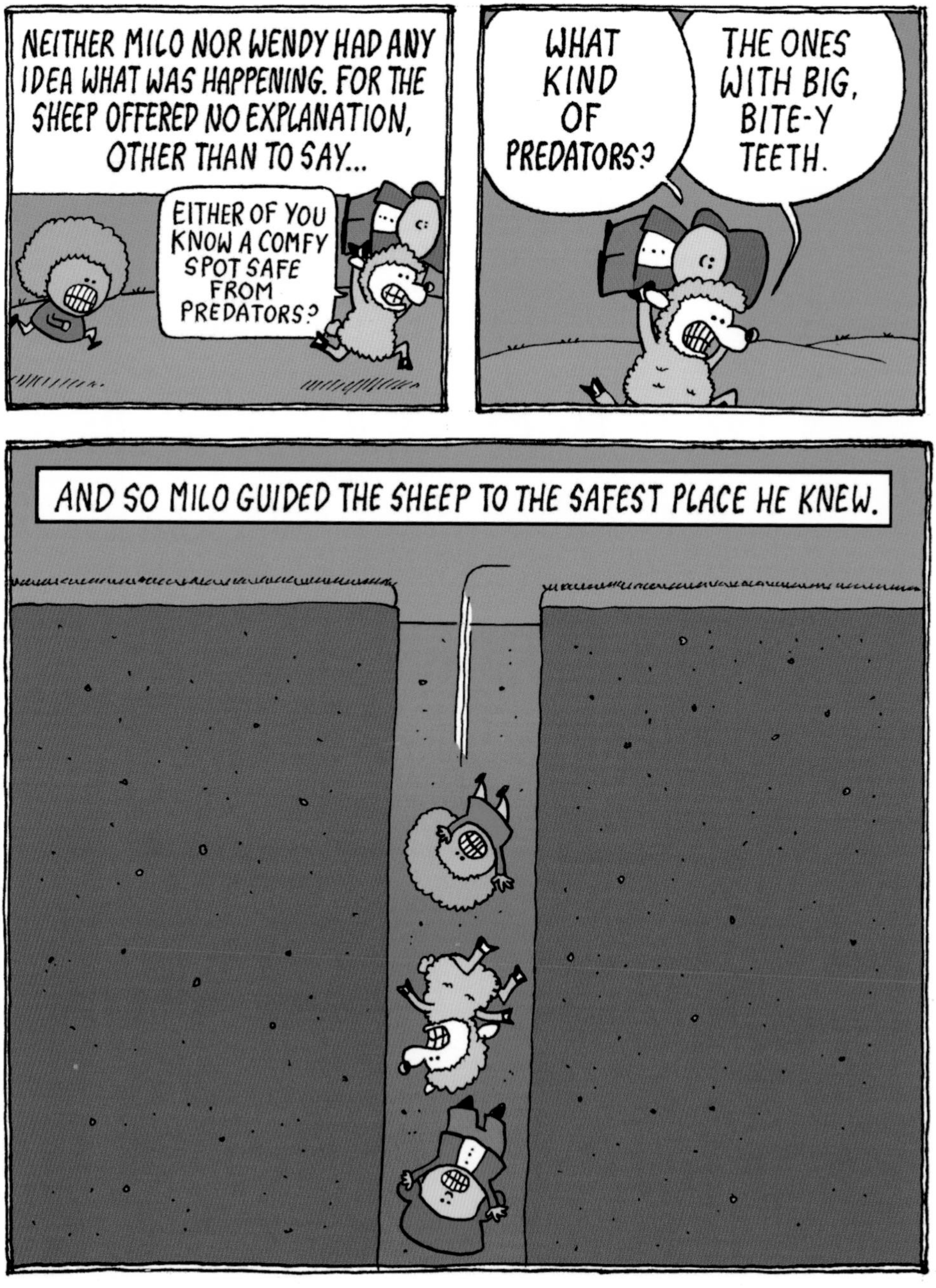
NEITHER MILO NOR WENDY HAD ANY IDEA WHAT WAS HAPPENING. FOR THE SHEEP OFFERED NO EXPLANATION, OTHER THAN TO SAY...
EITHER OF YOU KNOW A COMFY SPOT SAFE FROM PREDATORS?
WHAT KIND OF PREDATORS?
THE ONES WITH BIG, BITE-Y TEETH.
AND SO MILO GUIDED THE SHEEP TO THE SAFEST PLACE HE KNEW.

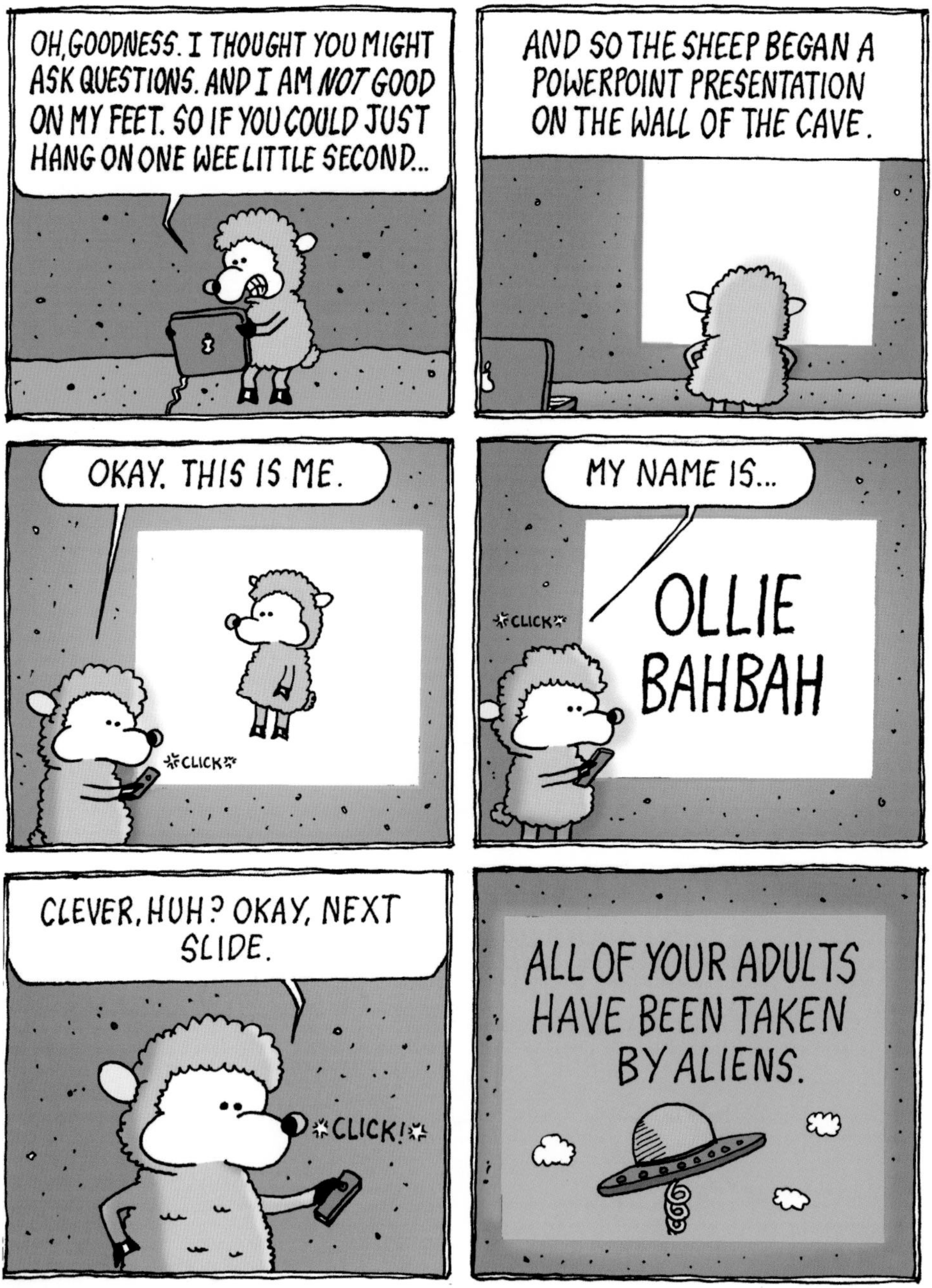
OH, GOODNESS. I THOUGHT YOU MIGHT ASK QUESTIONS. AND I AM *NOT* GOOD ON MY FEET. SO IF YOU COULD JUST HANG ON ONE WEE LITTLE SECOND...
AND SO THE SHEEP BEGAN A POWERPOINT PRESENTATION ON THE WALL OF THE CAVE.
OKAY. THIS IS ME.
CLICK
MY NAME IS...
CLICK
OLLIE BAHBAH
CLEVER, HUH? OKAY, NEXT SLIDE.
CLICK!
ALL OF YOUR ADULTS HAVE BEEN TAKEN BY ALIENS.

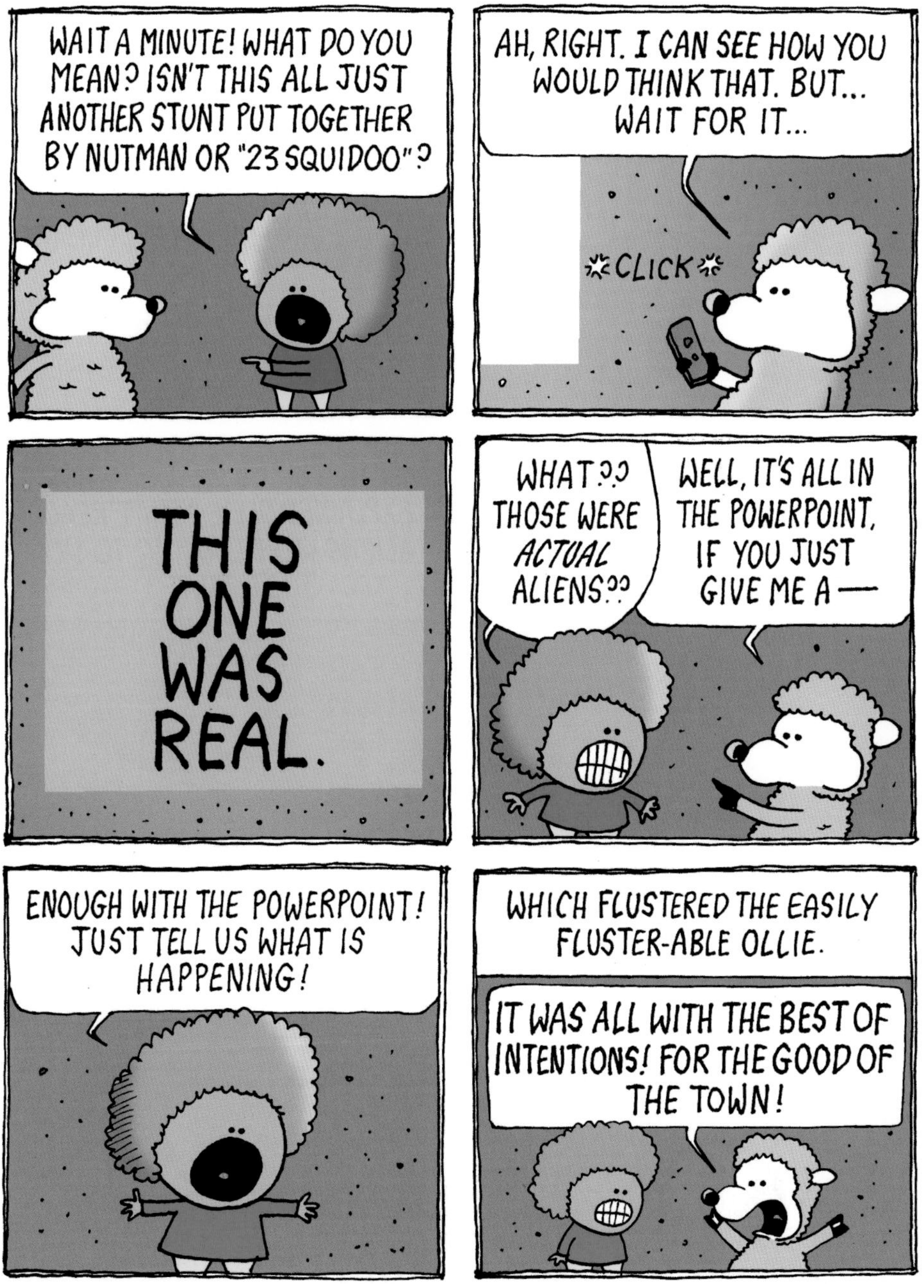
WAIT A MINUTE! WHAT DO YOU MEAN? ISN'T THIS ALL JUST ANOTHER STUNT PUT TOGETHER BY NUTMAN OR "23 SQUIDOO"?
AH, RIGHT. I CAN SEE HOW YOU WOULD THINK THAT. BUT... WAIT FOR IT...
CLICK
THIS ONE WAS REAL.
WHAT?? THOSE WERE *ACTUAL* ALIENS??
WELL, IT'S ALL IN THE POWERPOINT, IF YOU JUST GIVE ME A—
ENOUGH WITH THE POWERPOINT! JUST TELL US WHAT IS HAPPENING!
WHICH FLUSTERED THE EASILY FLUSTER-ABLE OLLIE.
IT WAS ALL WITH THE BEST OF INTENTIONS! FOR THE GOOD OF THE TOWN!

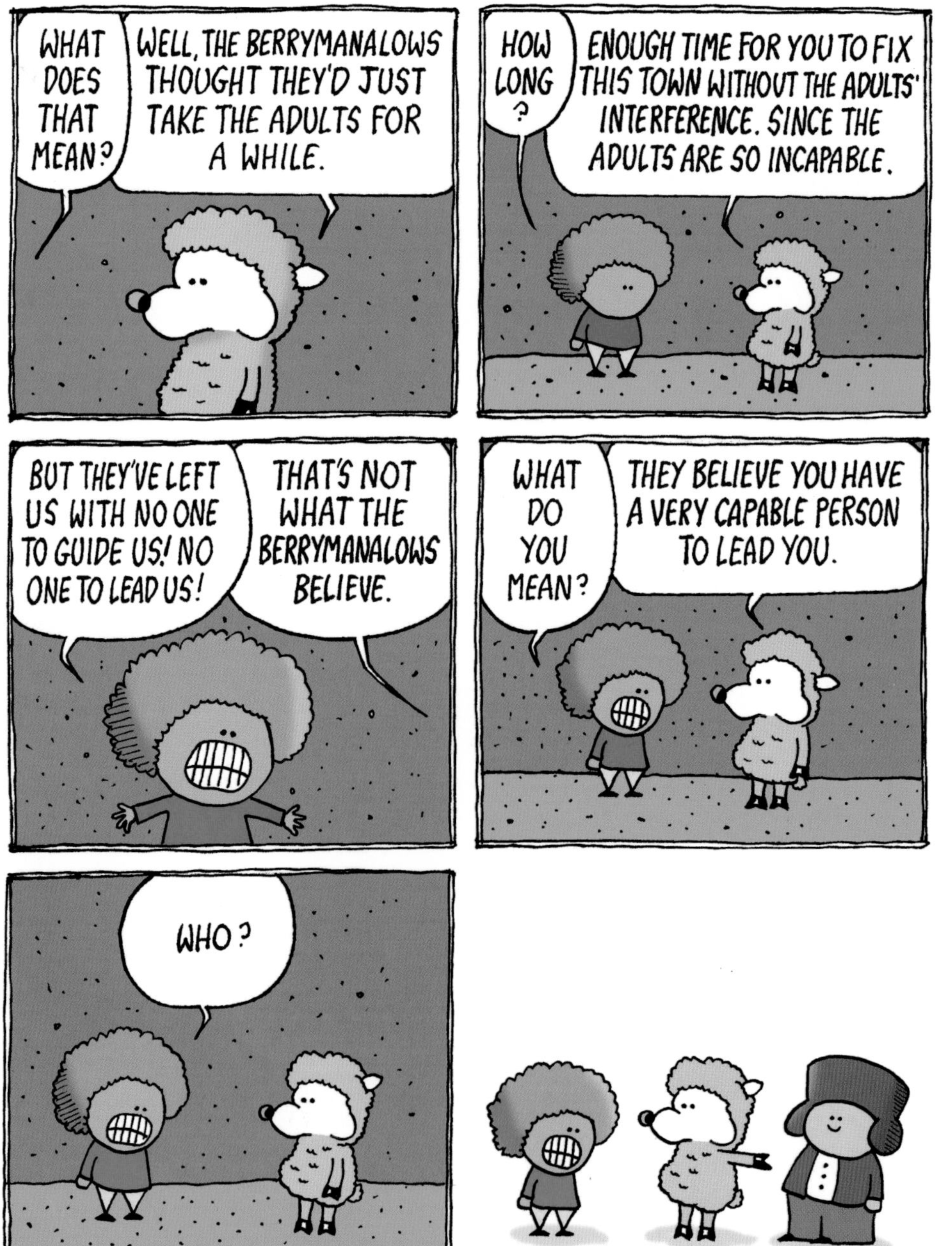
WHAT DOES THAT MEAN?
WELL, THE BERRYMANALOWS THOUGHT THEY'D JUST TAKE THE ADULTS FOR A WHILE.
HOW LONG?
ENOUGH TIME FOR YOU TO FIX THIS TOWN WITHOUT THE ADULTS' INTERFERENCE. SINCE THE ADULTS ARE SO INCAPABLE.
BUT THEY'VE LEFT US WITH NO ONE TO GUIDE US! NO ONE TO LEAD US!
THAT'S NOT WHAT THE BERRYMANALOWS BELIEVE.
WHAT DO YOU MEAN?
THEY BELIEVE YOU HAVE A VERY CAPABLE PERSON TO LEAD YOU.
WHO?

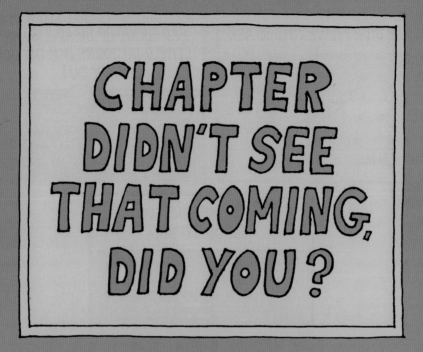

CHAPTER DIDN'T SEE THAT COMING, DID YOU?

IN WHICH...

WE CONTINUE TO AMAZE

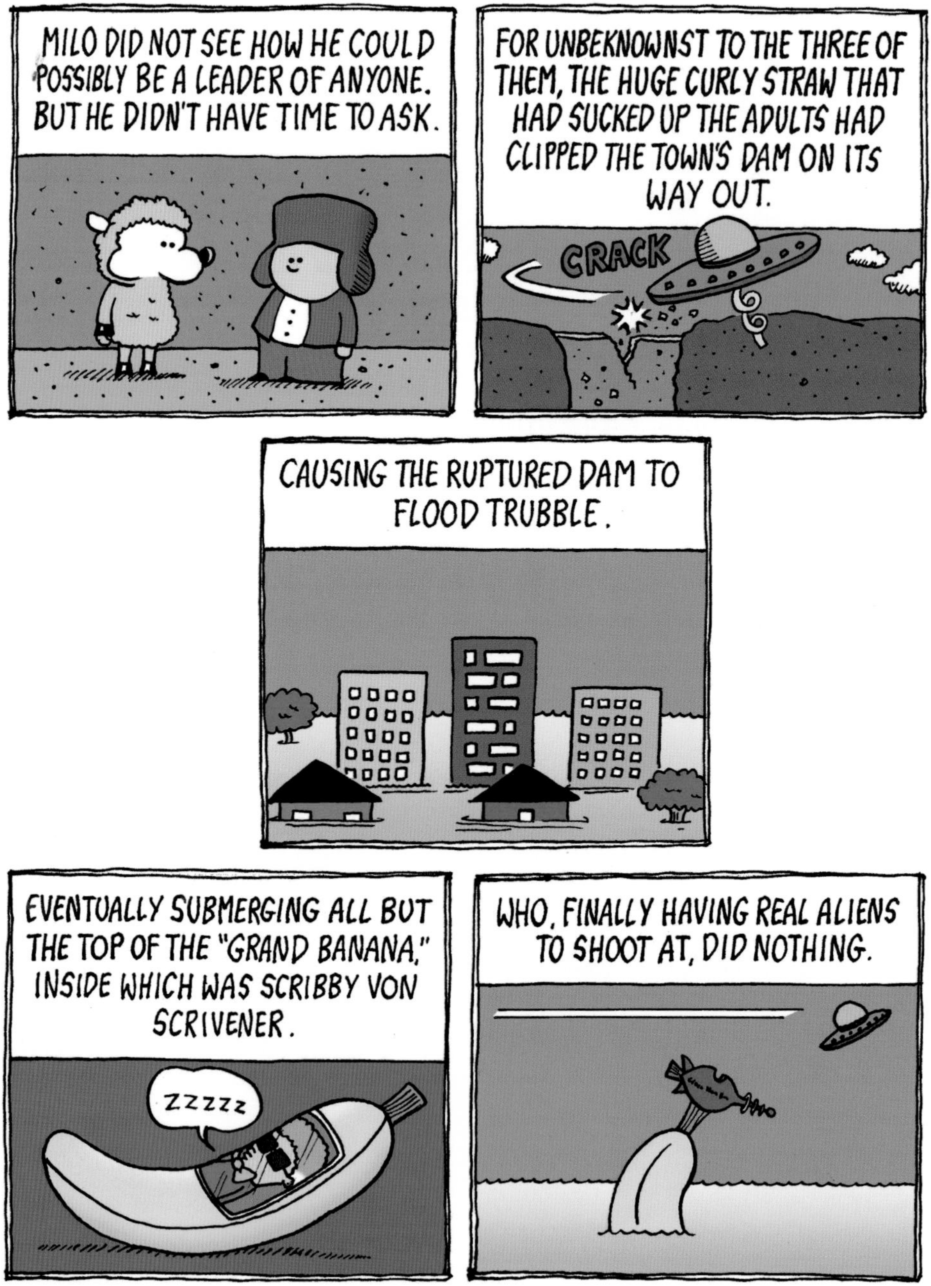
MILO DID NOT SEE HOW HE COULD POSSIBLY BE A LEADER OF ANYONE. BUT HE DIDN'T HAVE TIME TO ASK.
FOR UNBEKNOWNST TO THE THREE OF THEM, THE HUGE CURLY STRAW THAT HAD SUCKED UP THE ADULTS HAD CLIPPED THE TOWN'S DAM ON ITS WAY OUT.
CRACK
CAUSING THE RUPTURED DAM TO FLOOD TRUBBLE.
EVENTUALLY SUBMERGING ALL BUT THE TOP OF THE "GRAND BANANA," INSIDE WHICH WAS SCRIBBY VON SCRIVENER.
ZZZZZ
WHO, FINALLY HAVING REAL ALIENS TO SHOOT AT, DID NOTHING.

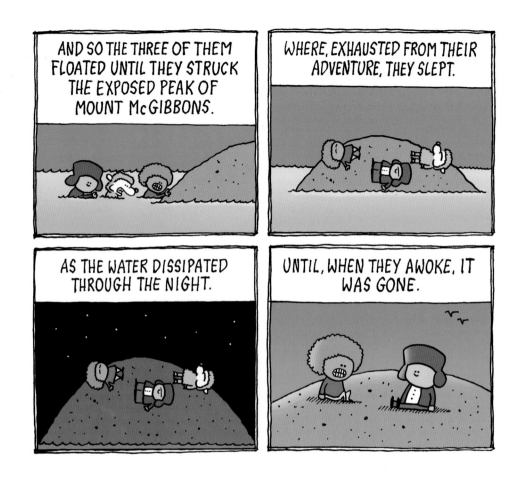

JUST LIKE OLLIE.

CHAPTER 33

IN WHICH...

WE MAKE NO ATTEMPT TO LOOK BACK AND SEE WHAT CHAPTER NUMBER THIS SHOULD ACTUALLY BE

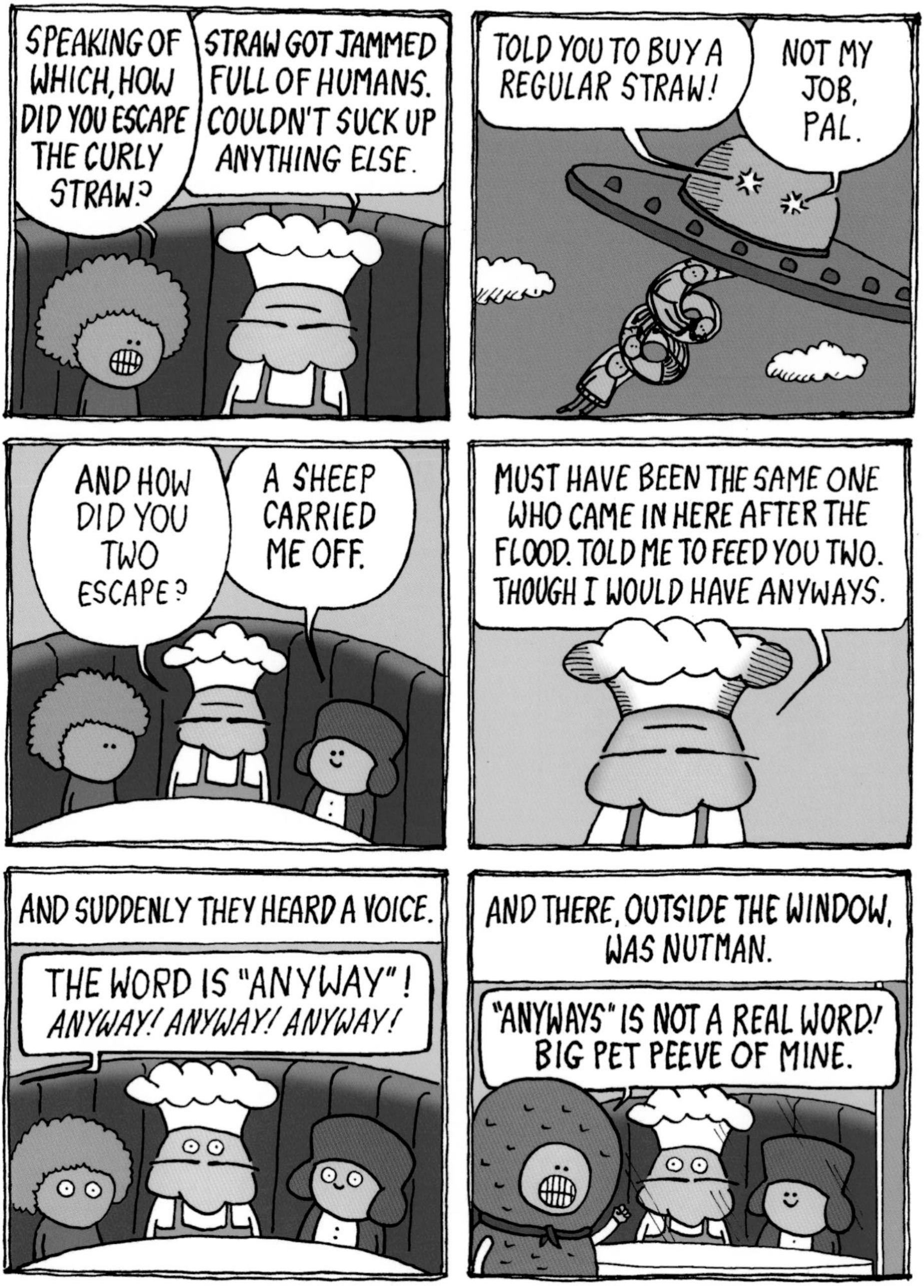
SPEAKING OF WHICH, HOW DID YOU ESCAPE THE CURLY STRAW?
STRAW GOT JAMMED FULL OF HUMANS. COULDN'T SUCK UP ANYTHING ELSE.
TOLD YOU TO BUY A REGULAR STRAW!
NOT MY JOB, PAL.
AND HOW DID YOU TWO ESCAPE?
A SHEEP CARRIED ME OFF.
MUST HAVE BEEN THE SAME ONE WHO CAME IN HERE AFTER THE FLOOD. TOLD ME TO FEED YOU TWO. THOUGH I WOULD HAVE ANYWAYS.
AND SUDDENLY THEY HEARD A VOICE.
THE WORD IS "ANYWAY"! ANYWAY! ANYWAY! ANYWAY!
AND THERE, OUTSIDE THE WINDOW, WAS NUTMAN.
"ANYWAYS" IS NOT A REAL WORD! BIG PET PEEVE OF MINE.

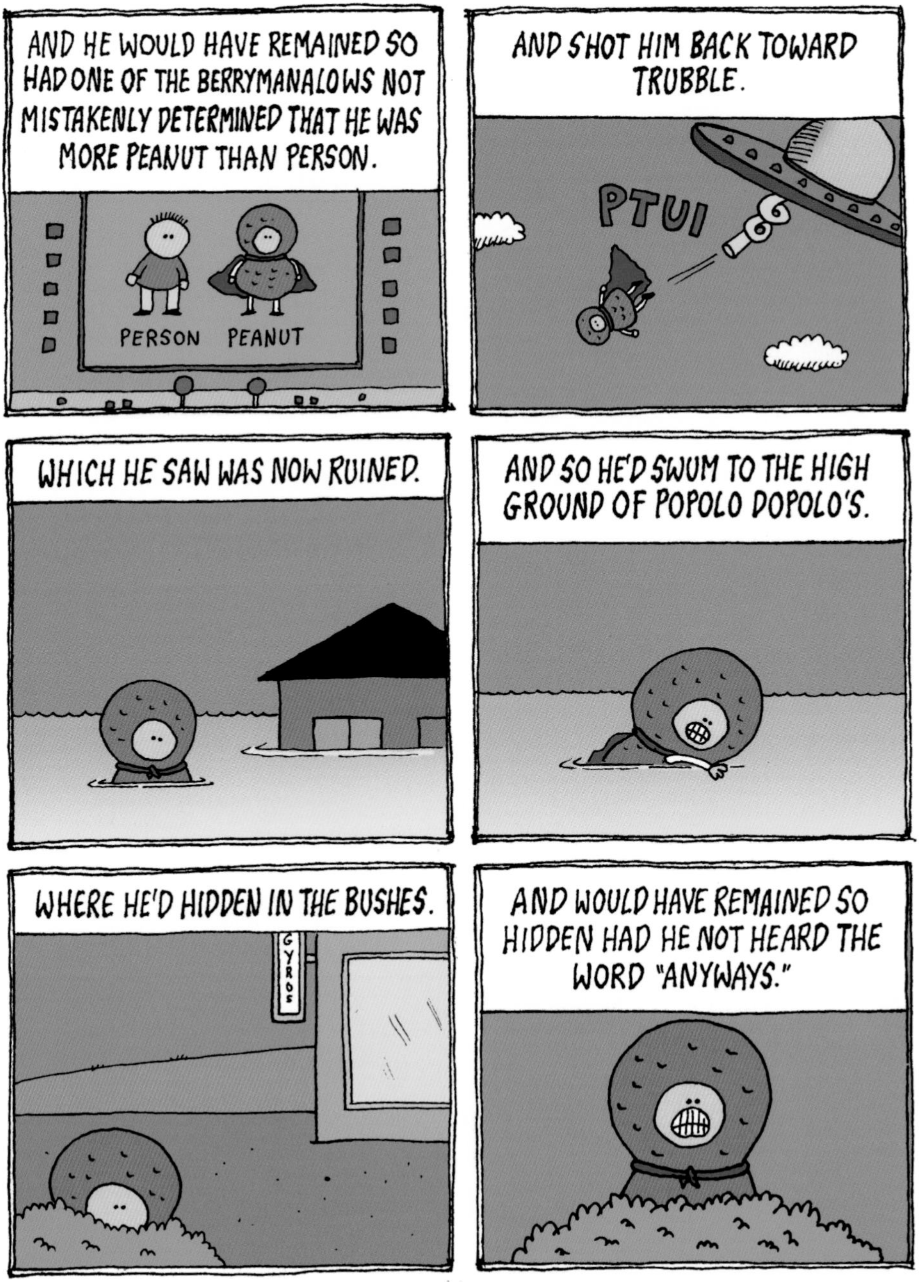
AND HE WOULD HAVE REMAINED SO HAD ONE OF THE BERRYMANALOWS NOT MISTAKENLY DETERMINED THAT HE WAS MORE PEANUT THAN PERSON.
PERSON
PEANUT
AND SHOT HIM BACK TOWARD TRUBBLE.
PTUI
WHICH HE SAW WAS NOW RUINED.
AND SO HE'D SWUM TO THE HIGH GROUND OF POPOLO DOPOLO'S.
WHERE HE'D HIDDEN IN THE BUSHES.
GYROS
AND WOULD HAVE REMAINED SO HIDDEN HAD HE NOT HEARD THE WORD "ANYWAYS."

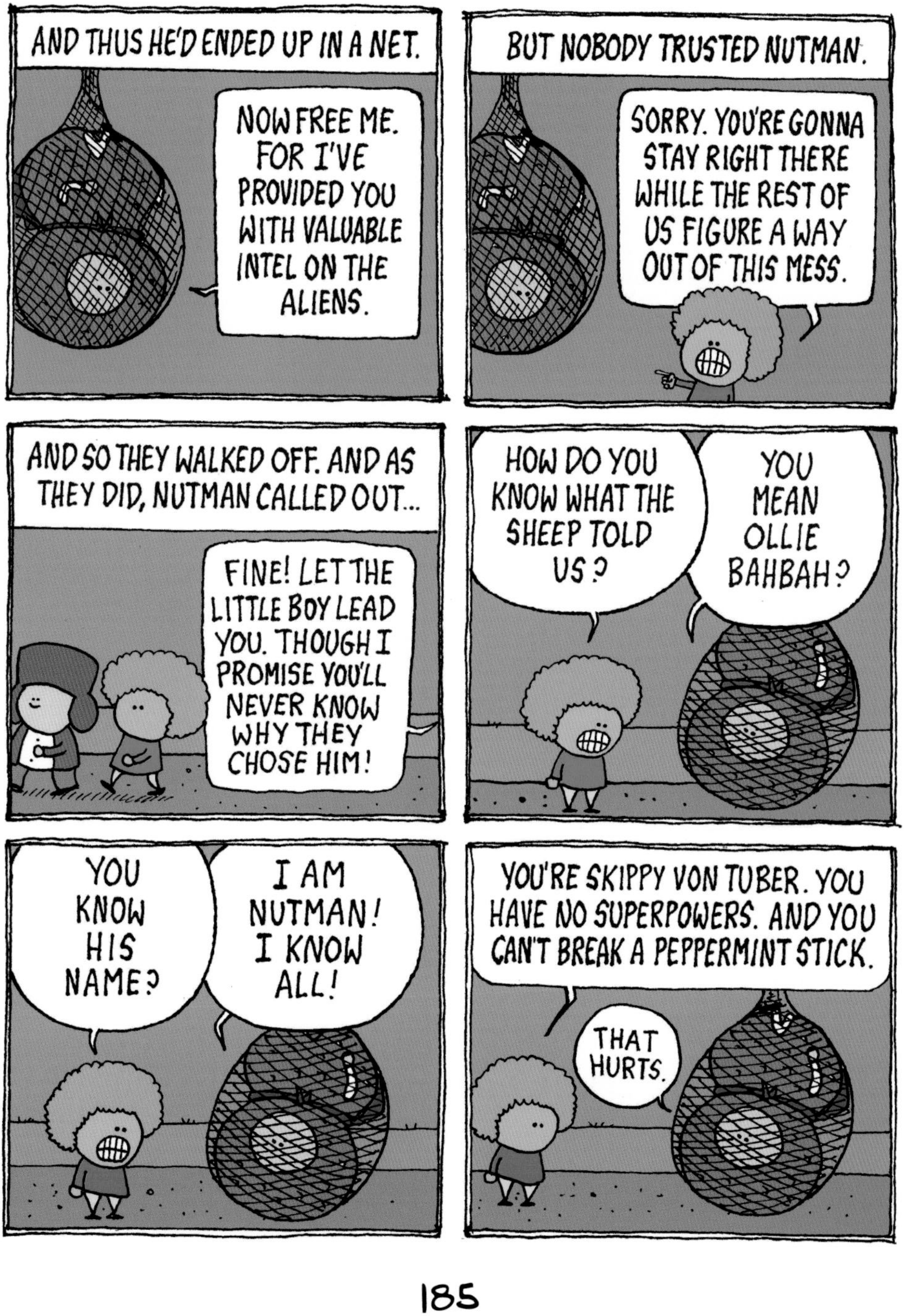
AND THUS HE'D ENDED UP IN A NET.
NOW FREE ME. FOR I'VE PROVIDED YOU WITH VALUABLE INTEL ON THE ALIENS.
BUT NOBODY TRUSTED NUTMAN.
SORRY. YOU'RE GONNA STAY RIGHT THERE WHILE THE REST OF US FIGURE A WAY OUT OF THIS MESS.
AND SO THEY WALKED OFF. AND AS THEY DID, NUTMAN CALLED OUT...
FINE! LET THE LITTLE BOY LEAD YOU. THOUGH I PROMISE YOU'LL NEVER KNOW WHY THEY CHOSE HIM!
HOW DO YOU KNOW WHAT THE SHEEP TOLD US?
YOU MEAN OLLIE BAHBAH?
YOU KNOW HIS NAME?
I AM NUTMAN! I KNOW ALL!
YOU'RE SKIPPY VON TUBER. YOU HAVE NO SUPERPOWERS. AND YOU CAN'T BREAK A PEPPERMINT STICK.
THAT HURTS.

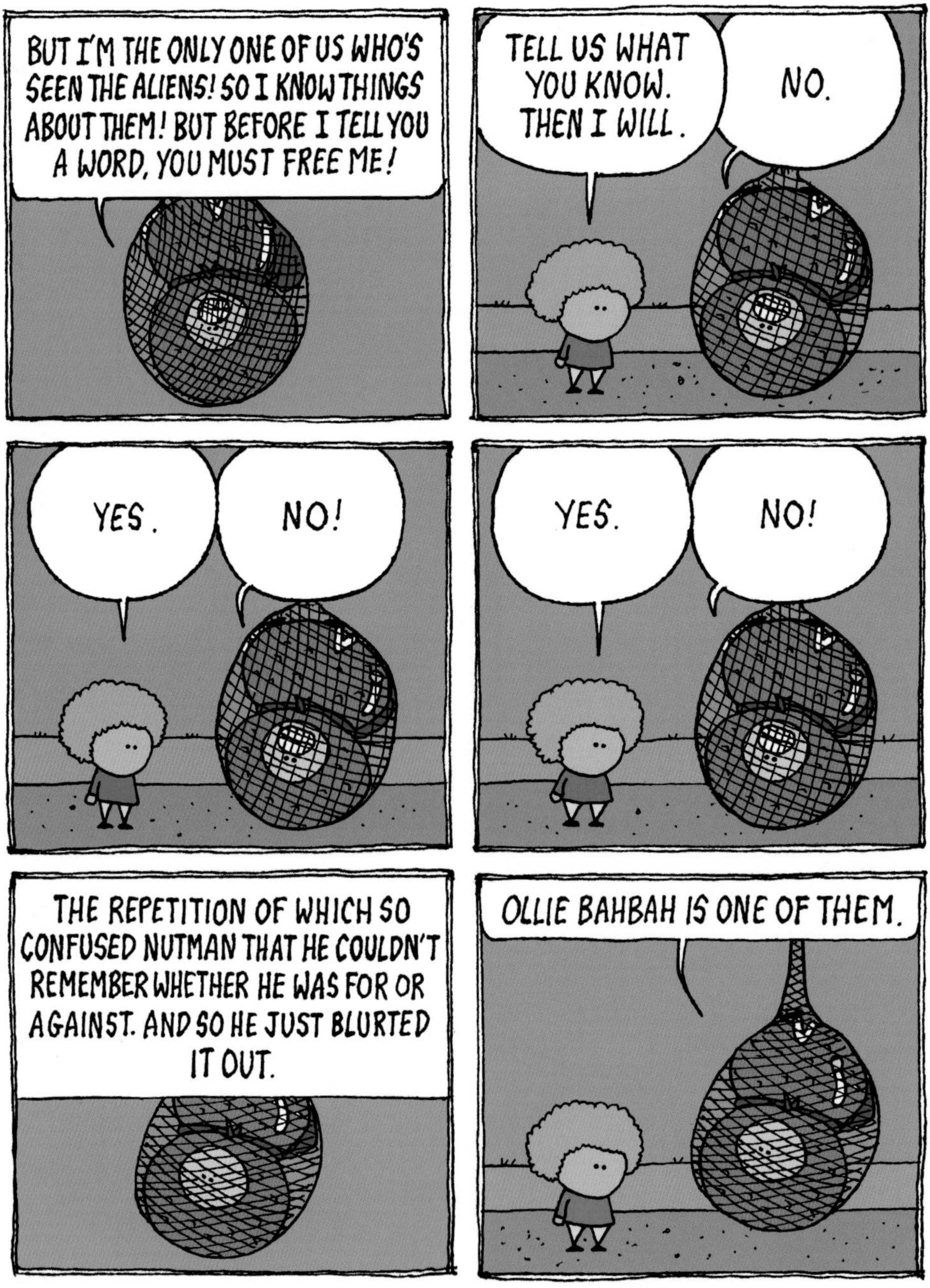
BUT I'M THE ONLY ONE OF US WHO'S SEEN THE ALIENS! SO I KNOW THINGS ABOUT THEM! BUT BEFORE I TELL YOU A WORD, YOU MUST FREE ME!
TELL US WHAT YOU KNOW. THEN I WILL.
NO.
YES.
NO!
YES.
NO!
THE REPETITION OF WHICH SO CONFUSED NUTMAN THAT HE COULDN'T REMEMBER WHETHER HE WAS FOR OR AGAINST. AND SO HE JUST BLURTED IT OUT.
OLLIE BAHBAH IS ONE OF THEM.

CHAPTER 34

IN WHICH...

WE PRETEND THAT CALLING THE LAST CHAPTER "CHAPTER 33" WAS CORRECT AND JUST KEEP GOING

189

CHAPTER 35

IN WHICH...

OUR STREAK OF NUMBERING CHAPTERS CORRECTLY CONTINUES

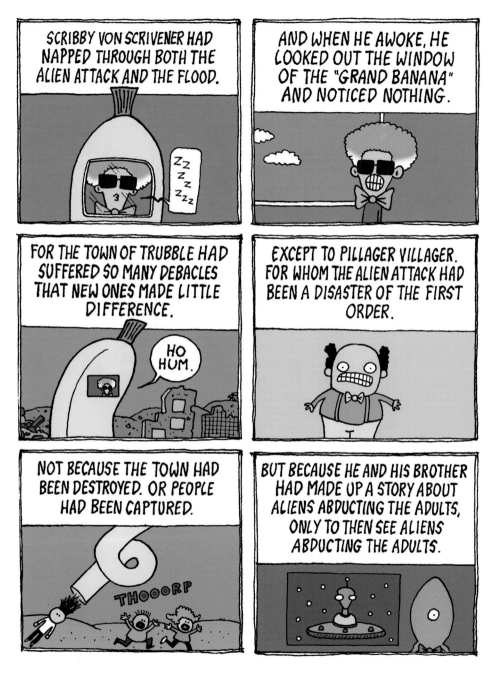

193

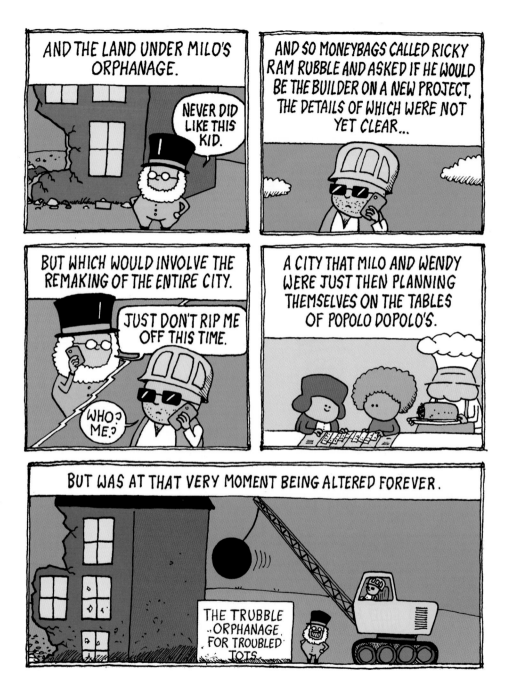

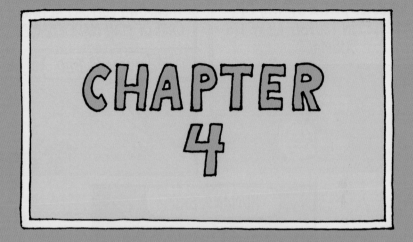

CHAPTER 4

IN WHICH...

OUR STREAK OF NUMBERING CHAPTERS CORRECTLY ENDS

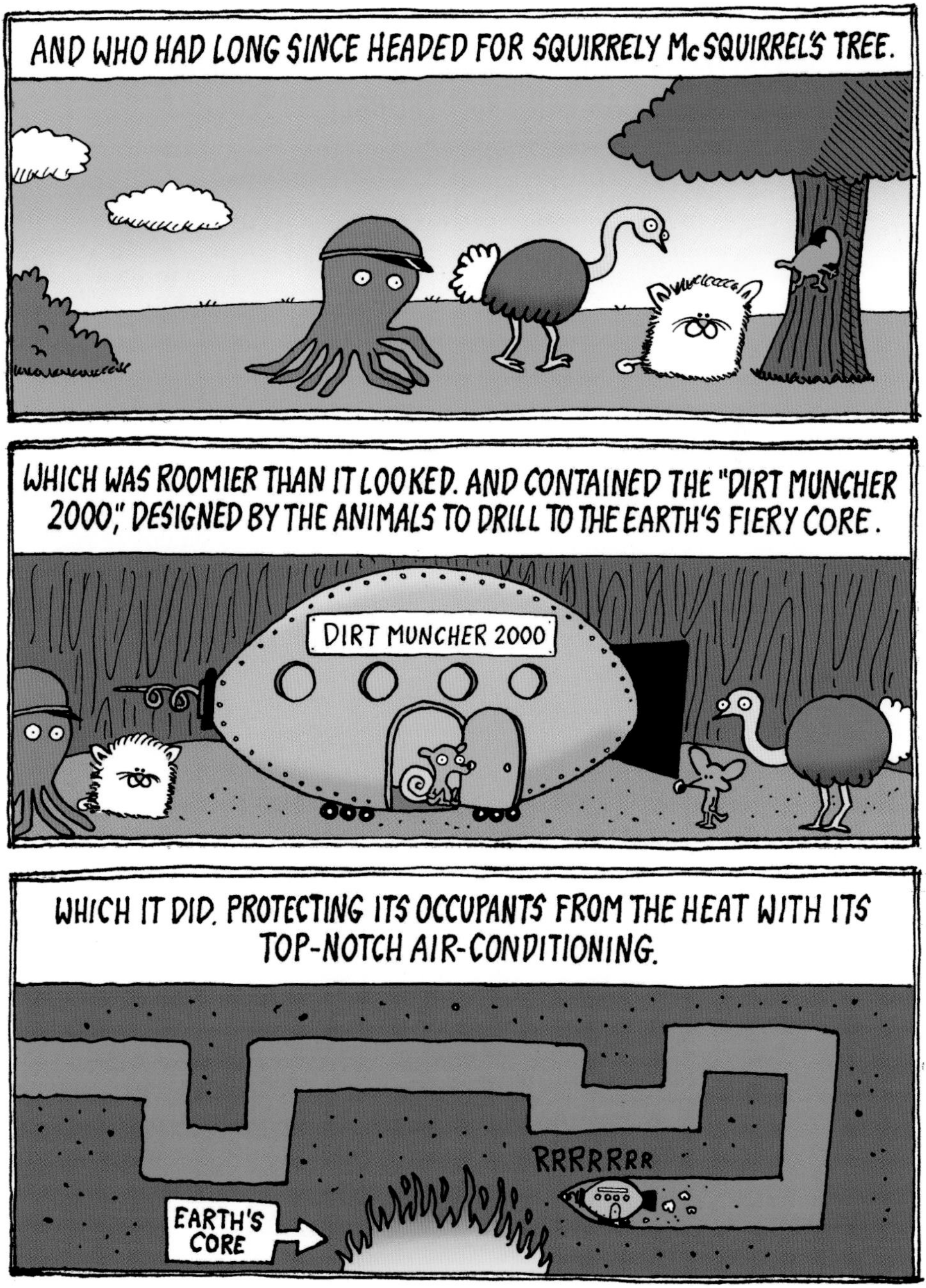
AND WHO HAD LONG SINCE HEADED FOR SQUIRRELY McSQUIRREL'S TREE.
WHICH WAS ROOMIER THAN IT LOOKED. AND CONTAINED THE "DIRT MUNCHER 2000," DESIGNED BY THE ANIMALS TO DRILL TO THE EARTH'S FIERY CORE.
DIRT MUNCHER 2000
WHICH IT DID. PROTECTING ITS OCCUPANTS FROM THE HEAT WITH ITS TOP-NOTCH AIR-CONDITIONING.
RRRRRRR
EARTH'S CORE

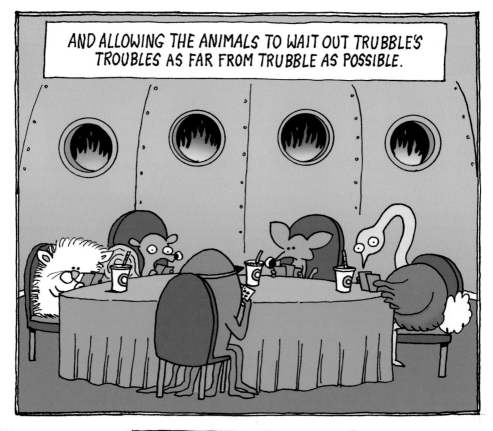

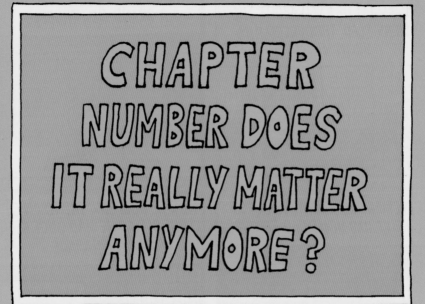

CHAPTER
NUMBER DOES
IT REALLY MATTER
ANYMORE ?

IN WHICH...

WE THINK YOU'LL
AGREE THAT
IT DOESN'T

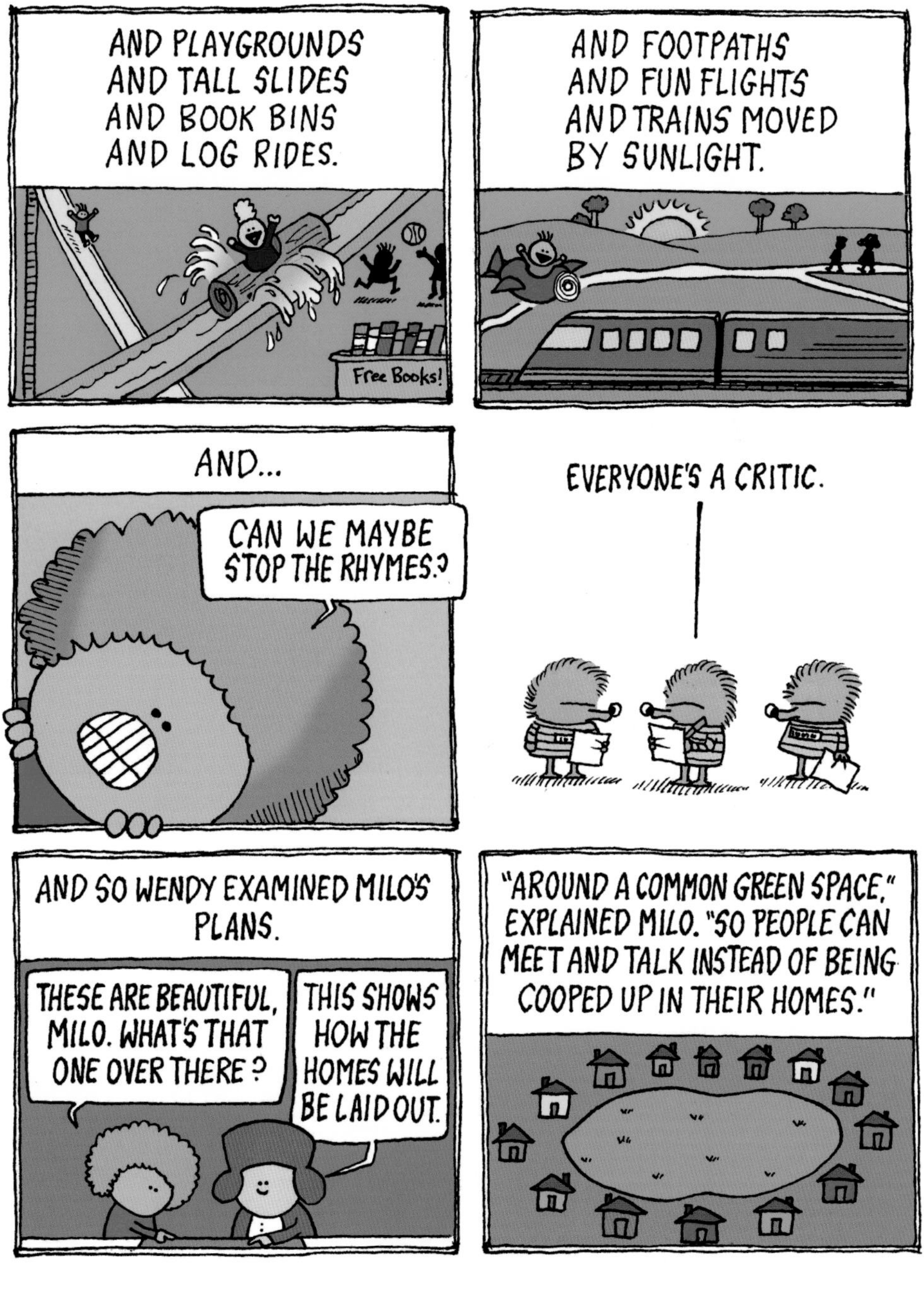
AND PLAYGROUNDS AND TALL SLIDES AND BOOK BINS AND LOG RIDES.
Free Books!
AND FOOTPATHS AND FUN FLIGHTS AND TRAINS MOVED BY SUNLIGHT.
AND...
CAN WE MAYBE STOP THE RHYMES.?
EVERYONE'S A CRITIC.
AND SO WENDY EXAMINED MILO'S PLANS.
THESE ARE BEAUTIFUL, MILO. WHAT'S THAT ONE OVER THERE?
THIS SHOWS HOW THE HOMES WILL BE LAID OUT.
"AROUND A COMMON GREEN SPACE," EXPLAINED MILO. "SO PEOPLE CAN MEET AND TALK INSTEAD OF BEING COOPED UP IN THEIR HOMES."

206

CHAPTER
4,000

WHICH IS...

A CHAPTER NUMBER WE'RE PRETTY SURE NO BOOK HAS EVER REACHED, SO WE THOUGHT WE'D TRY IT HERE

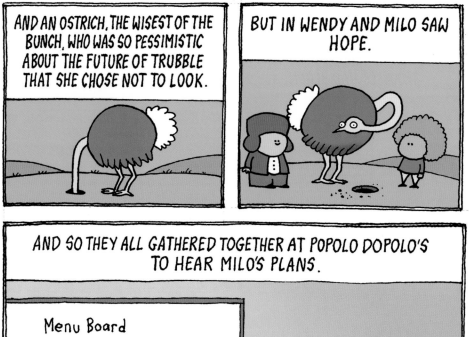

AND AN OSTRICH, THE WISEST OF THE BUNCH, WHO WAS SO PESSIMISTIC ABOUT THE FUTURE OF TRUBBLE THAT SHE CHOSE NOT TO LOOK.

BUT IN WENDY AND MILO SAW HOPE.

AND SO THEY ALL GATHERED TOGETHER AT POPOLO DOPOLO'S TO HEAR MILO'S PLANS.

Menu Board

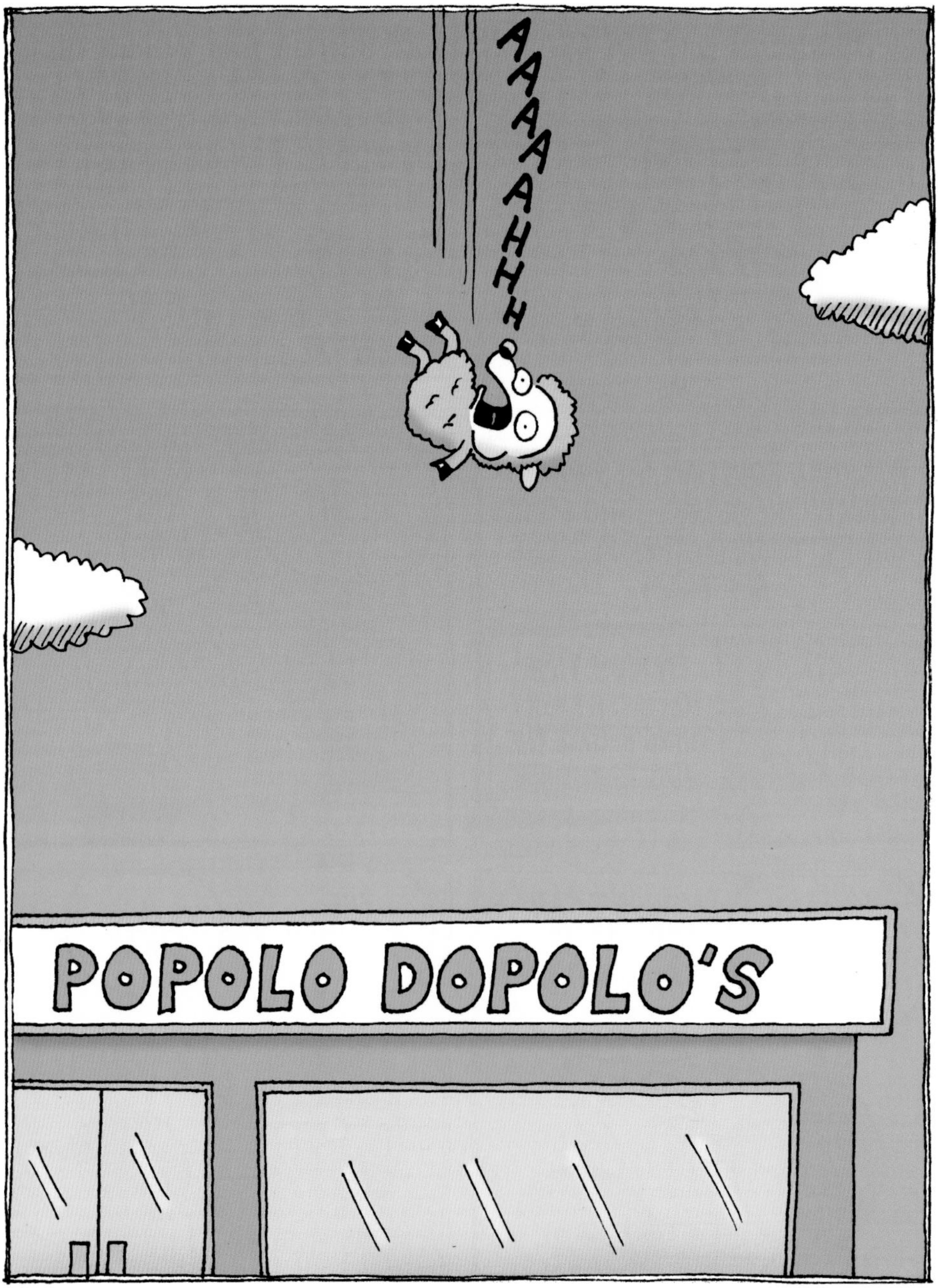
AAAAAAHHH
POPOLO DOPOLO'S

CHAPTER LOOKOUT

IN WHICH...

YOU SHOULD COVER YOUR HEAD FOR PROTECTION

KSSHHHH

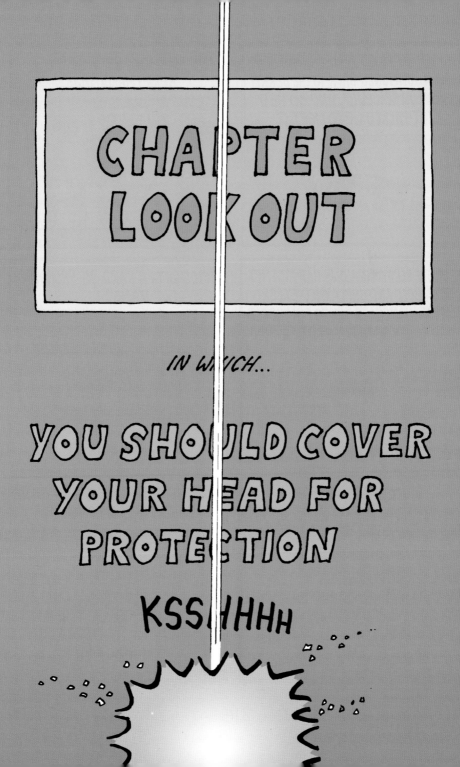

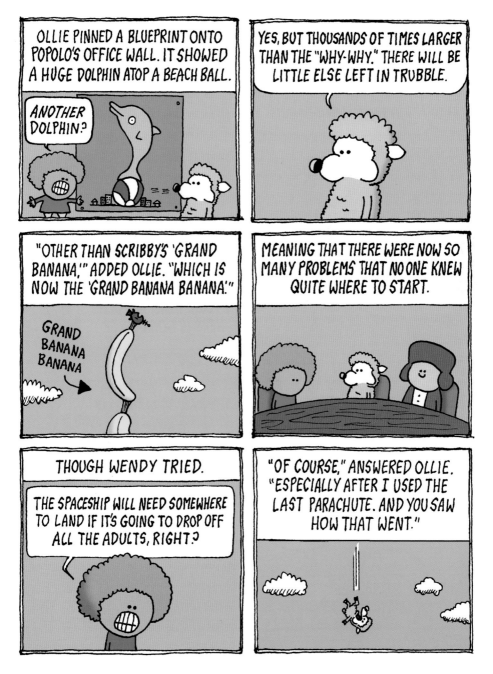

220

CHAPTER NOBEL PRIZE

WHICH IS...

... WHAT WE SHOULD WIN FOR WRITING THIS BOOK.

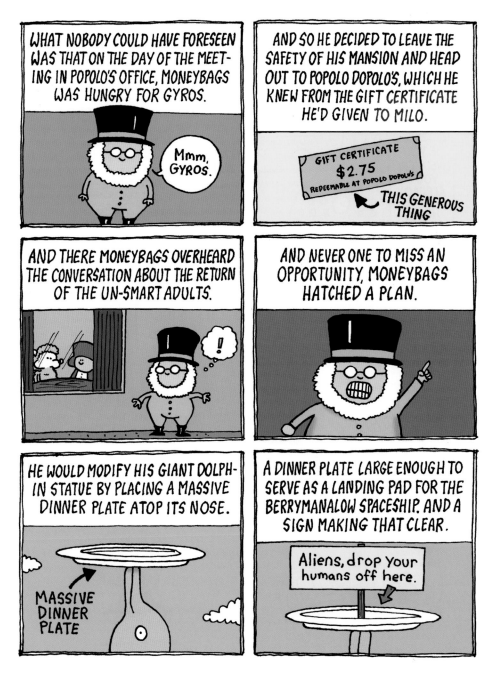

CHAPTER SHORT

WHICH IS....

SHORT

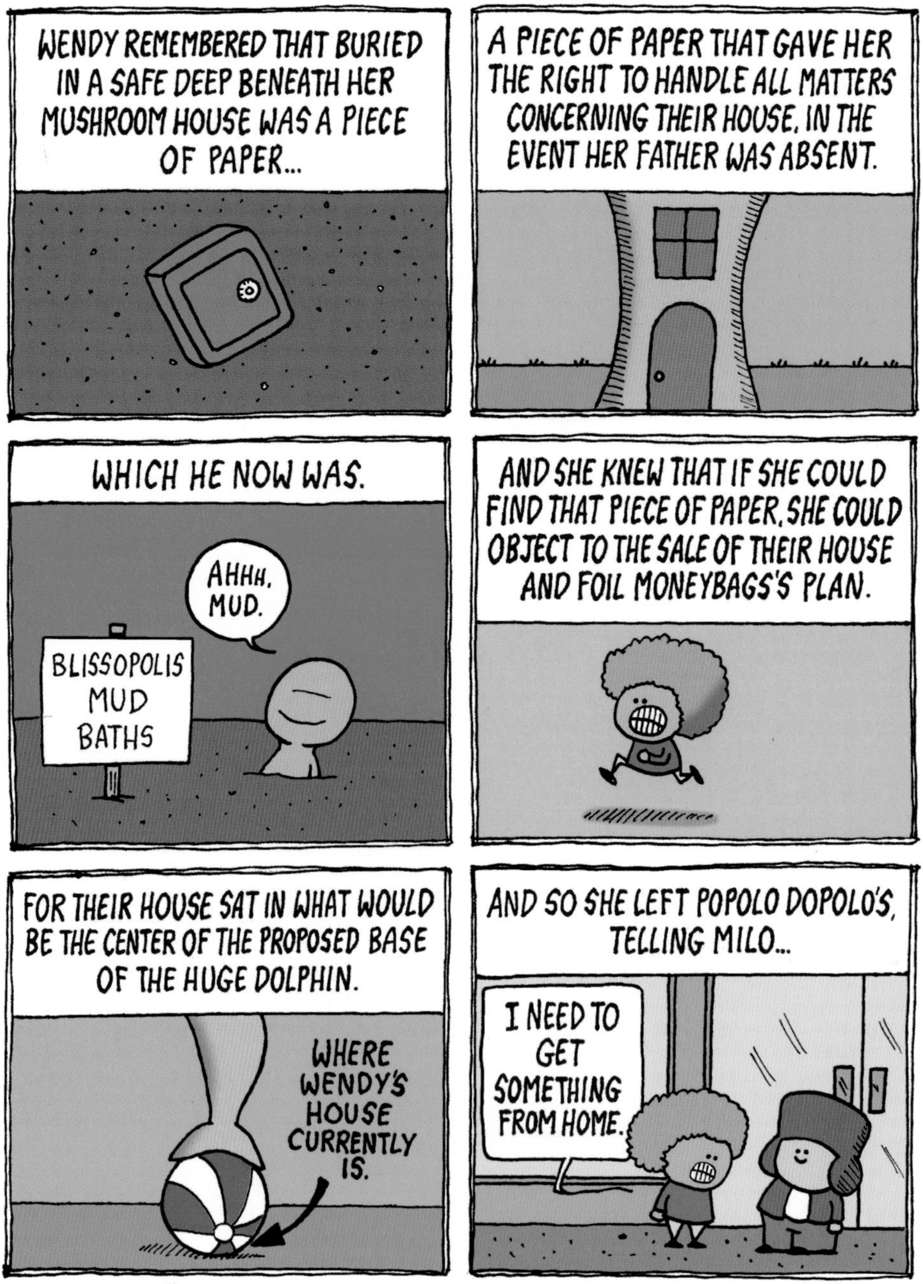
WENDY REMEMBERED THAT BURIED IN A SAFE DEEP BENEATH HER MUSHROOM HOUSE WAS A PIECE OF PAPER...
A PIECE OF PAPER THAT GAVE HER THE RIGHT TO HANDLE ALL MATTERS CONCERNING THEIR HOUSE, IN THE EVENT HER FATHER WAS ABSENT.
WHICH HE NOW WAS.
AHHH. MUD.
BLISSOPOLIS MUD BATHS
AND SHE KNEW THAT IF SHE COULD FIND THAT PIECE OF PAPER, SHE COULD OBJECT TO THE SALE OF THEIR HOUSE AND FOIL MONEYBAGS'S PLAN.
FOR THEIR HOUSE SAT IN WHAT WOULD BE THE CENTER OF THE PROPOSED BASE OF THE HUGE DOLPHIN.
WHERE WENDY'S HOUSE CURRENTLY IS.
AND SO SHE LEFT POPOLO DOPOLO'S, TELLING MILO...
I NEED TO GET SOMETHING FROM HOME.

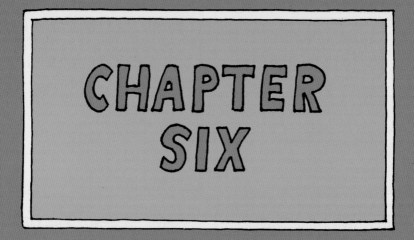

CHAPTER SIX

WHICH IS...

A
NUMBER
WE
DON'T
THINK
WE'VE
USED
YET

IT TURNED OUT THAT THE MODEST OLLIE KNEW MORE ABOUT CHEMISTRY AND PHYSICS THAN ANY OF THE OTHER BERRYMANALOWS.

AND SO OLLIE BEGAN DESIGNING THE "CATERPILLAR O' CHANGE," A LANDING PAD FOR THE ALIEN SPACESHIP.

SO NAMED BECAUSE WHEN THE PEOPLE LANDED ON IT, THEY WOULD BE TRANSFORMED FROM WHO THEY HAD BECOME TO NEW AND IMPROVED HUMANS.

JUST AS A LUMPY CATERPILLAR BECOMES A GRACEFUL BUTTERFLY.

A FEAT THAT WOULD BE ACHIEVED WITH THE "MIST O' GOODNESS," THE PRECISE INGREDIENTS OF WHICH ARE SO SECRET, THEY CANNOT BE LISTED HERE.

FOUR OUNCES
TWO SHAK
THR

CENSORED

BUT WHICH, IT CAN BE SAID, WOULD BE SPRAYED RIGHT UP THEIR NOSES.

FSSSHHH

229

230

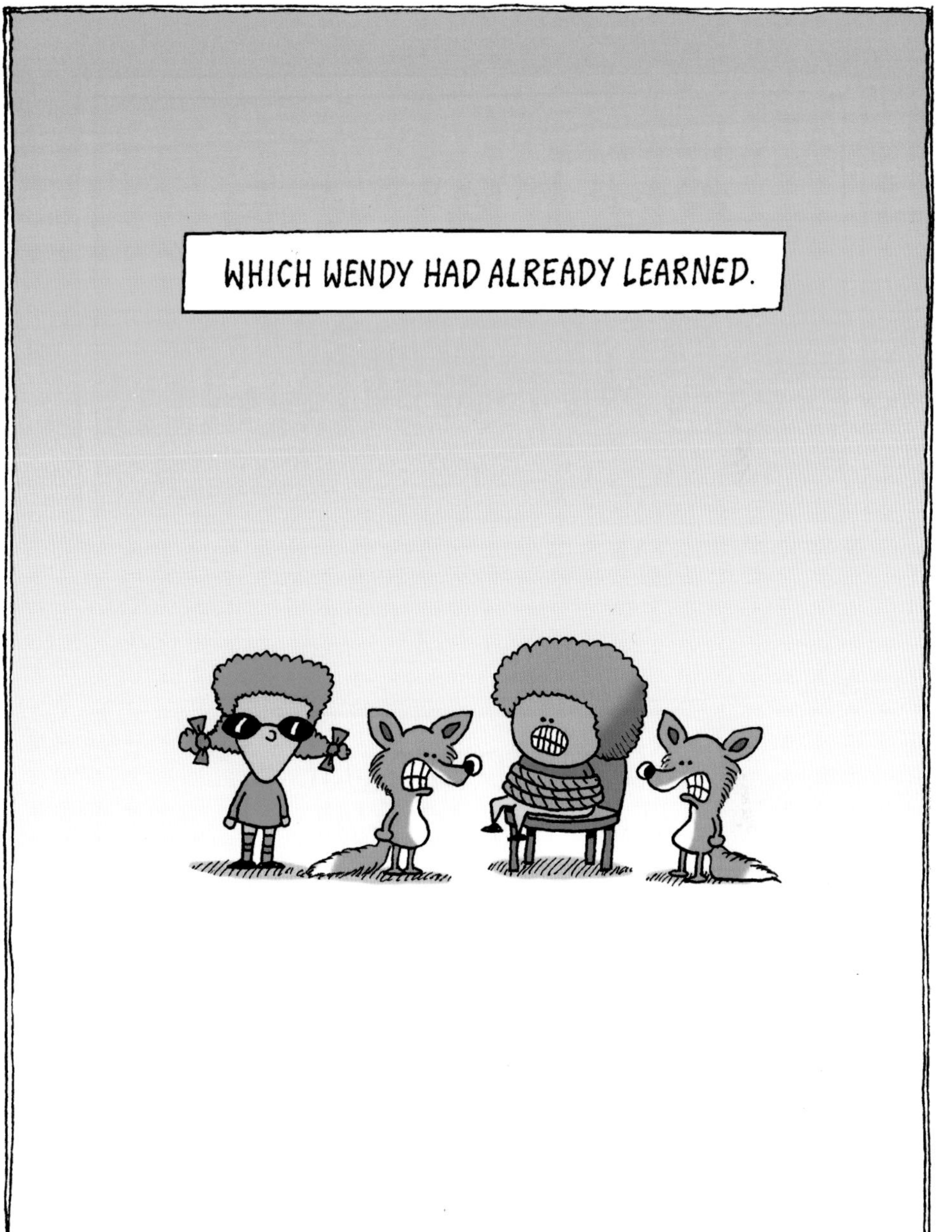
WHICH WENDY HAD ALREADY LEARNED.

AS MILO RAN TO SAVE WENDY, HE BEGAN TO FIGURE EVERYTHING OUT.

LIKE THE FACT THAT WHEN THE ADULTS HAD DISAPPEARED IN THE "GRAND TILT-A-TABLE," THE WAYNENOOTONIANS HAD CORRECTLY GUESSED THAT MILO WOULD RUN TO WENDY FOR HELP.

WENDEEEEEE!

WHICH IS WHERE THEY'D SOUGHT TO CAPTURE HIM.

THE ONLY THING HE DIDN'T KNOW WAS WHY THEY HADN'T JUST GRABBED HIM AT THE ORPHANAGE.

THE TRUBBLE ORPHANAGE FOR TROUBLED TOTS

AND THAT WAS BECAUSE THE WAYNENOOTONIANS FEARED IT. FOR THEY HAD HEARD IT WAS STOCKED WITH DYNAMITE.

DYNAMITE

DYNAMITE

IT WAS.

AND THOUGH THEY HAD HAD MILO TRAPPED AT WENDY'S, THEY'D BECOME DISTRACTED WHEN THEY'D HEARD THAT OLLIE—A BERRY-MANALOW ALIEN—WAS IN THE "GRAND BANANA."

240

241

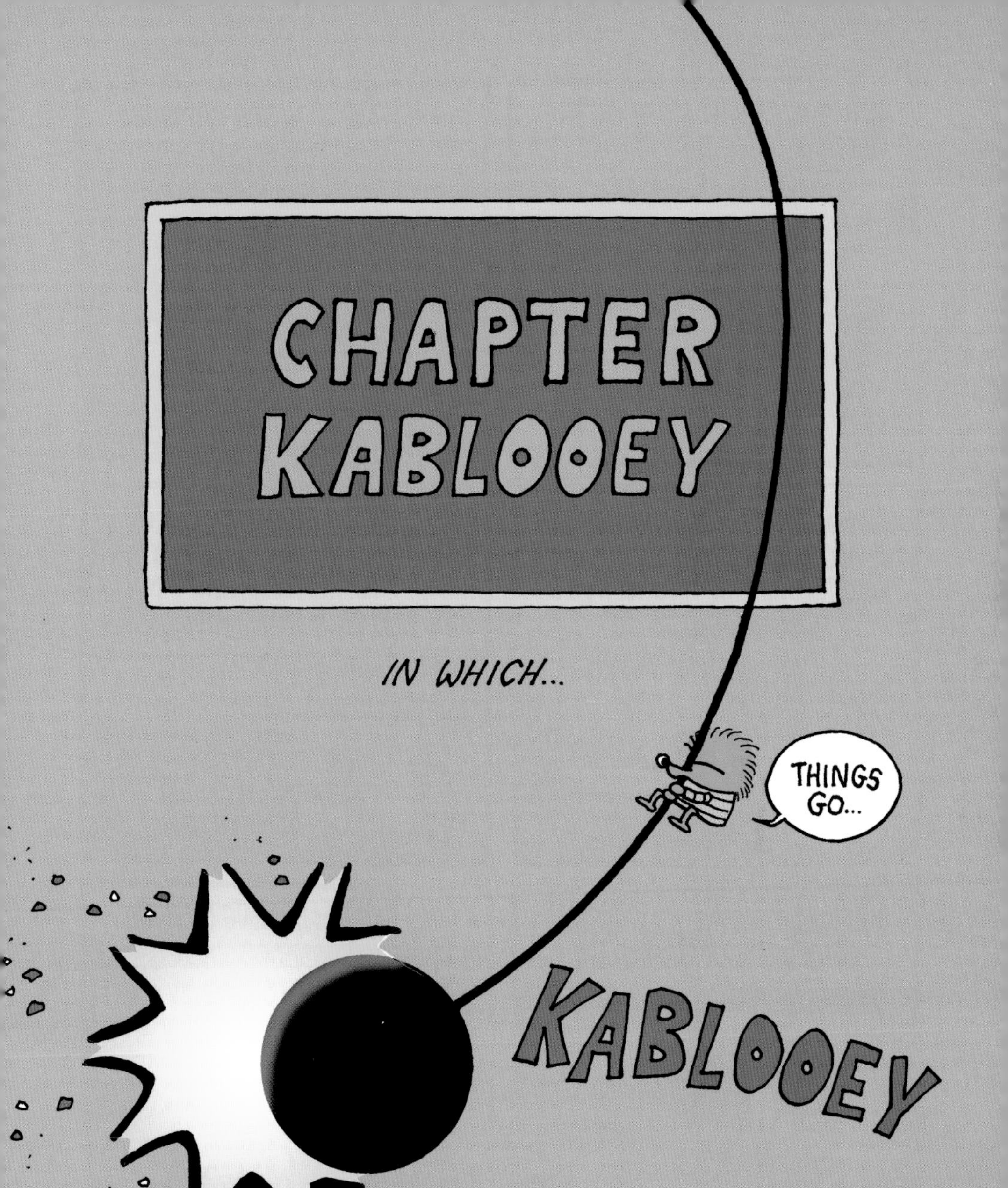
CHAPTER
KABLOOEY
IN WHICH...
THINGS GO...
KABLOOEY

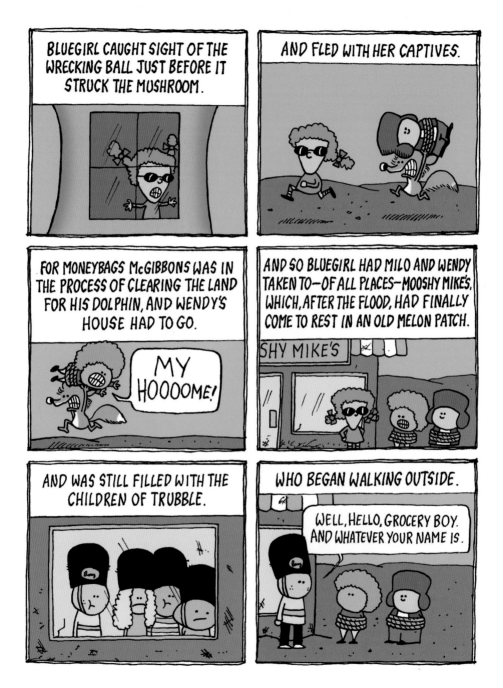

BLUEGIRL CAUGHT SIGHT OF THE WRECKING BALL JUST BEFORE IT STRUCK THE MUSHROOM.

AND FLED WITH HER CAPTIVES.

FOR MONEYBAGS McGIBBONS WAS IN THE PROCESS OF CLEARING THE LAND FOR HIS DOLPHIN, AND WENDY'S HOUSE HAD TO GO.

MY HOOOOME!

AND SO BLUEGIRL HAD MILO AND WENDY TAKEN TO—OF ALL PLACES—MOOSHY MIKE'S, WHICH, AFTER THE FLOOD, HAD FINALLY COME TO REST IN AN OLD MELON PATCH.

SHY MIKE'S

AND WAS STILL FILLED WITH THE CHILDREN OF TRUBBLE.

WHO BEGAN WALKING OUTSIDE.

WELL, HELLO, GROCERY BOY. AND WHATEVER YOUR NAME IS.

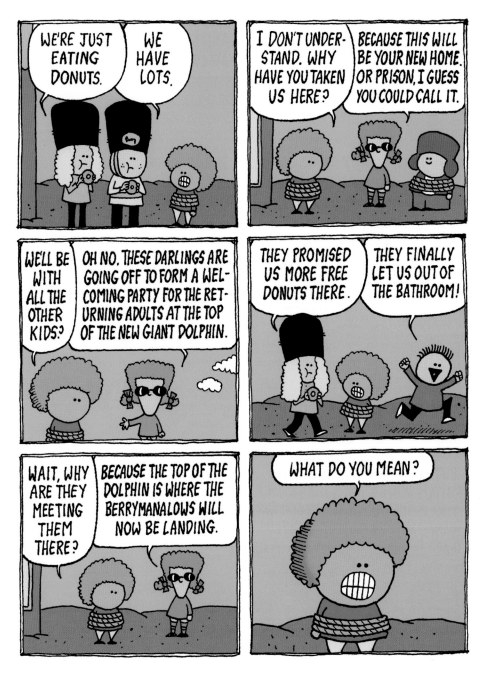

245

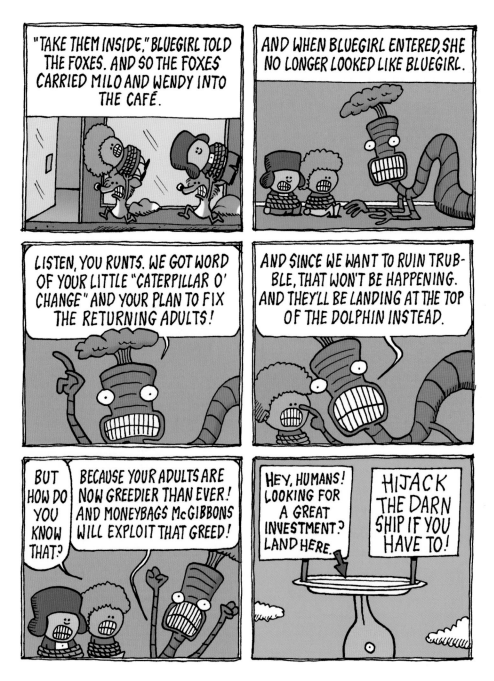

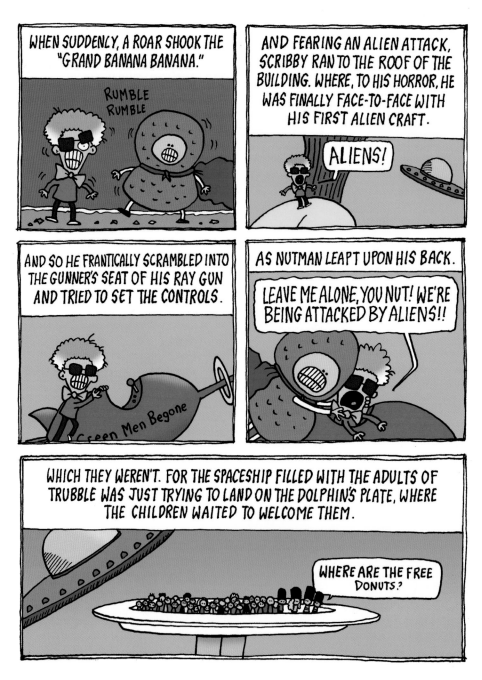

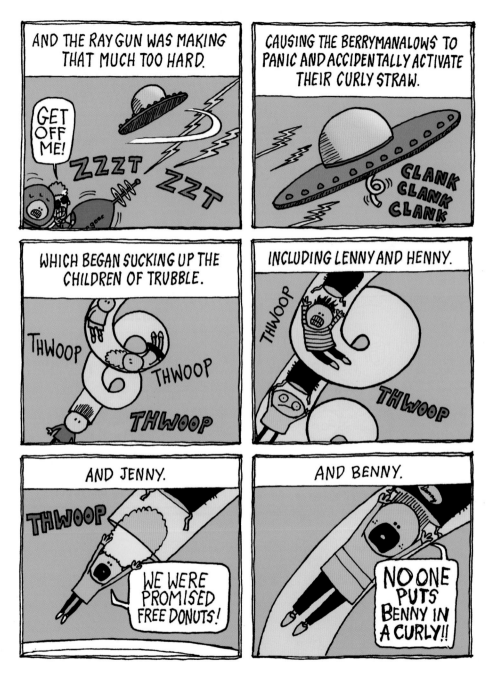

253

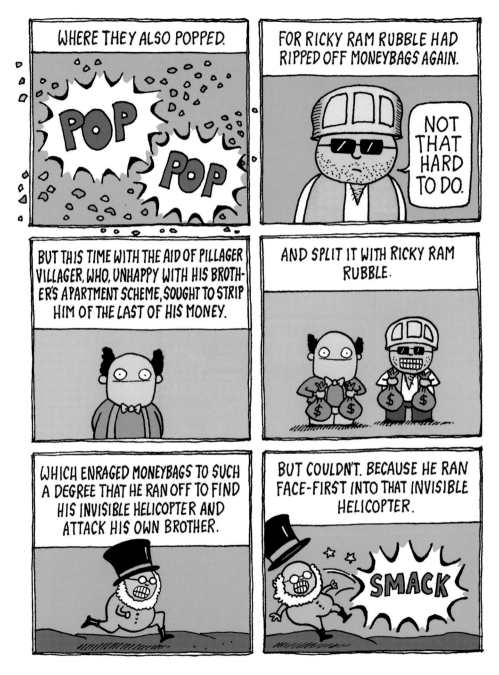

WHERE THEY ALSO POPPED.

POP POP

FOR RICKY RAM RUBBLE HAD RIPPED OFF MONEYBAGS AGAIN.

NOT THAT HARD TO DO.

BUT THIS TIME WITH THE AID OF PILLAGER VILLAGER, WHO, UNHAPPY WITH HIS BROTHER'S APARTMENT SCHEME, SOUGHT TO STRIP HIM OF THE LAST OF HIS MONEY.

AND SPLIT IT WITH RICKY RAM RUBBLE.

$ $ $ $

WHICH ENRAGED MONEYBAGS TO SUCH A DEGREE THAT HE RAN OFF TO FIND HIS INVISIBLE HELICOPTER AND ATTACK HIS OWN BROTHER.

BUT COULDN'T. BECAUSE HE RAN FACE-FIRST INTO THAT INVISIBLE HELICOPTER.

SMACK

AND DIED.

AND SO MONEYBAGS'S RESPONSE TO HIS ONCE-POOR BROTHER'S REQUESTS...

COULD I PLEASE HAVE MONEY FOR A PIE?

OVER MY DEAD BODY.

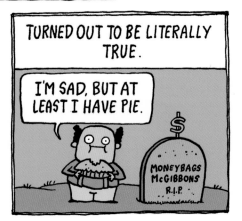

TURNED OUT TO BE LITERALLY TRUE.

I'M SAD, BUT AT LEAST I HAVE PIE.

MONEYBAGS McGIBBONS R.I.P.

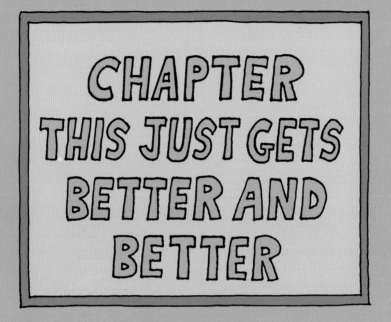

CHAPTER
THIS JUST GETS
BETTER AND
BETTER

IN WHICH...

WE THROW ALL PRETENSE OF
HUMILITY OUT THE WINDOW
BECAUSE THIS CHAPTER
REALLY IS THAT GOOD

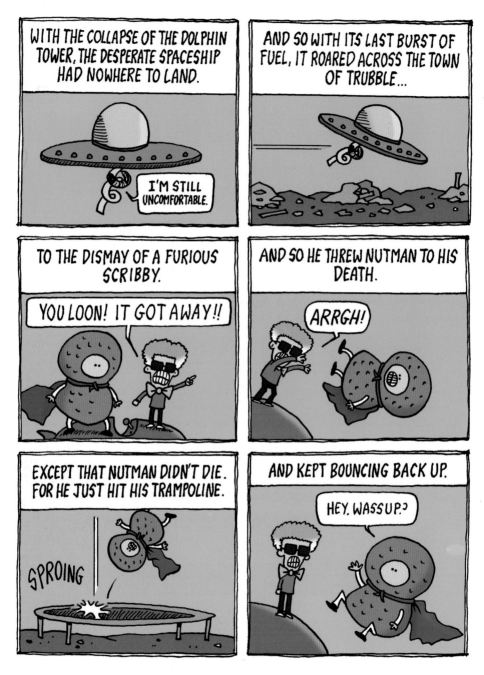

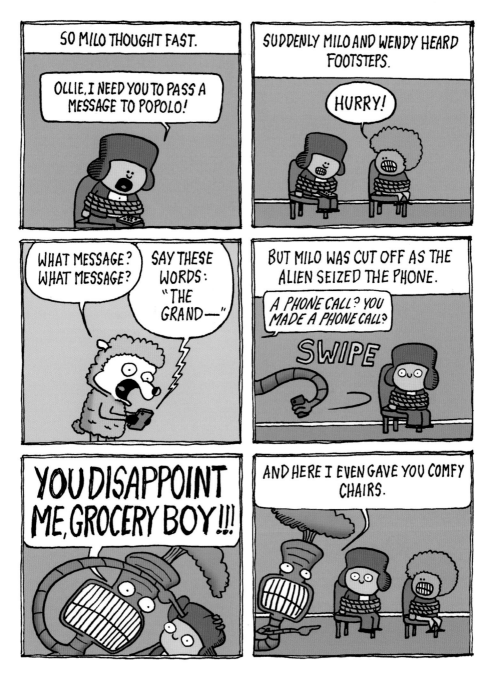

CHAPTER

SMALL

IN WHICH...

THE CHAPTER HEADING
STRAINS YOUR EYESIGHT

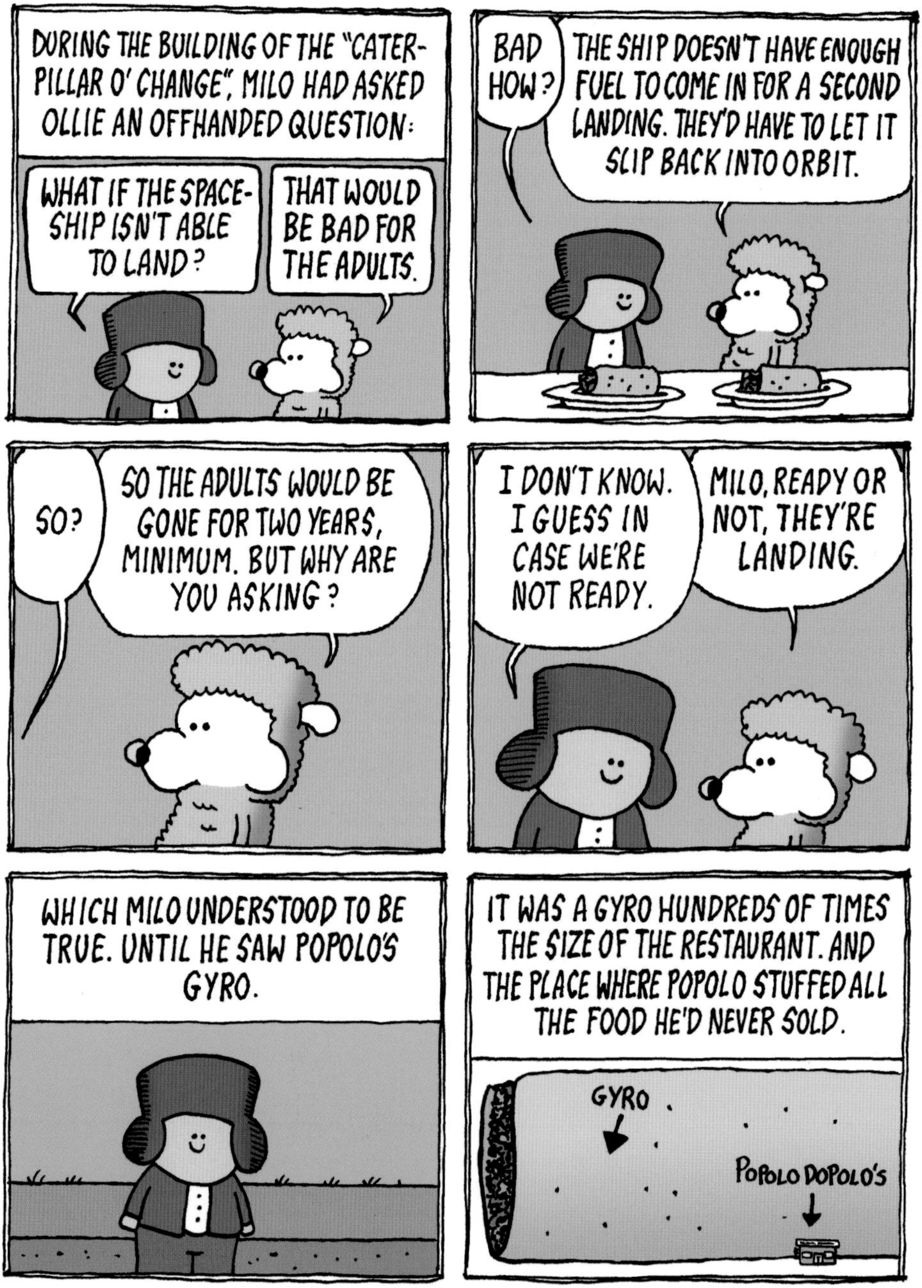
DURING THE BUILDING OF THE "CATERPILLAR O' CHANGE", MILO HAD ASKED OLLIE AN OFFHANDED QUESTION:
WHAT IF THE SPACESHIP ISN'T ABLE TO LAND?
THAT WOULD BE BAD FOR THE ADULTS.
BAD HOW?
THE SHIP DOESN'T HAVE ENOUGH FUEL TO COME IN FOR A SECOND LANDING. THEY'D HAVE TO LET IT SLIP BACK INTO ORBIT.
SO?
SO THE ADULTS WOULD BE GONE FOR TWO YEARS, MINIMUM. BUT WHY ARE YOU ASKING?
I DON'T KNOW. I GUESS IN CASE WE'RE NOT READY.
MILO, READY OR NOT, THEY'RE LANDING.
WHICH MILO UNDERSTOOD TO BE TRUE. UNTIL HE SAW POPOLO'S GYRO.
IT WAS A GYRO HUNDREDS OF TIMES THE SIZE OF THE RESTAURANT. AND THE PLACE WHERE POPOLO STUFFED ALL THE FOOD HE'D NEVER SOLD.
GYRO
POPOLO DOPOLO'S

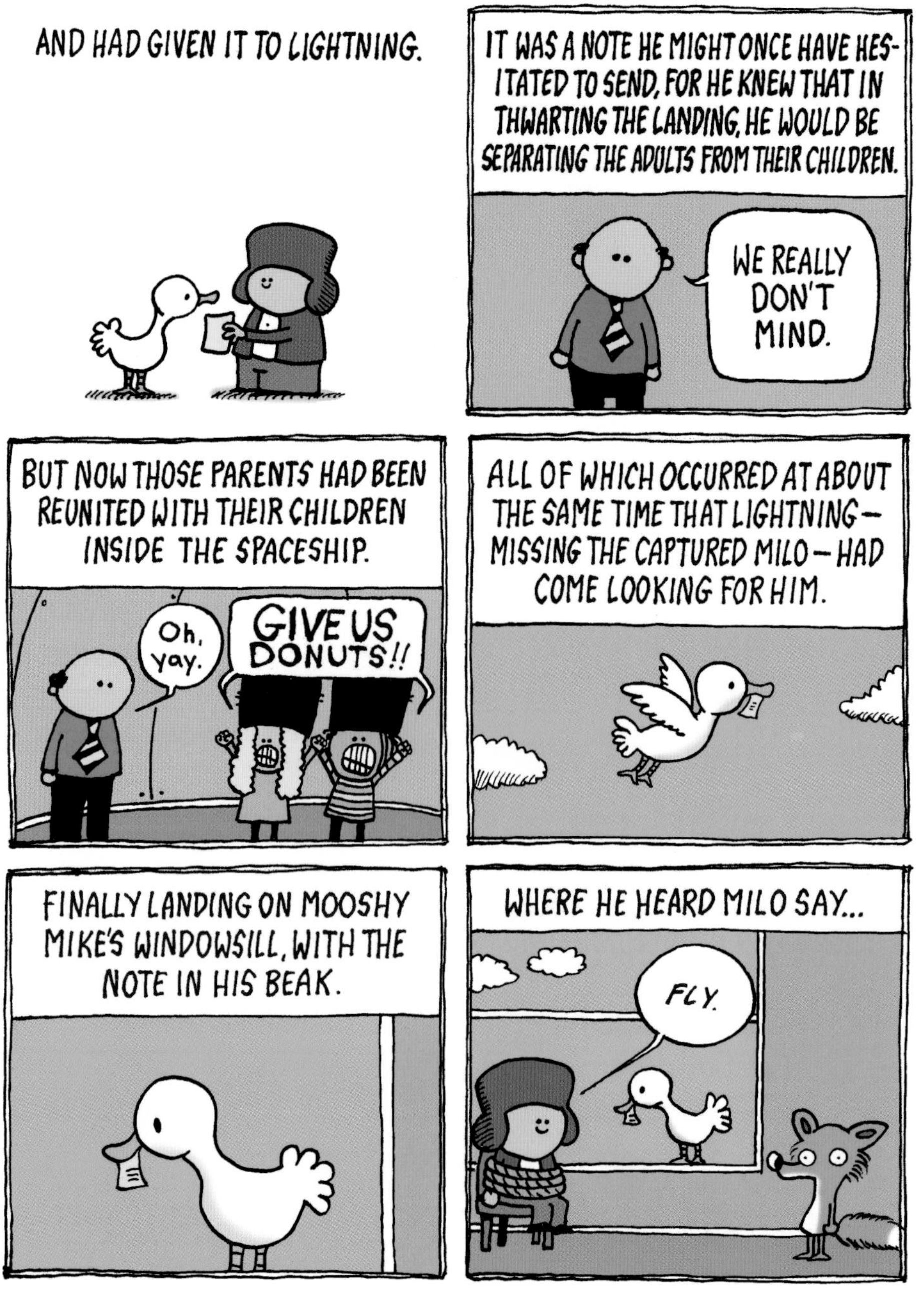
AND HAD GIVEN IT TO LIGHTNING.
IT WAS A NOTE HE MIGHT ONCE HAVE HESITATED TO SEND, FOR HE KNEW THAT IN THWARTING THE LANDING, HE WOULD BE SEPARATING THE ADULTS FROM THEIR CHILDREN.
WE REALLY DON'T MIND.
BUT NOW THOSE PARENTS HAD BEEN REUNITED WITH THEIR CHILDREN INSIDE THE SPACESHIP.
Oh, yay.
GIVE US DONUTS!!
ALL OF WHICH OCCURRED AT ABOUT THE SAME TIME THAT LIGHTNING—MISSING THE CAPTURED MILO—HAD COME LOOKING FOR HIM.
FINALLY LANDING ON MOOSHY MIKE'S WINDOWSILL, WITH THE NOTE IN HIS BEAK.
WHERE HE HEARD MILO SAY...
FLY.

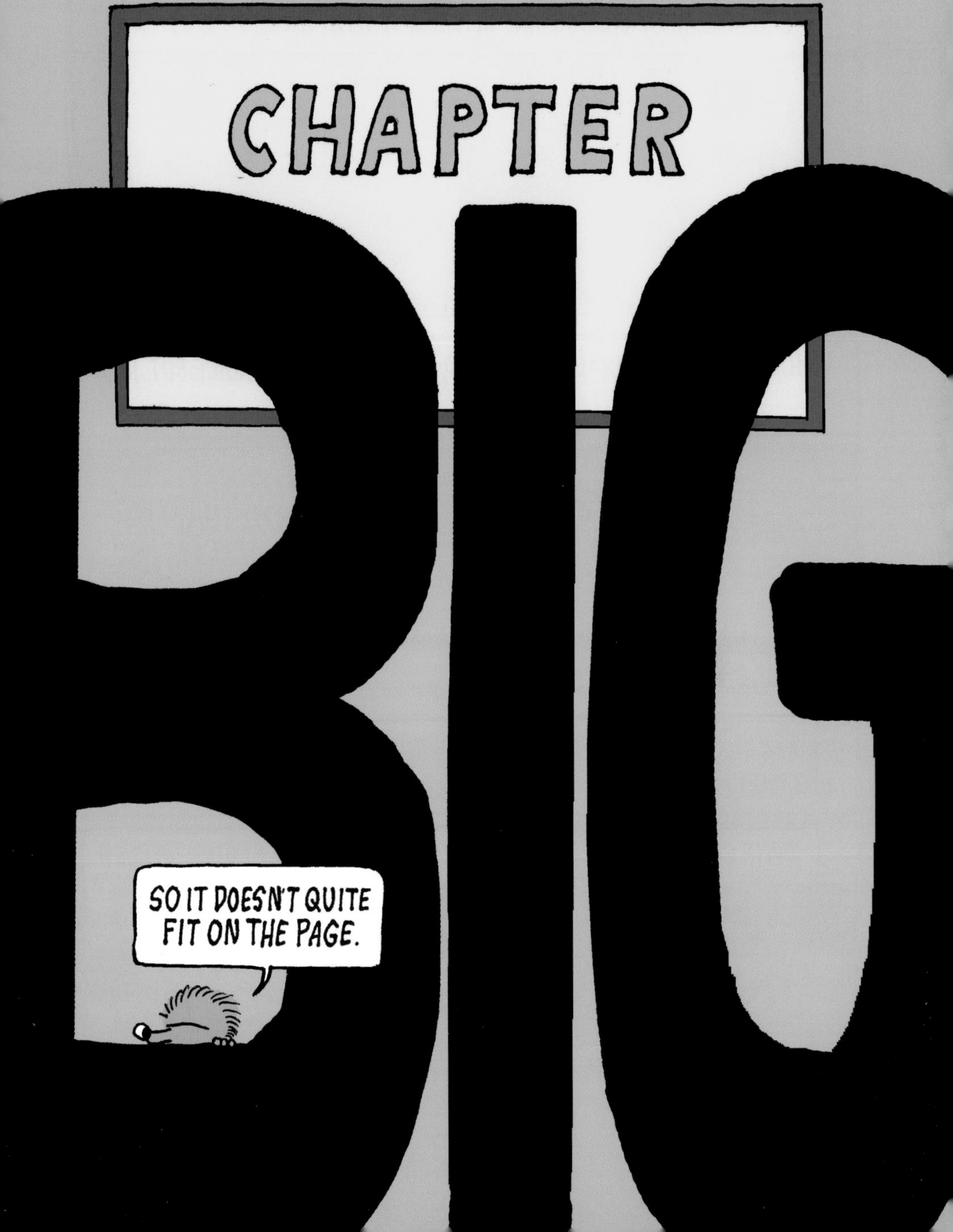
CHAPTER
BIG
SO IT DOESN'T QUITE FIT ON THE PAGE.

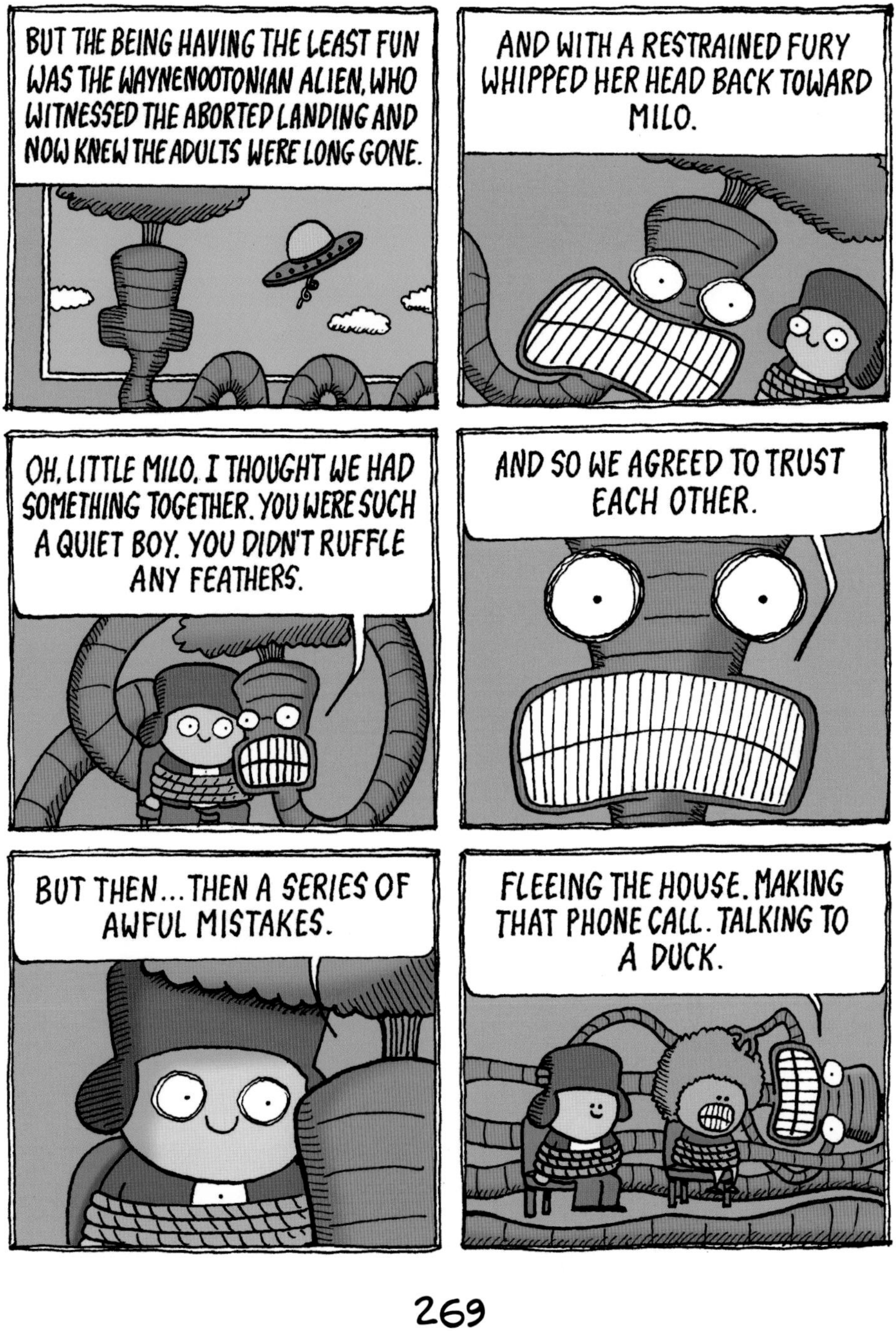
BUT THE BEING HAVING THE LEAST FUN WAS THE WAYNENOOTONIAN ALIEN, WHO WITNESSED THE ABORTED LANDING AND NOW KNEW THE ADULTS WERE LONG GONE.
AND WITH A RESTRAINED FURY WHIPPED HER HEAD BACK TOWARD MILO.
OH, LITTLE MILO. I THOUGHT WE HAD SOMETHING TOGETHER. YOU WERE SUCH A QUIET BOY. YOU DIDN'T RUFFLE ANY FEATHERS.
AND SO WE AGREED TO TRUST EACH OTHER.
BUT THEN... THEN A SERIES OF AWFUL MISTAKES.
FLEEING THE HOUSE. MAKING THAT PHONE CALL. TALKING TO A DUCK.

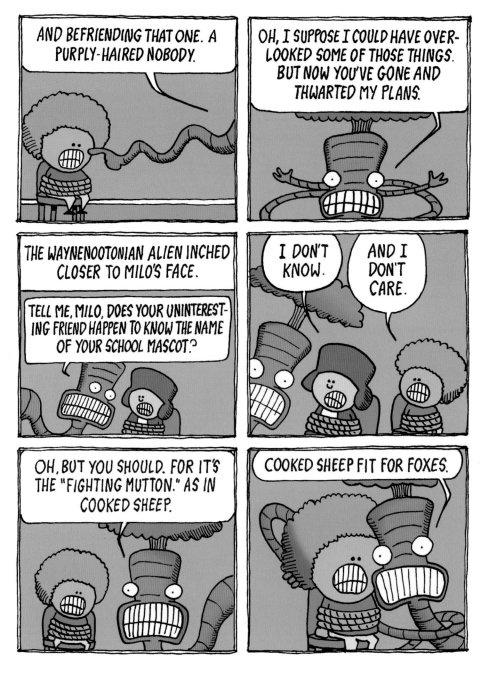

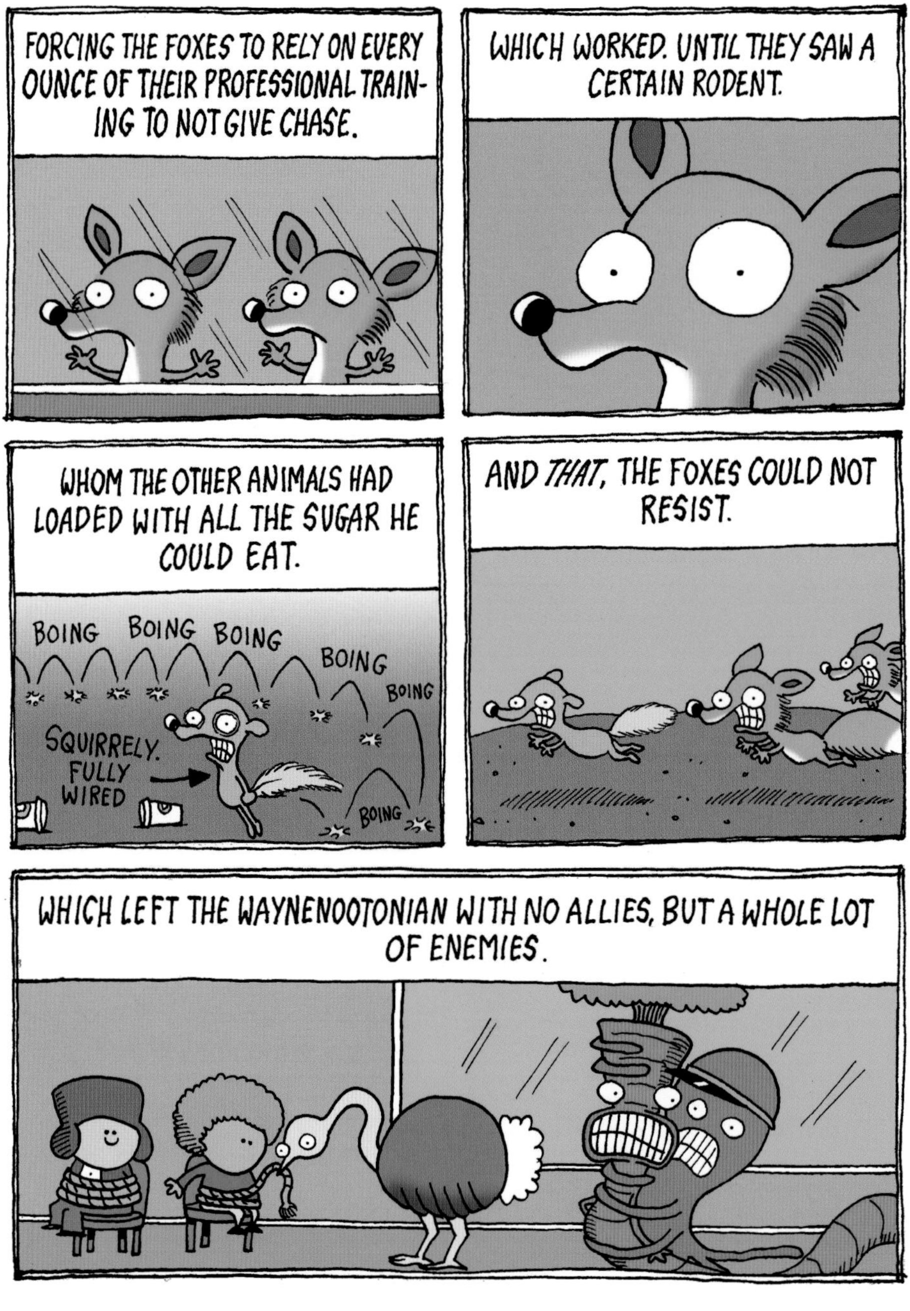
FORCING THE FOXES TO RELY ON EVERY OUNCE OF THEIR PROFESSIONAL TRAINING TO NOT GIVE CHASE.
WHICH WORKED. UNTIL THEY SAW A CERTAIN RODENT.
WHOM THE OTHER ANIMALS HAD LOADED WITH ALL THE SUGAR HE COULD EAT.
BOING BOING BOING
BOING
BOING
SQUIRRELY. FULLY WIRED
BOING
AND *THAT*, THE FOXES COULD NOT RESIST.
WHICH LEFT THE WAYNENOOTONIAN WITH NO ALLIES, BUT A WHOLE LOT OF ENEMIES.

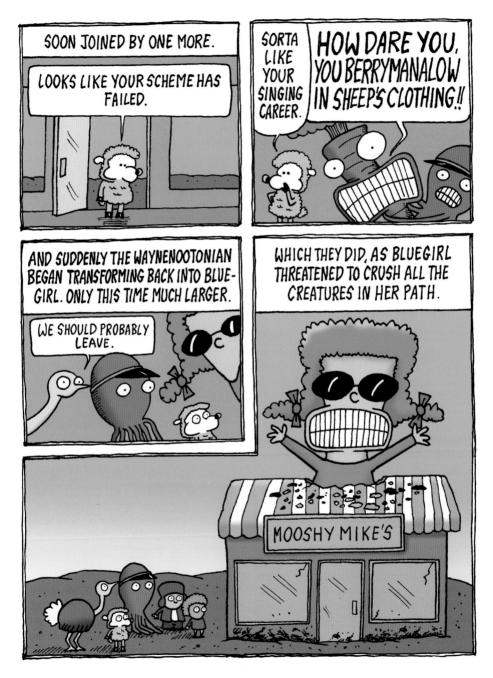

273

WHICH MILO AND WENDY HEARD FROM ABOVE AS THE DIRT UNDER MOOSHY MIKE'S CAFÉ GAVE WAY.

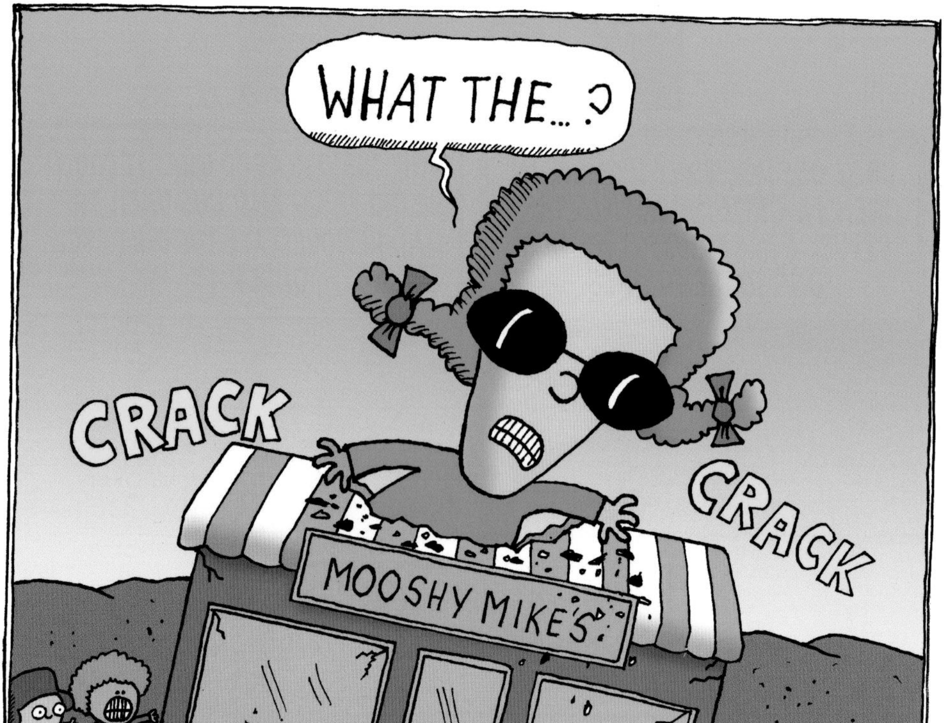

WHAT THE...?
CRACK
CRACK
MOOSHY MIKE'S

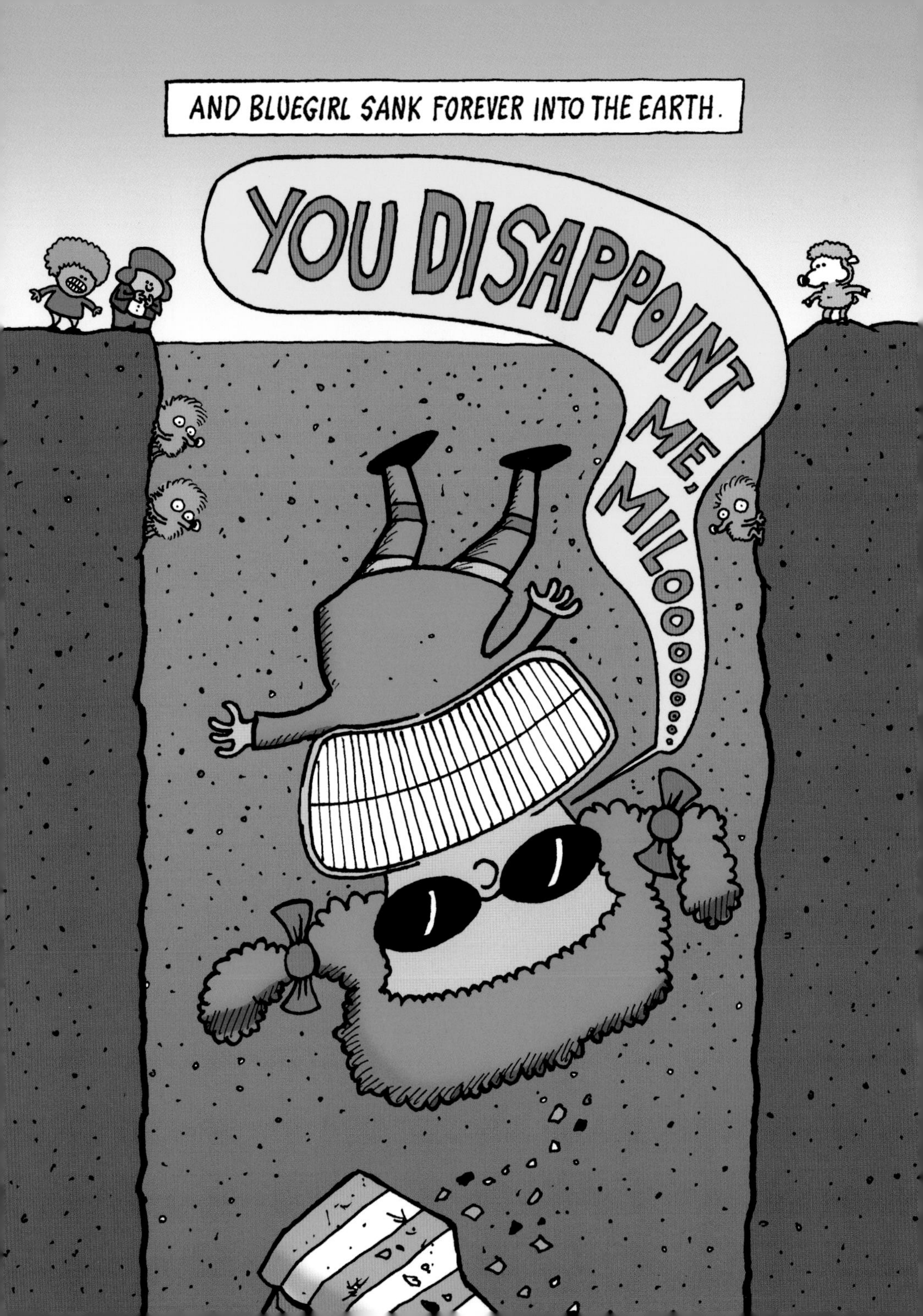
AND BLUEGIRL SANK FOREVER INTO THE EARTH.
YOU DISAPPOINT ME, MILOOOOOOOO...

CHAPTER
LAST
FOR
REAL

IN WHICH...

WE ARE NOT
KIDDING AROUND

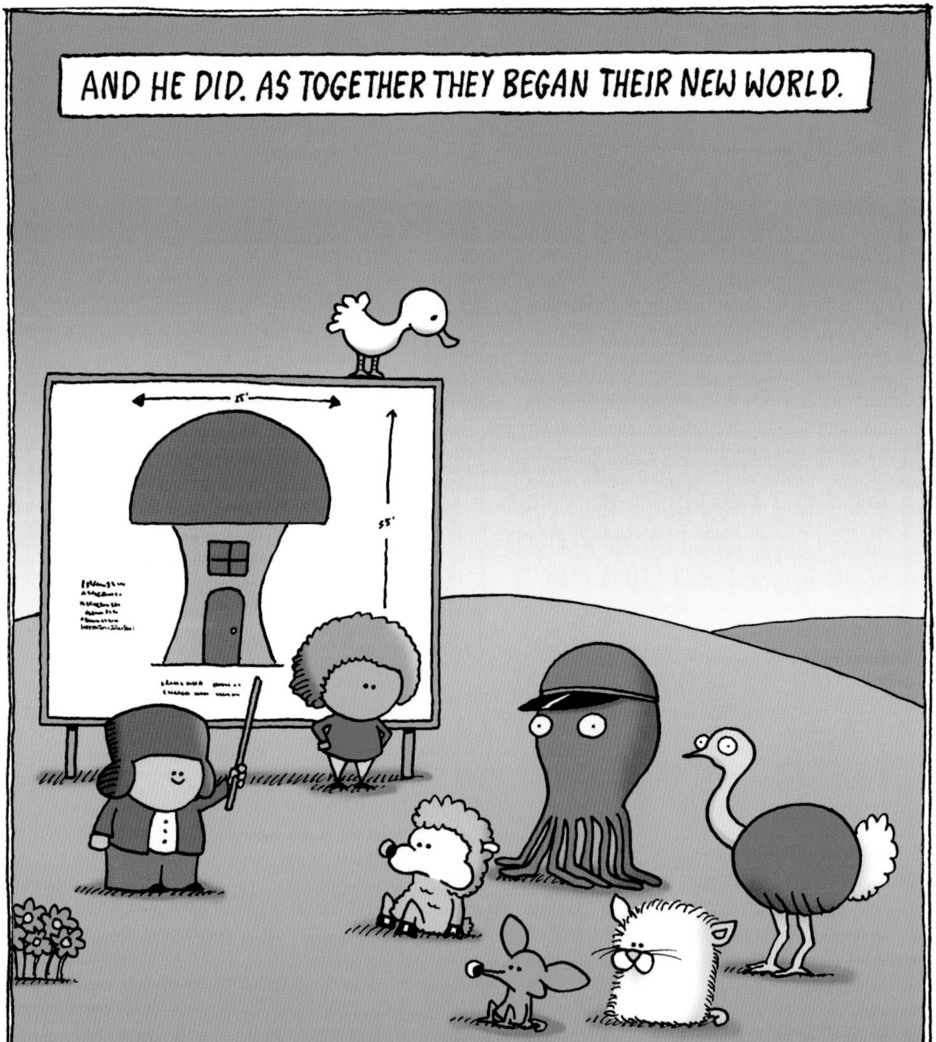
AND HE DID. AS TOGETHER THEY BEGAN THEIR NEW WORLD.

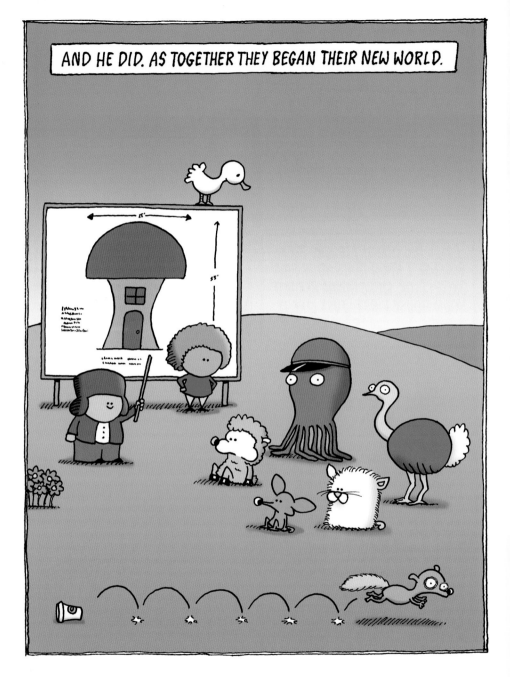

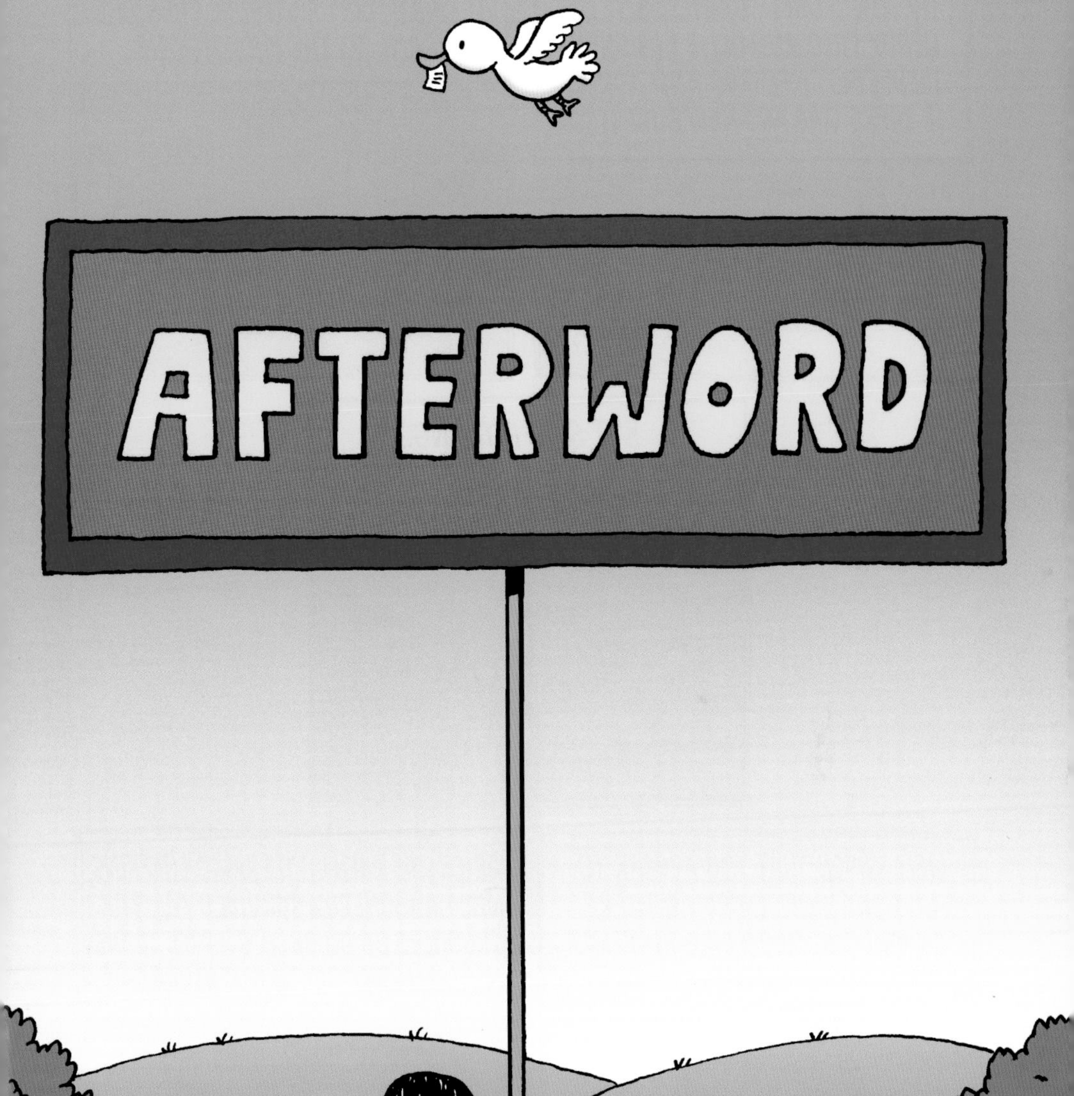
AFTERWORD

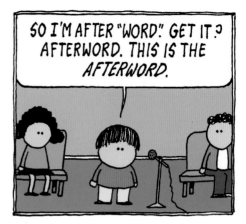

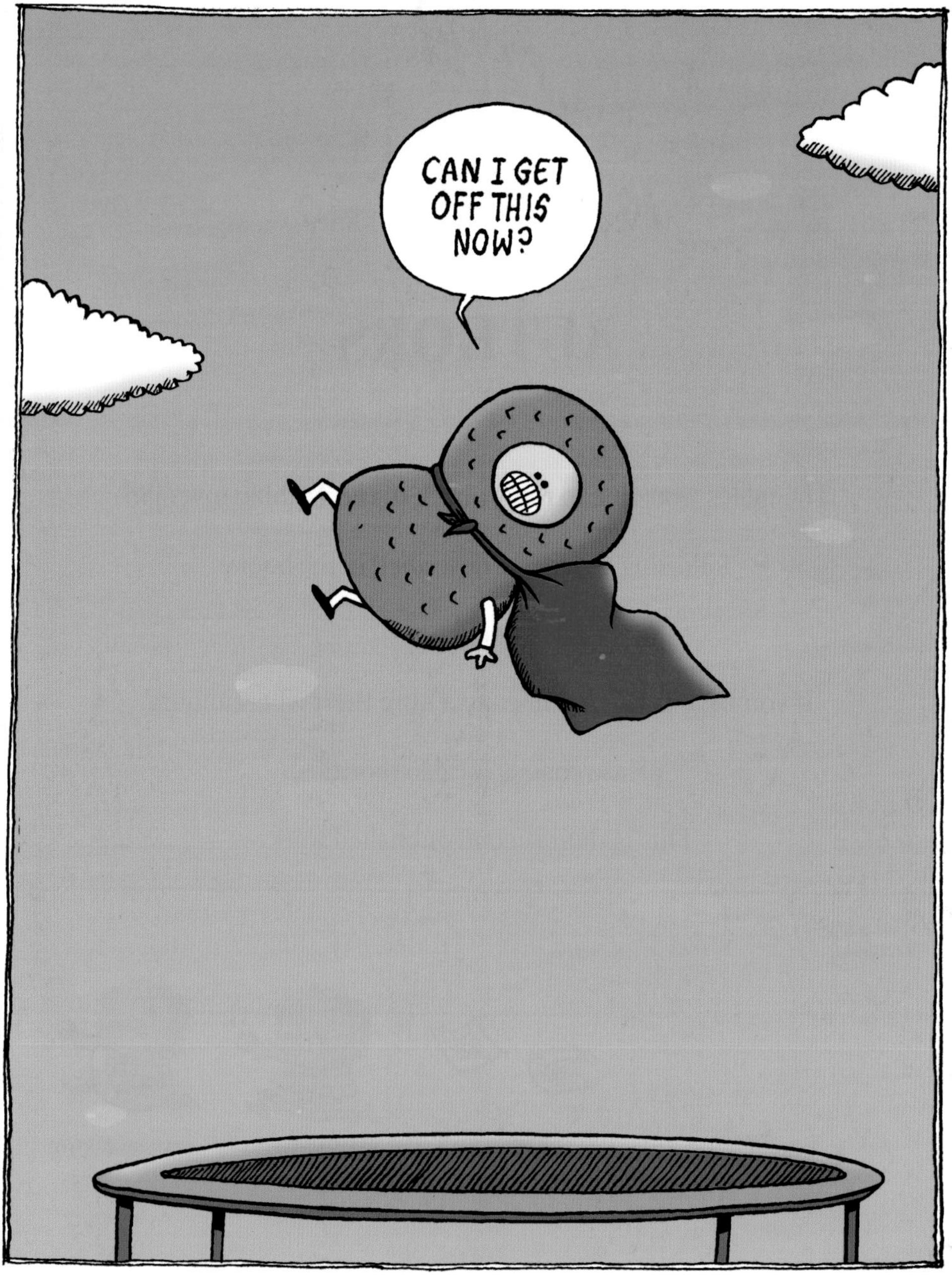
CAN I GET OFF THIS NOW?